ALL THAT LINGERS

Irene Wittig

ALL THAT LINGERS

for my Viennese family
whose memories lie at the core of this book

All That Lingers

LIST OF CHARACTERS

EMMA HUBER -
Catholic, born 1909, model, seamstress, close friend since childhood of Léonie Grünbaum Salzmann and Greta Hellmann Bruckner
FRAU HUBER -
Emma's mother
THEO BERGER -
Emma's fiancé, Socialist and activist
MARTIN TOWNSEND -
British army lieutenant in occupied Vienna
HANNAH HOFFMANN -
born 1935, child Emma's ward
STEFAN BÁRSONY -
Hungarian refugee
HANNS MENZLER - *doctor*
MAGDA -
16 year old girl found by Dr Menzler
XENIA -
her daughter
FRAU MANDL -
Emma's friend and her apartment building's concierge (Hausbesorgerin)

LEONIE GRÜNBAUM SALZMANN -
Jewish, born 1909, close friend of Emma Huber and Greta Hellmann Bruckner
JOSEF SALZMANN -
Léonie's husband, doctor
VALERIE SALZMANN -

Léonie and Josef Salzmann's daughter, born 1931
HERR GRÜNBAUM -
Léonie's father, businessman and Emma's boss
FRAU ANNA GRÜNBAUM -
Léonie's mother
FRAU LOTTE -
the Grünbaums' housekeeper

FRIEDRICH, GRAF VON HARZBURG -
German aristocrat, born 1908
MARION BRUCKNER VON HARZBURG -
Friedrich's wife, born 1919
KLAUS VON HARZBURG -
their son, born 1941
ELSA PACHEL BRUCKNER -
Marion's mother, second wife of Heinrich Bruckner, step-mother to Otto Bruckner
FRITZ -
Bruckners' and von Harzburgs' butler
TIBOR SZABÓ -
hotel busboy then barber to Friedrich
BERTHA -
Bruckners' and von Harzburgs' cook

SOPHIE BRUCKNER -
born 1932, daughter of Otto and Greta Bruckner
GRETA HELLMANN BRUCKNER -
born 1909, half-Jewish, close friend of Emma and Léonie
OTTO BRUCKNER -
anti-Nazi newspaperman, born 1906, Marion's brother
HEINRICH BRUCKNER -
Otto's father, wealthy businessman

RESI HELLMANN -
Greta's aunt
HARRY WHITTAKER -
Greta's boss, journalist, American.
BESSIE STONE -
Harry's sister
BILL STONE -
Bessie's husband
MATT MILLINGTON - *American graduate student*
MARGIE - *Sophie's shipmate, American*

1934

CHANGE AND TURMOIL

1.

VIENNA

Unaware that trouble was only days away, Emma was happier than she'd ever been. Once she might have described the early morning emptiness of their street as gloomy. Now she delighted in the dawn dancing silently on the cobblestones. The howling winter wind at the window would have frightened her. Now she greeted its icy arms around her and laughed. Even the scent of steaming bleach filling their small apartment every morning was comforting in its familiarity.

"Sing with me, Mama. It'll make you feel good."

Her mother looked up from the row of laundry baskets at her feet as two pots of soapy water continued to boil on the kitchen stove.

"Don't be silly, Emma, and close the window. The neighbors will complain if they hear us."

"Come on, Mama, don't worry about them."

Her mother pulled a pillow case from one of the baskets, smoothed and folded it, and added it to a stack of already folded laundry on the dining table.

"I have more important things to think about than singing, and so should you," she said, her voice weary.

"You work too hard, Mama, and don't get enough sleep."

Her mother straightened her back and put her hands on her hips.

"If I sleep, I don't get paid," she said, spacing her words as if she were speaking to a child. "I'm glad I still get work with so many people unemployed. We could manage when Papa was alive. I only had to do mending or alterations once in a while, but prices keep going up and without him—"

"That's why you should let me help. I'm working, it's only right."

"Absolutely not," her mother said, shaking her head. "You and Theo need to save for when you're married — though now people say there's no point with everything so unstable and inflation so high. Soon you'll have children. They cost money too, you know."

Emma's heart skipped a beat. Did she know? She and Theo hadn't told anyone yet.

Her mother brushed a lock of damp hair out of her face and adjusted the pins that held the rest of her hair in a bun. It hurt Emma to see her mother's hands so red and swollen from the daily washing and wringing out of other people's laundry, and flung her arms around her.

"You mustn't worry so much, Mama. We'll be fine, and after we get married we'll help you and maybe you won't have to work at all."

Her mother kissed her cheek but her shoulders seemed to slump as she answered.

"I think sometimes you forget that you aren't as well off as your friends. Greta and Otto may think they are Socialists but they live in a mansion. And Léonie's family has money and the shop, and her husband is a doctor. We are not in the same class."

Emma folded the last of the pillowcases and placed them on the table.

"We're friends, Mama. Theo says —"

"I know, I know. Theo thinks the working class should have the same rights as the rich. He's an idealist. That's why I worry. People will think he's a dreamer, or a troublemaker because he's so political, and he'll never get a proper job."

She pursed her lips and pulled an armful of towels from the still half-full basket. Emma took them from her and started folding them.

"He's not a troublemaker, Mama. You know that. He just wants to make things better."

Emma loved listening to Theo talking about his dreams for the country. His eyes would light up and he'd tell her how much better life will be for their children because of what the Socialists had already accomplished.

"Theo will be a responsible husband. And Léonie's parents pay me well enough that I can save and help you too."

"Modeling fancy clothes is fine when you're young and beautiful but that won't last," her mother went on, clearly not yet finished with her.

Emma reached out to hug her again. She knew it was out of caring and not anger that her mother said these things.

Emma would have told her that she'd already decided to ask the Grünbaums' tailor to teach her how to measure and cut so that she could work even after her belly grew too big for her to model. But her mother would only worry more if she knew about the baby. Nor did Emma tell her that the Socialists were planning a general strike to force the conservatives to negotiate. Some of Theo's friends were talking about emigrating if things did not improve. Theo said he'd never do that, but once their baby was born he might feel differently. She didn't tell her mother that either.

"Don't be so concerned, Mama. Everything will be fine. Theo is a good man. I know you like him."

Her mother softened, as she usually did in the end.

"I do. He makes me laugh—reminds me of your father when he was young." She stroked Emma's cheek. "But that's neither here nor there. Go on, it's time for you to leave for work."

"Don't forget, Greta and Sophie are coming over this evening and you promised to make them your best *Palatschinken*—the ones with farmer's cheese and vanilla sauce."

"I'll be curious to hear if things have improved at the Bruckner mansion."

"They haven't. Otto's father married Elsa after his wife died so she'd be a mother to Otto, but that never happened. She only focused on her own daughter. Marion is fifteen now and more spoiled than ever. Even though Elsa and Greta are very different, Greta hoped they'd all grow closer when Sophie was born but nothing changed. Greta says it's as if the house were divided in two, with only the servants knowing or caring what's happening on both sides."

Emma put on her coat and gave her mother another hug, then ran downstairs and through the inner courtyard to the front entrance, waving to Frau Mandl, the building's concierge, as she passed.

Theo was waiting outside, leaning against the wall, his hands in the pockets of his Loden coat, his dark curly hair disheveled by the wind. Emma reached up and kissed him.

"It's winter, remember?" she said as she pulled his coat closed. "Sorry I'm late but just as I was leaving Mama said to tell you that not everyone thinks Socialism is the answer, and Father Johannes said the Socialists are godless."

Theo laughed, a deep belly laugh that echoed down the street.

"Well, I hope you told her not to listen to him. You know it's just because he thinks the Socialists are all Jews."

"I thought Dollfuss outlawed discrimination against Jews."

Theo frowned. "Officially, although our dear chancellor also disbanded parliament and outlawed all the parties except his. He wants to be dictator, Emma. The Socialists should have overthrown him when they had the chance."

As they walked through the old streets, past St. Stephen's, through the Graben to Léonie's parents' store on the Kohlmarkt they passed a line of security forces.

"Don't drop the bomb!" Theo whispered mischievously, his brown eyes twinkling.

Emma poked him in the ribs with her elbow but couldn't help but giggle.

"Stop making jokes, Theo, they'll arrest us."

"Not me," he said. "I refuse to be arrested. Besides, they're too busy admiring each other's uniforms. The whole city center is full of them: police, army, and paramilitaries—both their *Heimwehr,* and our *Schutzbund.*

Emma squeezed his arm. "Will I see you tomorrow?"

"No, it's going to be a busy couple of days."

"You'll be careful, won't you?"

She reached up to adjust the collar of his coat.

"Of course. We're well prepared, and when the strike is over everything will change for the better. We'll get married and find an apartment, and have lots of Socialist babies. I promise. Meanwhile, I'll definitely see you at Léonie's for Josef's birthday."

"That's not until next week!"

He laughed and drew her into his arms again.

"You'll survive, my sweet. It's only a few days, and your friends will keep you busy."

She felt the warmth of his chest against her cheek and the beating of his heart in her ear and thought how much she loved him.

"Be careful, no bomb dropping, my big beautiful bear."

Life was good, and soon she'd have everything she'd ever wanted.

She gave him a last kiss, turned and opened the tall glass doors marked Grünbaum & Co.

2.

BERLIN

Weary, Friedrich von Harzburg dragged his feet through the city he'd called home for the past decade. Only twenty-six and already weary. A strange reaction to the energy infecting much of Germany. There in the midst of lingering poverty and degradation people felt hopeful again. Banners fluttered their swastikas in every nook and cranny of the city, promising to raise Germany from the ashes of war and depression. The ancient hooked cross they called a *Hakenkreuz* was the perfect symbol for Herr Hitler's invented myth of an Aryan master race.

The Germany Friedrich had been born into had once been an Empire consisting of four kingdoms, six grand duchies, five duchies, seven principalities, three free Hanseatic cities and one imperial territory. Due to a confluence of circumstances and decisions he found difficult to understand, Germany went to war and was utterly defeated. Poor Kaiser Wilhelm II, he thought. He was forced to abdicate and was quickly followed by all the other monarchs of imperial Germany, who in turn were replaced by a democratic Weimar Republic. Like all the nobles now struggling to find new roles and resources for their ebbing dynasties, Friedrich's father, Gottfried, Graf von Harzburg, found he was no longer guaranteed the aristocratic lifestyle he thought he deserved.

With war casualties in the millions, few workers remained to tend to the von Harzburgs' insignificant ancestral estate. No longer having the means to pay even their reduced staff, they left their centuries-old home to crumble, and made their way to the city. First one, then another and another until they settled in Berlin. That was in 1924. Friedrich was sixteen, and the German mark was worthless.

Friedrich's schooling had been intermittent due to war and the family's instability. Limited to his mother's instructions on the gentlemanly appreciation of the arts, he acquired few practical skills or qualifications.

His father had been equally unqualified yet gifted at making his living without actually working. The family's economic status had depended on his charm, which, after a while, became tarnished by age and alcohol. He died in 1930, leaving Friedrich with a title and a thousand stabilized Reichsmark in debt.

Reduced to living with his ailing mother in an unheated rented room, Friedrich became an *Eintänzer*, a taxi-dancer paid by the dance by single older women or women whose husbands wouldn't dance. His youth and soulful melancholy appealed to older widows especially and he soon found himself financially sheltered. Shortly after Christmas of 1933, his mother died of pneumonia, with a worn leather-bound volume of Heine poems in her hand—the last relic of a once-cultured life.

Friedrich was surprised at how much he felt the loss, and even more surprised at the kindness the most recent of his benefactresses showed him. Perhaps Frau Altmann, a widow who'd lost a son in the war, saw in him the son who would mourn her when she died. He might have had she not chosen to emigrate.

"Why now?" he asked.

"My dear boy, we Jews are no longer welcome here," she explained, as if he might not yet have grasped the full meaning of the Nazi placards warning citizens of the dangers Jews presented to Germany's economy and dreams of Aryan purity.

"Are you sure you won't stay? I can't imagine such coarse foolishness will last," he said, stroking the wrinkled hand of his cultured friend, with whom he'd spent many pleasant evenings enjoying theatre and ballet.

"It's happened before, I'm afraid," she said. "My parents were forced to flee Russia when they were your age."

"Where will you go?"

"Paris, for now," she said, and gave him the address of her favorite hotel.

Within days she was gone, and Friedrich had to resolve his financial situation once again. Perhaps he should have gone with her.

3.

VIENNA

It was on Monday, the 12th of February, that the trouble began.

In Linz—155 kilometers from Vienna—the police entered Hotel Schiff looking for weapons, knowing the hotel was owned by the Social Democratic Party. The Socialists' *Schutzbund,* responded by shooting at the police. The army responded by shooting at the *Schutzbund.* Dollfuss called in the artillery, and his *Heimwehr* was only too glad to add to the chaos by rampaging through Linz.

Soon the violence spread to other industrial areas, quickly reaching Vienna. At noon the Socialists canceled the strike.

Emma was at work when Herr Grünbaum ordered a taxi and asked her to go check on Léonie because he hadn't been able to reach her. When she arrived at Léonie's building, she found her friend nervously unlocking the front door as she held tight to her daughter's hand, a basket of potatoes and cabbages at her feet.

"This is all I could find," Léonie said. "Several of the vendors at the market had already closed. Everyone is afraid they'll get caught in the fighting."

Emma bent down to pick up the basket, as an almost empty trolley rumbled down Ungargasse behind them.

"Civil war, they call it," Léonie said. "Austrians fighting Austrians, Viennese against Viennese."

Emma felt a shiver of fear down the back of her neck.

"I'm afraid for Theo," she said, the muscles of her shoulders growing tense. "He called me early this morning to tell me the strike was canceled and he was on his way to Karl-Marx-Hof."

"Try not to worry. I'm sure he'll be careful," Léonie said.

Still holding Valerie's hand she and Emma walked through the building's unlit cobblestoned courtyard to the elevator. Through the open metal work they could see the elevator cage rising, until it stopped on the fourth floor. They heard the door creak open and then slam shut. They waited, listening in vain for the rattle of it being sent down again.

"Frau Maier always forgets to send it back," Léonie said. "We'll have to walk."

They trudged up the four flights to Léonie's apartment, their shoes clicking against the marble steps, their hands sharing the weight of the basket, while Valerie—three years old and overflowing with energy—ran ahead.

They heard the phone ringing as they reached the apartment door. Fumbling frantically with her key, Léonie managed to get inside and answer it before it stopped.

"Greta? I was just going to call you. You heard what's going on? Papa is closing the store, and Emma is here."

After a moment Léonie laughed and turned to Emma.

"Greta asked if she could join us. Said she'd rather face ten armies than be stuck in the house with Elsa and Marion." Returning to the phone, Léonie's voice was more serious. "Of course you can come, but hurry, before it gets worse."

Emma accompanied Léonie into the kitchen to unload her purchases and thought how lucky they'd been to find an apartment only a few doors from Josef's practice. When his schedule allowed he could walk home for lunch and catch Valerie before her nap—though she rarely took one.

In the third district, just over the Ringstrasse from the center—or the *Innenstadt,* as they called it —the apartment was elegant and spacious, with its tall windows and high ceilings, and a balcony that overlooked a peaceful back garden. It was no wonder that they always gathered there. Emma's was hardly fit for company, and at the Bruckner mansion they were made to feel like strangers— even Otto, who had grown up there.

Emma knew she and Theo would never be rich but they would make their home happy and welcoming—and without the smell of bleach.

Greta and Sophie arrived shortly before eleven and they settled themselves in the living room to talk over a late-morning coffee.

Valerie dragged in a large bag of building blocks and spilled it out on the Persian rug at their feet. With fierce concentration she built a lopsided castle for her doll, oblivious to the conversation around her. Sophie looked on, sucking the thumb of her right hand while holding on to the hem of Greta's skirt with her left. Emma always felt that as young and shy as she was, she took in every word. If she hadn't known better, Emma would have thought that the girls had been secretly switched at birth. Sophie's gentle quietness seemed a mirror image of Léonie's, while Valerie's confident determination was so much like Greta's.

Emma hoped her daughter would be like Theo, funny and courageous. The baby had to be a girl. Then there'd be three, friends from the start just like their mothers.

"I wish the men were here already," she said, looking at her watch.

"Have you heard from Theo?" Greta asked.

"Only this morning. He said he was on his way to Karl-Marx-Hof—"

"Oh no, I hope he didn't go there. They know it's a Socialist stronghold. It'll be the first place the *Heimwehr* will go. It won't be safe."

"Don't say that!" Emma cried out, startling Sophie. With her heart racing, she reached out to calm the child—and herself.

Karl-Marx-Hof was the symbol of everything Theo believed in. A kilometer-long apartment building with arches and lovely garden courtyards, it was the grandest of the many that the Social Democrats had built. Housing five thousand workers, it was a city within a city with stores, medical services, laundries, libraries, a post office, and schools. Its balconies, separate toilets and running water were luxuries the inhabitants had never known before. For Theo it was the future he'd been working for. One day, Emma and he would live there.

"Why don't you call Frau Mandl?" Greta said.

Emma nodded. She should have thought of that. Her mother was probably with her and might have heard from Theo.

Her hands were clammy as she picked up the phone.

Her mother and Frau Mandl were fine, but had no news. They would call if they heard anything.

Emma wiped the receiver on her dress and hung up.

Léonie's husband Josef returned at five, his face lined with worry that only one patient had kept his appointment.

"They will come tomorrow when things are calmer," Léonie said.

"Yes, perhaps you're right," he said, smiling weakly as he hung up his coat. "They'll call if there's anything urgent."

"Why don't you play with the girls a bit, Josef dear, while Greta, Emma and I start preparing dinner. After all, we're here to celebrate your birthday."

At seven Otto called to say he wouldn't make it. Things were chaotic at the paper, trying to verify or dismiss rumors before the next issue was published.

He asked Léonie if Greta and Sophie could stay the night because it wasn't safe to walk or even drive around.

"Of course," Léonie said, "Greta and I were just about to put the children to bed."

Emma stayed in the living room but couldn't sit still and found herself pacing the room while Josef pored over his medical journal.

"At least, Dollfuss is trying to keep the Nazis out," she said, needing to make conversation.

"Even so, the Nazis' influence is already inciting more anti-Semitism," Greta said, as she and Léonie returned.

"I'm a doctor," Josef said. "I can't imagine it will affect us."

"Don't be too sure," Greta said. "When I was driving here this morning I saw an enormous banner declaring that there were 500,000 unemployed and 400,000 Jews, and the solution was obvious: Vote for the Nazis. It's clear what they meant."

"Anti-Semitism is nothing new in Austria," Léonie said softly, twisting her Star of David pendant. "If we don't bother anyone, we should be all right."

"We can't ignore them, Léonie. It'll just get worse. If you read Hitler's "*Mein Kampf* you'd see how crazy his ideas are. Otto keeps writing articles warning people —."

"If his ideas are so crazy, do you think it's wise to give them so much attention?" Josef said.

"I do. We have to show that they're wrong. It's the only the way we can fight them. What do your parents think, Léonie?"

"Papa says his service in the Imperial Army proves he is a loyal Austrian. Deep down he probably thinks the Habsburgs will return to save the day. But come, let's not spoil Josef's birthday with all this terrible talk. We should eat before it gets too late. I'll put something aside for Theo. We'll wait with the cake so he can help Josef blow his many candles out—all thirty-four of them."

Josef, thin and pale, looked like he might need the help.

Léonie tried to keep the conversation light through dinner, but as the minutes and then hours passed, they could no longer ignore Theo's absence.

"I'm scared," Emma said. "If only he would call, then at least I'd know he was all right," She crossed her arms over her stomach as if that could keep her from panicking.

"Maybe he's not—" Josef began.

"I'll call Otto," Greta said, taking charge—but she could not get through.

Emma asked if they could turn on the radio.

"Of course," Josef said, "I should have thought of that. They'll probably report that the trams aren't running, and that's why…"

"I'll try Otto again," Greta said.

Finally, on her third attempt she got through.

"I've been trying to call you," Otto said. "Things are not good. Dollfuss called in the army and the *Heimwehr* and ordered them to shell Karl-Marx-Hof."

"People live there, for God's sake!" Greta said.

"Don't say anything to Emma yet."

Emma grabbed the phone out of Greta's hand.

"I can hear you, Otto. Tell me the truth, how bad is it?"

"Be strong. There's no reason to think the worst. Theo can take care of himself. Let me see what I can find out before you jump to conclusions."

She nodded and handed the phone back to Greta.

Josef turned up the radio and between flashes of loud static they could hear a voice filled with emotion:..*thousands of lives endangered…countless homeless…many injured…unconfirmed deaths…fighting in Vienna has ended…Socialists forced to surrender…hundreds arrested…*

Léonie gasped.

"Oh, God!" Greta cried out.

Only Emma sat frozen, not breathing—until the distant sound of a clock striking twelve broke through her shock. With a cry she jumped up, almost knocking over her chair.

"I have to go—he might be hurt—he might be dead!"

She rushed to the door and struggled to put on her coat while Greta tried to restrain her.

"Let me go, I have to find him! He might be hurt."

"If he's hurt, they will have taken him to the hospital. Let's try calling first."

"No! They won't tell you anything. I have to go myself. I have to see him."

"You can't, Emma. It's late. There won't be any trams now. It's better to call."

Gently but firmly Greta led Emma back to the living room.

"Josef will call, won't you Josef? You're a doctor. They'll tell you."

"All right," Emma said, but kept her coat on.

Josef was passed from one person to another until at last he was told that no, there was no Theo Berger among the list of wounded.

It was almost one o'clock now. Emma burst into tears.

Josef put his arms around her shoulders.

"But that's good, isn't it, knowing that he isn't hurt?"

"No!" Emma said, breaking into sobs. "Don't you understand? He might be lying hurt somewhere, or arrested or dead. I've wasted so much time. I should have looked for him hours ago. He'll think I've forsaken him."

Shaking, she buttoned her coat and ran down the stairs and into the street. The cold night air slapped her in the face. As if reprimanded, she stopped crying, pulled up her coat collar and start walking.

She would go directly to the police.

4.

VIENNA

Police headquarters was swarming with men—police, soldiers, prisoners, reporters. Emma pushed her way through, finally reaching a desk where a man with a pockmarked face and red, misshapen nose sat writing in a ledger.

"Please, will you help me?"

He looked up and winked.

"With pleasure, Fräulein."

He leaned back in his chair, and grinned. His teeth were yellow, and a missing button midway down his shirt exposed the wobbly flab of his belly. Emma swallowed hard as a wave of nausea swept over her.

"My fiancé…his name is Theo Berger. I have to find him."

"Have you lost him?" he laughed. "I'm sure you'll have no trouble finding another with such a beautiful face."

He raised his hand as if to touch her. Repulsed, Emma stepped back. She wanted to run but clenched her fists and fought off the panic she felt. Holding her arms tightly at her side, with her eyes fixed on his, she asked, as calmly as she could, "Is he here?"

He looked around.

"So many men here. I'm sure you'll find one to your liking."

"IS HE HERE?" She pounded his desk with her fist. "YOU HAVE TO TELL ME."

The man grabbed her wrist and pulled her toward him. His fingernails were filthy, and his knuckles were ink-stained and hairy.

"I don't have to tell you anything," he snarled, "and if you don't keep your fist off my desk I will have *you* arrested."

"I'm sorry, I'm sorry," she said. "I didn't mean...I'm just terribly worried." She tried to smile and undo the damage. "He was at Karl-Marx-Hof when —"

He gave her a sharp look.

"I should have known. You Jewish-scum-socialists are finished. Kaput. You'll all go to prison if I have anything to say about it. You'd better find yourself a good patriot instead." He rose from his chair and leaned with his fists on his desk like a gorilla.

"Now get out!"

The violence of his tone slashed through her. Anxious to escape, she crashed into a file cabinet, causing a stack of papers to scatter to the floor.

"I'm so sorry," she stammered, dropping to her knees. She felt tears trickling down her nose and wiped them with her coat sleeve.

"I don't have all day," he said flatly, having lost interest.

Her hands shaking, Emma replaced the papers on the file cabinet, terrified he'd notice they were no longer in order, then pushed her way through the crowd and out the door.

Newly fallen sleet coated the street. She shivered and pulled the collar of her coat up to her face. Not knowing what else to do, she began to walk home. She had done everything wrong.

It was five in the morning when she finally reached the top of Blutgasse, her streeet. Her feet were so cold every step felt as if she were walking on broken glass. Her ears ached from the wind, and her head was splitting.

Mistaking the rattle of a shutter for footsteps, she tried to run, but her feet were so stiff she could barely lift them from the cobblestones. When she finally reached her building and looked back, she saw no one. She unlocked the heavy door and slipped in.

Her mouth dry, her heart still hammering against her chest, she waited until her eyes grew accustomed to the dark and she was sure no one was coming, then ran across the empty inner courtyard and up the stairs.

She found her mother asleep at the table, a stack of folded laundry at her elbow.

"Mama," she whispered.

Her mother woke with a start.

"Where have you been? I've been so worried. After what I heard on the radio, I tried to call you at Léonie's but you'd gone."

"I couldn't find him. I'm useless. I should have gone to Karl-Marx-Hof but it was too far to walk."

"You're trembling, Emma, and cold as ice."

"It doesn't matter."

Her mother insisted she change into a warm nightgown and get into bed. She put wool socks on Emma's feet, pulled up the duvet and covered it with a wool blanket.

"Get some sleep, Emma. We'll decide what to do when you wake up."

Exhausted, Emma fell asleep right away but woke every few minutes, frantic that she was wasting time. After an hour, she couldn't stand it and got up, held a hot wash cloth to her face, and felt her energy returning. She put on fresh clothes and threw a scarf around her neck.

"I'm going downstairs to call Otto, Mama. He might know something by now."

They didn't have their own phone and used Frau Mandl's. She was not only their concierge but also their friend, so when Emma and her mother offered to pay her, she said if they could do her mending she would consider it a fair trade. Pleased with their work, she had quietly recommended them to her friends, which had helped them get through hard times after Emma's father died.

"Any news?" she asked, when she answered Emma's knock at her door.

"Not yet. Can I call Otto? I'm hoping he will have heard something by now."

Otto told her he'd been told that political prisoners were being sent to a concentration camp in Wöllersdorf.

"But that doesn't mean Theo is there, Emma. He could be anywhere."

Holding the receiver tightly in her hands, Emma begged him not to give up searching.

"I'm doing everything I can, I promise."

When she returned upstairs her mother had heated some soup.

"It'll make you feel better," she said.

"I can't eat. I'm going out."

"You don't know where to go."

"I do. It's where I should have gone in the first place."

5.

VIENNA

The slate gray sky grew lighter as Emma made her way to Karl-Marx-Hof. To her relief, the beloved fortress was still standing, though gravely wounded and shell-pocked. Dust filled her lungs as her eyes scanned the acres of debris. Everywhere people were on their knees searching through the rubble of concrete, bricks and glass for rescuable remnants of their lives— here a blanket covered with plaster dust, there a three-legged chair. The ground crackled and crunched as she stepped on photographs barely identifiable under shattered glass. Damn Dollfuss!

In the distance Emma heard the wail of sirens, as she spotted two men carrying a stretcher, with a body so small it could only have been a child. Her heart racing, she ran toward them.

"Where are you taking him? Where are the others?" she asked, her voice hoarse from the dust.

"Ask the police," they shouted back as they turned the corner.

"Where?" she said, too late for them to hear.

"Hohe Warte Station," an old woman said, pointing the way. "That's where those people are going, though the pigs there won't tell you anything."

Emma pushed her way through the crowds to the police station only to find another throng of people overflowing the steps leading to the front doors —- some desperately seeking loved ones, others begging for shelter.

Pressed together, the mass inched up the steps so slowly that it was almost eleven by the time Emma got inside. She filled out a form and handed it to the officer in charge.

"Are you a family member?" he asked, without looking at her, his voice tired.

"Fiancée."

He waved her aside.

"That is not enough. I cannot give you any information."

"Please, I just want to know if he's alive."

"Move on, Fräulein. You are not the only one here."

The woman behind her pushed her out of the way, muttering that she had been waiting all morning, her spot immediately filled by the person behind her.

Despondent, Emma wove her way back out through the ever-increasing horde and walked until she found a post office and an unoccupied phone. Every bone and muscle weary, she sat for a moment before she found the strength to dial Otto's number.

"Oh, thank God you answered. Have you had any news? No one will tell me anything. I don't know where else to look, or whom to ask." She choked back her tears.

"Where are you?"

"Still in Heiligenstadt, I think. I've walked around so much I'm not sure."

"Go back to Léonie's, please. Greta and Sophie are still there. I will call as soon as I know something. I promise you. Be strong, Emma."

Exhausted, Emma reached Ungargasse mid-afternoon.

"Any news?" she asked as soon as Léonie opened the door.

"Nothing yet. Come in. Otto told us you were in Heiligenstadt. Did you walk all this way? You must be frozen."

Léonie removed Emma's shoes and rubbed her feet.

"I am. I don't think I could have walked another minute."

"I'll get you Josef's slippers. Go sit down in the living room with Greta and the children," Léonie said. "I'll get you a hot water bottle and some tea with rum."

Greta made room for her on the sofa.

"The girls and I are having a tea party," she said, as she draped a blanket around Emma's shoulders.

The tightness in Emma's neck and shoulders slowly relaxed as she gazed down at Valerie, thoroughly absorbed in arranging a miniature tea set neatly on a napkin on the floor. With great seriousness, she poured imaginary tea into a tiny porcelain cup and handed it carefully to Sophie who just as seriously raised the cup to her lips and pretended to drink it.

Immeasurably comforted by the gentle innocence of the children's ceremony, Emma leaned back against the sofa's velvet cushions and closed her eyes. Her big strong Theo was smart and brave. Nothing could happen to him.

It was past six when the phone rang. Léonie rushed to answer. She nodded silently, her eyes filling with tears. With hands trembling, she passed the phone to Emma.

"It's Otto."

"Oh, God."

"I'm sorry, Emma. Theo was arrested in Heiligenstadt—"

Her hand tightened around the receiver.

"Thank God!" She was overwhelmed by a feeling of such relief that she could barely stand. "I could have stayed, if they'd only told me ... I'll go there now."

"No, Emma, he's not there. They took him to police headquarters —"

"Then I'll go there! I have to see him."

"You don't understand. You can't. It's too late... "

"It's only six o'clock," she said, trying desperately not to understand.

"They said he collapsed when they brought him in...he...he died two hours ago."

"They're lying, Otto! He's too young and strong—"

"There were injuries—"

She doubled over, as a spasm of pain radiated from her belly to her head. She squeezed the heels of her hands against her temples trying to silence the screams in her head before they shattered her skull.

"It's my fault! I shouldn't have told him!" she cried, now sobbing uncontrollably.

Léonie took the receiver from her hand and whispered to Otto that she would call him later.

"Told what to whom, Emma? What did you tell?" she asked gently, her own tears falling silently as she stroked Emma's back.

"His name. I told him Theo's name. He hated Socialists. He said he'd arrest all of us if he could."

"It wasn't him, Emma. It was the artillery. That's who…It was not your fault."

Léonie and Greta took turns sitting with her, trying to comfort her with their kindness, as the muscles in her belly contracted again. Pillows, sheets and blankets magically appeared transforming the sofa into a nest into which she burrowed. She could not stop shivering. She rolled herself into a ball and must have fallen asleep for when she woke she was alone and heard the clock strike three. As she tried to uncurl herself, her belly spasmed, the pain now radiating into her back. She breathed in and out slowly, but could not force the pain to subside. Bent over, her hands on her belly, she stumbled to the bathroom. As a wave of excruciating pain hit her, she felt a rush of something fluid or solid or both run down the inside of her thighs. She looked down and seeing a puddle of blood she must have screamed because before she knew it Josef opened the door. He called for Léonie to bring his medical bag, towels and a robe, and told Greta to prepare a bed. In a daze, Emma let Léonie undress and wash her and tried not to understand what had happened. Léonie slid Emma's arms into a robe, tied it loosely at the waist and led her to the guest room, where she held her hand as Josef examined her.

"I'm sorry, Emma," Josef said. "You've had a miscarriage."

"What have I done? What have I done?"

The sound of her wailing echoed in her ears.

"Nothing, dear girl," Josef said. "It is not your fault. Sometimes these things happen early in a pregnancy. In time, you will have other children."

Emma looked at him as if he were crazy. Theo was dead. Their baby was dead. There would be no others.

"My life is over, don't you understand?"

"You mustn't upset yourself. Let me call your mother—"

"No, no, don't tell her!"

"Tomorrow you must see your gynecologist— but now it is important for you to rest. I am giving you something so you can sleep."

Emma shook her head, afraid of what her mind would conjure if she closed her eyes—images of Theo bleeding, screaming in pain, forsaken, of blood running down her legs, her baby's blood … She was so tired. She could not keep her eyes open. She must have slept after all for it was growing dark when she heard Greta in the hallway saying the fighting in Vienna had stopped. And as it was not in her nature to be subtle, Greta added, "There've been so many casualties we may never know where Theo's body is."

Emma tried to get up but felt so weak her legs almost folded under her.

Léonie insisted she stay in bed, she needed to rest. Emma was grateful for she feared her mother would say Theo had brought his death upon himself.

She lay back against the pillows and felt herself sinking as if into a cloud of feathers. When she awoke, it was morning and her mother was sitting by the bed, her eyes red from crying.

She kissed Emma and let her sob as she cradled her in her arms.

"You will get through this," she said. "Léonie has ordered a taxi so I can take you home. Greta and Sophie went home, and Josef is at work. Come, let's get you dressed, I've brought you fresh clothes."

Emma thanked Léonie, and they went downstairs. Her mother held her hand all the way home, but they did not speak and Emma was grateful.

"Go lie down in my room," her mother said when they arrived home."Josef has arranged for one of his colleagues to come and examine you."

Emma stared at her.

"You know?"

"Yes. Now go lie down. He'll be here any minute."

She settled Emma in her bed, and tucked the blanket around her, as she had done when she was a child and ill. But now no doctor could make Emma well again. Her baby was gone.

When he arrived only minutes later, he shook Emma's hand and then went to wash his, as if she'd contaminated him.

"You're right," Emma wanted to say. "I ruin everything."

When he returned, her mother left the room, leaving the door slightly ajar. The doctor opened his medical bag and removed gloves and a speculum.

"There can be complications after a miscarriage. Josef thought it best to make sure there weren't any," he explained.

Slowly, gently, he examined her, with the fingers of one hand inside her and the other hand pressing on her abdomen.

Speaking in a soft, calming voice, he said, "If a miscarriage is incomplete it can lead to infection, but I see no sign of that, as it was so early in your pregnancy—so that is good news…but there is one matter of concern."

He pulled the sheet over her again, removed his glove, and wrapped the speculum in a cloth before replacing it in his bag, then sat down in the chair by her bed.

"Sometimes a woman's uterus is not fully formed. This was probably the reason for your spontaneous abortion."

"Abortion? I didn't! I wouldn't!"

"I know. It is a medical term. Forgive me if it sounded like a judgment. It was not. Sometimes, in the early stages of a pregnancy when a uterus is not a normal size or shape, the pregnancy cannot develop and is ... halted. The medical term for that is *aborted*. Physically, you will quickly recover from this event. Your condition is not dangerous to your health, but—and I regret having to tell you this —it will prevent your being able to have children in the future."

"I have no future," she said.

He patted her hand but said nothing. What was there to say?

Emma thanked him and her mother offered to pay, but he refused and mumbled something about friendship.

When he left, Emma turned to her mother and knowing she had listened through the open door, she said, "I don't want to talk about it."

Two days passed before she could make herself get out of bed. When she did, she found her mother had opened all the windows and let the cold air clear the smell of bleach from the apartment.

"Come," her mother said. "Eat something and then we can work together. Keeping busy will help you."

In the turmoil of those cold February days, no one ordered their laundry to be done, but there was still mending to finish so they closed the windows and sat down to work. For more than a week they sat side by side, barely a word between them, the silent repetition of their tasks both a bond and a balm. A lesson to remember, Emma thought, now that Pandora's box had opened and the future no longer shone with happiness.

Then one morning, her mother returned from Frau Mandl's and said, "I called the Grünbaums and told them you would be back to work tomorrow."

"Not yet, Mama, I can't."

"You have to, dear. The Grünbaums need you, and I can manage here. In the evening, we will help Father Johannes deliver parcels to all the poor people who were left homeless. They have nothing and need everything. The storm is over, Emma. Doing something for others will help you heal."

Emma shook her head. Had the short-lived civil war been merely a storm, she might have weathered it by standing fast against its battering winds until the sun returned. But it had been more than a storm. It had ruptured the very foundation of her life, sucking her future into its abysses—Theo into one, her child into another, forever stolen from each other and from her. How could she ever heal from that?

She did not return to her lessons in the Grünbaums' back room.

6.

BERLIN

A few weeks after Frau Altmann left, Friedrich made the acquaintance of a Prussian widow of a similar age, who allowed him to live on her estate and paid his expenses, although she considered him more servant and chauffeur than companion and regarded with suspicion the postcard he received from Paris.

My dear boy,
    A few words to tell you that Paris is as beautiful as I remembered—you would enjoy it — although Germans seem as unwelcome here as I was in Berlin. I will move on as soon as I can get a visa to somewhere.
    We live in difficult times, I'm afraid.
                Affectionately,
                Rosa Altmann

"Who is she and why was she unwelcome in Berlin?" the Prussian widow asked.

"I don't know. The name is not familiar," Friedrich said, throwing the card away.

But he remembered the name of the Paris hotel and replied.

My dear Frau Altmann,
    I was relieved to hear that you had arrived safely in Paris. You were right to leave here.

It is only getting worse. It grieves me to
think that someone like you does not feel
welcome everywhere.
May the future shine brighter,
I remain your friend,
FvH

His reply was sincere, but he was careful to sign only his initials and took it directly to the post office where the Prussian widow would not see it. There had been too many rumblings that people known to associate with Jews were being denounced and arrested.

He considered leaving Berlin himself. But where would he go? Not Paris—where memories of The Great War still lingered. Nor London, where people were insular and he did not speak the language.

Perhaps Vienna, where the wine and music were good and one still said *servus* and not *Heil Hitler*. But he had no money and neither did Austria. So why trade one former empire for another if there was nothing to be gained?

7.

VIENNA

As spring morphed into summer, Emma learned to hide her grief. If she did not speak of Theo or her unborn child, she could keep them in the ether around her. Invisible but still hers.

Outwardly, Vienna too seemed to return to its old self. Visitors spoke of its leisurely charm as if nothing had changed, unaware that the whole country's foundations were now rotting.

Austrofascism has brought an end to democratic parliamentarianism and party pluralism" is how Otto described the rot in one of his editorials.

One day in late spring when the chestnut trees along the Ringstrasse had begun to bloom, Otto learned that Theo had been cremated by the city, his ashes claimed by a relative who had thoughtfully added them to the grave of Theo's parents. That evening Emma knelt before the simple stone and begged Theo and his parents to forgive her.

Day after day she returned, bringing a flower for him and another for their child, pouring out her memories and love, comforted by the thought Theo was near—until early one morning she stood before the grave empty-handed.

"Yesterday, a man was buried in the plot next to you," she said.

She'd watched them lowering the coffin and thought how big it was, big enough for a man once full of life. His widow had looked over at her and said that when she died she was going to be cremated so that her ashes could be with her husband forever. Her name would be carved under his and everyone would know they'd always belonged together.

"I cannot come to this place of emptiness anymore," Emma said to Theo. She traced the letters of his name with her fingers. "Your name is here but you are not. You are in my heart and it is there that I will always find you. Rest in peace, my dearest, for we do not."

Emma's words were prescient for that very day, the 24th of July 1934, ten Austrian Nazis attempted a coup d'état. Chancellor Dollfuss was shot and died of his wounds.

German troops gathered at the border.

Mussolini rushed his army to the Brenner Pass and threatened war if Hitler invaded. Hitler backed off, abandoning Austria's Nazis to their unsuccessful rebellion.

Kurt von Schuschnigg was appointed the new chancellor.

"I'm not sure that's an improvement," Emma said to her mother.

"He says he'll keep Austria free from Germany."

"If he can. Things can change when you least expect it. I know that now."

"That's why you have to live life when you can, Emma. You're still young, whether you feel that way or not. You mustn't waste it."

"I'm doing my best."

Her mother glanced away, and said casually, as if the thought had just occurred to her, "Why not go out with that young doctor Menzler? You know, the one Josef introduced you to?"

"He's an intern. He has no time."

"Then meet someone who does. Go to the Sunday tea dances in the *Stadtpark Casino*. You are not the only one alone."

Emma glared at her.

"Mama, please. It's much too soon. I'm not ready. Don't you understand?"

"I do, dear, but things happen and life goes on, whether it's how we want it or not."

1936

THE OLYMPICS

8.

VIENNA

The first day of summer two years later was gloriously warm and sunny. Greta and Léonie organized a picnic for their girls in the *Stadtpark* and asked Emma to join them. Until then, Emma had declined such invitations. The sorrow of knowing she would never have a child of her own had sunk deep into her bones, even when outwardly she seemed to recover from her loss. In the privacy of her friends' homes, when a sudden tear could be wiped surreptitiously, she could be her old affectionate self with their girls, but in public, where the world seemed aggressively full of children she would never know, and an unexpected sob would draw attention, it had been too painful, so her friends were relieved that this time she accepted.

The park was crowded but they found a spot by the pond where they could lay their blankets and keep an eye on the children.

Valerie took Sophie by the hand and led her to the pond. Turning around to make sure of her mother's permission, she removed first Sophie's shoes and then her own. They sat down and wiggled their toes in the pond, giggling as they watched the water rippling toward a dozen newly hatched ducklings paddling behind their mother.

"The girls have grown really close, these last months," Greta said.

"Yes, just like us," Léonie said, glancing over at her friends.

Emma nodded and put her hand on her friend's.

"Papa always said a three-legged stool is the strongest," she said, grateful for the friendship that had seen her through the worst of the past two years.

They had let months pass before they gently suggested Emma meet friends of Otto's or Josef's. At first she'd said what she'd said to her mother — that she wasn't ready. When they urged her to reconsider, she said she couldn't begin a relationship with a man knowing that what he'd want most she could not offer him.

"Then tell him you can't have children," Greta had answered, in that direct way of hers.

"When? At dinner or during intermission at the opera? The first time we met? The second? After I tricked him into marriage?"

"If he loves you it won't matter," Léonie said.

Emma shook her head. Of course it would matter. It was all that mattered. She was aware of the admiring glances she still attracted, but love was something else. She had to face the fact that no one would love her again the way Theo had.

As she turned to look at the children, she suppressed those thoughts and said, "We were only a little older than they when we first met."

"Six," Greta said, nodding. "It seemed so grown up then. Do you remember our first day in school?"

"Every detail," Emma said. "I was so excited to be starting that I had practiced the walk there at least a dozen times. Mama had mended my favorite gray wool dress, and ironed a dark blue pinafore with so much starch it could have walked to school by itself. And I had brand new brown leather shoes."

"I don't remember my clothes but I remember not wanting any help getting ready," Greta said. "I insisted on brushing my hair by myself, which made it so frizzy that I had to wet my hands and pat it down before I could tie it back. It must have been completely lopsided but I wouldn't let my aunt fix it."

Emma laughed. "I would never have gotten away with that. Mama braided my hair so tightly that there wasn't a strand out of place. She even checked my fingernails, and must have told me a thousand times that I mustn't talk or laugh in class. I even remember what I ate—a bowl of warm milk with chunks of leftover bread and a big pat of butter, as a treat. Of course, it dribbled down my chin and my mother practically rubbed my face raw with a dishcloth cleaning me off. I think she would have killed me had I gotten it on my dress."

"No special treats for me," Greta said. "Farina with raisins is what the boarders and I ate every morning. But I didn't care. All I cared about was learning how to read so I could read the newspaper while I ate just like the boarders did."

Valerie and Sophie returned to the blanket to fetch some bread to feed the ducks. Léonie stroked her daughter's soft blonde curls, and the girls ran off again.

"Soon they'll be starting school," Emma said.

"Valerie is already talking about it. She's not afraid of it at all the way I was," Léonie said. "Frau Lotte came to dress me and told me I needn't be afraid. All children went to school. And since it was such an important day I was to eat breakfast in the dining room with my parents. She tied big satin bows at the end of my braids, and I wore the new clothes my mother had bought—a white lace blouse with a blue skirt, and a white smock, and new shoes, although I really wanted to wear my ballet slippers. When I entered the dining room I was surprised to see both my parents already dressed and asked if they were going somewhere too. Papa said they were walking me to school and picking me up when I finished and he was bringing his new camera. He only brought his camera on happy days. That's when I knew that everything was going to be all right."

"God, how innocent we were," Emma said. "Did we even realize we were in the midst of a war?"

"My aunt and the boarders talked about it when they thought I wasn't listening," Greta said. "So many young men lost...it changed the whole world, didn't it?"

Léonie nodded. "My father said that before the war everyone was filled with optimism, secure in the thought that life would keep getting better. So we weren't the only innocents."

"Weren't we lucky that alphabetical order put us together?" Emma said. "Grünbaum, Hellmann, Huber. Friends forever, we said—and here we still are."

"We should celebrate, go on a trip together," Greta said.

"Berlin! Theo and I always wanted to go there. We could go to the Olympics."

"Oh my God, Emma, not now," Greta said. "Léonie can't even consider going there. With the Nuremberg laws Jews have no rights anymore. None. They could arrest her."

"Forgive me, Léonie. I wasn't thinking. I am far too lost in myself sometimes."

Léonie reached out to squeeze Emma's hand.

"Never mind. We'll go someday. Hitler can't last. People will realize…"

"I don't know," Greta said. "The Olympics will make him even more popular. People will see glory and not look behind it. Elsa and Marion are all excited about going. That tells you something. "

9.

BERLIN

By 1936 Friedrich's finances were almost depleted. Unsure of his ability to maintain even the most reduced circumstances after the unexpected death of his most recent benefactress, he might have descended into despair had it not been for the Führer's Olympic plans. Such grandeur and pageantry might yet open the door to his financial salvation.

If he were to fail—which remained a possibility —he resolved to throw himself dramatically off the Palace Bridge, from the very spot where eight marble sculptures depicted the life and death of a warrior. Journalists—and perhaps even poets— would be moved to write of this tragically appropriate end to the life of a young and penniless nobleman.

Two days before the opening ceremonies, Friedrich moved to an attic room at the Hotel Esplanade that he had booked weeks before and practiced his charms on the young lady who cleaned the best rooms. She was able—he didn't ask how— to procure a press pass to the Olympics, for which he paid her with a kiss, and which he then traded for a proper five-day ticket.

The next morning he questioned the bell boys and doormen at length on which restaurants, cabarets, and shops were frequented by the hotel's finest guests. In the afternoon, he sold the silver cigarette lighter Frau Altmann had given him and treated himself to a balcony seat at the Ufa Palast cinema, although he did not care for Albert Speer's recent architectural changes. *Moderne*

Streamlining they called the stripped-down, utilitarian style the Führer so admired. The film was no more charming than the theatre façade. A sign, he feared, that it was only the beginning of a long week.

Eager to use the Olympics for propaganda purposes, Hitler had ordered the construction of a 326-acre sports complex in Grünewald, to be designed by the architect Werner March. This *Reichssportfeld,* as it was called, was to include an Olympic stadium with capacity for over 100,000; the 28 acre Mayfield, capacity 50,000; the Waldbühne amphitheater for 25,000; a 77 meter high Bell Tower, and facilities for various other sports and events.

On opening day the stadium was filled to capacity. Friedrich found himself facing the special stand built for Hitler and his associates, and seated diagonally behind a mother and her nubile daughter. Both women were attractively dressed in red and white, presumably in honor of the Austrian flag as their charming Viennese accents soon made their provenance clear. When the five thousand athletes marched into the arena, they turned to look at the Austrian-born Führer and raised their arms with shared pride. *Sieg Heil* they shouted. Feeling no affinity for the shrill little man himself, Friedrich gave in to a need to retie his shoe and forfeited the moment.

A specially composed Olympic Hymn was conducted by Richard Strauss, after which the Olympic torch arrived, having been carried from Olympia by three thousand relay runners over the preceding twelve days.

Other than to ask whether they would be attending again the next day, there was little time for idle conversation during such an impressive spectacle.

On the second day, Friedrich paid special attention to his appearance, slicking back his dark hair, clipping his mustache to curve neatly over his lip. He wore his father's best suit—slightly altered by the hotel's kindly maid for the price of a few more kisses.

He arrived in the stadium early and arranged to switch places so as to sit next to the two Viennese ladies.

"May I introduce myself," he said with a bow and a click of his Teutonic heels. "I am Friedrich, *Graf* von Harzburg."

"Frau Bruckner," the mother replied, her eyes sparkling as she held out her white-gloved hand for a kiss. "Elsa Bruckner. And this is my daughter, Marion."

There was no mistaking their relationship — both blue-eyed with wavy platinum-blonde hair à la Jean Harlow, and high-cheek bones hinting at eastern-European grandmothers. Czech, most probably. Marion was attractively dressed in a navy two-piece with large white collar and a white hat, while her mother wore a calf-length ivory linen dress buttoned off-center. Both very chic and *à la mode*.

Friedrich and Frau Bruckner chatted gaily for several minutes as they waited for the first event to begin, whereas Marion took little notice of him. She was more interested in the younger, blue-eyed, blonde Aryan smiling at her from a row below. Friedrich would have to do a little more than chat to turn her head his way.

As the event progressed, Friedrich noticed Marion's restlessness. Afraid she might ask her mother to leave, he said, "You've probably had many other invitations, but I would be greatly honored, if you would be *my* guests at an Olympic ball tomorrow."

"We had actually planned..." Marion began, but was quickly interrupted by Frau Bruckner's "That would be splendid, Herr Graf."

"Then I will send a car for you. I did not bring my car this time."

"We have a suite at the Kaiserhof," Frau Bruckner added.

"Ah, the Führer's favorite," he replied, with a knowing nod.

"And you, Herr Graf?"

"I have a room at the Hotel Esplanade—an old family tradition since Kaiser Wilhelm's days. Greta Garbo's favorite as well. She has often joined me there for tea."

Yes, he thought as he climbed to his room later that night, cheap rooms in grand hotels were an old family tradition.

He threw off his shoes and collapsed onto the room's narrow bed. Meaningless social exchanges were exhausting—yet necessary if he was to make a living. Until now his targets had been older women suffering a scarcity of suitors after The Great War. Hungering for affection, they rewarded his attentions with trinkets he could sell when needed.

Frau Bruckner was different. She and he understood each other immediately. He had class and she had money, so she overlooked the fraying cuffs on his sleeves, and the covetous look he'd cast on her diamond and sapphire brooch. She could accept his hungry intentions because she had plans of her own.

Friedrich was relieved that her interest in him was on her daughter's behalf, for the daughter was a far tastier morsel, with her enticing contradiction of angelic blonde curls and voluptuous figure. He wondered toward which attribute her character would most incline. If all went well, a match would be made and he would find out. Not that the answer mattered. Beggars can't be choosers.

Marion began to take interest in him when he suggested forgoing the canoeing, football, and greco-roman wrestling competitions so that he could introduce them to Berlin's finest shops.

"Leipzigerstrasse is Berlin's most fashionable," he explained. "Friedrichstrasse—as popular and well-known as it is—would not suit you. Its clientele is too provincial."

Mother and daughter were pleased at his assessment and made several purchases. In the evening, he delighted them with a promenade down Kurfürstendamm, before going on to a late night cabaret. Nothing too decadent, of course.

Marion had little interest in museums or cultural performances, so they repeated this routine twice again, changing only cabarets and cafés.

On the eve of their departure, he accompanied them to their hotel to bid them adieu. He expressed his sincere desire to meet again one day and gave them his business card.

As they walked toward the elevator he heard Frau Bruckner say, "Don't you find Friedrich terribly charming?"

"I suppose. He does have good taste," Marion answered, flinging the silk shawl he had bought her over her shoulders. As the elevator door opened he saw her twirl around and admire herself in the mirror on the elevator's back wall.

"He *is* more entertaining than any of the boys I know in Vienna," she added. "I should have him take me to the Opera Ball. I'm sure no one else would have a Count they could ask to their debut."

"Just what I was thinking," Frau Bruckner said, as the elevator door closed.

There would be no need to go to the Palace Bridge.

10.

VIENNA

"Otto, come look at all the things we brought back from Berlin!" Marion said, taking her brother's arm and dragging him to her room. "You too, Greta. Friedrich said Berlin's shops are as fashionable as in Paris."

"Who is Friedrich?" Greta asked.

"A charming gentleman we met on our very first day at the games," Elsa said, as she helped Marion spread her purchases on her bed. "Graf von Harzburg was quite taken with Marion— as you can imagine—and insisted on showing us the city. He's lived in Berlin for years, although his estate—"

"Mother, please, you can tell them later," Marion said. "This is more important." One by one, she held up half a dozen dresses, two suits, a coat, three pairs of shoes, and two hats. "Aren't they marvelous?"

"Very chic, Marion, but I hope you brought photos of the Olympic events, too," Greta said, sitting down.

"We didn't stay for many. Sports can be so boring."

"You didn't see Jesse Owens win? How I would have liked to see Hitler's face then."

Marion looked bewildered, Elsa annoyed, but then Greta regularly annoyed her.

"You're mischievous," Otto whispered to Greta as he put his arm around her.

"We had many other occasions for photographs," Elsa said.

"Especially at the ball Friedrich invited us to," Marion said. "I had nothing glamorous enough for that, so I *had to* buy a new gown. It's being cleaned now, but look." She pulled out two professional photographs, one of her alone, and one with Friedrich.

"So that's him," Greta said. "Very debonair. Like a French movie star."

"He's a count. That's much better. He comes from a very old family," Elsa said.

"Don't we all come from old families?" Greta said.

Otto nudged her foot with his. "There must have been quite an atmosphere of excitement in Berlin, and not only at the games," he said.

"Oh, there was," Elsa answered. "The city and the stadium were awash with Olympic flags and banners."

"Giant banners with swastikas. I saw the pictures in the paper," Greta said.

"Well, why not? The Führer was the host, wasn't he? He had reason to be proud. We could learn from him. Things have really improved in Germany. That's what everyone was saying."

"Everyone except the people that had been removed and sent to detention camps," Otto said. "They took down the *Jews Not Welcome Signs* that had been up all over the city until the tourists arrived."

"I saw no sign of anything like that at all," Elsa said. "Did you, Marion?"

Marion shrugged, uninterested. "I don't know why we always have to talk politics," she grumbled. "I thought we were going to look at my dresses."

"I'm sure neither of you asked any Jews what *they* thought," Greta said, ignoring her. "But then you would have had to obtain permission from the Gestapo to do so."

"And why would we have done that?" Elsa snapped, her voice quite icy now.

"You must have enjoyed all the cultural things in Berlin, Marion," Otto said, trying to change the conversation's direction.

"We didn't have time for anything like that. There were so many good shops to go to. Not just for me! Mother wanted porcelain and Rosenthal is the best, isn't it? More fashionable than Augarten. So that's what we got. She already put it in the dining room. Did you see?"

Before Greta or Otto could answer, Elsa said, "We're going to invite Friedrich to the Opera Ball."

"Won't Herr Bruckner be taking you?" Greta asked.

Elsa glared at her.

"Not for me, obviously. He'll escort Marion. It will be quite a coup for her debut don't you think?"

Greta looked at her watch with feigned shock at how the time had flown.

"Absolutely, but I really must check on Sophie and make sure she hasn't run away."

Otto followed Greta down the hall to their room.

"Marion's young. She doesn't understand," he said.

"I realize she's your sister, but she needs to understand. Ignorance is dangerous."

1937
THE MARRIAGE

11.

VIENNA

Frau Bruckner and Friedrich corresponded frequently regarding her invitation for him to be Marion's escort to the Opera Ball—an invitation he was given to understand could lead to a broader, more permanent association with the family. He accepted. If the relationship did not blossom, there must be any number of Viennese war widows looking for companionship.

Friedrich arrived in Vienna on 7 January 1937, a day earlier than expected in order to have time to arrange his accommodations without Frau Bruckner's further interference. She had insisted that only the Hotel Imperial on the Ring would befit his station, although he would have preferred a room in a simple boarding house. Fortunately, he had once met the assistant manager in Berlin and knew of his predilection for gambling to excess, so he had little trouble persuading him to let him reside in one of the several upstairs attic rooms once reserved for staff of visiting royalty. At no cost, of course, as his resources were limited. The little that he had would only see him through a short campaign to win over Frau Bruckner and her daughter.

His room was like all the other attic rooms he'd experienced— narrow and smelling of resignation to one's fate. He hung up his few shirts and suits, placed his cufflinks, gloves, and ties neatly in a drawer, and went downstairs to speak to the bellboy.

"I may be spending several hours a day in the lobby," he told the young man, slipping a few bills into his pocket. "Every so often, not always at the same time, I would like you to search for me in the lobby. You are to say that the ambassador of whatever country you choose is on the phone and wishes to speak with me. I will follow you slowly, as if it were a normal occurrence, and later you will tell me which eyes followed me in turn."

The bellboy, a hollow-cheeked, black-haired young Hungarian by the name of Tibor, arched one eyebrow but refrained from asking why, although it was clear the new guest had piqued his curiosity.

"One day, young man," Friedrich said, "you will understand the importance of such illusions."

It did not take long for Friedrich to ascertain that in Vienna there was no one *good society,* as the English would say. Instead, there were circles—cultural, scientific, aristocratic, as well as financial, commercial and industrial. The Bruckners belonged to the latter—a position of comfort he envied—but Frau Bruckner aspired to the aristocratic—a step up that he could provide.

Friedrich considered himself a keen observer of the human condition—a useful skill passed on to him by his father. *Knowledge is power,* he used to say, *but do not be distracted by the urge to judge right from wrong.*

His mother's skills in this realm had been diluted by an unfortunate tendency to forget ambition and show compassion for those in need of it. This weakness had not served them well, as she'd given most of her own fortune away and had gotten nothing but ill health in return.

His own talents were about to be tested at the Opera Ball—Vienna's most prestigious social event.

He had seen other opera houses but nothing could compare with Vienna's grandeur and the magnificent *Magic Flute* frescoes by Moritz von Schwind.

The ball began with a performance by the Vienna Opera Ballet, some of them in eighteenth century Imperial period costumes, others in long, flowing white ballet gowns. As debutantes, Marion and he were presented along with a few hundred other well-chosen couples. They'd been strictly trained and rehearsed at Elmayer's, Vienna's most prestigious dance studio. They did not disappoint and danced elegantly into the early hours of the morning.

For her debut at the ball, Marion Bruckner wore white satin, and danced on the arm of the handsome young Graf von Harzburg, recently arrived from Berlin—so stated the society news the morning after, thereby successfully easing them into Frau Bruckner's desired circle.

Frau Bruckner was delighted, and thought it only fitting now that she and Friedrich be on a first-name basis.

"It would be my honor, Elsa." Friedrich replied.

Marion complained that the photographs did not do her justice.

Due to deteriorating health, Marion's father had been unable to attend. Friedrich had met him only briefly, shortly after his arrival, but after the ball he was asked to visit the gentleman in his study— an imposing, dark-paneled room lined with books.

"What are your intentions, young man," Herr Bruckner asked, after staring at Friedrich intently.

"I assure you, they are serious. I wish more than anything to make Marion happy."

"The Reich has conscription. Will you be called to serve?"

"No, you need not fear that. I suffer from nyctalopia—night blindness."

Herr Bruckner chuckled and then grew serious again.

"And children? How do feel about them?"

Friedrich said he hoped one day to have a son as fine as his. Herr Bruckner stared again—as if seeing through him—and motioned to Fritz that his guest's time with him had expired.

Herr Bruckner stayed in his bed after that, and two days later, on the 19th of February 1937, at the age of sixty-seven, he suffered sudden cardiac arrest.

Frau Bruckner rushed dutifully to his bedside, but was later heard to say, "Thank goodness he didn't die before the ball. We wouldn't have been able to attend."

Even Marion was shocked at such coldness, and Friedrich found this unexpected loyalty to her father appealing and expressed his deepest sympathy. With the hope that it would bring her comfort, he took her hand and officially proposed.

Unsurprised, she nodded her acceptance. After all, it was what her mother had planned. Marion's enthusiasm for the merger grew when she realized that her life would become even more privileged once she was married, and that Friedrich demanded little of her in exchange.

So it was that in the summer of 1937, at the tender age of eighteen, Marion Margarethe Léopoldine Bruckner stepped up the social ladder to become Marion, Gräfin von Harzburg. A countess at last.

Friedrich left his attic accommodations and moved into the west wing of the Bruckner mansion. Adjustments were made as to the assignment of rooms, with Marion and he assuming her parents' bedroom, while Elsa transferred to a suite of rooms in the center of the house. He was given a room to serve as his study, had servants he could command, and was issued a bank account. He had no duties except to entertain his young wife and cultivate the proper social relationships. For the first time since his parents left their ancestral estate, he had a permanent address.

When Elsa asked about his furnishings and other belongings, he said that he would arrange for them to be packed and shipped. Why tell her that he had sold them long ago, and that in a moment of financial desperation his father had sold the old estate as well. Now that he had achieved his goal of marrying wealth, it no longer mattered.

12.

VIENNA

Léonie, Josef, and Emma were not invited to Marion's wedding and, as the happy couple spent some weeks away, their curiosity to meet the groom was not satisfied until Greta organized a small welcome-home party in early autumn.

"I was afraid they'd back out at the last minute, but they said they'd meet us upstairs," Greta said as she led her friends to her private living room in the east wing where Otto was already waiting. Valerie ran down the hall and joined Sophie in the nursery.

"What's your impression of him, Greta?" Léonie said. "Do you like him?"

Greta laughed. "I have no idea. I've hardly seen him. Marion said it's still their honeymoon and she wants to keep him to herself for a while—although it's probably just an excuse not to spend time with us."

"Do you think Marion loves him?" Emma asked.

"I doubt love had much to do with their marriage. With our little Austria on the verge of being swallowed by Germany, I'm sure Elsa thought a German title could prove useful."

"Now, now, Greta," Léonie said. "I'm sure all Elsa wants is for Marion to be happy. He's probably a very nice man. Where did they spend their honeymoon?"

"Bad Ischl, of course. Where else would Elsa send them but Emperor Franz Josef's summer place?"

"It *is* a romantic place. After all, he proposed to his beloved Sissi there," Léonie said.

"Here they are," Otto said, standing up. "The happy couple. Let me introduce you," he said.

After several expressions of *it's lovely to meet you,* and *welcome home,* Léonie turned to Friedrich and said, "Had you been to the Salzkammergut before? It is a lovely area, isn't it?"

"Not when it's raining, " Marion interjected. "We went to Munich instead. It's much more fun to be in a city, isn't it, Friedrich?"

"Oh yes, much more. Our days there were quite full," he said.

"And Hitler?" Otto said. "I hear—"

Marion turned to glare at her brother.

"Oh, stop it, Otto! No one cares."

Greta gave Marion a sharp look.

"I care," she said. "I'm no longer welcome there, you know. Under their new laws your brother wouldn't be allowed to be married to me. Even Sophie —"

No one spoke as Emma scanned everyone's faces. Elsa looked annoyed and Marion bored, as usual. Léonie and Josef seemed to be holding their breaths, and Friedrich probably wondered if every family gathering would be as tense as this.

After a few moments Emma felt she might be the only one who could break the uncomfortable silence.

"Now that you are settled here, Herr Graf, what will you do with your home in Germany?"

"You must call me Friedrich. We are all friends, are we not? I will sell it. I wouldn't dream of tearing Marion away from the city she loves so much. It's a huge old beast anyway and not really suited either for summer stays nor for skiing. We will look for something more comfortable."

"It must be difficult deciding what to do with all the furnishings. Have you—"

"It's the strangest thing, and quite awful," he said. "I had everything packed and shipped by a very reliable firm but was notified just today that the whole shipment has mysteriously disappeared. They have launched an investigation, of course, but … it really is most distressing. So many memories, you know…"

"I can imagine," Josef broke in—to everyone's surprise, since he was usually quiet. "One is so attached to family things. Things that have been passed down through generations … and with a rich history such as yours …."

Friedrich put his arm around Marion's shoulder.

"I'm sure my wife would much rather talk about her plans for the future…what was it you were telling me this morning, darling?"

Greta and Emma looked at each other. Perhaps Marion and Friedrich were well suited to each other after all.

13.

VIENNA

Friedrich found life in Vienna easy to adjust to. Its atmosphere was slower and far less colorful than Berlin's. He didn't mind, although he missed the movie palaces, where he had spent many happy hours. He didn't miss crowded beer halls, much preferring the more leisurely *Heuriger* evenings in the little inns of Grinzing and Nussdorf where the Viennese went with their friends to drink wine and listen to sentimental melodies.

And there were the cafés, of course. What would Vienna be without them? It was where he usually went when he was not needed for shopping or socializing. He sat for hours reading the many newspapers that were offered, eavesdropping on interesting discussions at neighboring tables. He envied them their wit and intelligence, knowing there was little chance he would ever have friends like that.

As the days grew cooler, he drove through the Wienerwald to see the trees change color and lose their leaves. The melancholy of that slow dying made him oddly nostalgic for the gray days of his childhood when his parents and he still lived together in their crumbling estate.

He settled well into the Bruckner household, flattering Elsa when needed, making few demands of his own, and acquiescing politely to all that was asked of him. He did not force Marion to attend operas he liked but that she found distressingly long—nor concerts, where she complained there was nothing to look at.

Marion preferred the theatre, although he found Vienna's offerings rather too traditional and would have enjoyed a Berlin-style cabaret now and then. Of course, even in Berlin the night life must have changed now that the Nazis banished degenerate art and entertainment of all kinds—though he wondered if it had just moved deeper underground—somewhere Goering would know to go.

Not that his own thoughts were pure. Marriage to Marion had awakened his desires. Her ripe body belied her youthful naïveté. Although she accepted the intimacies of marriage without complaint, there was a lack of enthusiasm that made him wonder whether it was he or the act itself that did not excite her.

On the rare occasions he saw the young Bruckners of the mansion's east wing, he wished he knew them better but they showed little interest in knowing him. Funnily, their quiet daughter Sophie had taken an unexpected liking to him. It touched him and made him want a child of his own.

Marion had no such thoughts. Shopping was all she longed for, and so he accompanied her when her mother couldn't. He always complimented her on her good taste and the quality of her purchases. Why not? It pleased her and it was not his money.

1938

THE BEGINNING

OF THE END

14.

VIENNA

The whole of Vienna must have stayed awake the night of January 25, 1938 as the aurora borealis lit the skies with flaming red curtains striped with white and shifting blues. The next day it was all people could talk about.

Not since Napoleon occupied Vienna has there been such a spectacle, one of the newspapers wrote.

Emma's mother said it was just as the Lady of Fátima had prophesied.

"She said a light would illuminate the night as a sign that God would punish us for our crimes by bringing us another war."

Emma tried to laugh it off as mere superstition, but when she arrived at work, she was surprised to see Léonie and the Grünbaums gathered in the back room of the store talking softly.

"We can't shake the feeling it's a warning we mustn't ignore," Frau Grünbaum said, her voice trembling, and her words incongruous for a woman normally composed.

"Ignore what, Oma?" Valerie chimed in from the floor, where she'd laid out paper and a box of colored pencils.

"Nothing, sweetheart, I was just being silly," she said, fingering the strand of pearls around her neck. "Would you go to the showroom and see if you can help Frau Mimi organize the scarves by color? You're so good at that."

Emma offered to go with her but Frau Grünbaum asked her to stay.

"Please sit down. What we have to say concerns you, too," she said, her voice steadier now. "We've come to the very difficult decision that we have no choice but to sell our business and emigrate while we still can."

Emma gasped. "Not because of some lights in the sky?"

"No, of course not, but it has become clear that we can no longer ignore the danger we are in." She looked at her husband and took his hand. "In Germany, Jews have lost all their rights. We've had desperate letters from some of our clients. They can no longer own anything or buy anything. Most jobs are forbidden to them, yet leaving has become more and more difficult—and for many unaffordable. We fear the same thing will happen here. It's already started and will only get worse. You know Hitler would like nothing more than to make Austria part of the Reich." She took her daughter's hand and said, "Léonie, we've talked about this. You must persuade Josef—"

"I've tried, Mama. He won't listen. But I'll try again, I promise."

"Can't Otto convince him?"

Léonie shook her head. "He's tried. In fact, he was the first to warn us."

Herr Grünbaum stood up and walked over to Emma's side of the table. He was not a tall man, barely the same height as she, but had always appeared strong. A man of substance who suddenly seemed smaller.

"My dear girl, I've known you since you were a child. It breaks my heart, but perhaps it would be best for you to look for another position. You shouldn't have any trouble. I will, of course, give you the excellent references you deserve."

Emma took his hand, held it in both of hers and thanked him, though they both knew his references would be of little use.

"I wouldn't think of leaving," she said.

As the day of the Grünbaums' departure grew near, Emma asked if she might be more help at their apartment than at the shop, an offer they gratefully accepted.

Together with Léonie, Frau Grünbaum and Emma sorted and packed until the elegance of the Grünbaums' apartment was dismantled piece by piece. Items to be sold—which included most of their furniture, carpets, and works of art—were wrapped and crated in the dining room, where they would be picked up by the Dorotheum auction house and sold at prices far below their value. In the foyer stood boxes and bags filled with kitchen items, curtains, towels, and clothing they wanted distributed to the poor. They asked Frau Lotte to oversee the disposal of whatever remained after their departure, but the poor woman, who had once been Léonie's nanny and had loyally stayed on as housekeeper, was much too distraught. So Emma volunteered as she didn't want Léonie to be forced to take on the burden.

On the second to last morning, after settling Valerie in the kitchen with Frau Lotte, the Grünbaums asked Léonie and Emma to join them in the living room. A long narrow table standing against an empty wall seemed to sag under the stacks of paper that covered it. On one of the table's delicately carved legs hung a hand-lettered tag: *for the Dorotheum.* Léonie put her hand on it as if to comfort it, remembering how the table had once stood in the foyer. A tall Chinese vase her mother had filled weekly with fresh flowers had sat in the center of it, under a Dutch still life of another tall Chinese vase filled with flowers. Soon it would all be gone.

Léonie turned on the radio. After a moment of static, Richard Tauber's tenor voice wafted through the room: *Wien, Wien, nur Du allein sollst stets die Stadt meiner Träume sein.*

"Please turn that off," Herr Grünbaum said.

"I thought you loved that song, Papa."

"Not anymore. Vienna is no longer the city of our dreams. Our dreams were an illusion, I'm afraid. But we have to go on and we will. I'm lucky for I have found a buyer for the store. And, although he's not paying anywhere near its worth, he has promised to retain what's left of the staff—so you should be all right, Emma. At least for now."

"I don't want to work for anyone else," Emma said.

"And I would not like to be the cause of your unemployment," he said softly.

Herr Grünbaum walked over to the long table and placed his slender hands on two piles of paper.

"This pile on the left concerns the sale. And this on the right contains all the documents we need to leave for England."

He picked up a folder and placed it in Léonie's hands.

"And here are instructions for what you have to do to follow us. Read them carefully and remember them. I fear you don't have much time."

"Josef won't leave yet, Papa," Léonie said. "He thinks that because Jews are half of Vienna's doctors and almost half of the university's professors, the Nazis will realize they need us. He firmly believes that the hysteria will pass and things will get back to normal in time. We just have to wait it out."

Her father banged his hand on a pile of papers.

"My dear sweet child, do not be naïve. Once they have power over us they won't change their minds. They have too many supporters. Look what's happened in Germany. It will be no different here, here where anti-Semitism is even stronger. You must come with us, Léonie, I beg you. If Josef refuses, then save yourself and Valerie and come without him. In England we'll be safe."

The weight of the terrible choice Léonie had to make fell on all of them as they watched her pace the room in silence.

Minutes passed before she answered, and then in a gentle but firm voice learned from her mother, she said, "You are right, Papa, Valerie must go with you to England."

"And you?" her father said.

"Josef is my husband. I can't leave him. I will persuade him in time, but in the meantime I will breathe easier knowing Valerie is safe with you."

"You will have to give us custody," her mother said softly.

"I know. I will have our lawyer arrange it."

"Will Josef agree?"

"He loves his daughter. He'll agree."

Léonie's mother took her daughter's hands firmly in hers.

"We will keep her safe until you come. I promise."

Silently, tears trickled down Léonie's cheeks. Her world was disappearing. In two days there would be nothing left of the home she'd grown up in. Where there had once been beauty and culture, laughter and joy, only bare walls and scuffed floors would remain.

Frau Grünbaum put her arms around her daughter, and the embrace seemed to give them both strength.

"Valerie and I had better go home now," Léonie said, kissing her mother once more. "Josef may come home for lunch."

Her mother turned to Emma and whispered, "Go with Léonie. She will need you."

Josef did not return for lunch. Léonie called her lawyer and packed a suitcase with Valerie's things while Valerie and Emma read fairy tales and drew pictures of princesses.

Emma stayed all day.

In the evening long after Valerie had fallen asleep, Léonie and Emma tiptoed into the nursery and saw that Valerie had kicked off her blankets. Léonie tucked them back around her.

"The cold always wakes her," she said. "I have to tell Mama to check that she's covered, and that one bedtime story is never enough—she always wants two. And she won't brush her teeth unless you do it at the same time."

"We'll make a list," Emma said, as they tiptoed out of the room. "When do you think Josef will be home?"

Léonie took a moment to answer, wrinkling her brow, as if the question confused her.

"He's always late in winter—everyone seems to get sick then. I worry that he will too. He was sickly as a child … He says that's why he became a doctor. He's a good man, Emma, but I'm afraid he won't forgive me for what I'm about to do."

She closed the nursery door and they walked down the hall to the dining room. She took a crystal decanter off the sideboard and poured them each a glass of wine.

"This wine is from Mama's favorite vineyard in Burgenland. She won't be able to find it in England."

When Léonie heard the front door key being put into the lock she jumped up and ran into the hall.

"You look tired, dear. Was it a bad day?"

"Exhausting. I'm hungry and glad to be home. Is Emma here? I see her coat."

"Yes, go join her in the dining room while I warm your dinner. She was an enormous help at my parents today."

Josef's coat hung loosely on his tall lanky frame and he seemed to have forgotten that he still had it on. Emma stood up and helped him off with it .

Léonie brought a bowl of soup, some bread, and a small plate of cold cuts and cheese.

Josef took a spoonful of soup and asked, "How was it at your parents?"

"Just about everything is packed and ready. By tomorrow the apartment will be empty and they will spend the night here."

"I don't think they've made the right decision, Léonie. Schuschnigg won't let the Germans in. He'll keep us free."

"Papa says —"

Josef spread out his arms, as if to encompass the room.

"Look around, Léonie. Every painting, every chair, every bronze and piece of porcelain we have means something to me. And why? Because they were handed down to me from my parents and their parents before them. If I lose them I lose my heritage, my history. This is our home and I treasure it as much as Kaiser Franz

Josef treasured Schönbrunn. We belong here. You understand that, don't you? You must feel the same."

Léonie put her hand on Josef's and in a soft, gentle voice said, "Papa says if we stay we will lose everything anyway, just like the German Jews. So many people we know have left already."

"Your father is a businessman. It's different for him."

Léonie's cheeks turned red, and Emma felt her own anger rising at his stubbornness.

"Otto has been warning us for months, and he's a journalist. They're afraid for us, don't you understand? It has nothing to do with business. Jews are being detained, put in camps."

"I can't go, Léonie. I'm a doctor. I can't—" He hid his head in his hands.

Emma blushed. She knew she shouldn't be there but she couldn't move.

Léonie rose and placed her hands tenderly on her husband's shoulders.

"I know, dearest. So I will stay with you until you are ready, but Valerie is just a child. We have to protect her. So I have made a decision. I have asked our lawyer to draw up papers giving custody to my parents so they can take her with them. You must sign them, and if you are not willing, I will take her and leave without you."

Léonie's voice was gentle but the fierceness of her ultimatum frightened Emma to the core for she knew in that moment that their world had broken beyond repair.

It no longer seemed right for her to be there. She slipped out of the apartment and ran down the stairs —and down the street, and through the park into the Innenstadt until she couldn't run anymore.

When she arrived home, Emma told her mother what Léonie had decided. Her mother didn't say anything, just held her and let her sob.

15.

VIENNA

On February 11th, 1938, only two weeks after the aurora
borealis burned the skies, and a mere thirty hours after Léonie's
ultimatum, she, Greta and Emma were at the Westbahnhof station
helping the Grünbaums load their luggage onto the train that would
carry them to the English Channel. Unable to face the last moment
with his daughter on a grimy platform surrounded by people, Josef
had said his farewells at home.

After hugs and kisses and last-minute whispered instructions,
the three friends left the Grünbaums' compartment and
disembarked. They stood on the platform looking up at Valerie,
who'd climbed up on her seat and was holding her doll out the
compartment window.

They'd kept the mood as light as possible. No talk of peril or
fear, or the end of their world, or Nazis, or how much they would
miss one another. Just happy plans for wonderful things to do and
see in London.

For Valerie's sake.

And theirs. They might never have made it through otherwise.

When the engine started and the conductor called for everyone
to board, Emma put her arm around Léonie's shoulders and Greta
put her arm around her waist and they stood together, waving until
long after the last speck of the departing train had disappeared and
the massive body of an incoming one chugged relentlessly into the
station, its whistle blaring. The wind it caused might have knocked

them over had they not been standing glued together as they had in the long-ago photograph taken on the day they'd become friends.

As they turned to leave, Léonie whispered, "I hope Valerie doesn't lose her doll. I stuffed the body with money."

Greta and Emma accompanied Léonie home and waited for Josef to return so she wouldn't be alone.

Although Herr Grünbaum had insisted she not give up her job, Emma couldn't bear the thought of Léonie alone, worried and torturing herself with thoughts that perhaps she'd made the wrong decision, so she decided she would call the shop in the morning and tell the new owners she was ill. Before she could do it, a letter arrived saying the store would be closed until replacements were found for the tailors, seamstresses, bookkeeper, and models— except her, the only non-Jew. So much for promises. She vowed never to step into the shop again.

"I'm going to Léonie's," she told her mother. "I have to make sure she's all right."

"I'm fine," Léonie said. "I'm sure I did the right thing, but I'll feel better once I know they're safe in London."

Otto and Greta joined them in the evening. Otto was outraged. Chancellor Schuschnigg had crossed the border into Germany hoping for a peaceful meeting with Hitler at his *Eagle's Nest* outside Berchtesgaden. Eager to win Hitler's cooperation, he'd encountered only threats. Thinking appeasement would prevent Germany's invasion and the loss of life, Schuschnigg had agreed — in a cascade of capitulations—to give amnesty to all Nazi prisoners, to appoint the Nazi anti-semite Arthur Seyss-Inquart, Minister of the Interior— which put him in control of the police— and to appoint Nazis to the Ministries of War and Finance.

"It's the beginning of the end for us," Otto said.

"All of Grünbaums' staff was fired except me," Emma told him in a whisper.

He gave her a sharp look. "And so it begins. Jews out, Aryans in."

"I'm not in," Emma said. "I quit. I'm just glad Herr Grünbaum doesn't know."

Nine days later the friends were gathered at Léonie's again as Hitler proclaimed the German Reich was no longer willing to tolerate the suppression of ten million Germans across its borders.

"He means us, of course," Otto said, and issued an editorial the next morning urging Schuschnigg to stand strong against the pressure and keep Austria independent. But in private, he despaired.

Trying his best to undo his surrender, Schuschnigg announced a plebiscite for March 13th, hoping that Austrians would vote to retain their national independence. Hitler demanded that he cancel it and resign, else he would order the German Wehrmacht to invade.

That night, Nazi thugs shouting *Heil Hitler* threw rocks through the windows of Otto's newspaper office.

By early March, they were returning almost nightly, smashing windows, defacing walls with swastikas. Still Otto kept writing and publishing, entreating his readers to remain firm in their resistance to Nazi interference.

With every day bringing another threat, the few remaining Jews on Otto's staff resigned in the hope they could still flee.

Again Otto urged Léonie and Josef to leave before it was too late.

"I can't. I have patients I'm responsible for. They'll see that," Josef said.

"They won't. You're a Jew. That's all that matters to them," Otto replied.

On March 11th, Schuschnigg warned Austrian citizens not to spill German blood by taking up arms against the Wehrmacht. When he began talks with Social Democrats to win their support, a slight hope glimmered that resistance was still possible—but Hitler, fuming with fury, called for his resignation.

At ten minutes to eight that very evening, Schuschnigg came on the radio and bade his country farewell with the words *God protect Austria.*

God abstained, and on March 12th, Schuschnigg was arrested and Seyss-Inquart, Minister of Security and Interior and long associated with the Austrian Nazi party, was made chancellor. Frantic, Greta called Emma, urging her to meet them at Léonie and Josef's as soon as possible.

When Emma arrived, the others were already gathered around the radio in the living room.

Otto rose to greet her and said, "SS Chief Heinrich Himmler and his deputy arrived in Vienna before dawn this morning. The Luftwaffe planes are circling, and the Germans have crossed the border. No one is resisting anywhere. Hitler will have full control before we know it." He placed his hand on Josef's arm. "We've run out of time, my friend. We have to leave—especially you."

"Thank you, I am grateful for your concern for us," Josef said, placing his hand on Otto's. "We will. I promised Léonie, but I have responsibilities ..."

"He won't let me pack any of our things," whispered Léonie. "He says they comfort him. I fear they only imprison us."

"Then pack up what you can carry yourself," Greta said, loud enough for Josef to hear. "Britain may close its doors if you wait any longer. What will you do then?"

"And you?" Léonie asked. "You're half-Jewish and Otto is the *Feinde Presse*—the enemy press."

"We know. We are trying to make arrangements to leave."

"When?" asked Emma.

"As soon as we can. We are no longer safe here."

Emma was overwhelmed by both fear and shame that she was the only one not at risk.

"Where would you go?" she asked, her voice breaking.

"To Lyon. Otto has friends there. After that, I don't know. Wherever we can get a visa."

Emma looked at her watch. "I'm sorry. I have to get home," Emma said. "I promised my mother."

Otto offered to drive her but she refused.

"I'll take the tram. You need to stay and persuade Josef to leave."

16.

VIENNA

Emma didn't know it until morning, but while her friends were talking about the threats they faced, the first German army units had already reached Vienna.

That morning, March 13th, Hitler stopped in Linz, his boyhood home, to announce that the *Anschluss* was complete. Ecstatic at his achievement, he marched on to Vienna. In the city that had denied him admission to art school, and where he had once lived in a homeless shelter, the streets now overflowed with people who welcomed their new Führer with thundering enthusiasm. Nazi banners and swastikas appeared everywhere as tanks filled the streets. The raucous noise of it all seeped into Blutgasse like the blood it was named for.

"I have to go back to Léonie's," Emma said, throwing on her coat.

"Stay here," her mother said. "It's too dangerous to be outside."

"If Theo were alive—"

"He'd be too smart to rush out and be crushed by a mob for nothing. Call Léonie. I'm sure they're safe at home."

Frau Mandl was at her window, pulling the shutters closed when Emma arrived downstairs.

"May I use the phone?" Emma asked.

"Yes, but quickly, before the hooligans shut it down."

Léonie answered on the second ring.

"Oh, Léonie, thank God, you're all right."

"So far. I'm boxing up as many of the things Josef loves most that I can. Maybe he will finally change his mind."

There was a hardness to her voice Emma had never heard before. Then she heard Léonie take a breath before she went on. "I wanted to send a telegram to my parents telling them not to worry, but I'm afraid to go out."

"Tell me the address and I will do it."

"No, you mustn't go out either. I will write them a letter. It will go out with the first post."

"Where is Josef?" Emma asked.

"Visiting patients, of course."

"Maybe he's saying good-bye."

"Perhaps," she said without conviction.

Mid-afternoon, Greta called Emma to say that Otto's paper had been ordered closed and stormtroopers were boarding up the office windows and doors.

"Now there's no one left to report the truth," she said.

Increasingly worried, Emma called Greta back later that evening. Otto and his staff had managed to escape being arrested, and he'd arrived home safely, after walking all the way through wind and sleet.

Realizing that she'd been monopolizing Frau Mandl's telephone, Emma offered to reimburse her.

"Nonsense," she said.

Emma hugged her and was about to go back upstairs when they heard a frantic knocking at the front gate.

"It's a man," Frau Mandl said, looking through the small window to the right of the front door. "He looks like he needs help."

The man's coat was covered with mud, his pant legs ripped at the knee. His head was bare and his hair, wet and disheveled, concealed his downcast eyes. Only when he looked up and spoke her name did Emma realize who he was.

"Josef! Oh God, what have they done to you?"

She pulled him in. Frau Mandl put her fingers to her lips and gestured with her head toward the two front apartments, and then the stairs.

"It's Dr. Salzmann," Emma whispered.

As she led him through the courtyard, Josef's knee buckled and he fell heavily against her. With Emma supporting him under one arm, and Frau Mandl under the other, they made their way up the stairs.

Hearing them approaching, Emma's mother opened the door.

"He is soaked to the skin, Frau Huber," Frau Mandl whispered. "Make sure you warm his hands and feet slowly." Turning to Josef she added, "No one need know you are here, but I will call your wife and tell her to bring fresh clothes."

Josef shook his head. "No, please. She mustn't see me like this."

"This is no time for pride, Dr. Salzmann," Emma's mother said. "Let's take off your coat and shoes. You can put on my husband's robe."

Like a child, he stood before her and let her undress him and put him in the old wool robe. Emma dried his hair with a towel and made him sit down. He rocked back and forth like a man at prayer, his hands crossed over his chest and tucked in his armpits.

Emma's mother brought over a pot of hot tea and a bowl of soup, poured him a cup and handed it to him.

"Tell us what happened."

He didn't answer, just kept his eyes on the cup in his hands.

"Where were you, Josef?" Emma asked gently.

He stared at her, his eyes red and full of pain. After a moment, he took a sip of tea, and began to answer, his voice hoarse and broken, the words coming out in short bursts.

"In the *Innenstadt*...I had to see Frau Lustig...she's so frail... she asked me why I was still here...her children left weeks ago... she was too old to start a new life...I tried to examine her...but she pushed me away... *Don't die here, Dr. Salzmann. Don't give them the satisfactio* ...she kept saying it..."

Josef began to cry and wiped his nose on the sleeve of his borrowed robe. Emma's mother took a handkerchief out of her apron pocket and handed it to him.

"And then?" Emma said, putting her arm around his shoulders.

"I made sure she had enough to eat...she kissed my hand when I left...I felt terrible leaving her alone...I was on my way home ... it was snowing and cold and I had no galoshes...I pulled my hat down and turned my collar up and walked as fast as I could...I kept my eyes down so I didn't have to look at anyone ... but there was a crowd...they were looking down at something...I thought perhaps someone was hurt and they needed a doctor...*Curious, are you?* a man said, and grabbed me by the neck...*Go and join them then, you dirty Jew*...He forced me to my knees and threw my hat into the gutter and pulled off my gloves..."

His words were tumbling out faster now.

"...there were at least twenty others on their knees in the icy slush, old men most of them...he shoved a scrub brush into my hand... *Scrub!* he kept shouting, pointing to the pro-Schuschnigg-anti-Nazi flyers as if *I* had stuck them to the pavement...all around us people were jeering, taunting...the storm troopers just watched and laughed...I scrubbed and scrubbed and kept telling myself *Don't die here. Don't give them the satisfaction.* Then I felt a sharp kick against my side and heard the kicker laugh, so proud of his power...I recognized him. It was our greengrocer's helper, that scrawny boy with pimples who'd always snuck Valerie an extra apple or handful of grapes. With his new-found swagger he went on to someone else while I crawled away in the slush...on my knees like a child..."

Josef buried his face in his hands.

"That's enough for now," Emma said.

Theo had been killed by people like that and she had been powerless to help him. At least now Josef was there with them and they could take care of him.

As if her mother had been thinking the same thing, she brought over a tub of lukewarm water. Josef winced with pain as Emma placed his feet into it.

"Please eat your soup, Dr. Salzmann," her mother said, pushing the bowl toward him. "You need your strength."

Silently, he ate a few spoons full, then stopped as if the spoon had suddenly grown too heavy.

"Forgive me, I can't manage any more."

"That's all right," Emma said. "Let me dry your feet, then you can lie down in my room."

"No, put him in mine," her mother said. "I'll get him a hot water bottle."

By the time Léonie arrived, Josef was asleep.

"How is he?" she asked.

"Exhausted."

Léonie took off her coat and tiptoed into Emma's mother's room. She kissed her husband's forehead, and pulled the blanket up over his shoulders.

"You're so cold. Thank God, you found your way here," she said quietly, then closed the door and went back into the main room.

"Come sit down at the table, Léonie, and have something to eat."

"Oh no, thank you, Frau Huber, I can't—but thank you for everything. I don't know what would have happened to him if —"

"He'll feel better tomorrow, you'll see. Tonight you'll both sleep in my room. Emma and I can sleep in hers. You two talk now and I'll see you in the morning."

She walked through the kitchen to the room behind it and closed the door.

Emma set out two glasses and took a bottle of wine from the cupboard.

"What will you do now, Léonie?"

"I don't know. I just thank God that Valerie is with my parents."

"We'll figure something out. Greta is coming in the morning. Perhaps you can go with them."

Léonie took her hand. "Won't you leave with us?"

"How? Mama and I don't have money. We don't even have passports."

No one slept very much that night except Josef.

In the morning his breathing sounded shallow. His lips were parched and his eyes glazed. It was clear that he was running a high fever.

"Should we call a doctor?" Emma asked.

Léonie shook her head. "Who would come? In any case, it's best no one knows he's here. We'll give him aspirin and fluids. And if I could have a pan of water and a wash cloth, I will try to cool him off a little."

She was so calm and courageous Emma wanted to weep.

Greta and Sophie arrived shortly after nine. Emma's mother took Sophie aside, while Greta and Emma joined Léonie at Josef's bedside.

"I tried calling you at home, Léonie," Greta said, keeping her voice low. "I was afraid something had happened when you didn't answer the phone so early. I told Otto I would stop by your apartment on the way here, but when I saw the police going into your building, I couldn't risk going in. Otto said that all around the city they've been arresting Jews, dragging them out of their apartments, taking whatever they want, leaving the rest in shambles. You can't go back there. Now that those bastards have closed Otto's paper we have no choice but to leave ourselves. They've made it as difficult as possible with all their permits and taxes and fees but we've managed to find someone to help us.

We're to leave tomorrow. Otto will ask them to add you, so try to get ready."

Léonie caressed Greta's cheek.

"My dear friend, I wish we could but Josef is too weak to travel."

"Then you —"

Léonie shook her head. "I won't go without him. I can't."

Emma put her arm around her. "Then you will stay here with us until he can. Later, I'll go and check on your apartment. They have no reason to arrest me."

"You can't count on that. You have to be careful," Greta said. "Forgive me, but Sophie and I have to go now. Tante Resi doesn't know we're leaving and I have to tell her. But I promise I'll see you tomorrow."

"Does Otto's sister know?" Léonie asked.

"Marion? No. I'm afraid to risk it—Friedrich is German, after all."

Léonie helped Sophie put on her coat and hat.

"Why are you crying, Tante Léonie?" Sophie said.

"Because you look so pretty," Léonie said, tenderly bending down to adjust the child's scarf.

Greta and Sophie returned the next morning around ten, carrying only a small suitcase and Sophie's teddy bear.

Josef was out of bed and sitting numbly at the living room table, a half-eaten bowl of farina growing cold in front of him.

"Are you feeling any better?" Greta asked.

He shrugged but didn't answer, as if he'd used up all his words the night before.

She put her arm gently on his shoulder and turned to Léonie.

"Otto talked to the man who is helping us. It wouldn't have been possible today, but as soon as he finds a way for you to leave, he will let you know. We told him to call Emma at Frau Mandl's."

"Thank you," Léonie said. "Are you...prepared?"

"Let's draw some pictures and let the grownups talk," Emma's mother said, taking Sophie by the hand.

Greta nodded her thanks, then turned to Léonie again.

"Our suitcases, yes. As you can tell, we packed only enough for a weekend in the country. Any more and we would raise suspicion. We've pinned our documents to our underwear and—thanks to you —I hid my jewelry and some money in Sophie's doll. But that was the easy part. In my head, I'm not so prepared. I hate leaving you but I know we can't stay. So here we are."

"Was it hard leaving your home?" Emma asked.

"Not really. I took a last walk around our rooms this morning. They are beautiful and the furniture elegant but I won't miss any of it. I was merely a visitor there. It was always Elsa's house. She is the queen of the palace and Marion the princess."

"And Friedrich?" Emma asked.

Greta smiled.

"Not the king, that's for sure—maybe not even the prince. But I don't think he cares."

Emma glanced at her watch. "When is Otto coming?"

"He was going to leave just after us, after he said good-bye to Marion."

"Should we wait then before we have coffee?"

As they waited, they drifted back and forth between questions no one could answer about what was coming and small reminiscences that only emphasized what they were losing. As the time passed, conversation became more awkward, and still Otto did not arrive.

At noon, Emma's mother brought soup and bread from the kitchen. After they finished, Emma cleaned up, while Léonie helped Josef back to bed, and Sophie and Emma's mother drew pictures on the backs of used envelopes. Greta reorganized the papers in her handbag, and made sure she could still feel the money she'd sewn into Sophie's teddy bear. And so, with such trivialities they passed the precious time they had left.

And still Otto did not arrive

.   "I think you should call the house," Emma said, finally.

"I don't dare," Greta said.

"Then I will. I'll invent some reason," Emma said and ran downstairs to use Frau Mandl's phone.

Elsa answered almost immediately. Emma made her voice sound as casual as possible.

"Oh hello, Frau Bruckner. May I speak to Otto, please? I've been trying to remember the name of a hotel in Tirol he told me about."

"He's not here," she answered curtly.

"I see. Do you know when he'll be back, or where I might find him?"

"No. I don't know anything."

"Perhaps Fritz would know."

"He's not here either, and I really must go."

Before Emma could say anything more, Elsa hung up.

"She couldn't tell me anything," Emma said, when she returned upstairs. "Maybe I should have asked for Marion."

"It wouldn't have made any difference," Greta said. "If Otto doesn't come, Sophie and I will go as planned. We have to meet the man at five. If we're not there, we'll lose our chance to leave."

"You can't go without Otto," Léonie said.

"I have to. Sophie is in danger here."

"Maybe Otto is waiting for you there," Emma said with little conviction.

Her mother came out of the kitchen with Sophie and handed Greta a bundle. "Sophie and I made this for you so you don't get hungry on the trip," she said.

Greta lifted her daughter into her arms and gave her a kiss.

"What a good idea, Sophie. Thank you, Frau Huber."

They embraced one by one.

"Pray for us," Greta said. "We will meet again. Hold on to that and I will write when we reach Lyon."

"Friends forever," Emma said, her throat so tight she could barely breathe.

That night Emma posted a letter to Léonie's parents asking them to address all letters to her from then on. They would have heard enough to understand why.

17.

VIENNA

Friedrich had moved his study from a large room upstairs to a small room downstairs just to the right of the foyer. One might conjecture that he had chosen that spot so he might slip away and return without being noticed, but he had neither need nor interest in doing that. He chose it because of the unusual acoustics resulting from the new heating vents which allowed him to overhear every word spoken in the foyer.

Marion and Elsa were at their most newsworthy when they returned home from meeting friends and eagerly exchanged gossip. One never knew when such knowledge could prove useful.

Friedrich rose far earlier than his wife and liked to spend those early hours in contented solitude. As Marion found the smell of cigarettes distasteful, she avoided his little domain. They often did not see each other until it was time for an aperitif together before dinner as her days were busy with activities more suited to her mother's interests than his. Never having found boredom to be a burden, he was happy to have few demands placed on him other than his presence at social gatherings.

Friedrich was reading about the enthusiastic welcome the Viennese had given Herr Hitler—a shrill little man whose appeal he would never understand—when he heard Greta whispering in the foyer. He put his ear to the door to listen.

"Are you sure we should tell Marion that we are leaving, Otto?" she said. "I don't trust her or Elsa—and all we really know about Friedrich is that he's German."

And if they knew more, would they be more or less worried, Friedrich wondered.

"He doesn't seem so bad. Sophie likes him," Otto answered.

Otto was a good man—much like his father, Friedrich supposed, just as he was like his own—-except for drinking to excess and gambling all his money away at casino tables.

"Yes, that's odd, isn't it?" Greta went on. "As shy as she is, she took to him right away. But even so, why say anything?"

"Because Marion's my sister. I can't just disappear without a word."

"Be careful, Otto. Just tell her we're going out of town for a few days."

"Yes, that's probably wiser. Now go on and ask Fritz to call you a taxi. I'll follow you in the car and be at Emma's in an hour or so. Don't tell Fritz anything."

When the taxi arrived, Friedrich looked out his study window and saw Fritz shaking Greta's hand with both of his. He stooped down to say something to Sophie and she threw her little arms around his neck and kissed him on the cheek. Fritz stood and waved until the taxi rounded the driveway and disappeared down the street. Both Fritz and Friedrich understood that they were leaving for more than a few days. Neither would tell anyone.

Several minutes later the doorbell rang.

"Is it my package?" Friedrich heard Elsa call out as she ran down the stairs. "I ordered some dresses to be delivered."

Fritz unlocked the door and said—quite gruffly—"Yes? What do you want?"

Wondering whom he would talk to that way, Friedrich cracked open his study door and saw Fritz was blocking the door with his foot. Looking through the window, he saw several men in uniform standing outside.

"We have orders to bring Otto Bruckner in for questioning," said a voice.

"He's not here."

"We will look for ourselves," a tall, burly man said, pushing roughly past Fritz.

Elsa stepped forward.

"There's no need for that, gentlemen. He's upstairs," she said, her voice inappropriately friendly.

"I believe he already left for his office," Fritz said.

"What office?" the burly one asked, making the others laugh.

Fritz tried to shut the door, but Elsa stopped him.

"He's here, I tell you. I heard him making a phone call." She smiled and pointed up the stairs. "Last door on the left."

Friedrich could make out scuffling on the landing, then saw Otto being dragged down the stairs—the burly one on one side of him, a skinny boy no older than eighteen on the other.

Silently, he closed his study door, then listened as the front door slammed and a car started up and drove away.

There was nothing he could have done. They would have found Otto one way or another. At least the child was already gone.

"Get back to work, Fritz." Elsa's voice was no longer friendly now. "It's over. Tell Bertha to clean out their rooms. And don't bother with lunch. Marion and I are going out...And there's no need to tell her about this."

18.

EN ROUTE

Bewildered, Sophie sat on her mother's lap and stared at the empty seat opposite them as the evening train pulled out of the Westbahnhof station. Where was her father? Why wasn't he with them?

For days she'd heard her parents whispering, even when no one was around or sleeping. She'd asked them what they were talking about. Just grown-up talk, they'd say. Nothing for her to worry about.

One morning she woke to find that her dolls and books were missing.

"They're not missing, sweetheart," he mother had said. "They're just tucked safely in the attic for when we come back. See, tomorrow we are going on a little trip—but it's a secret, so don't say anything to Oma Elsa or Tante Marion. We want it to be a surprise."

Yet when they left, they didn't say good-bye to anyone except Fritz, who looked very sad. His hand was shaking when he took hers. She hugged him and told him not to be afraid. They'd only be gone for a few days.

They'd gone to Emma's house after that and Tante Léonie and Uncle Josef were there. He must have been very tired because he was wearing pajamas. Frau Huber took her to her room. She said that now that Sophie was almost six she was old enough to learn how to embroider. She showed her how to make Xs with a needle and thread, and said she could make lots of pretty designs with Xs.

Sophie liked embroidering—but it was hard on her fingers after a while so Frau Huber said she could draw instead.

Everyone looked sad when they left but her mother said they had to go because they were meeting a man at the train station. When they got there her mother said to look for a man with a book under his arm. The station was very crowded, but they found him.

"Ah, you've come for the book," he said, so loud everyone could hear. But then he whispered, "Your papers are inside. Board the third car from the rear of the train on Track 4—and hurry, if you miss this train it won't work. Third car, remember." So that part must have been a secret.

And then he disappeared.

"Come, Sophie. We have to go," her mother said, pulling her by the hand as she ran.

"Wait, Mama! Isn't Papa coming? I don't see him anywhere."

She was scared and her mother must have been too because she didn't let go of her hand and held it really tight.

They boarded the train on Track 4 and found the compartment with three free seats in the third car. Before they even sat down the train started to move.

Her father's seat stayed empty.

Opposite them were two women and a boy. No one said anything.

"Mama, what about—" she whispered, trying hard not to cry.

"Shhh. No talking now. Lean against me and try to sleep."

When the conductor asked to see their tickets, her mother took something out of the book the man had given her. The conductor looked at it, and at her mother and her, and then winked and punched a hole in their tickets. She could feel her mother taking a deep breath as she squeezed her hand.

Sophie fell asleep after that.

When she awoke different people were sitting across from them, and a different conductor was saying *passaporti, per favore.* They must not have been in Austria anymore.

And her father's seat was still empty.

19.

VIENNA

The Viennese life Emma and her friends had known ceased to exist the day Austria became a part of the Führer's greater Reich. Léonie and Josef's once cultured world was now compressed into the square footage of the Huber apartment. Together they waited for word from the people they loved.

The Grünbaums wrote often those first months, comforting them with the news that Valerie was adjusting well, that they'd taken an apartment near Hyde Park, and found a lovely school for Valerie to attend in the fall. But when an unsigned postcard arrived from Lyon in October with the words *mother and child safe*, their thankfulness was overshadowed by the devastating realization that Otto was not with them.

There was no point in calling Elsa again.

"There might be someone from Otto's newspaper staff who's still in Vienna and might know something," Léonie said.

Emma recalled an old typesetter who'd worked at the paper since Otto's father ran it.

"He's known Otto since he was a child. He would tell us if he'd heard anything."

Frau Mandl found his number in the phone book. When Emma placed the call, his wife answered.

"My husband is at work—they've reopened the paper. Who are you? Why do you want to speak to him?"

"I'm a friend of Otto Bruckner —"

Before she had a chance to explain further the woman had hung up.

"She's afraid," Frau Mandl said.

"Then I'll go see him at work."

"No, *I'll* go and say he forgot his medicine. I'll insist on seeing him and they'll assume I'm his wife."

"Be careful."

When she returned, she said she'd had no trouble getting to see him.

"But he didn't know anything. Hadn't heard anything. Poor old man. His eyes filled with tears when I asked why there was hardly anyone there. All he could do was point to the Nazi banners hanging in every window. This is what they are publishing now."

Frau Mandl handed Emma a copy of the morning's issue. What had once been a newspaper whose editor and reporters sought the truth, was now filled with Nazi propaganda, with Otto listed as editor-in-chief—as if he'd betrayed all his principles and crossed to their side.

"He would never have agreed to that," Léonie said.

"No," Emma replied, realizing the only explanation was that Otto was imprisoned or dead.

Propaganda was all there was on the radio as well. Soon they could rely only on Frau Mandl to tell them the reality of what was going on outside —Jewish teachers and students dismissed from the university; Himmler opening a concentration camp in Mauthausen for Jews and other enemies of the Reich; Jewish bank accounts frozen, all assets to be declared.

"How are people supposed to live?" Josef said.

"Or escape," Léonie said softly. "Everything we had is inaccessible now—our money, our home, our things."

Then, on the 9th of November 1938, Austrian anti-Semitism exploded with a fury, turning their once beloved city into a smoke-filled labyrinth of broken glass. This night of murdered Jews, smashed businesses, and burned synagogues was ironically given the poetic name of *Kristallnacht*.

Good riddance. The sooner the rats leave the ship, the better, Emma heard a woman say as she spat on an old man in a long black coat, carrying a battered suitcase. How far would the poor man get? The image of her spittle on his stunned face haunted Emma for days. She should have done something. Helped him. Saved him. Said something, at least.

Those who still might have been able to flee had their fortunes and valuables confiscated or, at best, seized as exorbitant payment for an exit visa from the Office for Jewish Emigration. Those who had no such resources were hunted, arrested, and sent to labor camps, or Mauthausen.

Wherever Emma went to deliver laundry or pick up clothes to be mended, she passed shuttered shops, with stars of David and the words *JUDE RAUS*—Jews out!—painted in black on their walls and remaining windows. Signs were posted declaring apartments and businesses aryanized—mostly by Nazi party members, of course.

Soon it seemed the only Jews who remained were Léonie and Josef.

They might as well have been in prison, but not wanting to appear ungrateful for the enormous kindness Emma and her mother had shown them, Léonie would never have said that. And Josef barely spoke at all.

One morning, Josef woke and thought he could rouse himself enough to leave, but his fever still lingered and his lungs had filled with fluid—as if he were drowning in the terrible regret he felt.

"I am a burden to everyone. I should be working. Forgive me, Léonie, I should have listened. We should have gone to England when you said. I was a fool. I am useless. Let me die so you can leave before it's too late."

Gently, patiently, Léonie soothed him and he would sleep again. She did not tell him that for them it was already too late.

Every evening Léonie wrote Valerie and her parents, and every morning Emma posted it. Every letter she received in return kept alive the hope that the insanity would pass and they would be reunited.

THE WAR

20.

VIENNA

Hitler invaded Poland on the 1st of September 1939, making clear that Czechoslovakia and Austria were not enough for him.

Britain and France declared war on Germany.

The postman delivered no more letters from Valerie after that.

In that terrible silence, Josef fell into an even deeper depression. By mid- November, his health had so deteriorated that he could no longer raise his head from the bed. Every night Léonie would sleep beside him, cradling him, until one morning she woke to find his body cold, his suffering ended.

All that day and night, she did not move from his bedside. At times, Emma and her mother could hear her talking softly, as if to comfort him still.

When Léonie came out of the bedroom the next morning, she was dressed and composed. Whatever tears she'd shed were no longer visible.

"I am going downstairs to talk to Frau Mandl. Please forgive us. Josef was right. We have been a terrible burden."

Emma tried to object but Léonie shook her head.

When she returned from downstairs she went back into their room and placed a photograph of Valerie in her husband's hands.

"Forgive me, Josef, but I cannot stay," she said and gently kissed him. Then turning to Emma, she said, "Frau Mandl has made arrangements…Will you let them in? I don't have the strength."

"Here, put on my coat, and go to my church," Emma's mother said, dressing Léonie as if she were a child. "No one will look at you there, but be careful outside. It's not safe."

Léonie walked out wearing Frau Huber's green Loden coat, a kerchief tied under her chin, looking like any other Viennese *Hausfrau*.

It was shortly after noon when Frau Mandl came upstairs with two men.

"They've come about your carpet," she said, loud enough for nosy neighbors to hear.

The men walked in, went to the bedroom and closed the door. A few minutes later they walked out, with one of the men carrying the rolled carpet over one shoulder. Emma followed them downstairs.

"I'm not sure this is the kind of carpet they need," said the other man loudly as he opened the front door. "So I may bring it back, but your desire to help with the war effort is greatly appreciated."

Emma thanked him and they left. She didn't ask where they were going.

A few minutes later her mother went out wearing Emma's coat and hat, hoping no one would notice and ask questions.

"I went to church," she said when she returned. "Léonie and I lit two candles. One in remembrance and one for forgiveness. God will understand. She offered to move out but I told her it would break your heart."

"You're right, Mama. Where would she go? She can't go to England now."

Léonie did not return until dark when the streets were empty.

"Are you all right, Léonie?" Emma asked. "I was so worried."

She nodded and hung up Frau Huber's coat. They ate supper in silence, waiting for Léonie to speak.

"I have not been doing my share," she said, when she finally spoke. "You must give me more work."

Emma and her mother understood that it was work that would keep her going, so they came up with a plan to rotate chores, but after a while they fell back into their old ways. Emma's mother washed, Emma wrung out and hung the laundry, Léonie ironed, Emma and her mother fetched and delivered. In the evening they sat together and sewed.

Emma wondered if this was what life was like in a convent.

21.

VIENNA

One morning in March of the new year, Frau Mandl knocked on the Hubers' door, holding a large basket.

"Here are the potatoes you wanted," she said and came inside. She put her finger to her lips and closed the door behind her.

She removed the potatoes and lifted a towel-wrapped object out of the basket.

"This was my husband's short-wave radio," she whispered. "He loved listening to it but I put it away after he died. I don't understand most of the stations and can't use it now. People might hear it when they walk by and have me executed. You must be careful and never leave it out when you are not home. You will have to tell me what your friends on the BBC are saying."

Emma embraced her and her mother immediately covered the radio with a towel.

Léonie pulled off her wedding ring and the gold chain that held her Star of David and held them out to Frau Mandl.

"You have risked so much for us. Please sell these and use the money for what you need. I only wish I had more to give you."

Frau Mandl curled Léonie's fingers back over the jewels.

"Keep those for your daughter. They will mean everything to her."

Later that morning, Emma brought back one of the new *Volksempfänger* radios which only broadcast propaganda and music acceptable to the Führer.

"That way we can turn it on every time the neighbors are about."

Afraid the shortwave might be discovered, they moved it frequently, only daring to bring it out for the BBC's evening broadcast when curtains were drawn and people were home, listening to their own *Volksempfängers*.

Their deception was almost discovered one evening when a neighbor knocked on their door looking for her cat. The next morning, Emma devised a permanent hiding place by building a false wall in the wardrobe by the front door in which they kept their coats.

In April, the BBC reported the German invasion of Denmark and Norway. By May, German forces had entered Belgium, Luxembourg, the Netherlands, and France. On the 19th of May, they listened to Winston Churchill's first broadcast as Prime Minister.

> *The Germans have broken through French defenses north of the Maginot line. We have formed a coalition of every party and point of view. One bond unites us all to wage war until victory is won and never surrender ourselves to servitude and shame whatever the cost and the agony may be. Conquer we must as conquer we shall.*

The countries had fallen like trees in a storm. With the Germans now in France, Emma and Léonie feared that Greta and Sophie might not have gotten out in time. They'd heard nothing from them since the postcard from Lyon.

Yet Churchill's speech moved Léonie profoundly, and—despite her fears and the force of Nazi propaganda—both she and Emma believed that this man would somehow keep the Grünbaums safe.

But on the 29th of May, the news grew grimmer as the BBC issued an appeal for men with experience with motorboats and coastal navigation.

A week later an American journalist named Edward R. Murrow broadcast from London that because of the brave men who had answered the appeal, 335,000 soldiers had been rescued from Dunkirk, although 30,000 had been killed. He paid tribute to the young flyers *greater than the knights of the Round Table or Crusaders of old* who had helped make the rescue possible.

Emma and Léonie wept at the numbers of dead —Emma's mother and Frau Mandl perhaps even more, recalling all the lives lost in the terrible war of their youth.

The first German bombing raid over Britain occurred in early June. To their relief London remained untouched.

Only days later, Hitler marched into Paris and their diminished world felt even darker without the city of lights to dream about. Where were Greta and Sophie?

In August, the Reich bombed airfields and factories in England and declared a blockade of the British Isles.

In a speech in Berlin on 4 September 1940, their zealous Führer announced that:

> *The other night the English had bombed Berlin. So be it. But this is a game at which two can play. When the British Air Force drops 2000 or 3000 or 4000 kg of bombs, then we will drop 150 000, 180 000, 230 000, 300 000, 400 000 kg on a single night. When they declare they will attack our cities in great measure, we will eradicate their cities. The hour will come when one of us will break – and it will not be National Socialist Germany!*

They cursed him and prayed for England.

The first attack on London came on the 7th of September—a bright, sunny day. The planes looked like glistening birds against the blue skies, the BBC reported, until the city filled with flames and smoke.

Day after day after day, bombs rained over London. Léonie was so overwhelmed with fear for her daughter and her parents that it almost destroyed her. If she could have swum the Channel to save them or at least die with them she would have, but they were trapped and powerless, like animals spinning wheels in a cage.

Then one day in October, the BBC broadcast a speech by Princess Elizabeth—at fourteen just a child herself—to the children of Britain:

> *Thousands of you in this country have had to leave your homes and be separated from your fathers and mothers. My sister, Margaret Rose, and I feel so much for you, as we know from experience what it means to be away from those we love most of all. To you living in new surroundings, we send a message of true sympathy; and at the same time we would like to thank the kind people who have welcomed you to their homes in the country.*

Léonie grabbed Emma's hands and said, "That means that Valerie is safe. I'm sure of it. She's somewhere in the country and my parents are with her. They would have never let her go alone."

They had no proof, of course, but the speech gave them comfort. They kept their hopes up by imagining how life would be for them in the country—Valerie running over fields with her dog —she had to have a dog—a black and white spaniel whose ears would fly in the wind when he ran. Frau Grünbaum would plant vegetables for the war effort, dressed as if she were a guest at an

English Lord's garden party, while Herr Grünbaum gave local businessmen advice.

And so it was they could wash and mend without going mad.

When Frau Mandl brought reports of executions and suicides in Vienna, Emma tried to shut out the images of streets littered with unclaimed bodies. She did not tell Léonie. And she wept for Theo again who'd died because he'd resisted. It had been a war of ideas they'd thought then, though it probably had been as much a fight for power as any other war. Under the Reich, friends turned on friends, neighbors on neighbors, because they hungered for power of their own—or merely because they were told to do so. To Emma and Frau Huber it was clear that Léonie was never to be left alone.

Yet, one day, in the second year of the war—perhaps because the sun shone so brightly after days of rain—and in a moment of unthinking recklessness, Emma and Léonie defied the strutting little Führer and claimed their freedom by walking around the city as they used to, even stopping in a café—although by then they looked so ordinary and war-weary that no one noticed them. So invisible had they become, that when Emma grabbed Léonie's arm and stifled a cry because Marion suddenly stepped out of a small hotel in front of them, they made no more of an impression on her than the shadows on the wall behind her.

"She was too busy with some young Nazi officer to notice us," they told Emma's mother that evening. "We slunk away as quickly as we could, but we could hear that they were arguing, and just as we turned the corner we saw him kiss her. Oh, and she was pregnant!"

They might have lingered over that titillating bit of gossip had Emma's mother not slapped her daughter hard in the face.

"How dare you risk Léonie's life like that!"

22.

VIENNA

In November of 1940 Europe had been at war over a year, yet Friedrich was happier than he'd ever been. Marion was pregnant. He watched her tender bulge grow, knowing that inside her his son was growing. He knew it was a boy, a boy that would carry on *his* name. He felt such pride, as if no one had ever sired a son before. Poor Marion seemed less pleased, complaining that her bladder always felt full and she couldn't sleep. She moved into her own room—out of concern for him, she said. How could he mind? Nothing was more important than her well-being—and his son's.

The war had changed things for them as well. As was to be expected. An SS officer resided in their house now—a part of the agreement Friedrich had made with the Party. Declared *UK— unabkömmlich (*indispensable), Friedrich was exempt from military service. In exchange he was to pass on information that would be useful to the Gestapo. Gossip, mainly, that might reveal which persons in their milieu were or could be working against the Reich and the Führer.

Friedrich had detected glimmers of dissatisfaction and disappointment at how the Germans treated the Austrians. As annexed partners, they'd probably expected to have an advantage over the Germans, as the Führer himself was born in Austria, forgetting that Hitler considered himself a German nationalist. As their dissatisfaction did not lead to even the mildest insurrection or resistance as far as Friedrich could tell, he saw no purpose in mentioning such vague observations. And besides, denunciation was not a sport he cared to engage in.

While he avoided firm political commitments, finding them both unnecessary and unwise, Marion courted the Nazis whenever she could, not realizing that they who won at the beginning often lost in the end.

One morning in January of 1941, Marion left for a doctor's appointment. Friedrich offered to accompany her, but she said she was perfectly capable of going alone. He expected her back for lunch, but when she did not return he was not concerned, thinking that she'd probably gone on to lunch with a friend—though he was surprised that she had not taken Elsa with her.

It was three o'clock when Marion called. Tired of reading, he'd laid down to take a nap.

"Did you have a nice lunch, my little chrysanthemum?" he asked.

"Don't tell my mother, but you must come here immediately!"

He could barely hear her.

"What is it? Why are you whispering? Where are you?"

Marion must have raised her voice, or put her mouth closer to the receiver, for her next words were quite clear.

"Hotel Rosenhof, right by the hospital, I don't remember the street, room 412. Come right away. By yourself and don't say anything to anybody."

"Oh, God, is it the baby?"

She hesitated.

"Yes. Come quickly."

He rushed out of the house, jumped into his car, and raced the Daimler through the snow-covered streets, skidding around corners, and almost hitting three pedestrians, until he reached the hospital, where he stopped, rolled down his window, and shouted at an old man crossing the street.

"Quick! Where's Hotel Rosenhof?"

The man pointed to the right, waving his hand in a circle to indicate it was a little further down.

Friedrich parked in front, ignored the man at reception and ran up the stairs to room 412. Marion must have heard him coming because she opened the door before he reached it and pulled him in.

He tried to take in everything he saw as he caught his breath.

Marion's dress was splattered with blood over her bulging belly. Her cheek had a red streak from the corner of her mouth to the corner of her left eye, as if she'd wiped her cheek with the back of her hand.

Siegfried, the officer assigned to them, lay on the floor, his shirt soaked in blood, his jacket on one side of him, a revolver on the other, as if he'd thrown it there.

Friedrich grabbed Marion's arms and made her look at him. She was trembling.

"What happened? Why is Siegfried here?"

"He—"

"Did he hurt you? How did you get here?"

"Oh, Freddy!" she flung her arms around his neck and began to cry. "He forced me. He forced me to come here. He was going to attack me. I kept saying he mustn't hurt the baby, but he didn't care. He tried to throw me on the bed…then suddenly I saw he had a revolver in his hand. I don't know how it happened but before I knew it, I had taken his revolver and shot him. He was going to kill me!"

She began to sob uncontrollably.

"I'm so frightened, Freddy. What are we going to do? They'll arrest me. I'll go to prison. Our baby will be born in prison."

Friedrich's head was spinning.

"Let me think, Marion. You'll be all right. I promise."

He looked around. His eyes fell on the revolver again.

He picked it up and wiped it off with his handkerchief. Carefully, he placed it in Siegfried's hand, pressing his fingers to the handle, and his index finger on the trigger.

"Did the man at reception see you come up together?" he asked.

"I don't know. I don't think so. Siegfried wouldn't have wanted him to see him forcing me, would he?"

"Of course not," Friedrich said. "Wipe your face with your sleeve, then put on your coat and go downstairs. Walk. Don't take the elevator. If the man is at the desk, don't look at him. Just go outside, get a taxi and go home. I will wait until you are gone and then I'll call the police. I will tell them Siegfried called me and was distraught about his gambling debts, but by the time I got here it was too late. He had shot himself. The man at reception will vouch for the time of my arrival. I will tell them how sorry I am. If Siegfried had only told me, I would have helped him."

When he returned home hours later Marion was asleep. He did not disturb her. In the morning, she came downstairs looking quite well, considering.

She touched his face gently.

"Thank you, Freddy," she said. "But it's over now, and I don't want to talk about it. Ever."

And so they didn't. Not then.

It was Elsa who called the doctor and midwife in the middle of the night as soon as Marion felt the first twinge of discomfort. Friedrich was not awakened until dawn.

He rushed to her room but was told that it was not customary for husbands to be present at a birth.

Fritz and Bertha brought him coffee and breakfast in his room. He tried to read while he waited but could not concentrate and went downstairs, where he was joined by Siegfried's replacement, a coarse, older man named Ulrich, who told him he had four children of his own. All daughters he couldn't wait to marry off. He was quite envious when—shortly after noon—they heard a baby cry and Friedrich was told he had a son. It was the 3rd of February 1941.

They named him Klaus Heinrich (for Marion's father) Lothar (for Friedrich's) von Harzburg. It was the happiest moment of Friedrich's life.

AND SO IT ENDS

23.

VIENNA

The tentacles of war spread far—Europe, Asia, Africa—with soldiers being pulled in from almost every country.

In their quiet, unobtrusive ways, Emma and Léonie were the enemy within, hoping from the first day that the country that had so betrayed them would be defeated. Their hope was strengthened the day America entered the war after being attacked by Japan—for it meant that Britain was no longer alone..

Even as the world perished around them in ways their darkest dreams could not have imagined, they eked out a life as they waited for the war to end—which it must, they told themselves. They were much too civilized, weren't they, to believe that endless death was the answer to anything?

Day after day, month after month, they washed and ironed, mended and delivered bundles of other people's linens and clothes. Every morning at dawn, Emma and her mother heaved two large pots of water onto the stove to boil, filling the kitchen with the heavy smell of wet wool and cotton and soap. In the main room, a large table was covered by a thick wool blanket and a sheet held in place by clothespins. There Emma ironed and folded, while Léonie sat by the window's light and mended garments with tiny exquisite stitches taught to her when she was a girl and had no need to sew.

When the laundry was ready for delivery, Léonie entered each piece in a ledger while Emma wrapped the bundles in brown paper and addressed them. Her mother delivered to and picked up from the nearby customers. Emma delivered to the more distant clients by bicycle—until one night her bicycle was stolen from its hiding place under the stairs. The thief was never caught, the bicycle never seen again. After that, she had to spend some of their hard-earned money on tram fare.

As the months went by, food became scarcer as did their laundry soap. They lined their shoes with newspaper to cover the holes in the soles. Their faces grew gaunt, their hair thinner, their fingernails brittle. Only when they looked in the mirror did they see the full damage to themselves. In each other they still saw who they used to be.

Clothing was rationed and even then, there was little they could find or afford. Their clients sent items they might have used as rags before to be cut, altered and reused. Emma's tailoring training at Grünbaums'—incomplete as it was—made this possible. A grandfather's shirt could be reworked into a little girl's dress, old trousers opened and resewn as skirts. They added lengtheners to coat sleeves and hems for growing children, and combined fabrics in new and imaginative ways—though after a while, everything seemed to take on the same tired gray color. Moth holes were sewn closed or covered with small patches—or ignored.

Slowly they got used to everything. At least they were together and had the BBC. They no longer listened to the other side.

The Allies landed in Sicily in the summer of 1943. It was the beginning of the end, they thought. The war couldn't last much longer now. In September, Allied forces reached the mainland. In October, Italy declared war on Germany. Yet the war dragged on.

Almost a year passed before the Allies trudged their way up to Rome—nine months, in fact. Long enough for a baby to be conceived and born. Then, two days after the liberation of Rome—the invasion of Normandy.

When news came that the Americans and British had crossed the Rhine and the Soviets were closing in from the East, Emma and Léonie began to talk about the future—first in cautious whispers, then more bravely and with real hope.

In February and March of 1945, bombs began to fall in Vienna. Thousands were killed. On the 12th of March, they hit the opera. They mustn't die now. Not now. Not when it was almost over.

On April 2nd, they heard the Russians were approaching Vienna from the south. The end was definitely, finally near. They would make it through.

Perhaps it was nerves, or fear that they were wrong, but on April 4th Emma came down with a fever. The next morning she felt too sick to get out of bed. Her mother could not make all the deliveries alone, and only took those bundles that were needed immediately, leaving three that could wait another day.

Léonie was laying out the things to be mended when she noticed that a bundle had fallen under a chair.

"Oh no! Your mother left this one behind."

"It doesn't matter. I'll take it tomorrow with the others," Emma called from bed.

"But it's Frau Wagner's wash. She'll be furious if we're late."

Emma groaned. "She'll just have to understand..."

Léonie hesitated, then said, "I'll go. We can't have her coming here."

"No, I'll go. It's too risky for you." Emma dragged herself out of bed. "Where are my clothes? Why can I never find anything?" She felt dizzy.

"Be sensible, Emma, and get back into bed. She's not far. I'll ring the bell and leave it at the door before anyone can see me. You need your rest."

"All right," Emma said. All she wanted was to lie down and pull the cover over her head.

Léonie turned, buttoned her coat, took the bundle and slipped out the door without another word.

Emma shivered and pulled the blanket tighter. Léonie should have worn a scarf. As soon as she got back Emma would apologize for being so selfish. Léonie would forgive her.

24.

VIENNA

Friedrich knew they were going to lose the war — but even the defeated must welcome an end to misery. Not that anyone in their household had been especially miserable. To them the war had been more of an inconvenience than a catastrophe. After all, they had suffered no massive shortages, no bombs through their roof. They had water and electricity and enough money to procure everything they needed—even things they merely coveted. In fact, on April 5th, when the Russians were approaching and the smell of defeat was in the air, Friedrich was returning home from purchasing—at a greatly reduced price—a painting Marion had admired, when old Emil, their chauffeur, turned the car onto Blutgasse to avoid the debris on the other streets.

"I'm going to have to wash the car again," Emil grumbled. "Even on a white car you can see every speck."

Blutgasse was deserted and dark, although it was the middle of the day. As they neared the end of the block Friedrich noticed a woman looking both ways before she crossed. Her blonde hair was pulled back into a bun at the nape of her neck. She wore a long coat, and was holding a bundle wrapped in brown paper in her arms. She looked strangely familiar. Perhaps it was the fine features of her face.

"Stop!" Friedrich said, putting his hand on Emil's shoulder and rolling down his window.

"Léonie Salzmann, is that really you?" he called out.

Startled, she clutched the bundle to her chest, stepped back and must have twisted her ankle for she lost her balance and fell. Unable to catch herself because of the bundle, she hit her head against the curb.

"Help her, Emil," Friedrich said.

"Are you sure I should, Herr Graf?" Emil said, "Isn't she Frau Greta's Jewish friend?" he added in a whisper.

"What does it matter anymore?" Friedrich said, opening the car door. "There's no one here to see."

He stepped out of the car and reached for Léonie's hand.

"Here, let me help you. You are hurt."

"I'm sorry," Léonie said, looking frightened, and stumbling again as she tried to get to her feet.

He took a handkerchief out of his pocket and placed it on the cut on her head.

"You're bleeding."

"No, no, please, it's nothing," she said, pushing his hand away.

"At least, come sit in the car for a moment until you feel better."

"I can't. I have to deliver this package."

"We'll take you. What is the address?"

"Oh no, please. I can do it, it isn't far. "

He held out his hand and smiled. "Then it will be no trouble. What is the address?"

Her brow wrinkled, as she weighed the risk of telling him, then sighed and accepted his hand.

"Singerstrasse 12 … It's too kind of you."

Once they'd reached the apartment building, Friedrich sent Emil to the door with the bundle.

"Thank you, Herr Graf, I can manage now," Léonie said, reaching for the door handle.

"No need for such formality. We're old friends, aren't we? Your head is still bleeding. Let me take you home … or to the hospital."

He put his hand on hers and felt her flinch.

"No! I mean, you've already done so much, and I'm feeling much better."

"Then come back to the house and we can have dinner together. Emil will take you home afterwards. Ungargasse, if I remember?"

"I really shouldn't." Léonie gripped the door handle.

As if the challenge of persuading her was now too enticing to ignore, he put his hand on hers, ignoring the fear in her eyes, and motioned Emil to drive on.

"It's very kind of you," she said, although they both knew it wasn't.

25.

VIENNA

Emma was drifting off to sleep when she was startled by a loud knock at the door, followed by the sound of a key turning.

"Léonie? Did you forget something?"

"No, it's me," Frau Mandl said, gasping for breath from running up the stairs. "Léonie was talking to someone in a car down at the corner. I couldn't see his face. I was afraid to say anything—he might only have been asking directions—but she shouldn't—"

Emma grabbed her robe, pushed past her, ran down the stairs and onto the street. She ran barefoot to one corner and then the other but Léonie was gone, as was the car.

She hurried back upstairs where Frau Mandl was waiting, holding a pair of slippers in her hand.

"Here, put these on before you catch your death. Did you find her?"

Emma shivered and wrapped her robe tighter.

"No. She wasn't there. You don't think she got into the car, do you? Do you have any idea who it might have been?"

"No, only that it was someone who has a Daimler."

"Oh God, the Gestapo." Emma sat down, afraid she would faint.

"No, no, the car was white, private—but she should never have gotten in."

"Maybe it was someone she knew. She wouldn't have gotten

into a car with a stranger."

"She'd be safer with a stranger, someone who doesn't know who she is...what she is—don't you understand?"

Emma stood up again. "I have to look for her."

"You can't." Frau Mandl's voice dropped to a whisper as she grabbed Emma's arm. "Remember what happened with Theo. If you don't draw attention to her, she might get away."

"No! I can't take that chance again. There must be something I can do, someone I can trust," Emma said, staring at her old friend as if she could will her into revealing a name.

"There's no one," Frau Mandl said. "No one at all. Why did she go out, anyway?"

"It was my fault. I never should have let her. Frau Wagner would turn in her own mother if the Nazis asked her to, but I couldn't think. My head was pounding and every bone in my body ached."

Frau Mandl placed her hand on Emma's forehead. "You're burning up. Get back into bed. You'll be of no use to anyone if you end up in the hospital. I'll see what I can find out. Someone might have seen something. I'll let you know."

It was dark when Emma heard her mother frantically jiggling the front door key and calling her name. She'd been running and was out of breath.

"Where's Léonie? She has to hide. I saw the Gestapo breaking open cellar doors up and down the street. They found three old men hiding in a coal cellar and took them away. It happened so fast I couldn't even see their faces."

"She's gone!" Emma began to sob. "You forgot Frau Wagner's linens and she saw it. I felt so sick I let her deliver them. I should never have done that! Frau Mandl saw her talking to someone in a car. I ran downstairs to stop her but she was gone!"

Her mother scowled and shook her head, "Oh, Emma."

26.

VIENNA

Friedrich leaned back in his seat as the car sped up and said, "Marion and I have a little boy now. His name is Klaus."

Léonie didn't answer at first, then said "He must bring you much joy."

Friedrich smiled. "Yes, he does. I remember your daughter very well, you know—such a vivacious little child. Well, not so little any more, I suppose. How is she?"

Léonie turned and stared at him as if he were mad.

He looked down and saw her hands were clasping and unclasping, as if trying to decide which hand could best protect the other.

"Here we are," he said, as Emil turned into their driveway.

Léonie gasped as she saw the two Nazi banners that hung on either side of the front door, flapping in the wind like the wings of a giant predatory bird. She grasped the handle of the car door and tried to steady herself.

"The lilacs are in bloom," she said.

"Makes one remember happier times, doesn't it?"

"Greta planted them," she said, daring him to remember.

"Ah yes, how it annoyed Elsa. She thought only a gardener should do such work," he said and thought he saw the semblance of a smile in Léonie's eyes.

They stepped out of the car just as Fritz opened the door.

"Frau Doctor Salzmann? I thought...what a pleasure to see

you. Your head…are you hurt? Let me call Bertha to help you."

"It's nothing, Fritz. I hope you've been well. It's been a long time."

"Yes, very long," he said.

"We'll have drinks in the garden room," Friedrich said.

Fritz reached out to take Léonie's coat, but she shook her head and held it closed. He nodded, understanding. Friedrich took her arm and as he led her through the foyer, she turned her head to glance at a group of small paintings.

"I see you've noticed our new acquisitions," he said. "Marion is determined to become an art connoisseur."

The garden room was filled with light and flowers bloomed in terra cotta pots on the deep window sills. He walked over to the tea cart that served as a bar with a wide selection of liquors and liqueurs.

Léonie raised an eyebrow.

"Do sit down, Léonie. What may I offer you? Are you wondering if we think the war has been a mere fiction invented for our entertainment"

"No…I …"

"I have some excellent French cognac, I recently acquired."

"I couldn't."

"A small glass of wine, at least? A nice Bordeaux perhaps while we wait for Bertha?"

He reached for the crystal decanter.

"Why are you waiting for Bertha, Freddy?" Marion said, sweeping into the room in a long, pink satin dressing gown and fur-trimmed slippers. A scowl furrowed her brow as she took in the image of Léonie, bundled in her oversized winter coat, holding a handkerchief against her head, and sitting on the edge of a chair, her knees together, one foot slightly behind the other, as if she were about to spring up and run a fifty meter dash.

"Léonie? What are you doing here? I thought—"

"We ran into each other in the city and I invited her to join us for dinner," Friedrich explained as he handed Marion a glass of cognac.

Marion ignored him and turned to Léonie.

"Freddy's mind is a sieve when it comes to social engagements. He never remembers any of them. I'm afraid we have plans."

Léonie stood up. "Then I mustn't keep you."

"There's plenty of time," Friedrich said. "Besides, I'd like you to meet Klaus before you leave."

"I doubt he wants to be seen in his bath," Marion said.

"Darling, he's four years old."

"So big already?" Léonie said. "I remember seeing you when you were pregnant. You were talking with a young officer in the city."

"Was that—" Friedrich began.

"I have no idea who that was," Marion said, practically spitting out the words.

"I really must get back," Léonie said, standing up. "I didn't mean…it's later than I thought."

"Are you sure you can't stay and finish your wine, at least?" Friedrich asked, always ready to annoy Marion.

"Léonie wouldn't have said it if she didn't mean it," Marion said.

"Then I will accompany her home."

Marion glared at him.

"No. You have to get ready. I'll take care of it," she said, her eyes blazing.

He sighed. "Then I must bid you adieu, Léonie. I hope I have not inconvenienced you."

Léonie shook her head and walked toward the door to the foyer.

27.

VIENNA

Emma waited for word of Léonie until long after midnight, finally falling into a fitful sleep. When she rose at dawn, her nightgown and sheets were wet with perspiration, her fever broken. She dressed and went into the kitchen to find her mother already bent over the sink.

"How long have you been up, Mama?"

"Hours. I kept hearing noises and thinking Léonie was back. Help me wring this sheet out," she said, handing Emma one end. They twisted the wet sheet in opposite directions, and then folded it into the wash basket to be hung up later.

"Do you think Frau Mandl has had any news, Mama?"

"She would have come up if she had."

Emma burst into tears.

"I'll never forgive myself!"

Her mother pushed a lock of hair off her forehead with the back of her hand.

"Feeling sorry for yourself won't help her. Go hang up these sheets and figure out how you're going to tell Frau Wagner that her bedlinen has disappeared."

An hour later Emma was making her way through the *Innenstadt,* growing angrier with every step.

Stop walking! she wanted to scream at the crowds crisscrossing the streets. *One of you might be Léonie, if you'd just let me get a look.*

But no one was, and she found herself standing in front of Singerstrasse 12 wondering whether they—whoever *they* were—would let Léonie go now that the Allies were near. She was about to ring the doorbell for the Wagners' apartment when Frau Wagner opened the front gate.

"Fräulein Huber, what are you doing here? You know I pay at the end of the month."

"Of course, Frau Wagner. I just came about your bedlinen," Emma said, still unsure how she was going to explain its disappearance.

"Yes, that certainly was a surprise. A chauffeur making deliveries, Fräulein Huber? Who would have thought you could afford such luxury? I must be overpaying you."

"I don't understand…"

"I'm a busy woman, Fräulein Huber. I can't stand here all day chatting. I'll expect you to pick up on Monday as usual." And with that she walked off.

"I stood there like an idiot," Emma told her mother afterwards. "I didn't even think to ask if the chauffeur had driven a white car."

"Even if you had, and she said yes it was, what could you have done? We still have no idea who it was."

There was no news of Léonie or the men in the coal cellar in the days that followed; only whispers of more last-minute arrests and cold-blooded shootings.

On the eighth of April, fierce fighting broke out in the streets of Vienna as the Soviet Army battled the German Panzer Corps.

By the tenth all but two of the bridges over the Danube had been destroyed.

The next day, fire that started in neighboring shops spread to St. Stephen's, destroying the roof. Then came the terrible whistling sound that preceded the bomb that crashed through where the cathedral's roof had been and landed on the floor.

The crash reverberated with such force that it knocked Frau Huber's crucifix off the wall above her bed. Afraid to get too close to the windows, she and Emma huddled together and watched as smoke and dust swirled through the air outside. What if the next bomb hit Blutgasse? Who would look for Léonie?

On April 12th, while the Americans, British, and French pushed into the rest of the country, Vienna fell to the Third Ukrainian Front.

Buildings lay in ruins, electricity lines were cut, water and gas pipes broken. With no police force in evidence, there was nothing to stop the liberators from their plundering and assaults.

When the second wave of Soviets arrived, they brought an even greater orgy of violence, looting, and raping with them.

Perpetrators, liberators; liberators, perpetrators. To Emma there seemed no difference any more.

On the 7th of May, Germany finally surrendered — unconditionally—with all operations to end at 23:01 on the eighth. The Third Reich lay crushed and defeated. The war in Europe was over at last. But to Emma without Léonie it was meaningless.

AFTERMATH

28.

VIENNA

"I'm walking to the market, Emma. Come with me. It's summer and it would do you good to be out in the sun," her mother said.

"We can't both go, Mama. What if Léonie comes and no one is here?"

"We won't be long, and Frau Mandl is downstairs. I don't think —"

"We don't know for sure."

Three times Emma had gone to the Red Cross to ask about Léonie, but each time they would not tell her anything because she wasn't family. Her mother said that might mean it was bad news and that's why they could only tell the family, but Emma refused to give up hope. Not yet. It would mean facing that everything that had ever happened had been so much worse than what she'd feared. First Theo, dead. Then losing the baby and being told there could never be another one. Then the worst of all...

All those hours listening to the BBC, thinking they knew everything, they hadn't known anything at all. They knew the Reich had labor camps, and concentration camps. Dachau had been the first, long before the war began. Mauthausen was frighteningly near. She and Léonie had talked about how the English word camp meant a place where *people* were temporarily housed, whereas in German the word was *Lager,* a warehouse where *things* were stored—and wouldn't it make people more easily cruel if they called camps *Lager*? How clever of them to recognize the power of words—but how blind they'd been not to recognize there was no end to the terrible depths to which human beings could fall.

Only when Emma saw photographs of the killing centers at Auschwitz, Belzec, Treblinka, Chelmno, and Sobibor did she even begin to grasp the horrors that had been perpetrated. And death had not been limited to the camps whose names she now knew. Prisoners in uncountable number of camps all over Europe had been shot, or beaten, or starved to death.

How could anyone forget what they'd seen in photographs? How could they go about their business as if they didn't know? Didn't they care? she asked naïvely, like a child horrified to find out her pet chicken had been served for Sunday dinner.

"I really worry that it will destroy you if you just sit home thinking about this all the time," her mother said. "If you don't want to come with me, at least work on those alterations Frau Schmidt asked for. It will do you good to work, and we still have to eat, you know."

"You're right," Emma said, knowing it would make her mother feel better. She could still sew and wash and iron *and* wait for Léonie to return. People were being found every day, the radio said.

Emma stopped talking about Léonie. No longer so worried that she was abandoning her daughter, her mother left to visit her sister in Graz.

A few days later, Frau Mandl knocked on Emma's door to tell her her mother was on the phone.

"It took me ten hours to make the trip because we were constantly stopped to have our papers stamped. Thirteen times in all, as if we were going through all of Europe, not just from one town to another. If you are sure you are all right, I would like to stay here and help my sister for a while."

"As long as you need to, I am fine," Emma said, relieved she would no longer have to explain why she never went out

One day in July, she filled a basket with wet laundry to take up to the attic to dry. As she opened the door she saw a young boy looking lost,

"I'm looking for Emma Huber. I have a letter for her and was told to give it to her in person. To no one else."

"That's me."

"Are you sure?"

"Yes."

Satisfied, the young man handed her an envelope and left before Emma had a chance to thank him or ask who he was.

She turned to go back into her apartment. Her hands began to shake as she recognized Greta's firm handwriting and a New York address on the envelope.

Thank God! Thank God! Thank God! The words seemed to bounce from wall to wall and Emma had to wipe her tears with her sleeve before she could even attempt to open the envelope. She closed the door and went to sit down.

The letter was written on six sheets of onion skin airmail paper and was dated 16 May 1945.

My dearest Emma, Frau Huber, Léonie and Josef.

Not a moment has gone by that I have not thought of you. I am desperate for news and write you with the fervent hope that this letter finds you safe.

Sophie and I are well and have been in New York since late November 1941—only days before America's entry into the war—but Otto is not with us. With a heavy heart and for Sophie's sake we left Vienna without him when he did not meet us at the appointed place. We stayed with Otto's friend in Lyon for quite some time, still he did not come. Not knowing whether he'd been able to leave Vienna, we continued on to Spain, Casablanca, Cuba and finally New York.

I have not been able to find out anything about Otto since then. If there is anything you know or can find out I would be so grateful. I still hold out hope.

I'm sure you have as many questions to ask me as I have of you, and I will answer them all when I write again, but for today I will tell you about Sophie and our new American friends.

Our little Sopherl is twelve already. Can you imagine? She is tall and lanky, but must still think of herself as small for she often bumps into things, as if she didn't expect to take up as much space as she does. This clumsiness will pass, of course. I see the swan in her already.

She is bright, but she missed school for three years, and was very shy when we first came, so when I heard about a little school not far from us whose director was also Viennese (she left in '37) I thought it might make starting school a little easier. She's gone on to public school now, loves to read and has caught up to her classmates, but she's more serious than she should be. Being separated from Otto has been the worst, of course, but it's also because she hears all the refugees' stories, hears the news on the radio, reads the newspaper. I worry that she can't accept what we can't change. And we are the lucky ones. We escaped the war. So I'm torn. On one hand I want to shield her from it all, on the other I think she needs to know so she'll be prepared for what life could still present her with.

Shortly after we arrived, we were told about a weekly newsletter that provided immigrants and refugees like us information about apartments, jobs, doctors, schools, how to work through official channels, etc. I had a million questions and thought it best to go see the publisher in person. The publisher turned out to be a man named Harry Whittaker and he was the best thing that could have happened to us. When I told him that I had sometimes worked with Otto at the paper he offered me a job. With his help we found a small, walk-up apartment nearby, in a part of Manhattan called the Upper West Side.

He introduced us to his sister Bessie Stone, who lives with her husband Bill in a small town along the Hudson River, about two hours from New York. We have been there several times and I keep hoping Sophie will agree to accept their invitation to spend a whole summer there, where they are kind to her and where she would have the freedom and peace to be a child—but she won't leave me. So I worry about her, but I also know how lucky we've been and am grateful. My daughter is safe and healthy. We have a roof over our heads, and I have a job in which I can be useful. And now at last, the war is over, and I wait anxiously to hear from you.

One of Harry's friends who was working in London tried to find your parents, Léonie, but did not succeed. With all my heart I pray it is because they evacuated to the country like so many others. I have enclosed a photo of Sophie for Valerie.

How was the 1943 Moscow Declaration received in Vienna? Did declaring the Anschluss null and void inspire Austrian resistance as the Allies hoped? I pray that it somehow helped Otto, and that Austria will recognize its complicity in what Hitler unleashed. Being independent again should make that easier.

Friends forever, we used to say. Remember those sweet days?

I love you all, wherever you are. Whoever can, please write as soon as possible and tell me if there is anything I can do for you.

Yours always,
Greta

They were safe. Greta and Sophie were safe.

Emma pressed the pages to her heart.

"Thank God, thank God!" she cried again, overwhelmed with joy.

Every morning after that she carefully laid each page out on her dresser so as not to smudge even one precious word with her fingers. Every day she read each detail until the images in her mind were as clear to her as the photo Greta had enclosed.

Love is blind, they say, but joy is blinder. Three days passed before she let herself remember that she had no good news to offer Greta in return. How could she tell her that Otto and Léonie had disappeared and Josef was dead? She should have protected them. She felt both ashamed and relieved that telling her she had failed was out of her hands for now. Postal service had not been restored yet. She couldn't write.

29.

MILLERSVILLE, NEW YORK

Sophie's cough started the day her mother sent her letter. One had nothing to do with the other but Sophie knew her mother worried about two things more than anything—Sophie's health, and her friends in Vienna.

"Maybe if I stop coughing, you'll hear from them," Sophie said. Her mother said it didn't work that way, but almost three months later Sophie was still coughing and her mother still had no word from her friends. So maybe her mother was wrong and it did work that way.

When her mother took her back Dr. Löwy for advice, he held his stethoscope to Sophie's chest and then her back.

"Your cough has lasted too long, Sophie. A little country air would do you good. Manhattan in the summer can be hard on young lungs. I understand you have friends in Millersville, Frau Greta—that's along the Hudson, isn't it?"

Her mother nodded. "Bessie and Bill Stone. My boss' sister and her husband. They've been very kind to us."

But they're not *her* friends, Sophie thought. Aunt Bessie was not a serious person like her mother. Sophie had heard Uncle Bill tell her not to be such a chatter box, gossiping about people she didn't even know. Movie stars, mostly, which was really silly, Sophie thought.

"I'll call them tonight," her mother said, as they left the doctor's office. "We'll take the morning train, but I'll have to get back by evening. I have work I need to finish."

"I don't want to stay there without you, Mama," Sophie said.

"It'll just be for a few days — three or four at the most. I'm sure Aunt Bessie will make you the blueberry pancakes you like so much, and Uncle Bill likes to take long walks just like you do. Take a good book along and sit and read in the garden. Before you know it, I'll be there to pick you up."

Uncle Bill met them at the Millersville station, and after an early lunch at the house, they took her mother back in time for her to catch the afternoon train.

"Be good. See you in a few days," her mother shouted from the window as the train pulled out.

On the way home, Uncle Bill asked if Sophie would like to help him hang some bird houses he'd built.

"Someplace where the squirrels can't get to them," she said.

"Yes, that's the challenge, isn't it? Go on and unpack and we'll take a tour of the garden. Once we decide on the best spots we can draw a map."

Sophie was hanging up her clothes in the upstairs guest room when her mother's train derailed twenty minutes outside Manhattan. Aunt Bessie didn't have the radio on so they didn't find out until Uncle Harry called that evening that her mother and the woman beside her had been killed..

They were in the living room with all the windows open because it was hot. Uncle Bill had just started teaching Sophie gin rummy when the telephone rang.

"I'll get it," Aunt Bessie said. "Hi, Harry. No, we didn't, why? …Oh, God!" She shrieked, and then for a minute—it felt like ten —she didn't say anything, just sat and nodded until finally she looked at Sophie and said, "No… I'll tell her."

She motioned for Sophie to come to her.

"Honey, I'm afraid I have some bad news…"

She took Sophie's hands in hers and Sophie heard her talking but none of the words made sense. They couldn't have anything to do with her. Soon her mother would call and tell them it was all a mistake. They'd mixed her up with someone else.

Sophie tried but couldn't shake free of Aunt Bessie's hands.

I have to go back to New York she thought she screamed but no words came out so Aunt Bessie didn't understand that's what she wanted, and said, "Don't worry, sweetheart, you can stay here."

Sophie wanted to pound her fists against Aunt Bessie's chest and tell her she was wrong, terribly wrong, and that she hated it there, hated it, hated her —but Aunt Bessie kept holding her, rocking her like a baby until the screams in Sophie's head quieted down.

"It's a blessing you weren't on the train as well," she said, her voice kind and soft as she stroked Sophie's hair.

"No, it's not," Sophie said, her voice breaking. "Blessings are supposed to be good."

Be good, Mama had said when she left, as if she knew what was going to happen. But if she knew, why did she go? The train after hers didn't derail. In fact, it probably couldn't even leave because of the accident. If they'd waited for the next train she'd still be there.

Aunt Bessie was patting her hand now.

"Come, I'll run you a nice warm bath. That'll make you feel better."

She led Sophie upstairs and gave her a terry cloth robe to wear.

"I dried it in my new dryer so it's nice and soft," she said, as if that would make up for anything. "When you're ready, I'll come tuck you in."

Sophie nodded, glad she didn't have to talk. Aunt Bessie didn't understand that nothing would ever make her feel better.

The next morning Aunt Bessie's friends began to come by. That lasted several days. Their eyes were filled with pity and Sophie knew they meant to be kind when they gave her little pats and said how sorry they were but not to worry, Aunt Bessie would take good care of her. She'd just nod and say thank you and try not to cry when they told her what a wonderful woman her mother was. She knew that! She knew that better than anyone. But the worst was what they whispered to Aunt Bessie when they thought she couldn't hear.

Only twelve and an orphan, poor thing. Such a tragedy. But aren't you brave to take her in? Doesn't Bill mind? If it's too much for you, you can always send her to an orphanage. It's not like she's a relative...

And then one of them asked, *is she Jewish?*

Did that matter here? It hadn't mattered in New York. Almost everyone she met was Jewish, or part-Jewish, like her, or didn't care, like Uncle Harry. He didn't care. Couldn't she live with him? She could clean his apartment and learn how to cook. Should she ask Aunt Bessie? Or would she be hurt and think she was ungrateful for asking? Maybe she'd ask later, when she was better and her cough was gone. Meanwhile, she'd have to stay. It was better than an orphanage. She'd read Oliver Twist. She knew what they were like—children were whipped for saying they were hungry, and the big kids picked on the little ones. Not that she would ever do that but there might be others...

Of course her mother didn't know the train would derail. She just said *be good* because that's what mothers did. But they loved their children even when they weren't good. Sophie wasn't so sure Aunt Bessie knew that—after all, she wasn't a mother. So Sophie would have to be extra good just in case, so they wouldn't send her away.

She'd be brave. She had to be. It's what her mother would expect.

30.

VIENNA

It was August when Emma began counting time —five years, nine months the war had lasted; three months and twenty-three days since Léonie disappeared; two months minus one day for Greta's letter to reach her; four weeks since the Allies occupied Austria; twenty days since she stopped going to the Red Cross; four hours since the last time she read Greta's letter. Fifty-eight minutes since she stepped outside, fifty-seven since the young American soldier asked her for directions and she, without thinking, asked if he could get a letter to America for her.

"You writing to family, ma'am?"

"Yes...my cousin...in New York."

"No kidding. Where? I'm from Rockaway myself. Just got here on Monday. You got the letter with you?"

She shook her head.

"That's okay, you can bring it to headquarters tomorrow. Ask them to hold it for Private Vinny Palermo—that's me. I'll send it home and my ma'll be sure to get it to your cousin. They must be dying to hear from you."

"Yes, they must be," she said, finally ready to face her fears. She ran home and had already taken out pen and paper when Frau Mandl knocked at the door.

"A telegram," she said, then waited while Emma ripped it open.

TERRIBLE TRAIN ACCIDENT STOP
GRETA DEAD STOP
SOPHIE SAFE WITH US STOP BEST NOT TO
WRITE STOP
BESSIE STONE

Emma clutched her stomach and looked down as if she expected blood to pour through her fingers. Her head spun and she would have fallen had Frau Mandl not grabbed her arm. Emma turned and stared, hardly recognizing her.

"Greta," is all she said, but Frau Mandl understood for she slipped her arm around Emma and held her tightly to her.

Emma aged ten years that day—the same day an American atom bomb wiped out Hiroshima, stopping 100,000 people from aging at all. Charcoal shadows under her eyes resembled the scrawls of a child gone mad. Her once black hair grew dull and streaked with gunmetal gray. It was all that death.

When a second bomb devastated Nagasaki, she could not grasp it at all.

"The war is over in the Pacific," Frau Mandl said.

She also told Emma that fifty countries had signed the United Nations Charter, with the promise they would work together to maintain peace.

May it be so, Emma said, though for her it came too late. Everything that mattered was already dead.

There was no point in counting time after that.

31.

MILLERSVILLE

Sophie stopped coughing three days after the train accident—not because of the fresh air—but because she only coughed when she talked, and she didn't talk any more. Aunt Bessie wouldn't let her. At least not about her mother.

She didn't exactly forbid it, but when Sophie had questions—and she had a lot of them—Aunt Bessie would stop her and say that dwelling on things she couldn't change would just make her sadder, and she should concentrate on the future. So Sophie kept her questions to herself. And her memories.

She heard one of Aunt Bessie's friends say, *she's young, she'll forget.* Sophie thought that was a terrible thing to say. She didn't want to forget her mother and was sure none of them had ever forgotten theirs. Sometimes memories were all you had.

Aunt Bessie was a great believer in keeping busy and encouraged Sophie to join the Girl Scouts or 4H or the youth group at her church, but Sophie didn't want to, and said if it was all right she would rather read or go for long walks. Aunt Bessie was probably disappointed Sophie wasn't more like her. Uncle Bill didn't say much. Sophie thought it was because he wasn't used to children and wasn't sure what to do with her.

August finally passed. In September, Sophie started school. Aunt Bessie said she'd make friends there but there was no one there who was like her—foreign and an orphan. Everyone in Millersville seemed to have lived there forever, surrounded by cousins and aunts and uncles. One boy's father had been killed by the Japanese in the war, but he had a mother, four older brothers, and a sister, and an uncle, so he didn't need her to talk to.

Sophie told Uncle Harry that it really wasn't fair that she was an orphan. Why her?

"Why someone else?" he said.

She didn't like it, but knew he was right. Fairness had nothing to do with anything.

Uncle Harry was always right. She wished she lived with him.

32.

VIENNA

Emma opened the kitchen window and found her mother's towels hanging stiffly on the clothesline, all mottled and gray. She pulled at them and felt their grime under her fingers. How long had they been hanging there?

There was a sharp coolness in the air. Had summer come and gone already? Just as well. The cold truths of fall and winter suited her better than the foolish promises of spring and summer—as people often referred to youth. Happiness was an illusion.

Being cynical and lying around depressed won't make anything better. Be grateful the war is over, her mother had said—when was that? Before or after her trip to Graz? *You were such a happy girl once. Léonie and Greta would want you to get on with your life,* she'd coaxed.

"I will," Emma had answered, knowing she meant well, but why would they? Anyway, she couldn't. She was trapped in her grief as if it were a physical thing—a dark and narrow abyss so deep that to climb its cold dank walls only to fall— climb and fall, climb and fall—required strength she no longer had or deserved.

Her mother had done her best to lift her out of that hole. Emma pretended to be rescued, and when her mother's sister begged her mother to return to Graz to help her run her shop, Emma had insisted she go. *Enough laundry, enough Vienna, Mama. You deserve better and I'm fine.*

But as soon as she'd gone, Emma let most of their customers

go, save for a few old ones who were too blind to do their own mending or too weak to do their own wash. Once done, she surrendered to the abyss again and felt an emptiness she mistook for peace.

Yet now, weeks later Emma found herself restlessly pacing back and forth in the cold air of the open window, thinking of Léonie again, sitting at the table, quietly sewing as they listened to the BBC.

She slammed the window shut and pulled the drapes closed. Those days were gone and she'd put the radio away long ago. The news no longer mattered.

You shouldn't have gone, Léonie! Emma cried into the stillness of the room, pressing her hands tightly against her temples as she tried to erase the image of Léonie slipping out the door. *No, forgive me. It was my fault. I should never have let you.*

A floor lamp flickered as she walked around the darkened room. One more chore before the last of her lightbulbs burned out. One by one Emma removed photographs from the walls, leaving only their grimy ghosts to shimmer dimly in their stead. She discarded the frames, wrapped each image in paper, and placed them all in a wooden box on the table.

Forlorn, she sat down and held the last two in her lap. The first had been taken by Herr Grünbaum on their first day of school: three happy little girls standing arm in arm. *Friends forever,* they'd said. The second was of Theo, his arm around her shoulders, on the day he'd asked her to be his forever. Forever? There was no such thing for the living. Her heart filled with pity at how innocent they'd been to make such foolish promises. Tenderly, she wrapped the two photographs in cloth.

She had no right to look at them, these pretty pictures of a once pretty life, while every newspaper was still filled with photographs of death and destruction.

Sixty million dead; another 20 million displaced, wandering from one country to another, hungry and afraid.

There was no way to absorb such things, no way to ever be happy again. Someone should wrap *her* in cloth and put her in a box.

During the war, when they were still together, Léonie and her mother and she had kept their hopes alive even as they listened to reports crackling through the static of their secret radio. They'd weighed the radio's news against rumors they heard, and naïvely thought they knew both the best and the worst. What they hadn't known, could not even imagine, was the cold-blooded organization all the round-ups and camps required. Millions upon millions of mothers, fathers, children, babies had been numbered and robbed of their humanity so they could be worked or starved to death, their bodies thrown into pits; or herded into showers to be gassed and cremated. Someone had to plan that, do that, document that. Where were they now, those planners and doers? How could they go on knowing what they'd done?

When Greta's letter arrived from New York, hope had flown out of it like a bird released from its cage. If she and Sophie were safe, there was hope—until that too was destroyed, crushed by Bessie Stone's telegram. Greta dead for no reason at all. Didn't God ever have enough of death?

Emma sat at the table staring at the photographs she'd wrapped.

A loud knock broke into the silence.

"I'll get it, Papa," she said out of habit.

Hurriedly, she placed the photographs in the wooden box, closed the lid and slipped it under her bed.

And then a second knock.

"Just a moment," she said as she looked through the peepholes —one at the top to see how many heads there were; one at the bottom to see how many feet.

One head, two feet. British uniform. A liberator? *Too late*, she wanted to say. *The enemy already won.*

"How did you enter the building?" she called in English

through the door.

"Your gatekeeper let me. I told her I was looking for Emma Huber. So sorry to disturb you, but is that you?"""

"What do you wish?"

"I've been sent by a friend to speak to you."

She watched the soldier remove his cap, leaving his sandy hair disheveled like a schoolboy's, then turned the tumbler four times, unlocked the door, and pulled it open, though only a crack.

The soldier leaned forward and squinted, trying to make out her face through the narrow opening.

He pushed lightly against the door—a gentle move but it startled her and as she fumbled for the door handle she breathed in too quickly and felt her head begin to spin.

"Are you ill, Miss Huber?" he asked, reaching out to steady her. She saw him glance at her open bathrobe. She pulled it closed with one hand while she held the door more tightly with the other.

"Who are you?" she asked. She felt nauseous and could barely hear herself speak.

The soldier made a small bow. "I do beg your pardon, I should have said. I'm Lieutenant Martin Townsend, British Army, and I've come to see you on the behalf of Mrs. Anna Grünbaum."

"Oh, God, Is she here?…I cannot see her. Not yet. Not like this."

Emma's heart was pounding as she moved to close the door again. He put his hand out to stop her.

"She's not here, Miss Huber," he said. "They're still in Watersmeet."

"Watersmeet? In London?"

"No," he said, stepping into the apartment and closing the door behind him. "She and Valerie left London before the Blitz. Only Mr. Grünbaum was there when the bomb struck their apartment. They were safe in the country."

Safe...killed. Climb ... fall.

Emma's eyes filled with tears. "Herr Grünbaum was killed? I

did not know."

"Oh. I'm terribly sorry, I wouldn't have—"

"And Valerie?"

"They are well, both of them. They live in Watersmeet, the same village as my uncle. It's in Buckinghamshire. That's how we became acquainted. When Mrs. Grünbaum learned I was to be posted here, she asked me to find you and make sure you were well — and to ask what you knew of her daughter and son-in-law."

Emma turned away.

"Léonie is gone." The words burned in her throat. She couldn't look at him. "I don't know where."

"Surely, there is something you can tell me. Mrs. Grünbaum has waited so long."

"I did not want her to go." She began to sob.

He hesitated, then placed his hands on her shoulders, forcing her to face him.

"Go where? When did you see her last? When did Léonie and her husband leave you?"

Emma closed her eyes and saw Léonie in front of her, picking up the bundle and walking to the door.

"I begged her not to go..."

"You didn't want them to leave?"

She stared at him. Why didn't he understand?

"Them? Only Léonie was here...she was taking the linens to Frau Wagner..." She began to tremble and folded her arms tightly to her chest. "I should have stopped her...but I did not know. I swear I did not know..."

"I don't understand. How long was she with you? What didn't you know?"

"I cannot talk about it ..."

He leaned forward, his face now close to hers.

"Please, you must. Mrs. Grünbaum knows Léonie is dead, but there's so much else she needs to know."

Emma felt another wave of nausea wash over her and tried to steady herself against a chair, but it moved and the young soldier caught her before she fell. He helped her into the chair and gently wiped the perspiration from her forehead with his handkerchief.

She grabbed his hand.

"Are you sure? Are you sure she's dead?"

He nodded. "The Russians found her body at Gestapo headquarters."

"Oh, God." Emma forced herself to breathe. "How did Frau Grünbaum find out?"

"The Red Cross."

She dropped his hand.

"They would not tell me anything…I would have looked for her—I wanted to—but I did not know where…you have to tell Frau Grünbaum that. I was afraid I would make things worse if I drew attention to her…just as I had with Theo…You have to believe me…" She began to sob again.

"I understand, but if you can just tell me—"

"I can't tell you anything, Lieutenant. Not today."

She struggled to stand up but felt her knees buckle.

"Do sit down, Miss Huber, you've had a shock," he said. "Is your father here?"

"My father? What do you mean? He died long ago."

"When I knocked you said—"

" Oh. Just an old ruse to make them think there was a man in the house."

"If you're alone then perhaps it's best I stay," he said.

She shook her head and waved him away. Gestapo headquarters? Frau Mandl said it was a white car. Why would Léonie …? She looked up. Why was the young man still there? Did he think she'd change her mind?

"Please, you must go now," she said.

He opened the door to let himself out. "Who is Theo?"

Emma slammed the door behind him. For a moment there was silence, and then she heard his footsteps as he ran down the stairs. What did he mean, who is Theo?

Only later when she finally went to bed did she fully comprehend that Valerie and Frau Grünbaum were safe. If only Léonie had known. She would not have taken any chances then.

When Emma woke the next morning her sheets were off the mattress and her blankets lay crumpled in the corner of her room, as if she'd had to struggle to escape them. She pulled aside the window curtain and saw puddles in the street. It must have rained but the wind had cleared the sky, leaving only a gray streak of a cloud moving slowly toward the sun.

She made her way to the kitchen, filled a kettle with water and set it on the stove to boil, then wiped some hardened grease off the tiles on the wall behind it and saw the sun reflected on their surface. As the strip of cloud covered the sun, the kitchen grew dark and made her tremble. She drew her arms to her chest as if to stop the sudden violent hammering of her heart, then ran into the bathroom and locked the door. Grateful for the windowless walls around her, she sat on the rim of the bathtub, her eyes shut, her hands over her ears in a futile attempt to stop the sound of her pulse. Swoosh...swoosh...swoosh...In time, she found the repetition calming. Her panic subsided. She rinsed her face with cold water until her heart thumped normally again.

When she opened the bathroom door the kettle was whistling impatiently while a steady rapping at the door was urging her to obey it instead.

She wavered, feeling oppressed by the need to decide, but then turned the kettle off and walked toward the door.

"Miss Huber? Are you there? It's Lieutenant Townsend again."

"Why are you here? I cannot talk to you."

"I'll only stay a minute."

She didn't answer.

"You might as well let me in, Miss Huber. Otherwise I'll have to wait here until I know you're all right."

"Why? I do not matter to you."

"You matter to Mrs. Grünbaum and I promised her."

Emma hesitated but then relented and let him in.

"I brought you something to eat," he said, walking to the table. "You'll feel better if you eat."

He opened his Army satchel and took out a loaf of bread, a box of English biscuits and a small tin of meat.

"I can't —"

"You don't have to eat it all at once, Miss Huber."

She saw his eyes wandering from the dust-covered sideboard to the old *Kachelofen,* its tiles long cold because she had nothing left to put into the firebox, then to the chandelier, with its three burnt out bulbs covered with cobwebs; and then finally to her in the washed-out robe she'd been wearing since the last day she'd been outside.

"If you have a couple of light bulbs, I can do that for you," he said.

She shook her head.

"I will come and check on you again. Maybe then," he said. "I'm billeted nearby, though I did have to make a few detours to get here. Some of the streets are quite damaged. You were lucky."

"Lucky?"

"That your house wasn't hit."

She stared at him, as if he'd purposely spoken a language she couldn't possibly understand.

"Well," he said, looking at his watch, "I'm afraid I have to be going, but we'll talk again when you are feeling better."

"You don't have to. You have already been very kind," she said, pulling the phrase out of some memory of good manners.

She closed the door behind him and returned to the table. Pushing his food offerings aside, Emma sat down and laid out a two-deck solitaire she'd learned from Frau Mandl, who played it for hours at the table by her window where she could keep watch.

"Someone has to know what is going on," she'd always said. "How else could we know whom to trust?"

Resistor? Collaborator? Victim? Perpetrator? Conqueror? Liberator? How could one ever know? Certainly not just by looking out the window.

Emma glanced down at the cards and saw she was at an impasse.

Could one have a liberator and not feel liberated?

She gathered the cards into a ragged heap, tapping first one side and then the other against the table, until she forced the cards into submission. Then she laid them out again and again until it grew dark and the remaining light bulb was no longer enough for her to see.

33.

VIENNA

Even after the war, Marion and Friedrich continued their weekly visits to the Dorotheum auction house which seemed forever filled with furniture, porcelain, paintings, sculpture, jewelry, and furs their owners had once greatly prized but were forced to sell. At the beginning, many of the owners had been Jews hoping to earn enough to pay for their escapes. Now it was war widows barely able to support themselves and their children, or old people forced to leave their once grand apartments to move into small, cramped places with no room for memories. It reminded Friedrich of his parents selling off the family treasures in a futile attempt to keep the von Harzburg ancestral home afloat, so he took little pleasure in profiting from the pain of these poor sellers. Marion, on the other hand, viewed their acquisitions as opportunities—not as opportunistic.

"Aren't we lucky, Freddy, to have found such an exquisite commode? It might be the only one like this in Vienna," she gushed on their way home after her most recent purchases.

"Louis XIV, Marion? Don't you think it's a bit too ornate even for us? All that gold?"

"No, it isn't. It's October and this dreary war has been over for months. It's time we show everyone what a showplace our house can be."

"Half of it is your brother's, remember?" he said, although he knew that thanks to Elsa Otto would not be back to claim it.

Marion glared at her husband. "That's unfair. Otto left and never even sent a postcard. I would share with him if he were here. Really, Freddy, every time I'm feeling happy you find a way to spoil it."

As Emil pulled the car up to the front door, she jumped out and almost slammed the door in Friedrich's face. He laughed. He rather enjoyed her little fits of anger, much like a child enjoys capturing a cat by its tail and and watching it hiss as it tries to escape. Not one of his admirable traits, he had to admit.

Marion ignored him and turned to Emil.

"Before you park, take the porcelains to Bertha and tell her to be careful unpacking them."

"Yes, Frau Gräfin," Emil said as he hobbled to the servants' entrance.

Marion sighed as she watched him, still annoyed Friedrich hadn't replaced him yet with a younger chauffeur, someone she could gossip with, the way her mother did with the maid.

"And wash the Daimler," she called after him, then turned to Friedrich and said, "Don't forget that we have a dinner engagement."

"Don't we always?" he said—under his breath, of course. He'd vexed her enough.

They walked up the stairs in silence, she to her room, he to the nursery to look in on Klaus. He was a bright and lively child, with Marion's looks but none of her less pleasing personality traits. He was Friedrich's greatest joy and they spent most afternoons together, building with blocks, or coloring, or just pretending, which was Klaus' favorite thing to do.

Klaus' childhood was a happy one—even during the war, which he'd been too young to understand. To Klaus, soldiers had been nothing more than fancy uniforms, and the cellar a place for adventure when the air raid sirens sounded.

He was playing with his toy train when Friedrich walked in and joined him on the floor. Marion heard them laughing and came in to tell them not to be so loud.

.   "Mama, play with us," Klaus begged, tugging at her skirt. "Papa is the train conductor and I just bought a ticket. We are going to Salzburg. You can come too, if you want."

"Isn't it time for your bath?"

"I don't want a bath. I want you to play with us."

She stroked his hair absentmindedly.

"Another time, dear, I have to get ready for this evening. Go on now. Fräulein Helga is waiting for you."

Klaus looked up at her and saw what Friedrich already knew. She wouldn't change her mind. He looked at his father and ran out of the room, leaving him sitting cross-legged on the floor.

"We were playing trains," Friedrich explained. "He bought a ticket to Salzburg and said he wanted to visit Mozart. Isn't that something? He's only four but he's very bright for his age, don't you think, darling?"

"Of course, which is why I have been thinking that we should hire a proper nanny. An English one. I hear they're very well trained. It would make a good impression."

"On whom?"

"I was also thinking," she said, ignoring him, "that we should change his name, call him something more English or American sounding."

"Something like Cary Grant?" he suggested.

"Don't be stupid."

"How foresighted of your mother not to name you Brunnhilde. Then we would all have been uncomfortably Teutonic."

"Get up off the floor, Freddy, and stop talking nonsense. I'll expect you in the living room in fifteen minutes."

She talked to him as if he were a child, so he acted like one and took his time.

By the time he joined her, she'd already poured herself a second glass of their finest French cognac, leaving only drops for him.

"We need more of this," she said.

"I'm afraid our supplier has fled to Germany, my little rose petal."

"Then you'll have to find a new one. Now that the Allies have settled themselves in Vienna we have to start entertaining them. One of them can surely help you acquire what we need."

"Which Ally would you prefer? Not the Russians, I assume."

The Allies had parceled Vienna into different zones and they'd been lucky to end up occupied by the Americans. The *Innenstadt* was the international zone, in which the occupation forces changed every month,

"Don't be tiresome, Freddy. I was thinking how before the war the right people always had their large parties on Thursday. They called it *Nobeltag*. Even the Opera Ball was on a Thursday."

He took a fresh cigarette from the silver etui Marion had given him.

"Yes, sweet pea," he said. "I remember. You told me your father had to work on Fridays just like common people, so your mother couldn't be noble and entertain on Thursdays. Poor thing."

Marion frowned. "That's exactly why we're going to make up for it now. Don't look at me like that. It's important. Now that the war is over we have to set the right tone and make the right friends."

How things had changed. When Friedrich first arrived in Vienna, he had spent the last of his money to rent white tie and tails to accompany Marion to the Opera Ball so they could impress Viennese society. And now here they were buying Louis XIV antiques and planning parties at Palais Bruckner to impress the Allies.

"This is just the beginning, Freddy. Let's toast to that... Freddy, are you listening?"

"Yes, of course, always."

"It's very important we make the right connections now. You'll help, won't you?"

"With pleasure, my little fox."

They sat in separate chairs. He would have preferred to sit on the sofa with Marion's surprisingly soft body leaning against his, sipping champagne and talking about making love. But it hadn't been like that for a long time. Gone was the thrill that the unexpected voluptuousness of her young body had brought him on their wedding night. It had seemed delightfully vulgar for her to be so fleshy. He didn't tell her that, of course. She wouldn't have liked it at all.

He fought the temptation to reach for her and squeeze her breasts.

"Well, that's enough," she said. "I'm going upstairs. I haven't even seen Mother yet. I'll be down for dinner. Put on some shoes. Only old men wear slippers during the day."

He followed her and heard laughter coming from the nursery bathroom. He opened the door to find his son sitting happily in the bathtub, his blond hair all tousled and wet around his neck.

He looked up and smiled.

"Papa! Fräulein Helga and I are playing with bubbles! Do you want to play?"

"Yes, I do. More than anything."

34.

VIENNA

Every evening for a week, the young English lieutenant came. Every evening he knocked at Emma's door and asked to speak to her, and every evening she refused to let him in—until, defeated, he stopped.

Emma continued to ignore Frau Mandl's entreaties to go outside, and only obeyed her instructions to eat by boiling the last of her rotting potatoes one by one. She left the lieutenant's tin of meat and box of biscuits unopened on the table and let his once fresh loaf of bread grow moldy and stale. It was only when she found herself picking at it, that she realized the depths to which she had fallen. She could not go on like this.

She removed her robe and held it to her nose. Even her sweat smelled sour. She ran a bath, then washed and scrubbed herself until the water grew cold. Shivering, she stood naked before the mirror and combed the knots out of her wet hair, barely recognizing her emaciated self, then threw her robe and underwear into a basket to wash and got dressed.

Suddenly overcome by long-ignored hunger, she opened the lieutenant's tin of meat and finished the whole thing. She was starting on the biscuits when she recognized the sound of his footsteps on the street outside, and moments later on the stairs leading to her door.

Emma hid the evidence of her gluttony, and composed herself before opening the door.

"I thought you had given up, Lieutenant," she said. Her voice had the hoarse, broken sound of someone who hadn't spoken for days.

"I wouldn't do that, Miss Huber. I was just called away for a few days."

"Please come in then, Lieutenant. I have been unfair. I will answer your questions now as best I can. Please," she said, gesturing for him to sit down at the table.

She brought out a dusty bottle of Schnapps, poured out two glasses, and began to explain all that had happened, her words coming out in rapid spurts as if that would make them less difficult to speak. Or perhaps less true.

"It was a frenzy when Hitler arrived—mobs everywhere, cheering him—Josef was coming back from visiting a patient when he was caught in it—they threw him to the ground like a piece of garbage—he managed to escape and came here—I almost didn't recognize him—he and Léonie should have left after that but he was too sick, too broken—we couldn't call a doctor, they were arresting Jews, others wouldn't come—Mama pretended she was ill so the pharmacist would give her medicine—"

She stopped to catch her breath.

"They stayed here with you?"

She nodded.

"Weren't you afraid?"

"I could not think about that. They were my friends."

"And your neighbors?"

"Yes, we worried about them—big eyes, big ears—swastikas in their windows—but Frau Mandl, our *Hausbesorgerin,* let it be known that Léonie and Josef were my mother's relatives from Graz. Léonie wore my mother's housecoat over her clothes. We braided her blond hair so that she looked like a Gretchen from the country in case someone saw her…One morning, she was in the attic hanging up clothes, when there was a terrible pounding on our door. I had to open it. Six SA in full uniform demanded to see my documents and search the apartment for Jews...Someone must have said something. Josef was in bed and my mother was in a chair reading to him. When they walked in, she jumped up, raised her crucifix, and screamed *Get out, get out, can't you see my husband is very ill!* They clicked their heels and left. I think I didn't breathe the whole time they were there." She looked up at the young man and smiled. "It was one of those moments, you know, Lieutenant. A slight shift of circumstance—Léonie returning, a neighbor watching through the curtains...It had felt like a glorious victory at the time."

In its memory she raised her glass and took another sip of schnapps.

"I noticed the woman downstairs near the gate peering through the curtains ... was she the one?"

"Oh no. Frau Mandl was our protector. You called her our gatekeeper the first time you came—that is exactly what she was. Still is. She was the only person I was sure we could trust."

He looked toward the door and asked why she had two peepholes.

"That was our friend Greta's idea, so we could check if the number of feet matched the number of heads. Checking gave *us* time to hide someone. Once I helped Léonie hide in the wardrobe, inside a coat, with her feet inside my father's old boots, while my mother pretended she was having trouble with the locks."

"And Josef?" he asked.

"You don't know? He died—not long after the war started— pneumonia, probably. We could hear the fluid rattling in his lungs. He'd been sick so long by then that he had no strength—or will— left...He was only forty."

"Forgive the question, Miss Huber, but how did you dispose of his body?"

Emma had become so accustomed to death that the question did not startle her.

"Léonie arranged it with Frau Mandl. Men came. That's all we knew."

"I see. That must be why the Red Cross had no record of him. And Léonie? She stayed here?"

Emma nodded.

"She offered to leave, but by then it was far too late to escape. The order had already been given for Jews to be deported. Staying with us seemed the only way to protect her."

"How did you manage?"

"We did laundry and mending for other people and only dealt with the outside world when we needed to. Mama and I picked up and delivered, otherwise we mostly lived in isolation, with Frau Mandl as our sentinel."

"It must have felt like prison."

"Sometimes—though I think in reality it was a cocoon in which we were sheltered from the worst around us … In March, when we heard the Allies had crossed the Rhine, we were filled with hope. Soon the war would be over and Léonie would join her family…but it was all an illusion. The war wasn't over, won't ever be over for me, no matter how many surrenders and treaties they sign."

They sat in silence for a few moments, until the lieutenant asked, softly, "You once said that you should never have let her go. What did you mean by that? Where was she going?"

Emma turned away.

"To deliver a package to one of our customers—I was sick and couldn't do it but I shouldn't have let her…"

"When was this?"

She looked down at her hands. "April 5th… she was only gone a moment when Frau Mandl came up and told me she had seen Léonie talking to someone in a car. She shouldn't have done that …I ran downstairs but she was gone…I didn't know what to do. I was so afraid that if l called attention to her it would make things worse but what if she was waiting for me? She must have felt so forsaken."

The young man placed his hand gently on her shoulder.

"If the Jerries had her I doubt there was anything you could have done, Miss Huber."

"Please don't tell Frau Grünbaum. She'll never forgive me."

"You took an enormous risk, Miss Huber, keeping Léonie and her husband with you. It will be a great comfort to her mother and Valerie to know they were never in a camp. It was their greatest fear."

She took his hand from her shoulder and held it to her cheek. His touch was warm and soothing, like the sun on a summer afternoon. She closed her eyes and for a moment her demons were banished, chased away by a stranger's kindness. She floated weightlessly, at peace—until he moved and startled her. She leapt up, embarrassed, and dropped his hand.

"I've kept you much too long, Lieutenant," she said, almost pushing him out the door.

"I'll check on you again soon."

"It's not necessary," she said—although when he left, the room felt cold and empty. She rushed to the window to listen to the echo of his footsteps as he strode down the street, taking his youthful strength and energy with him. When she could no longer hear him, she pulled the curtains closed and sat alone in the dark.

It was early evening when he knocked on her door a few days later.

"Miss Huber, I have some food for you. You wouldn't want it to go to waste. Do let me in."

"You are too kind to me, Lieutenant, but how do you find all this food? Do you work in the Army kitchen?"

He laughed. "That might be more useful. I arrange entertainment—a trivial job, I'm afraid, when there's so much of importance to be done."

"Escaping reality can be better than food, Lieutenant. Once I found an old Baedeker guide for London in a book shop, and Léonie and I spent hours planning all the things we would do and see there with Valerie—although my mother did not encourage such dreaming. She was much too practical."

She cut a few slices of bread and put the cheese on a plate. She noticed the edge was chipped and turned the chip away from him.

"Where is your mother now?" he asked.

"In Graz helping her sister run her shop."

"What kind of shop?"

"Household goods."

She took a bite of the bread and cheese and was surprised how good it tasted.

"Why didn't you go with her?" he went on.

"I couldn't. I had to be here in case Léonie returned...I didn't know she wouldn't...I used to love Vienna. Isn't that strange?"

"No. I heard it was a lovely city before the war," he said.

"Lovely? In theory perhaps, but not in truth—not even then. We just didn't know it."

She fidgeted with the tablecloth, rolling and unrolling the hem.

"Mrs. Grünbaum said there were three of you," he said.

"Friends, you mean? Yes. Léonie, Greta and I..."

"Do you know if—?"

She felt her stomach tighten.

"Yes. Greta and her daughter made it to New York in 1941."

"How wonderful! And how relieved she must have been to hear from you."

Emma looked into the young man's face. For the first time she noticed his clear green eyes, and the freckles across his nose. So young—mid-twenties at the most. It was no wonder he saw life in such simple terms.

Her eyes filled with tears.

"I never answered," she said. "I couldn't bear to tell her..."

Emma stood up and walked over to the sideboard and took an envelope out of the top drawer.

"When I finally had the courage to respond I received this telegram telling me that Greta died in an accident. I knew then that God was punishing me for Léonie."

"Miss Huber, I think God has far worse sins to punish than any you think you are guilty of…but won't you write to Mrs. Grünbaum? She needs to hear from you."

"To say what? Your daughter disappeared because of me, and I did nothing, and now Greta is dead and I never even answered her letter?"

Her voice was harsh, cold even to her ears. She was sure he'd give up on her then. Instead he was kind.

"They need to hear from you. It's been months since they were told of Léonie's death. I've written them that she and Josef were never in a camp, but only you can tell them how—except for the last day, maybe just hours—Léonie was safe with you, with someone who loved her; that she and Valerie were always on her mind. Don't you think you owe them that little bit of comfort?"

Emma felt her cheeks grow hot with shame.

"Forgive me. You are right. I will have a letter ready for you tomorrow, I promise,"

Emma sat at the table for an hour after he left before she could make her pen touch the paper. Even then, every page she wrote seemed wrong— the tone, the words, her handwriting. Frustrated, she ripped them up and started again until, exhausted, she went to bed. When she woke she saw she had only a few sheets of paper left. She could postpone it no longer.

The letter was ready when the lieutenant returned that evening. In it she had placed the photograph of Sophie that Greta had sent. He thanked her and said he would make sure it went out the next morning. When he left she turned out the light and sat in the dark again.

She could not understand why the young lieutenant returned after that. She had done what he'd asked, told him all she knew. She had nothing else to offer. Why bother with her anymore? But he kept returning. Perhaps he was lonely—a soldier far from home. Or just a young man who remembered how to be kind.

On good days, she'd be dressed and her hair would be washed, and she'd open the door at the sound of his footsteps.

"You have color in your cheeks. That's good," he'd say.

"I've been going out," she'd answer. "I would have made you something to eat, Lieutenant, but there's nothing to buy, so I brought you this instead."

She'd hand him an etching or print of a long-ago Vienna she'd found for pennies in a second-hand shop.

"It's my way of rescuing forsaken bits of happier times," she'd explain, though those days meant nothing to him.

In early November she decided it was time she reentered the world. Outside, the world, as damaged as it was, was teeming with activity as the Viennese tried to repair the damage their liberators had caused. Or rather, to repair what would not have had to be repaired had they not made their catastrophic choices. But Emma did not speak of that. She joined the *Trümmerfrauen*—the women who cleared up bomb rubble—and tried to find peace of mind with a pick and shovel. The physical labor was boring but cathartic.

One evening she took the young lieutenant to the streets where she'd been working. For every house that stood miraculously intact another lay damaged or destroyed.

"I don't like my good fortune," she said, and looked around, wondering if others felt that way.

"It's survivor guilt. Soldiers feel it all the time," he said, pulling an unopened pack of Players Navy Cut out of his jacket. "Cigarette?"

She shook her head.

"No, don't waste them on me, Lieutenant. You can accomplish a lot with a few cigarettes. Especially American ones, if you can get them."

"Don't you think it's time you called me Martin?"

She nodded. "Emma, then."

They started walking again, silently side by side, their feet in step.

"What are you thinking?" Martin asked.

"Just remembering. I used to walk to work this way."

"You worked at the Grünbaums' store?"

"Yes, I was one of their mannequins."

"You were a model? I should have known. Photographers must have loved you."

She blushed.

"No, no, I only modeled fashions at their salon. Customers would order the dresses, or coats, or whatever, made to their size...the Grünbaums were very good to me..."

"And Greta? Did she work there, too?"

"Oh no. She was much too serious for fashion, though she once wrote a letter to Otto's paper saying how wonderful it was that women were wearing trousers." The memory made her smile. "Do tell me about England, Martin, and what your plans are when you get home again."

Martin looked pleased.

"My uncle has a print and framing shop. He has no children and wants me to come work with him and maybe take over one day."

"Do you like the idea?"

"Very much."

"And that's where they are, Frau Grünbaum and Valerie?"

"Yes, in a village called Watersmeet."

"I can't imagine Frau Grünbaum in a village"

Martin laughed.

"She's definitely more sophisticated than our average residents. When she and her husband first bought their house there was a lot of talk, my uncle said, about the rich couple from London, immigrants and Jewish at that, buying the grandest house in the village, coming only on weekends at first, and keeping to themselves. The villagers didn't take too kindly to that. But everything changed when the Jerries bombed London and Mr. Grünbaum was killed. Mrs. Grünbaum opened the house to several evacuees and their children and had them teach her English. It won her many friends."

"Léonie and I used to practice speaking English…"

"So that's why yours is so excellent," he said. "I've been wondering where you'd learned it."

"What is Valerie like?" Emma asked, trying to remain in the present. "She was just a little girl the last time I saw her."

"Quite grown-up for her age, and full of life If she's ever sad or worried she doesn't show it."

"Then she hasn't changed. That's wonderful."

"You should come and visit."

Emma shook her head. "It would be too hard."

"Traveling will get easier again. They've already started repairing train tracks," he said.

She nodded. There was no point in explaining.

35.

VIENNA

The soft yellow facade of Palais Esterhazy looked washed out under the gray November sky but not even the threat of rain could diminish Marion's excitement at attending Fred Adlmüller's first post-war *haute couture* show.

She put her arm in Friedrich's and pressed her body against him with an ardor one might have taken for affection, though affection was rarely on her mind.

As they entered, she whispered with unnecessary harshness, "Everyone who is anyone will be here today, Freddy—so you *will* do your best and not squander your charms on useless people."

"Yes, darling."

Marion pulled her arm from under his and removed her sable stole so as to reveal the splash of sequins her dressmaker had meticulously applied to her best black crepe dress.

"There he is," she whispered, as she approached the acclaimed costume designer and couturier.

Fred Adlmüller had been commissioned to create costumes for a film called *Wiener Mädeln*— Viennese Girls. Warned that there was nothing in Vienna to work with, he'd met the challenge by tracking down bolts of fabric that had been hidden away in warehouses all over the country during the war. From this cache of rediscovered treasures he'd designed and completed seventeen hundred costumes, even managing to leave enough fabric to design his own collection, which he called *Roses from the South*.

Attractive models draped in silks and satins and lace-trimmed velvets, each with a bracelet of roses on her wrist, walked gracefully through the grand salon, stopping periodically so that the audience could admire the workmanship of his creations. Friedrich thought of Greta's friend Emma, who'd been one of Vienna's more beautiful models before the war, and wondered what had become of her. She no longer came to the house, of course, with Greta gone.

As his eyes traveled around the room he recalled his mother wearing her best to fashion shows such as this, sitting with her hands folded in her lap, hoping no one would notice the worn spot on her skirt, or the dinginess of the jacket cuffs at her wrists, as she dreamt of the high life no longer within her reach.

Where were the Viennese Frau Altmanns, he wondered, remembering his friend's tired eyes as she told him she was no longer welcome in Berlin, the city they both loved. Vanished. Replaced by women pretending that if they smiled and were polite the last years could be ignored.

With a pang, Friedrich thought of Léonie. She would have come to such an event to check out her father's competition. His store was gone now, of course. It closed before the war, so they must have left. Why hadn't Léonie? What circumstances had caused her to deliver paper-wrapped bundles? And where was the child?

The sound of applause shook him out of his reverie. He saw Marion rise so he suggested they might leave.

"Don't be silly, Freddy. I have to place my order, but not yet. I don't want to be first, that would make me seem too eager."

"Why order anything?" he asked. "What do you need?"

"Need? I'm twenty-six, I *need* to start living."

And with that she turned and walked toward the couturier, list in hand. Friedrich saw Adlmüller's pencil-thin mustache twitch a little, and his jaw muscles stiffen, as if preparing for unpleasantness. He even imagined he heard the poor man sigh.

After all, Adlmüller knew Marion from the years she and Elsa had frequented the Stone and Blyth store he'd managed before. But as she reached him, he also knew to bow and kiss her hand, as any Austrian gentleman would. And Marion knew enough to flatter him in return. It was the Viennese way.

"I'm quite overwhelmed by your glorious designs, Herr Adlmüller," Marion gushed as she made her final purchase.

"You'll be the most elegant woman in Vienna, Frau Gräfin."

"Then you absolutely *must* reserve one of your dressmaker's dummies for me—for future purchases."

"They're limited in number, I'm afraid, each one made precisely to a client's measurements and kept carefully up to date."

"Then I absolutely must have one if I'm to wear only *your* designs. As enjoyable as it might be, I can't possibly spend all my time at fittings."

"Of course, Frau Gräfin. I would not think of inconveniencing you. It will be an honor and a pleasure to have one made for you. I will have someone measure you immediately."

Friedrich smiled, for he too knew that success could rise from small defeats. He went outside to tell Emil that they were almost ready, and he could pull the car up to the entrance. The November gray had lifted and he lit a cigarette and watched the last of the guests leave the Palais until, at last, as the sun was setting, Marion appeared, snapping her fingers for Emil to carry her packages.

"I thought the dresses had to be ordered," Friedrich said.

"Dresses need accessories, you know that…We have to start making plans for the Red Cross Ball, Freddy. February will be here before we know it."

Emil opened the car door and they settled in for the drive home. Marion closed her eyes and leaned against the window on her side, while Friedrich looked out the window on his. Such was the state of their marriage.

36.

VIENNA

It was Emma's last day cleaning rubble as a *Trümmerfrau*. She should have held on longer as she'd hardly made a difference, but some of her old customers called to ask if she could refashion their war-weary clothes. She needed the money and couldn't manage both, and she liked the idea of using the skills she'd learned at Grünbaums'. It was a way to keep them with her.

When she arrived home that evening, Frau Mandl was sweeping the stairs to the second floor. Centuries of use had sculpted gentle valleys into the stone steps, and Emma was reminded of the marble steps just a few houses away that had been crushed by bombs, leaving the upstairs not only uninhabitable but also unreachable. Downstairs, two families were living in a three-walled room, barely sealed off from the street and the cold by old sheets.

Frau Mandl bent down to pull the clumps of dust out of her broom with a tired sigh.

"Look at the dirt people's boots leave behind! It's all I notice now. When I was young it didn't bother me. I imagined a young pianist—Schubert perhaps—carrying his music, a muffler around his neck, leaping up these stairs two at a time eagerly anticipating a meeting with the beautiful young lady who lived upstairs. Someone like you, Emma."

"Hardly me, Frau Mandl, but I never knew you were such a romantic."

Frau Mandl shrugged and went back to sweeping briskly, giving an extra little whisk to the floor in front of Emma's door.

"I heard the tickety-tick of your sewing machine early this morning," she said. Putting the broom aside, she put her hands together across her belly like a school mistress about to give a lecture. "I'm pleased you have work again—but even more pleased about that nice young soldier who comes around. It's time you were happy again and you two look good together, both so tall and slender. He fair and you dark."

Emma shook her head. "He's a friend of Frau Grünbaum, that's all. I'm much too old for him."

"We'll see," she said, reaching for her broom again.

"It's been days since I've seen him."

Frau Mandl merely smiled and kept sweeping.

More days passed with no word from Martin until one Saturday morning he knocked at Emma's door, eager to have her join him on his day off.

"I have work to do, Martin."

"You have to come. I've brought you a surprise."

"I can't. It's almost noon and I have to finish three dresses by Monday."

"Doctor's orders, Emma. You need fresh air."

He handed her her coat. She pushed it away.

"I'll go tomorrow."

"Frau Mandl said it might snow."

"How would you know? You don't speak German."

He laughed and pushed her coat toward her again.

"It doesn't matter. She and I understand each other."

"All right. I can't fight both of you—but just for a little while."

Emma put on her coat and followed Martin down to the courtyard, where he had hidden two bicycles under the stairs.

Though one was scratched and the other dented, they had been carefully cleaned and polished.

"One for you and one for me," he said. "Take your pick—rusty silver or dented blue."

She couldn't take her eyes off them.

"Silver. How in the world did you get them? I haven't had a bicycle since mine was stolen just after Josef died."

"I bought them. Go on, choose one."

"They must have cost you a fortune," she said, with her eyes still on the silver bicycle.

"Ten packs of cigarettes," he said. "You told me they'd come in handy, so I've been saving them. I even got you a basket for your deliveries."

She held the bicycle while he attached it.

"So where should we go?" he asked.

"Everywhere. I haven't been far in a long time."

"It won't be pretty. I'm afraid you'll find that 200,000 tons of bombs, the Russians, and SS setting fires when they were retreating caused more destruction than you probably realize. There's not a street that doesn't have piles of rubble."

Four days of steady rain had left puddles everywhere, but the skies had been scrubbed clean and the air was crisp, so Emma said she was ready to face it.

She led the way past the burnt out St. Stephens to the *Pestsäule,* the high-baroque tower of clouds, saints, angels and Habsburgs that stood on the Graben. She explained that it memorialized the end of the plague of 1679.

"The Grünbaums' store was near here, wasn't it?" Martin asked.

She nodded and led him to the end of the Graben and left onto the Kohlmarkt to number 2. She had avoided going there for so long that she'd almost forgotten how lovely the three-story *Sezession* building was, with its tall arched windows, polished black granite façade, and two female majolica figures crowning the gable on either side. Miraculously undamaged.

"It's a lovely building," Martin said. He started to put his arm around her shoulder but certain she would cry if she stayed any longer, Emma got back on her bicycle and told him to follow. She led him through Michaelerplatz, past the Habsburgs' Imperial Palace to the Ringstrasse. As they wove around randomly, young girls waved at the British soldier hoping for who knows what, while old women hunted for usable junk in the rubble.

When they reached Karlskirche, Emma was stunned by the size of the black market.

"This is where the Russian soldiers come to buy," Martin said. "After not being paid for months they now have money and seem to be willing to pay enormous amounts for things they haven't seen in years—cameras, jewelry, cigarette lighters, stockings for their girlfriends. It doesn't matter."

"Where should we go now?" Emma said.

"Can you show me where Léonie lived so I can tell Mrs. Grünbaum that I saw it?"

She stopped.

"All right," she said after a moment. "It's time I faced it."

As she led him through Schwarzenbergplatz, down Zaunergasse, Neulinggasse, past Modena Park, her stomach tightened and her hands began to perspire. Without realizing it, she'd gone the route Theo and she had always walked together.

"What's the matter? You're suddenly white as a sheet, " Martin said, as he pulled up beside her.

"This is it. Ungargasse…I haven't been here since…"

"Should we leave?"

"No. That's their building over there…I have to see it."

Emma got off her bicycle, walked past the bombed-out shells of what had once been Josef's office and another building she couldn't remember, to the four-story building she had once known so well. It was damaged but still standing. A handwritten list of names hung crookedly by the bell. She passed her finger down it. No Salzmann. No Berg. No Jellinek. Only names she didn't know.

"Not one of them Jewish…"

She was holding onto the door handle when the door suddenly opened, pulling her inside. A large woman in a housecoat stepped forward, a mop in one hand and a bucket in the other.

"Yes? What do you want?"

Emma stared at her blankly. "Nothing…I just…"

"I know you. You were a friend of the Salzmanns, weren't you? I'm the *Hausbesorgerin,* don't you remember?"

"Forgive me, it's been a long time, Frau um...Frau...?"

"Novak. Elfriede Novak. I'm not surprised you don't remember after the terrible years we've lived through," she said, almost eagerly, as she leaned forward, her face practically touching Emma's. "You and I weren't as lucky as your Jewish friends, were we? They took their filthy money and disappeared without a word, leaving me to take care of everything. The SS must have known about them because they came the day after Frau Doktor left and emptied their apartment. I cried when I saw the mess they left— broken dishes and papers strewn about, scratches on the walls, broken glass in the windows—they must have lived like pigs. I did keep a few items for myself. I thought it only fair, after all I had done for them over the years."

She waited for Emma to agree, but Emma could barely breathe, her lungs and nose filled with the poison of the woman's malice. When she swallowed it felt like broken glass.

"We're lucky to be alive," the woman droned on. "The bomb just missed us, but the house shook so hard the walls cracked, and the roof has a big hole. Now they're talking about dividing the apartments into smaller ones. I don't know that I would want to stay here, if they did that. Who knows what rabble would move in then. Refugees, probably. They've been swarming in like locusts— most of them from the east, they say…They're not like us, you know."

Stammering that she felt sick, Emma clutched at the air, looking for something to hold on to, then turned and stumbled over the threshold as she ran back across the street toward Martin.

"What is it?" Martin said.

He grabbed her arm but she shook him off and burst into tears as she ran down the street.

Holding one bicycle handlebar in each hand he ran behind her until, finally out of sight of Ungargasse, she stopped and let him catch up.

"I'm sorry, Martin. I've been a fool. They were all collaborators—all of them! The rot infected everyone! I never should have come here. Please, I have to go home."

37.

VIENNA

Emma was so shaken by her brief excursion that she vowed never to go anywhere again. She would give Martin back the bicycle next time she saw him. But the next time was not until days later when he came with tickets to the re-opening of the State Opera.

"Put it on your calendar, Emma—the 5th of October."

"I won't go," she said, but when he told her that *Theater an der Wien,* where Beethoven himself had once performed *Fidelio,* had been chosen to stand in for the Opera House, and that Josef Krips was to conduct that very same opera, she thought back to the happiness music had once given them. It was not music that had betrayed her, she told herself when she agreed to go—although it did not stop her from smelling the bitter scent of her own hypocrisy.

From a box Emma kept under her bed, she pulled the gown Herr Grünbaum had given her before he sold the store. She had never worn it and it took two days before an open window for it not to smell of a decade's worth of mothballs.

When the theatre curtain rose it seemed to lift the brutality of the war with it. For a precious few hours the audience could convince itself that civilization existed after all.

During intermission the halls buzzed with excitement and people hummed the familiar melodies as if they were new hits. Filling the stairways and foyer, they exchanged memories of singers and performances they'd seen before the war. There was no talk of war or hating Jews or refugees.

"Jan Kiepura and Maria Jeritza were our favorite singers," Emma told Martin, though the names meant little to him. "When we were girls, Greta, Léonie and I asked for their autographs so many times they knew us by name."

As they neared one of the boxes a door opened and a woman seemingly surrounded by men— though in actuality only three— stepped out wearing a purple evening gown and a long sable coat draped casually over her shoulders. Diamonds sparkled on her ears and fingers, and around her right wrist. And lest they not make enough of an impression, a far larger diamond hung from an intricately braided platinum chain so as to nestle inescapably visible in the small depression under her throat.

"Who is *that*?" Martin whispered. "She's wearing twenty years of my salary."

"Marion. I don't want to talk to her."

But before Emma could escape, Marion stepped toward her.

"Emma? My goodness, I hardly recognized you … but then it has been years, hasn't it?"

She passed a finger over a gray streak in Emma's hair.

"Yes, war ages one, Marion—although *you* seem to have survived well."

Emma lifted her chin and turned to walk away, but Marion caught her by the arm.

"What happened to Otto? Do you know?"

Emma gasped.

"You ask *me* that? As if you didn't have anything to do with it."

Emma shook off Marion's hand and spun around toward Martin. "Let's go. I can't stay here."

She pushed her way through the crowds of people, with Martin behind her until he caught up to her outside.

"I don't understand," he said, finally. "What happened? Why were you so sharp with her?"

"Because I'm sure it's her fault that Otto is dead."

"I thought you didn't know what happened to him."

She glared at him. "I know he stayed to say goodbye to her and never came to us—so she must have done something. Denounced him. Had him arrested. Killed him herself for all I know. There's no other explanation. And she didn't even ask about Greta or Sophie. That proves she knows Otto didn't go with them, doesn't it?"

"Not necessarily...Come, let me take you home."

"You don't have to," she said. He didn't understand. How could he?

38.

VIENNA

"What did Emma say to you, Marion? Why do you look so upset?" Friedrich asked, once they'd returned to their seats.

"She implied that somehow it's my fault we haven't heard from Otto. It's not my fault he snuck out like a thief and never even told me where they were going. He was my brother. He should have told me."

"Maybe he couldn't."

"Yes, he could. It was months before the war started. There was no problem writing. They've probably been in America all this time, never even giving a thought to everything we were going through."

"You're right, my darling, quite inconsiderate of them."

Seven years had passed since Elsa's betrayal. He'd kept silent all these years. There was nothing to be gained by telling Marion now. She might even blame him for not saving her brother, although there was nothing he could have done.

39.

VIENNA

Martin came by less often after that, and when he did Emma turned down his invitations to performances or bike rides or walks through town. He was busy and so was she, she told herself.

But one morning in the middle of December, Martin came and asked her help with children at the hospital.

"I'm too busy, Martin. Look how much work I have." She pointed to the piles of clothing she had to mend or alter. "Besides, it's been years since I've been around children."

They would just be a painful reminder of what her life would never be. But she didn't tell him that.

"Can't you spare an hour or two, Emma? These children have suffered so much and the nurses are overburdened. A Christmas celebration would do them good."

She felt a flush creep up her face.

"Forgive me. I'm a selfish cow. Of course, I'll come. When do you need me?"

"Right now, if you can. I'm supposed to be there in an hour and we'll have to walk."

Emma was unprepared for what greeted her in the hospital. Bandaged children sitting in wheel chairs, standing on crutches, limping, their arms in slings, their legs in casts or missing, moaning, singing, whispering, screaming, crying, laughing, or—worst of all—making no sound at all. Healthier children shared beds that spilled out of the wards into the halls. The sounds and smells permeated her every pore, like water saturating a dry sponge. There was no hiding from the present here, no escaping into oblivion. Pain and blood were signs of life, the pungent smell of disinfectant proof that bodies and souls were struggling to survive—even heal.

A little boy pulled at her skirt and asked who she was. She leaned down to answer and found herself instantly surrounded by a dozen other children. How easy it was to listen with interest to the news that Hansi had peed in his pants, and Poldi had cried when they played hide and seek between the long rows of beds. She nodded and caressed one child's arm, another's cheek, and was devastated when she realized some no longer expected more than that. When the nurses came to take their temperatures, she asked if there were any children in isolation, remembering her own weeks in the hospital with scarlet fever when she was a child.

"Yes, we've had many cases of diphtheria as well as scarlet fever. I'll show you where they are," an elderly nurse said, "You can wave to them through the glass. They like that, but you can't go in because they're still contagious."

Most of the children in those rooms were sleeping, shut off from the noises of the wards by thick panes of glass. In one, Emma saw a pale blonde girl sitting in a wheel chair, one thin, bare leg hanging down, the other, rolled in a thick bandage, stuck out straight and stiff. A black-haired little boy, flushed with fever, was curled on her lap. Emma watched as she rocked him softly, moving her lips in a silent lullaby.

"That's Hannah," the nurse whispered. "She shouldn't be in there anymore, but she says he'll die without her. She's probably right. He was one of the poor children that had been experimented on at Steinhof. Most of the others are dead. Hannah has been here since March. Too long for a child to be here. We thought she'd lose her leg, it looked so bad for a while. But it's finally getting better and now we worry what will happen to her once she's discharged.

Her family was killed in an Allied bombing. She's only ten, but so good with the little ones I almost wish we could keep her here."

The nurse shook her head wearily and walked away, muttering about the insanity of it all.

Hannah looked up just then, surprising Emma with the deep darkness of her eyes. Theo's eyes. Emma placed her hand on the window pane, as if to touch the child, but the girl looked away again, still rocking and moving her lips. Only ten—the age their child would have been, hers and Theo's.

She rushed out of the ward to look for Martin and found him in the entrance foyer, putting up a small, spindly Christmas tree.

"It's the best I could find, but we'll decorate it, and keep the children out of here until Christmas Eve," he said. "Then we'll sing Christmas carols and hand out some sweets. What do you say, Emma? Will you come and help us give out gifts, or are you trying to figure out how not to?"

She blushed, ashamed of how she had resisted before.

"I'll come. I want to come."

The children's faces swam before her eyes as she hurried home. She wanted to make something for every one of them. Most of all for the girl with Theo's eyes, the one that could have been hers.

She ran up the steps to her apartment, and was so lost in thought she almost forgot to wave to Frau Mandl. She threw her coat on the chair nearest the door and pulled out the large trunk in which she kept her sewing supplies. She kept it neatly organized, just as her mother had taught her. Scraps of fabric were neatly folded and organized by color. Spools of thread and yarn, buttons and clasps, needles and pins—were all sorted into boxes. She had everything she needed.

With so many children, there was no time to waste. She put her other work aside and began.

When Martin came by the next day, buttons were spread out on the table, pieces of fabric lined up in rows by color. Snippets of thread were strewn everywhere. And standing at attention against one wall was a chorus line of cloth dolls that resembled well-fed stick figures in black, white, brown, red, yellow, and more exotically, striped, plaid, polka-dot, and paisley.

"Good heavens, Emma, what is this?"

"Dolls. You said you needed Christmas presents."

Martin grinned. "They're quite… unusual."

"That's because they don't have eyes yet. That's where you come in. Can you sort through those buttons, and put together pairs? With some help, I can have them ready in time for Christmas Eve."

"I'm not...I don't really… sew. "

The look of panic on his face made her laugh.

"Don't worry, you don't have to. I thought I'd ask Hannah, a young girl I saw."

When Emma arrived at the hospital the next morning she was told that the black-haired boy was improving and no longer infectious. He and Hannah had been scrubbed clean and disinfected and were back in the ward.

The elderly nurse remembered Emma and led her to Hannah and the boy, who were in adjacent beds. The boy was sleeping peacefully, while Hannah was sitting up, watching everyone who walked by. Her pale blond hair was still damp and lay in braids over her narrow shoulders.

"You've come back," she said softly.

"Because we didn't get a chance to talk yesterday, and I have a secret I want to tell you."

"Will we get into trouble?"

"No, why would you think that?"

"My mother said telling secrets was dangerous."

"Oh, but not this kind of secret. This is one I have to tell you because it will make you happy."

Hannah's dark eyes lit up. "Really, will you tell me now?"

Emma nodded and looked dramatically to the right and to the left.

"It's a surprise for Christmas." She leaned closer and whispered in Hannah's ear. "I've been making dolls for all the little children but they don't have any eyes, and I don't know what to do. I was hoping you could help me."

Hannah thought about it, wrinkling her brow. "You could use buttons..." she suggested finally.

"Buttons! What a wonderful idea. I have a whole box of them. Do you think if I brought them you could help me sew them on?"

Hannah nodded eagerly.

"Do we need anyone else?" Emma asked.

Hannah shook her head.

"No, just us. We can make room in the broom closet, so no one will see us. We can finish them all if you come every day."

Emma took her hands in hers.

"You're right. There's no other way. I'll bring everything we need first thing tomorrow morning."

The next days passed quickly, with Emma working days in the hospital and evenings at home.

On Christmas Eve morning, she arrived at the hospital to find Hannah waiting for her in the broom closet. There were no dolls to be seen.

Hannah whispered in Emma's ear. "One of the nurses helped me wrap them in napkins last night so they'd be a surprise; and then one of the soldiers put them all in pillow cases and took them downstairs. Do you think they'll let us put them under the tree?"

"Of course. As soon as we get you dressed. I brought you a robe and a pretty ribbon for your hair."

As Emma helped her take off her hospital gown, she had to bite her lip to stop from crying when she saw the bony little arms, and the jagged scar on one of her legs.

Hannah put her arms around Emma's neck for support and slipped on the robe.

"It feels so warm," she said, and caressed it with her hands while Emma brushed her hair and tied it back with a wide velvet ribbon that matched the roses on the robe.

"How is your little friend, Hannah?"

"He's gone—to a safe place, the nurse said."

"You took good care of him," Emma said.

She wheeled Hannah down to the foyer, and found the overflowing pillow cases leaning against a wall. One by one, she pulled the dolls out and handed them to Hannah who placed them neatly under the tree.

Martin and his fellow soldiers arrived in the afternoon and set up chairs and loudspeakers.

At six o'clock, the nurses brought the children in. Soon the foyer was filled with the sounds of laughter and delight as each child was given a gift of his own.

The room grew hushed as the loudspeakers began to crackle and Chancellor Leopold Figl's voice came over the radio. Thin but penetrating, it was marked by the pain he himself had suffered at the hands of the Gestapo.

> *I can give you nothing for Christmas. I can give you no candles for your Christmas tree, if you even have one; I can give you no gifts for Christmas, no piece of bread, no coal for heat, no glass to etch...we have nothing. I can only ask you: believe in this Austria.*

As his voice grew still, nurses and children began to sing *Silent Night*. Emma held Hannah close to her and her eyes filled with tears. Austria was poor and broken; its families ripped apart. Destroyed from within and from without, it had slaughtered its own and was now occupied by strangers; but it was a Christmas without the thunder of cannons or the hail of bombs.

All around anxious parents, homesick soldiers, exhausted doctors and nurses held on to the children as their hope for the future.

40.

VIENNA

Friedrich had originally chosen to create a study out of a room that had once been a cloakroom for guests, so that he could listen to conversations in the front hall without being noticed. But now he found its main advantage was its easy access to the servants' quarters.

The servants' narrow hallway was hidden behind a wall in the foyer, and was reachable only through doors on either end. Marion and Elsa rarely entered it, preferring to ring for the servants through an antiquated bell system. Along the hidden hallway were several small rooms once occupied by a far larger staff. The first room had been the butler's and was now occupied by old Fritz, who had had to take on the duties once performed by four men. The room next to it had been that of Herr Bruckner's valet. Friedrich had replaced its simple bed, dresser, and high-backed wooden chair with a well-cushioned club chair, a mahogany bookcase filled with children's books, a floor lamp, radio, and a chest filled with toys so that Klaus and he could meet there in the morning before Marion awakened.

On the morning after the February 1946 Red Cross Ball, Klaus climbed up on Friedrich's lap and asked, "What's a ball, Papa?"

"It's a big party where people dance."

"Mama said it was in a palace."

"That's right. In the Hofburg, where Emperor Franz Josef used to live. You should have seen it, Klaus. There was a long line of Daimlers just like ours spilling guests onto the Hofburg steps—"

"You mean they fell out?"

"No, I just meant there were so many. Inside the Hofburg was a big curved staircase that led to red and gold rooms with ceilings as high as the sky and chandeliers that sparkled like diamonds. The ladies wore fancy dresses and very expensive jewels."

"Mama, too?"

"She was the fanciest of all."

"And what about the men, Papa? Did they wear jewels?"

"Some of the officers wore their medals on their chest."

A gentle knock made them turn to the door.

"Come in," they said together.

Fräulein Helga poked her head in and announced shyly that it was time for Klaus's breakfast.

Klaus jumped up and happily took her hand. She'd been his nursemaid since he was a baby and he loved her. She reminded Friedrich of a Viennese apricot dumpling—warm, sweet and round. How lovely it must be to be married to someone like that, he thought, someone simple and uncomplicated— but then, there'd be no money in that.

"Would you enjoy being married to a count, Fräulein Helga?"

"Whatever do you mean, Herr Graf?"

The poor girl was so startled by his question she blushed hotly and led Klaus out the door without another word.

Friedrich sat in his chair by the window and thought back to the night before and the man serving champagne. He'd looked familiar, but Friedrich didn't fully recognize him until the man addressed him by name and asked if he remembered their mutually beneficial relationship during Friedrich's stay in the garret of the Hotel Imperial. He was the bellboy Friedrich had engaged to create the impression that he was a man of importance. He had to admire the young scoundrel's nerve at bringing it up.

"I remember," he said, "but not your name. It's been almost ten years."

"Tibor Szabo," the man answered, without the slightest hint of a bow.

"You've gone up in the world since we last met, Herr Szabo," Friedrich said, though he saw in his sunken eyes and gaunt cheeks that it was probably not true.

"And as have you, Herr Graf."

"You are right, Herr Szabo." Friedrich laughed. "And here we are, both of us mingling with the richest and most powerful people in Vienna."

"Most of whom have something to hide," Szabo replied, as if he'd already gathered incriminating evidence on all of them.

Before Friedrich could answer that final bit of impertinence, the young man had gone off to serve champagne to an American general and his wife.

Toward the end of the evening, when Friedrich was on his way to the lounge, he noticed Szabo wrap a dozen pastries in a napkin he then hid under a table. He did not see Friedrich so when he crossed his path again later he felt no awkwardness at making his bold suggestion.

"I am here on assignment from Soviet High Commissioner Kurasov, Herr Graf," he began.

"I didn't realize he was hiring waiters."

Szabo scowled.

"A mere ruse, Herr Graf. My assignment is to ask for your cooperation in obtaining information. As before, our relationship will be mutually beneficial. Knowledge for us, safety for you. It's quite simple."

"Why safety for me?" Friedrich asked. "I have no damming war record to expunge. And the Moscow Declaration was quite forgiving of Austria, don't you think? First victim and all that."

"Ah, but you are German, Herr Graf, and for the Allies every German was a wolf at the door. Your title—your sheep's clothing, one could say—may have fooled others but not High Commissioner Kurasov. You yourself told me—knowledge is power."

"How clever of you to remember."

Friedrich decided not to tell Marion about this unsettling conversation until the next evening, after dinner and a few glasses of wine, but Fritz woke him in the morning with a message that he was to meet his wife in the dining room for breakfast. Not ready to face her yet, Friedrich dawdled as long as he could, so that by the time he joined her, she was already buttering her second piece of toast. She looked peeved.

"What took you so long? I am so excited, I could barely sleep."

"About what, my little breadcrumb?"

"Don't be stupid, Freddy. The ball, obviously! Give me a cigarette. Do you realize how many important people I met? I told all the Allied wives how grateful we Austrians were to finally be liberated. They were very sympathetic, especially when I told them how my own brother had been against the Nazis from the start."

Friedrich raised his eyebrow at this, but lit his cigarette without comment.

"Everyone was talking about my diamond necklace and how beautiful it looked with the earrings. I told them the jewels had been in the family for years."

Friedrich leaned back in his chair and rocked back and forth, knowing Marion hated that.

"It's good you didn't tell them it was war loot," he said with a smile. "It might have spoiled your image."

"Don't start, Freddy."

"You're right, darling. It's too trivial. I have something more important to tell you."

"Not now. I need..."

"Very important."

He usually took delight in watching Marion react to sticky situations, as long as he wasn't directly in the path of her temper.

This time he might be, but he had no choice. She had to know. She might look pampered and dainty, with her hair all rolled and twisted into one of those fashionably complicated hairdos, but he knew she could be as hard and sharp as a surgeon's knife when she wanted to be.

"All right," she said, jiggling her leg up and down, "but no long introductions. Just get to the point."

"Remember how often I warned you we shouldn't get too involved with the Nazis?"

"Too involved? You wouldn't even join the party. You could have been important, just as Mother suggested a million times. Instead, you did nothing but gossip."

"I was an informant, as they asked."

"Not a very good one. If it weren't for me, you'd have had no contacts at all," she said, still not understanding that he had been a good enough informant to avoid going to the front, which was why he'd agreed to it. Had he told her that then, she would have thought him a coward, so he'd feigned sympathy for the cause as his true motivation.

"You're right, my little dove, but now your contacts might be considered war criminals. Subtlety would have been better."

"Don't be boring, Freddy. They can't charge you with anything," she said, leaning back to take a long drag from her cigarette.

"It wouldn't just be me—and the Russians think otherwise."

"What Russians? How would you know what they think?"

"Because they told me."

"You're just saying that to be annoying."

He laughed. "No, my sweet, as much as I like to tease you, this is the real thing. One of their agents talked to me at the ball yesterday. He said he knows all about us and what we've done."

Marion glared at him and crushed her cigarette into the ashtray.

"That's ridiculous. We haven't done anything."

"But your friends have. And, of course, there was that incident we made to look like suicide— what was the poor fellow's name?"

"For God's sake, Freddy," she glowered. "That was years ago. I don't know why you even mention him."

"I was just remembering, that's all. But it might matter if they knew."

He put a fresh cigarette in his cigarette holder and lit it.

"Can't you get rid of this Russian?" she demanded.

Friedrich affected his most innocent, uncomprehending look and took a drag.

"What do you mean get rid of him, darling? Do you mean shoot him? Or strangle him? Even if we got away with it, it wouldn't make any difference. They'd just send another one. And if I tried to pay him off I'd end up having to pay off the whole Russian army. Then they'd spend it on vodka, and all of Vienna would be filled with tottering..."

Marion stamped her foot.

"Stop talking nonsense! I can't think when you do that. If this is serious, we could lose everything."

"You're right, if he talks, we could even be arrested. If it were the Americans, we could hope that they would just de-nazify us. But if the information stayed in the hands of the Russians, we could end up in a gulag. What would poor Klaus do then?"

"Stop it!" she screamed, putting her hands over her ears like a child. "Just tell me what they want."

"They want me to work with them. Re-enlist in the spy corps, so to speak."

"My God, you didn't agree, did you?"

She was clearly exasperated, so he stopped his taunting and spoke in his most soothing voice.

"Yes, I did, my angel. It was the only way. I won't have to do much. No big secrets. Nothing dangerous. They know I'm not the type for that. It'll just be a little gentlemanly spying. Hand over a few Nazis, listen in on the Americans, that sort of thing. It won't be difficult.."

"So you're letting them win?"

"No, Marion, we're the ones winning, don't you understand?"

We'll see," she said coldly, regaining her composure. "Who is your contact? I don't want any Russians lurking about."

"He's not Russian, actually. He's a clever little Hungarian named Tibor Szabo. He'll pretend to be working for me. We'll tell him just enough gossip to keep his bosses satisfied. It doesn't even have to be correct. It just has to sound believable … Tibor's rather handsome, by the way, in a roguish sort of way. You'll probably like him."

Marion raised her hand to slap his face, but Friedrich caught her by both wrists and pulled her toward him.

"Too working class for you?"

She kicked his shins with her bare feet. He laughed and kissed her full on the mouth.

"Ooh sometimes you are delicious! Don't worry, my darling. As long as we pay him, we can deny we ever knew his real identity. We'll beat them at their own game. You'll see."

41.

VIENNA

As she'd done every day since December, Emma worked early in the morning, then made her laundry deliveries en route to the hospital to see Hannah in the afternoon. Three months had passed since they'd sewed button eyes on all the Christmas dolls, and Hannah had come to depend on her—and she on Hannah.

On her way home, Emma often stopped at Frau Mandl's to talk before returning to her apartment and her sewing machine.

As she sat at the scrubbed pine table under the front window, Frau Mandl filled two large bowls with steaming broth.

"It's amazing how much flavor you can get out of one old bone," Frau Mandl said.

Food shortages had barely improved since the war, and they'd often survived on dried peas handed out by the Russians. Emma could see the toll it had taken on her old friend. She'd grown thin, and her clothes hung loosely over what had once been strong arms and an ample belly.

"You were lucky to get a bone. There's nothing left in the shops—even on the rare days they are open," Emma said.

"It wasn't luck. I traded my husband's tattered old coat for it. You can't get anything anymore."

"You shouldn't waste it on me then," Emma said, pushing her bowl toward her.

"Eat, Emma. It's only fair. You shared with me every time Martin brought you food."

Frau Mandl peered at her over her glasses.

"I haven't seen him in a while," she said.

"We've been busy."

"You seemed to be growing so close…"

"Only as friends."

Frau Mandl placed her hand on Emma's, her veins blue against her skin.

"Friendship can develop into something more, you know," she said.

Emma felt a blush rise to her cheeks.

"He's just a boy. I'm no good for him."

"He's a soldier. He's seen things far worse than you or I could imagine."

"Then he deserves someone young who's not broken like me. But it's silly to even think about it. He's never asked me, and British soldiers aren't allowed to marry Austrian girls anyway. In fact, the Army is arranging for English girls to come over here."

"Wouldn't you like to go to England and get a fresh start ?"

"Things are not so easy there either. Besides, I couldn't, you know that."

"Frau Grünbaum wouldn't mind, Emma. She told you in her letter how grateful she is to you."

Emma broke off a piece of stale bread and dropped it into her soup, stirring it until it was soft.

"That may be, but every time she saw me she would think that it should have been Léonie with her, not me. I couldn't bear that … But it's not only that. I have Hannah to think of now. She needs me. Martin doesn't. It's as simple as that. She's been growing stronger every day. Soon they'll be releasing her and I want her to come live with me."

Frau Mandl shook her head. "Hannah can't take Léonie's place, dear. Nor Greta's."

"And I can't take the place of her parents—I know that— but she has no one else and I can't—"

"Take Hannah and leave this damn place!" Frau Mandl said, banging her spoon on the table. "You saw how they cheered when the Allies liberated us, as if they weren't to blame for the state we are in. Do they really think we have forgotten how they cheered in '38?"

Frau Mandl stood up and carried their bowls to the sink.

"The Russians certainly haven't," Emma said, thinking of the orgy of rapes the Russians had brought with them. "Sins heaped upon sins, as if that were justice."

Frau Mandl shrugged and began washing the bowls.

"It's revenge they want, not justice. Then the revenge will be avenged, and so it will go on…Does Martin know about Hannah?" she asked, handing the bowls to Emma to dry.

"Not yet."

"When was the last time you saw him?"

"When he took me to the Red Cross Ball. I didn't want to go and be with all those people pretending everything was all right again. But Martin said the money people paid for tickets would help the Red Cross."

Frau Mandl wiped her hands on her apron.

"The von Harzburgs must have been there."

"Oh yes, they wouldn't have missed it. I didn't talk to them this time. Thankfully, Marion was too busy mingling to notice me. Friedrich seems to have given up trying to ingratiate himself for he sat in a corner most of the time, looking unhappy."

"Did I tell you that my cousin who works in the Dorotheum saw him walking with a little boy. Did you know they have a son?"

"So it was a boy. Don't you remember? Léonie and I saw Marion once when she was pregnant. He must be about five now."

Frau Mandl shook her head.

"Poor little thing. Can you imagine being raised by those two vultures? But maybe he'll rebel and be a socialist."

Emma smiled but wondered what good it had done her to have good parents. They'd tried to make her strong but she wasn't—not then, not now. Where was she when Theo was beaten, or Léonie taken? Why hadn't she protected them? And why hadn't she searched for Otto once she knew he hadn't joined Greta? Even a vulture might have succeeded at some of that.

"I'd better get back to work," Emma said. She hugged Frau Mandl and felt how thin she'd gotten. She determined to find her something more nutritious than broth to eat.

As she walked through the courtyard on her way back to her apartment, she noticed tiny green sprouts pushing their way through the cracks in the concrete. With the eternal optimism of nature, those little sprouts were fighting for life and would even burst into bloom soon. It was a lesson she had to learn herself if she was to care for Hannah.

Emma received a letter from Frau Grünbaum a few days later asking if she knew what had happened to Léonie's apartment. Emma dreaded returning there and learning that the apartments had all been divided and occupied, but found that the hateful Frau Novak had been replaced by a far friendlier *Hausbesorgerin*.

"Most of the apartments are still empty due to the bomb damage, so the city is looking for people who can help pay for the necessary repairs. In exchange, they will be able to buy the apartments at low prices, or rent them on long-term, low-rent leases."

Emma wrote Frau Grünbaum and asked if she and Valerie were interested. If so, she would help arrange it in any way she could.

In return, she received this telegram:

INTERESTED STOP WILL TALK TO BANK STOP HAVE IDEA STOP IF POSSIBLE WILL LET YOU KNOW STOP REGARDS ANNA G.

Weeks passed. Emma heard nothing more. Of course, they weren't coming back. Why would they? They probably just wanted to sell it.

42.

VIENNA

The sun shone brightly the late June day Emma brought Hannah home, fully a year after the war ended. Frau Mandl greeted them at the front gate and Hannah swung her crutches in front of her, as they slowly made their way through the courtyard and up the stairs.

Emma had made the front room look as welcoming as she could, with her mother's best tablecloth and a small vase of flowers on the table usually covered with folded laundry.

"Is this all yours?" Hannah asked as she looked around.

"And yours now," Emma said, and led her to the room off the kitchen she'd brightened with fresh new curtains and a coverlet she'd made from a pair of white linen sheets Frau Mandl had given her. As a welcome gift, Emma's mother had sent a pillow case embroidered with flowers and Hannah's name.

Emma put Hannah's meager possessions away and placed her button-eyed doll next to the pillow.

"Do you like it?" she asked.

"Where do you sleep? Is it far?" Hannah asked.

"Just off the front room. Come, I'll show you."

Hannah asked why Emma had such a big bed. "It's big enough for two people," she said.

"It's where my parents slept. I used to sleep in your room."

"Weren't you afraid?" she asked.

Emma understood then why she had seen an anxious flicker in Hannah's eyes before, and suggested she move her pillow case and doll to the big bed. When a nightmare woke Hannah that night, Emma held her until she fell asleep again. In the morning, Emma woke to find Hannah cuddled up against her, the button-eyed doll nestled in her arms.

"Should we sign you up for school today?"

Hannah shook her head.

"They'll take me away if they know you're not my mother."

Afraid she might be right, Emma agreed to wait for now.

They soon fell into a quiet routine. Mornings, while Emma washed and ironed for her customers and the apartment filled with steam, Hannah worked on lessons Emma devised. She was a willing student, liked to read and was surprisingly good at numbers.

When Emma's customers started giving her their moth-eaten sweaters to repair, Hannah was eager to help. She offered to unravel the wool while Emma sewed or mended. Emma taught her how to knit and read a pattern and they spent their evenings knitting side by side. It was a peaceful life that veiled the wounds they could not talk about.

One August morning, after Emma had sent Hannah downstairs to help Frau Mandl, there was a knock at the door. She no longer peered fearfully through the peepholes and opened the door immediately, assuming it was Hannah coming to fetch something she'd forgotten. But it was Martin, his hair disheveled from having just removed his hat—reminding her of the first time she'd seen him.

"I thought you'd left," Emma said, fighting off the flutter in her heart. "I haven't seen you since the Red Cross Ball."

"I'm terribly sorry, Emma. It's because they've been shipping me from one post to another without a moment's notice. Last week I was in England, which was brilliant timing, it turned out." He took a large envelope out of his satchel. "Mrs. Grünbaum apologizes for not having gotten this to you earlier but she wasn't sure until the last minute that it would go through and then there was the problem of how to get the documents to you safely."

"I don't understand."

"She took your suggestion and bought Léonie's apartment."

Emma's heart leapt. "They're coming back?"

"Oh no, the apartment is for you."

"Are you mad? That's impossible." Emma said, pushing the envelope back into his hands.

"She said it was the only way she knew to thank you. You risked your life hiding Léonie and Josef. I'm not sure you realize that."

Emma's eyes welled with tears. "It wasn't enough in the end."

"That was not your fault. But the apartment is not just for you, Emma. Mrs. Grünbaum said it's also for Hannah."

Martin cast a glance around the room.

"Where is she? I thought she was living with you now."

"How did you know?"

"I have my spies," he said, smiling.

"She's downstairs helping Frau Mandl."

Martin looked at his watch.

"Crikey, I have to go, Emma. I'm leaving for Germany tonight, but I'll stop in and see them on my way out."

"Be careful," Emma said and put her hand on his arm.

"The war is over, Emma," he said and kissed her on the cheek.

She watched him run down the stairs, and wondered if she would ever hear his footsteps again.

That night, after Hannah had gone to sleep Emma wrote to Frau Grünbaum.

I have read all the documents and papers Martin brought and am overwhelmed. By all rights the apartment is and always will be Valerie's and I will do my best to take care of it the way Léonie would have. I can hardly believe that the repairs have already begun and we will be able to move in so soon.

I will be sorry to leave Frau Mandl who has been our most faithful and trusted friend but I will not be sorry to leave my apartment. It is too full of sadness even for my mother, who writes often but has decided to stay in Graz permanently. Léonie and Josef's apartment will be filled with ghosts of a gentler sort and I think Hannah and I will find comfort as well as beauty there. We will be forever grateful for your incredible generosity.

When Emma told Hannah in the morning that she was going to have a beautiful sunny room all to herself, the poor child looked frightened and asked if she promised to be very quiet—could she please stay with Emma in her room there too. Emma wanted to hold her and tell her not to be afraid, but she was smiling so courageously Emma thought it might make her cry. Or herself, which would frighten her even more. So she told Hannah she was clever, for that big sunny room would serve them much better as a sewing room and she looked forward to not finding pins and needles everywhere.

Emma and Hannah left Blutgasse in November. They couldn't afford to hire a moving company and were considering leaving the furniture behind and sleeping on the floor for a while when Frau Mandl came to the rescue, as she had done so many times before.

"The grocer's nephew is bringing a wagonful of wine from Burgenland," she said. "He'd appreciate earning a few groschen once it's empty, so I've arranged for him to move you."

Emma reached out to embrace her old friend but felt her resist as if her arms were too harsh against her bones. She let go and kissed her on the cheek, realizing for the first time how frail she'd become.

"We'll never manage without you, Frau Mandl. Why don't you move to Ungargasse with us? We have room."

She shook her head. "I'm too old to start another life. That's for you and Hannah to do. But I will visit—in the spring when it's warm."

Emma soon found work with some of the American wives. They were friendly and open, and it made her glad to think that Greta's shy little Sophie was with people like that, and no longer touched by war.

Always eager to help, Hannah often suggested ways to expand their business.

"You're too young to have to worry about such things," Emma said.

"I like to work because then I don't think about the war."

It was how Emma felt—but Hannah was not even eleven. It was terribly hard sometimes not to think of how things should have been.

1947
MOVING ON

43.

VIENNA

Tibor Szabo had reported for duty only days after the Red Cross Ball, surprising Friedrich. He hadn't expected the Russians to be that efficient.

"I've been instructed to be your barber and dresser."

"As if I were a Russian nobleman before the revolution? How un-Soviet, Herr Szabo."

Tibor had scowled. "You will pay me, of course, comrade, so as not to cause suspicion. And you will report your findings, as agreed."

"Yes, just as I did before. It's clear only the ears have changed. I advise you not to call me comrade, if you wish this charade to succeed. And I do hope you have learned proper barbering skills for this assignment."

Tibor had, and his manner quickly became less stern, making their daily sessions strangely amicable. But as the brutally bitter winter of 1946-47 dragged on, he lamented how difficult it was to find—let alone afford—the necessities of life.

"Not that I care for myself, but on what you pay me," he said, as he clipped dangerously close to Friedrich's ear, "I worry that I cannot give Vera the life she deserves."

Tibor had been entertaining Friedrich with stories of how he'd wooed and won—against all odds—the beautiful and faithful Vera, the Juliet to his Romeo. It both fed and tore at Friedrich's soul to hear that such pure love could exist, so what was there to do but to raise Tibor's salary a bit, and let Bertha send him home with a basket of food once in a while.

As the weeks and months passed, Friedrich noticed that Tibor stayed on after tending to him, to chat with Fritz or Bertha in the kitchen, or to Emil in the garage. Fearing that it was to collect evidence he could use as further leverage against him and Marion, Friedrich snuck into the secret playroom off the kitchen to listen and discovered that there was nothing to discover. He and Marion were rarely even mentioned. Tibor mostly spoke of Vera, or his neighbors, or how expensive everything was.

Friedrich began to wonder when Tibor had time to report back to his superiors. And didn't he get paid for that? With two incomes he should be managing, shouldn't he?

Having been far too lazy to have actually spied for the Nazis, Friedrich was not skilled at deducing things from evidence presented him, so it took him until the summer of 1947 to realize that Tibor's blackmail had been a sham, a ruse to obtain a job. When he did finally realize it, Friedrich felt sorry for him, for Tibor had outsmarted himself. Friedrich would have paid a straightforward blackmailer a lot of money to keep quiet.

He could have fired Tibor then and told Marion that she no longer needed to worry that they were under threat, but she'd just sent Klaus off to the country with the nursemaid without consulting him and he was angry—so he kept Tibor on to spite her —and because he was lonely and enjoyed his company. But mostly because he did not want to cause the lovely Vera any further hardship.

One late summer morning, when Klaus was back and they were coming out of the playroom, Friedrich heard Bertha say, "You can leave it on the table, Vera."

He took Klaus' hand and hurried him into the kitchen. Bertha was standing at the sink next to a woman leaning on a wooden crutch.

"Klaus was hoping he could watch you bake," he said, "but I see you have company."

The woman turned around slowly. One of her legs was shorter and thinner than the other, and Friedrich wondered whether she was born that way or it was the result of an accident. Or perhaps even the war.

"Vera Szabo," she said, curtsying awkwardly. On the left side of her face, a thin scar ran from her eye to her jaw and crinkled slightly as she smiled. A shy, unattractive smile, yet Friedrich was touched by it. And by the fact that to Tibor she was truly the beauty he so lovingly described. Or was that also a sham? How sad if it were.

44.

VIENNA

Frau Mandl did not make it to spring, dying peacefully in her sleep one snowy night in March. Emma did not return to Blutgasse after that.

Martin must have passed by Ungargasse once for Emma found a small package with marmalade and biscuits marked *For Hannah* hidden in the umbrella stand outside the apartment door.

Then one day in May a large box with jars and tins was left downstairs with the *Hausbesorgerin. For Miss Emma Huber*, it said in a large block letters. Nothing after that—not until summer when a thin blue envelope arrived, postmarked Watersmeet and addressed in Martin's hand. Emma put it in her pocket and did not open it until Hannah went to bed. Then she poured herself a glass of wine, and sat down at the kitchen table to read.

> *Dear Emma,*
>
> *I've been staying with Mrs. Grünbaum and Valerie for a few days while my uncle fixes up the little flat above his shop so that I can take over when he retires next month.*
>
> *Sadly, my father died shortly after my return to England. He'd been ill a long time and I was grateful to the Army for making it possible for me to be there at the end, though I think it was a part of their*

decision to "lessen overseas commitments" rather than any compassion for me personally. There are many who would need it far more. After my return I worked in different parts of England until I was finally discharged last week.

I'm glad to be a civilian again, and am happy to be home, but I hated not being able to say goodbye. I was working outside of Vienna when I was notified that my father was failing. I had barely a day to pack up and no way to reach you. I asked some friends to make sure you two had enough food. I hope they kept their word.

I know you will take good care of Hannah. Let her do the same for you.

your friend always,
Martin

Emma didn't realize she was crying until she unfolded the second sheet of paper and saw that the words were stained with tears.

My dearest Emma –

It is a pleasure to have Martin here so we can thank him for all he has done, as a soldier and as a friend.

Forgive me for not writing more often. I hope you and Hannah are well and survived the terrible winter. Remember when we thought the winter of 1929 was the worst ever?—29 degrees below zero on the Hohe Warte. This past one was even worse. England was paralyzed by blizzards. And when the snow melted we were overcome by floods. There was little food, and even less coal. Many businesses had to close, throwing hundreds of thousands of people out of work, which made them even poorer and hungrier than before. An "economic Dunkirk" someone called it. Life is especially grim in London where people wonder why victory seems no better than defeat. Safe in our little village, I can only imagine how bad it must be in cities where half the homes no longer exist. Deep in my heart, I fear that Man will never be cured of war no matter how we wish it to be otherwise, and our young people will see the likes of this again.

I never expected to once more live in a country seeing an end to its empire, although I think England will fare better than Austria. Churchill once said the English have "the spirit of an unquenchable people." They are brave and have been remarkably cooperative—even about rationing—but Churchill's election loss after the war made it clear that there was a limit on how long one could expect it of them.

My husband and I were so optimistic when we were young, firmly believing things would continue to get better forever—but the Great War shattered that belief. Our optimism was further trampled upon by depression, civil war, and Hitler, whose monstrosity had been unimaginable before. There were times I felt I could not go on without my husband and my daughter, but then I would think of the love and care you showed Léonie and Josef and I was comforted that such compassion and generosity still existed. And of course there's Valerie—so full of life, reminding me of all the good I've known. "Don't worry, Gram," she'd say, as she cartwheeled down our front path. "I'll take care of you." And I'd be touched again by joy.

May it be like that for you and Hannah. You deserve to be happy.

Please write when you can. You are always in our thoughts.

your old friend,
Anna Grünbaum

Emma placed her head in her hands and wept, overwhelmed by both gratitude and grief. And as she dried her tears, she could not help but think of Sophie and how Greta had described her, now alone in a strange land without her. She longed to reach out to her but realized that she did not even have an address.

The next morning Emma unwrapped the photographs she had hidden away during her darkest hours and hung them over her bed. She would have to get one taken of Hannah. If only she'd thought to ask Martin. Perhaps one of her customers had a camera.

1955
INDEPENDENCE

45.

VIENNA

On the 16th of May 1955, while Friedrich and Marion were having lunch at the Hotel Sacher, the Soviet Union, Great Britain, the United States, and France signed a treaty granting Austria independence, fulfilling plans they'd made in 1943. Occupation forces were to be withdrawn with the understanding that Austria would declare its neutrality, making it a buffer zone between the East and the West.

Marion felt quite celebratory and ordered a bottle of champagne.

As the sommelier poured two glasses, Marion raised hers and said, "Austria is free again!"

"Free of what?" Friedrich asked, knowing neither guilt nor shame were in her vocabulary—nor in that of her fellow Austrians, as far as he could see. But who was he to judge?

"The Russians, of course," she said, giving him a blank look.

Ever the chameleon, Austria had managed to survive her mutations, morphing from mighty empire to poor republic to parliamentary democracy to dictatorship. Swallowed up and made a part of the greater Third Reich, she had used the Allies' words to transform herself from perpetrator to victim. Liberated and then occupied by her former enemies, she had succeeded in freeing herself from their occupation—the only country that had managed it. She was an independent republic once more. A little one. Neutral. Like Switzerland or Sweden, people said, ignoring all the compromises fear and greed had triggered during the war. Friedrich wondered if neutrality in times of peace would be any easier.

"We can finally get rid of Tibor," Marion said, breaking into his historical ruminations.

Friedrich should have found it easy to agree. Tibor was a sly, dishonest little man but he made Friedrich laugh and was the only man he'd ever thought to call a friend. Despite his strutting and boasting Friedrich knew Tibor envied him his money. He hated that after so many years he still had to watch what he spent and needed Friedrich to have the little money he did have. Yet Friedrich felt affection for him because his many schemes had always failed. He would have been too much like Marion if they hadn't.

"I don't know, my darling Marion. I think caution is a wiser course of action. Stalin wants to annex all the countries of Eastern Europe that the Red Army captured during the war. He will use any means to achieve that. We would merely be an inconsequential cog in his machine. If we don't squeak neither Stalin nor the West will notice us."

To Friedrich's surprise, Marion saw his point. Tibor could stay.

Elsa might have seen through his argument but she had not lived to see Austria's freedom, having suffered a fatal stroke the previous summer while on her annual trip to the baths in Bad Ischl. Too much of a good life, Friedrich supposed. She'd grown quite heavy after the war, when money had real power in the black market. Their pantry and liquor cabinets were continually stocked and restocked with only the finest.

Marion had arranged a suitable and well-attended funeral for her mother and grieved her loss quite visibly as the casket was lowered into the ground. But realizing that without her mother, she was queen, the palace hers alone, she regained her composure. Perhaps she felt monarchs ascending the throne must remain strong, unweakened by tears.

Friedrich's standing in the palace remained unchanged.

1957
Still Living with Shadows

46.

VIENNA

Emma finished polishing the brass plaque on the wall outside her building door, tucked the rag into her apron pocket and put her hands on her hips, happy with the results of her labor.

PENSION FÜR JUNGE DAMEN
4. Stock - Tür 7

The guesthouse for young ladies had been Hannah's idea and attested to her growing self-confidence, which pleased Emma as much as the idea itself.

Emma turned and saw a woman waving her umbrella at her, muttering that in her day there never would have been a boarding house in a building of such standing.

Of all the armies that had marched through Vienna, this army of old women, robbed by two world wars of their fathers, brothers, husbands and sons, was the one that had truly survived. Uniformed in raincoats and *Tiroler* hats, armed with umbrellas and vinyl shopping bags, they occupied every street, every market, every café. They were expert in schedules and routes of buses, trains and trams, and traveled from district to district in pursuit of their rights. Sharp-thinking and shifty eyed, they focused on every detail that disturbed them. No incongruence was too trivial. If a person sat sideways in a tram, or laughed too loud in public, he was deemed to be a foreigner. They were convinced all market vendors cheated their customers and beggars hid their wealth, proving that Man was by nature dishonest. They maintained that the world was only getting worse, and despite unemployment, depression and wars, the old days had been better. Children weren't fresh then, music was melodic, and dialect was restricted to the mouths of the proletariat.

Emma felt an odd affection for this army of grumpy survivors —now that both Frau Mandl and her mother were gone—for who else would remember the imperial Vienna of old?

After a final glance at the brass plaque, Emma went back in, closed the door behind her, and walked through the courtyard to the elevator, that splendid wrought-iron shaft that rose from ground to fourth floor. Inside, a smaller but no less splendid, wrought-iron cage with wooden floor, wooden railing and one small leather-covered seat, carried its passengers upwards -- but only up. As they exited, passengers had to send the elevator back down—empty. Riding down was still *verboten,* as it had been when Léonie and Josef first lived there. But last year little Frau Wöhrer, from the ground floor apartment by the garden, said she'd bowed to enough rules in her life and rebelled. Every morning after that, as the other tenants were walking down the stairs to go to work, she rode the elevator up just so everyone could see her ride it back down. The *Hausbesorgerin* scolded her repeatedly, warning her that the elevator would surely crash to the bottom someday, but Frau Wöhrer persisted. One victory for the resistance, Frau Mandl would have said.

Emma reached the fourth floor, pushed the lever down and to the right to unlatch and open the door, then pushed the return button, closed the inside cage door and then, finally, the outside door. The elevator groaned as it descended, settling into place on the ground floor just as she unlocked the double lock to *Tür 7*—a suite of clicks and grumbles that never failed to remind her of when it was Léonie who lived there.

She put away her rag and polish.

"Hannah? Are you ready?"

"Ready," Hannah said, coming out of the pantry with her cane in one hand and a straw basket in the other. "I put on lipstick and combed my hair a different way. What do you think?"

Hannah was twenty-two and no longer the frail little girl Emma first met in the hospital.

"As lovely as Princess Grace," Emma said.

Hannah smiled happily and held on to Emma's arm for support as they walked slowly down the marble stairs. Her leg had healed enough over the years to cause her little pain, but her mobility had remained limited.

Their first stop was at the greengrocer in the Landstrasse Market, an ill-tempered man Emma always vowed never to frequent again except that he had the freshest fruits and vegetables.

"Two kilos of potatoes, two cauliflowers, one radish root and three kilos of apples, if you don't mind," she said.

He glared at her, her request just one more unwelcome irritation.

"Finally we're free of the occupation, and what do they do? Send us a hundred and seventy-five thousand Hungarians asking for asylum!" he groused as he wrapped her purchases in newspaper. "We're just a little country, what are we to do with them all?"

Emma glared back at him, paid him what she owed, and said, "Put them in the places you emptied twenty years ago—an immigrant for every outcast—a refugee in for every refugee out."

He shook his head but did not reply.

Emma turned to Hannah.

"Don't people realize that those refugees walked from Hungary, carrying their children and their meager belongings so they could escape yet another dictatorship? Are we doomed to be like Sisyphus, forever pushing a boulder up a hill, never reaching the top, never winning the struggle against the powers that rule...

We're *never* buying from him again," Emma added for all to hear, as they made their way to the cheese vendor.

Hannah's eyes fell on a young man in muddy boots buying bread, his clothes still damp from the rain that had ended earlier.

She squeezed Emma's arm and nodded in his direction.

"Doesn't he look mischievous—but nice somehow—with his scruffy clothes and curly black hair?"

The young man turned and caught Hannah's glance and grinned. Flustered, her hand slipped off Emma's arm and she lost her balance on the wet cobblestones. She tried to raise herself with her cane, but her leg gave way and she fell again. Before Emma had time to put down her bag, the young man rushed over and picked her up.

"Are you all right, dear?" Emma asked, as the young man helped Hannah to a bench, then dashed back to retrieve her cane.

"Oh, yes!" Hannah said, then added in a whisper, "Wasn't that gallant?"

"Allow me to introduce myself," the young man said, when he returned with her cane. With a little bow he kissed her hand, making her blush. "My name is Stefan Bársony. What is yours?"

"Hannah Hoffmann," she said, lowering her eyes.

"It was kind of you to help," Emma said. "But we mustn't keep —"

"We often go to the café across the street," Hannah broke in. "Would you like to join us? We have time, don't we, Emma?"

"I would like to very much," the young man answered, not waiting for Emma's reply. "But I am not alone," he added, pointing to a man in a shabby suit waiting for him by the fruit stand.

"He's welcome, too, isn't he, Emma?" Hannah said.

"I suppose—"

"I'll tell him then," Stefan said. He ran over and brought the man back.

"Herr Bársony, your son is a gentleman," Emma said, reaching out to shake the man's hand.

He removed his hat, and kissed her hand.

"He is that, but he is not my son, I'm sorry to say. Just a friend." The man's lips curved into a small smile. "I believe we know each other."

"I don't think—," Emma began, although he did look familiar.

"My name is Hanns Menzler."

"Oh, my goodness! Forgive me. I did not recognize you. You were Josef's colleague, weren't you?"

"Yes, colleague and friend—long ago. I was much younger then. You, on the other hand, are as young and lovely as ever."

She felt her cheeks grow warm, remembering that he had once been interested in her, and could not think of how to answer.

Stefan hooked Hannah's arm in his as they crossed the street to the café. Several elderly men were seated alone at tables along the paneled walls, reading their morning papers, while two small groups of ladies in hats were clustered together in the middle, chatting in low voices as they drank their coffees. Stefan led the way to an empty table in the corner, helped Hannah to her seat and sat down beside her, leaving Dr. Menzler and Emma to sit together on the other side.

An elderly waiter took their order and Hannah and Stefan were soon lost in conversation, hardly noticing when their coffees arrived.

"How do you know the young man?" Emma asked.

"I found him trying to make a bed for himself in a quiet corner of the Prater and offered him a bed."

"He's from Hungary?"

"Yes. He fled after the riots in Budapest, when the Russian tanks rolled in. Like so many others, he arrived with nothing but a satchel of clothes. He's been with me ever since, working whenever and wherever he can."

"What does he do?"

Dr. Menzler looked over at Stefan and smiled.

"Anything and everything. He's clever and good with his hands, which has been very useful since I live in an old building. But besides that, I enjoy his company."

"If he needs work, we might be able to use his help. We will be renting out a few rooms and have little things that still need to be completed. Would you really recommend him?"

"Absolutely." He gestured toward Hannah and Stefan, who were still deep in conversation. "And under the circumstances I'm sure he'd be more than delighted. Where do you and your daughter live?"

Emma hesitated, decided not to explain about Hannah but wrote down their address.

"Is this not where Léonie and Josef lived?" he said, with a look she could not interpret.

"Yes ... Hannah and I...it's a long story," she said, afraid he thought she'd somehow stolen it. "And you?"

"I live in Leopoldstadt. I moved there after the war."

The second district had been the old Jewish section before the war, and under Russian occupation after it. Emma wondered what had made him move there, but he offered no explanation.

"It's getting late," she said, when she noticed how long they'd lingered over coffee. "We still have so much—"

"Perhaps Stefan could come and fix that faucet we were having trouble with?" Hannah said, nudging Emma's foot with hers.

"Yes...we'll tal ..." Emma said, although their conversation had disoriented her. Where had Dr. Menzler been during the war, what had he done? When had the war ended for him?

Her mind went back to the summer of 1947 when the first prisoners of war had come back from Russia. She'd had a moment of irrational hope that Otto would be among them; that he'd fled east instead of west and had been taken by the Russians. Month after month the prisoners had arrived, until by the end of 1949 almost half a million had been released, with the last coming in

1955 — but not Otto. Why only those who had fought and killed for Hitler? Where was the justice in that?

Her mother often talked about the young boys she knew when she was young, who were sucked into a war they didn't understand or know the cost of.

"We mustn't forget," she said, "that even the mothers of the defeated welcome their sons home, happy they survived when so many didn't."

Emma found it difficult to forgive those on the wrong side.

Stefan turned out to be as creative as he was practical in his approaches to both mechanical and carpentry problems; and he was so willing and filled with *joi de vivre* that his every visit became an event Hannah looked forward to and talked about for hours afterwards. It wasn't until then that Emma realized in what isolation she and Hannah had been living. Like two moles never exposed to sunlight, they were unprepared for the effect of the young man's dazzle. Hannah was smitten, and Emma worried that Stefan would suddenly fly off, leaving Hannah doomed to spend her days with an aging spinster long bereft of dreams.

As they worked in the foyer, setting up a table with Vienna brochures and maps for their prospective guests, Emma gently broached the subject of Stefan.

"He's a very nice young man, Hannah, full of fun and energy, but I don't know how serious he is or how reliable. You mustn't get your hopes up, my sweet girl, it may not work out."

"You're just jealous and don't want me to be happy because then you'd be alone!"

Hannah threw down a handful of maps, picked up her cane and stormed out of the apartment, slamming the door behind her.

The fierceness of her outburst stunned Emma. They'd had so few disagreements over the years. Afraid of hurting each other's feelings, they'd dealt with differences by withdrawing or remaining silent. It seemed kinder though perhaps it was merely cowardice.

Hannah was right that Emma was afraid—not of being alone, as she thought—but of once again not being able to protect someone she loved. She wanted to run after her, insist she come back, but Hannah was not a child anymore. She deserved more of a life than Emma could give her. It was 1957. The army wasn't shooting socialists, and Daimlers weren't lurking at the corner. Even the Russians kept their distance now that Austria was neutral.

Hours passed and Emma waited. When she heard a key in the door, she rushed out of her room and found Hannah in the kitchen setting the table for dinner.

"I'm sorry," they said at the same time.

Hannah embraced her and said, "Stefan really likes me, Emma, and I feel the same about him. I am not afraid and neither should you be."

By May, Hannah and Stefan were making wedding plans, every detail of which Hannah reviewed with Emma every morning after they'd cleared the breakfast dishes.

"We thought September would be good, and we want it to be just us," Hannah said. "Stefan and I, you and Dr. Menzler. We'll have a civil ceremony and then come back here to celebrate. I want everything to be pretty—but not fancy. Stefan and I are going to look for dishes at the flea market. Then I can make a tablecloth and napkins to go with them. We'll have big vase full of flowers, and if it's a sunny day we can eat on the balcony—as long as it's not too windy. What do you think? Or do you think we have to include our boarders?"

"I don't think so, but don't you want to marry in church?" Emma asked as she put the last of the dishes away.

"They wouldn't let me," Hannah answered in a soft voice.

"Why not? Did you already marry someone else while I wasn't looking?"

When she didn't answer, Emma turned around and saw that she was crying.

"What is it, Hannah? I didn't mean anything by that."

"I know. It's not that…it's that I'm Jewish," she said.

Emma sat down. "Why didn't you tell me, Hannah?"

"It's not that I didn't want to, but my mother said it was a secret and I mustn't tell anyone. Only the Hoffmanns knew."

"What do you mean only the Hoffmanns? Weren't they your parents?"

Emma could see that Hannah was struggling with how to answer until the words not spoken for so many years tumbled out.

"They were our neighbors. My real parents were arrested by the Gestapo while I was in school. When I came home, Frau Hoffmann was waiting for me. She told me that from then on I would be their child and I mustn't ever mention my real parents. They kept me safe—until a bomb fell onto our house and killed them…that's when I was taken to the hospital."

'When I first met you," Emma said, "you told me it was dangerous to tell secrets…I should have known what it meant…I only wish you could have trusted me enough to tell me."

"I trusted you more than anyone, Emma. I don't know what would have happened to me without you."

"We should have talked about those days…"

"I couldn't. Not then." Hannah put her hand on Emma's and gently stroked it. "And I think you couldn't either. I'm not sure what made me tell Stefan, but when I did I felt free for the first time and realized I didn't have to keep secrets anymore."

Emma put her arms around her.

"I'm so glad, Hannah. I am really happy for you."

Yet Emma's happiness was tinged with regret that she had not been the one to free her.

47.

VIENNA

When Friedrich and Marion were first married he'd offered to work in one of the Bruckner businesses, thinking it might be enjoyable to have a position in an office, with a secretary and co-workers, but as he possessed no marketable skills, he found himself retired before he ever worked—an accomplishment many a laborer would have envied. His only task was to be available for Marion's social calendar.

Marion's father had built several businesses, the largest of which manufactured paper—something of enormous value before and after the war, and perhaps especially during, when every death and crime was diligently recorded. And so it was that the Bruckner fortune—and thus his—never waned.

When Klaus, now sixteen, joined friends for a week-long summer hike in the Alps and Marion went for a cure in Bad Gastein, Friedrich found himself alone. He gave Tibor the week off, and told Fritz, Bertha and Emil he would only need them mornings. Afternoons and evenings they'd be free.

When the phone rang his first afternoon alone in the house, Friedrich realized he had to answer it himself. It was the Bruckner lawyer.

"My wife is away," he said, as Marion normally handled such matters.

"I see. The thing is, I am missing a property deed. I don't like to bother you, Herr Graf, but do you by any chance know if any of

Frau Bruckner's papers were left in the house inadvertently, as she made the purchase shortly before her death?"

"Some of her papers have been taken to the attic...I suppose I could look."

Friedrich had never been to the attic and was surprised at how vast it was as it stretched over both wings of the house. Suitcases, trunks, and hatboxes were stacked on and under tables and chairs that had outlived their usefulness downstairs. Although all the containers appeared to be his or Marion's, only a few identified their contents. None of them were Elsa's.

In the farthest corner, under a sheet, and untouched for years, he discovered a pile of boxes marked Otto, Greta and Sophie. Imagining them to be filled with clothes and toys he might recognize, he felt a twinge of sadness and did not open them.

Finally, to the far left of the attic stairs he found Elsa's belongings, labeled in her own handwriting. W*inter clothing. Summer clothing. Shoes. Handbags.* No documents there ... Then, tucked between two suitcases, he found a large *Lebkuchen* tin, inside of which was a a large brown envelope and a green leather album with the name *MARION* engraved in gold.

He opened the album first. Its spine was still stiff, and had probably only been opened once or twice. On the first page was an old newspaper photograph entitled *Marion Bruckner, Best-dressed Child of 1921.* A mere toddler, but not too young to compete for attention. Only a few photographs on the next few pages, then nothing. Elsa must have lost interest.

The brown envelope was unsealed. No deed. Just another yellowed newspaper clipping, with a photograph of a man, shackled, his mouth open as if caught in mid-word, under which it said:

> *Johann Pachel, street car conductor, is led out of the courtroom, having been convicted of accidentally killing a pedestrian while intoxicated.*

'My wife and daughter will starve if I am in prison!,"
he cried. Sentencing to take place in a week.

Clipped to the clipping was a small photograph clearly of the same man, albeit younger, this time with a young woman and child in front of a church. Shabby but radiant, the young couple held an infant in a long white gown between them. On the back, *Elsa's baptism day, Altottakring.*

Poor Marion, Friedrich thought, as he digested—with some glee—what these items meant. She'd always described Elsa's father as an upstanding government official who—impoverished by the collapse of the Empire—had died broken-hearted, leaving young Elsa an orphan (strangely, there had been no mention of what fate had befallen poor Frau Pachel). According to Elsa, she'd been taken in by the Sisters of the Sacred Heart as a child, and had attended the prestigious Sacre-Coeur School, though in their position there would have been little chance of that.

One could only wonder what fairy tale Elsa had invented to hook old Papa Bruckner. His wife had only been dead a year when he and Elsa married. Loneliness must have blinded him. Friedrich would have to ask Fritz. He would know.

Friedrich understood Elsa much better after his discovery. Her raw greed had come from feeling disgraced as well as poor. Mere poverty was far more acceptable when accompanied by a good name—especially one with a title. He might have had sympathy for her but could not forget how heartlessly she'd handed over her step-son merely out of greed.

Marion had inherited her mother's drive to accumulate as she climbed the social ladder, although she had no excuse, having suffered no deprivations whatsoever. Yet Friedrich could not imagine her being as ruthless as her mother.

Klaus did not share Marion's ambitions, nor did he seem to have any of his own yet, which might prove to be a failing—but like father, like son. Again.

48.

VIENNA

As the wedding grew closer, Dr. Menzler called and said he would like to contribute to the celebration in some way. Emma suggested they meet for coffee.

"I am on call all week, but I could take an hour off...," he said.

"It's best I come to your office then. My guests are off to the Wachau tomorrow."

"That would be wonderful. Tell me when and I will meet you at the tram so we can walk back together."

It was a five-minute walk from the tram stop to his apartment, but it took more than fifteen as one patient after the other stopped to talk to the good doctor and ask about his health, or thank him for theirs.

"It appears your patients consider you a friend," Emma said.

"I've been here a long time."

"I thought familiarity bred contempt," she teased.

He laughed.

"Perhaps I haven't been here long enough for that."

As they turned the corner onto Odeongasse, an elderly man carrying three bulging cloth sacks stopped and put them down.

"You have a lovely companion this morning, Herr Doktor," he said, with a little bow.

"Yes I do, Herr Freund. May I present you Frau Emma Huber."

"Good morning, Herr Freund," Emma said. "I see you've been to the market."

"Oh no," he said, pulling the sacks closer to him. "I always carry them. You never know when they'll come after us again."

He wished them well and walked on.

"He survived the war by hiding in cellars. All he managed to save he has kept in those bags," Dr. Menzler said, as they walked the last few steps to his apartment building. He pulled a large bundle of keys out of his pocket and had to jiggle the door handle repeatedly before the lock clicked open.

"I should have Stefan replace this lock," he said. "A hundred years of service has taken its toll."

He held the heavy door open and they slipped into the dark cobblestone entryway.

"Come," he said, "my apartment is on the other side of the courtyard."

He offered Emma his arm and as she took it she was overwhelmed by a feeling of loneliness she had long suppressed.

As if he knew, Dr. Menzler drew her closer and said, "We were on a first-name basis once. Do you think we can be again?"

"I'd like that, Hanns."

Laundry hung from clotheslines strung from one side of the inner courtyard to the other. Pots of flowers and herbs perched on window sills. Children with dirty faces and patched and mended clothes laughed and shouted in different languages as they played with marbles and sticks on the cobblestones. The smells of exotic cooking filled the air.

"It's a surprise, isn't it, Emma?" he said. "From the outside, it looks like every other bleak Viennese building on a long street of old, bleak buildings. But here in the second district, the buildings are full of life. Many of the apartments still share toilets and baths so you hear people wandering the halls all through the night. The refugees and immigrants who live here aren't like the old Viennese, who think that making noise is a crime, and muffle the sounds of their lives even behind closed doors. I can't remember if we were always like that or only after there was so much to hide."

Emma gave him a sharp look. He understood.

They walked up the stairs on the far corner of the courtyard, pushed the light button, turned left and walked down to the apartment marked *Tür 6/7, Doktor Hanns Menzler, Arzt for Allgemeinmedizin.* General Practitioner.

"Six is my little apartment, seven my office," he explained, holding the door to number six for her to enter. "My nurse will come get me if I'm needed."

The main room of his apartment was small but comfortable. A sofa and two upholstered chairs were arranged around a coffee table on a red-and-blue Persian rug. Framed prints covered one wall. Shelves stacked with books lined another. On a shelf directly behind his desk, surrounded by old, formal portraits of his parents, was a photograph in a simple wooden frame of a group of young people dressed in summer whites, seated on a blanket in the dappled shade of an old tree.

Emma gasped.

"That's us!"

"Yes," he said, handing the photograph to her. "You, Greta, Otto, Léonie and Josef. And that's me, in the back, the one with the mustache. You probably don't remember —"

"I remember," she said, biting her lip and fighting back tears.

His forehead wrinkled with concern as she fumbled with her handbag and tried to hold on to the photograph at the same time.

"We were celebrating something…" she said.

"Yes, my first real assignment. Léonie even brought a cake… They were always so kind to me. I knew no one when I first came to Vienna. They took pity on me and often inclu—"

"They're all gone now," Emma stammered, tears running down her cheeks.

Hanns pulled a handkerchief out of his pocket and handed it to her. She blew her nose loudly like a child.

After a few moments, his voice older and more tired, he said, "During those first ugly days after the Anschluss I looked for them, but there were signs posted at both their home and Josef's office that the apartments were to be aryanized. I told myself that they'd gotten away and there was nothing I could do anyway …"

He turned away and placed the photographs on his desk.

"When I was drafted, I was almost glad. On the front, with the wounded dying all around me, I did not have to decide what I should do, that part was clear It didn't matter who was bad or who was good—but when I returned to Vienna at the end of the war, the world I had loved was gone and I had to face the fact that I had done nothing to prevent it."

He sat with his hands in his lap, his eyes downcast.

Perhaps another day Emma might have judged him for his weakness but she was overcome by sadness for all the good people who'd given in to fear. Had she not done the same?

They remained silent for several minutes.

"Why did you come here to Leopoldstadt, Hanns?" she asked. "With so many men lost in the war, and all the Jewish doctors gone, you must have had many offers."

"Here among survivors and refugees, I thought I could do some good, and atone for what I hadn't done before … When I learned that of the 185,000 Jews in Vienna before the Anschluss only a few remained at the end, I actually thanked God we'd been defeated. I thought it meant that evil itself had been defeated—as if evil were limited to one group of people in one place at one time."

Hanns rubbed his forehead. "How naive I was," he said. He turned and pointed to his overflowing bookshelves. "I read a lot now—especially history and philosophy—so I can understand the world."

"And do you?"

He shook his head. "Not at all. I looked evil in the face and asked how it could happen, as if I hadn't been involved. How can people do such terrible things? Don't we all ask that? Yet we detach ourselves and blame The Others—other generations, other cultures, other circumstances—not grasping that we will always share the guilt, for we share the human weaknesses that make evil possible."

He shrugged, his mouth twisting into a sheepish smile.

"Forgive me, Emma. I don't know what's possessed me. I don't always pontificate. It must be the emotion of being with an old friend again after all these years. Nor am I as despondent as I must sound. In my heart—despite everything—I still believe people are capable of reason and compassion, and can learn from their mistakes."

"I hope that's true," Emma said. She opened her handbag on the pretext of taking out her gloves so that she would not have to look at him. "So many of my sweetest memories are clouded by regret."

"I hope you know you can talk to me about such things," he said.

She looked up at him. His eyes were kind and sincere.

"Thank you, Hanns. One day, perhaps."

They stood up and Emma held out her hand to shake his. He held it for a moment then raised it to his lips and kissed it.

On her way home, the memory of that small gesture made Emma realize again in what isolation Hannah and she had been living. In their peaceful but narrow existence, they'd repressed all the memories and feelings that could cause them pain. It was no wonder Stefan's youthful, unafraid vibrancy had dazzled Hannah, awakening dreams and emotions she'd never dared to have before. Unearthing dreams that could no longer come true was much more difficult.

Hannah was clattering around in the kitchen when Emma returned.

"I can't sit still," she said. "I have such exciting news! Stefan has inherited a farm! Well, almost inherited. If he works it, his great-uncle will leave it to him. He's been too sick to farm it himself, so there's nothing to harvest this year, but there is a house. And a cow, and a horse, two goats, and some chickens."

"Not in Hungary, I hope."

"No, in Burgenland, on our side of the border, near the Neusiedlersee."

Emma was relieved it wasn't far, but Burgenland had been under Russian occupation and remained very poor.

"Does Stefan know anything about farming?"

"No, but he can learn. And until then we'll have a house and milk and eggs, and I can sew for people just like here, and Stefan is so clever, he can always find work. We were thinking we could have summer guests. People like going to the country in the summer, don't they? Especially children. I already wrote down some of my ideas. I'll show you."

Emma watched Hannah hobble down the hall and thought she'd never seen her so happy.

Later, as they were finishing dinner, the doorbell rang.

"Telegram," a voice said through the door.

Emma's heart raced with fear as she opened the door. *Not again, please God, not again.*

She tore it open.

VALERIE AND MARTIN GETTING MARRIED SEPTEMBER 14 STOP PLEASE COME STOP ANNA

Emma held it against her breast, filled with gratitude that Léonie's little girl had found happiness with a man as fine as Martin. So why this pang of regret for not having taken a path only Frau Mandl had thought possible? It was Theo and the life they'd planned that she'd loved, and that she'd missed all these years. Not Martin.

> *Dearest Frau Anna,*
>
> *What joy your happy news brings us! Hannah and I send all our love and a world of good wishes for the happy couple.*
>
> *I'm overwhelmed with memories—of Léonie and Josef, of Valerie so suddenly (it seems) grown into womanhood, and of Martin, young and healthy, saving me from despair.*
>
> *We would so like to accept your invitation, but change must be in the air for Hannah and Stefan have chosen the same day to be married. After the wedding they will move to a small farm in Burgenland. A year ago I would have worried that my timid little Hannah would hide herself away and not get to know anyone, but Stefan has opened up the world to her and will make sure she blossoms. I might have been tempted to become a hermit myself with Hannah gone, but running my little Pension will save me from that. It was your generosity*

during my darkest days that makes also this possible.

All these changes and your news have made me think of Greta's daughter again, who, because of Bessie Stone's request not to contact her, has been lost to us. I hope, being far away and safe means that Sophie has been spared the dark memories that still fill the recesses of our minds.

With deepest affection,
your Emma

1958
Changes

49.

NEW YORK

It was a hot July afternoon, and Sophie was dressed in her favorite light-blue shirtwaist and white ankle-strap sandals. She felt quite chic as she climbed aboard the Poughkeepsie-to-New York train carrying her new London Gray Samsonite Streamlite suitcase. It was the first time she'd taken the train since June 11,1945—the day her mother brought her to stay with Aunt Bessie and Uncle Bill, and the day she had had to shut her mind to everything that had come before. She knew they'd meant well, but they——or at least Aunt Bessie—hadn't understood that losing memories was even sadder than remembering. She should have tried to explain but she'd been afraid they'd think she was complaining and send her away to an orphanage.

Sophie could have lived with Uncle Harry if her mother had married him. Sophie had wanted her to but her mother had just smiled and said she was already married. She was still waiting for her father then although they hadn't heard anything from him, not even a letter, after they left Vienna. After a while her mother had hardly talked about him at all so Sophie assumed that he must have died. She told herself he'd been killed trying to save someone else like in the movies—but she didn't want to tell her mother that, so she said maybe they could just marry Uncle Harry in the meantime, just until the war was over. She was only a kid then and it was a silly idea, but she was sure that if her mother had married him, she wouldn't have had to leave her in Millersville. And she wouldn't have taken the train that day—even though the two things weren't related.

Sophie smiled thinking how horrified Aunt Bessie would have been if Sophie had asked to live with Uncle Harry. *What would people say,* she'd have said, *a young girl living with an unmarried man who isn't her father!*

She couldn't have done it anyway because Uncle Harry gave up his paper and took a job as a roving foreign correspondent. Sophie was sure it was because he couldn't bear staying in New York after her mother died, but sometimes it made her feel like he'd died too.

Sophie was grateful to Aunt Bessie and Uncle Bill for taking her in, even if she didn't always show it. She had plenty of food to eat, her own room, and new clothes when she needed them. Not many people would have done that for a sullen twelve-year old who wasn't related to them. It probably made them sad to know that no matter how nice they were to her she would have rather been with her mother. She felt bad about that.

Going to school helped—the studying part of it. The social part was harder and Sophie wasn't good at it, so she mostly avoided it.

Uncle Bill didn't talk much, but sometimes he understood how she felt better than Aunt Bessie did which is probably why he came home one day with a dog that had been abandoned. The dog had long ears and a funny white spot on her back that looked like a daisy, so that's what Sophie called her. Daisy limped a little but she was a great listener. She and Sophie took long slow walks and Sophie would tell her about her mother and what their lives would have been like if only … she was just daydreaming, of course, but Daisy didn't mind. She died of old age a week after Sophie finished high school. Uncle Bill helped bury her near her favorite tree. Sophie was grateful he didn't ask if she wanted another dog. She wouldn't have wanted Daisy to think she was replaceable.

Aunt Bessie and Uncle Bill insisted she go to college. They said if she lived at home they could afford the fees. Sophie decided to study history so she could understand how she'd ended up in the life she was in.

On the last day of her junior year, she overheard Uncle Bill telling Aunt Bessie that his work hours had been reduced and they'd have to cut down on their expenses. Sophie didn't want to be more of a burden than she'd already been, so she told them college was not for her after all and she would rather get a job.

She had taken typing and shorthand in high school and found a job with *HairBright*, a funny little company that marketed to local beauty parlors an herbal shampoo that the owner had developed. It took Sophie a full month just to go through paperwork the owner had placed in random piles around the office. By the end of three months she'd created a filing system, done a complete inventory and paid all the bills. Her boss was so grateful he gave her raises two months in a row. Soon she was earning enough to help out at home and put money in the bank, too.

Saturdays, Sophie would drive to the Poughkeepsie Public Library and read some more about the war. It depressed her but if a movie about the war was playing, she'd go see it and feel better. Things seemed simpler in the movies. You knew the good guys from the bad guys. She wondered if she could ever be as courageous as the hero or heroine.

She didn't think so as she didn't even have it in her to leave MIllersville. She applied for a job in Poughkeepsie once but her boss begged her not to take it, said *HairBright* could never manage without her. So she stayed on, until one day he announced he'd sold the business and was moving to Florida.

It was her chance to do something new, but she'd been in a rut for so long that she had no idea what that new thing should be.

Then Uncle Harry called and gave her hell.

"You're almost twenty-six, Sophie, and you're wasting your life. Get off your behind and do something!"

"I was thinking of moving to New York," she said, though inertia had her so firmly in its grasp that it hadn't even crossed her mind until that moment.

"Perfect. You can stay in my place. I'm hardly ever there."

Sophie had no choice then but to move to New York, which she did—very appropriately on Independence Day—although she had no idea what she would do once she got there.

She arrived at Grand Central Station early on that hot Friday afternoon. Following Aunt Bessie's detailed instructions, she took the shuttle to the West Side and waited for the IRT. The heat was even more intense underground, relieved only by the wind created by incoming trains. The uptown express arrived first. She heaved her suitcase in and collapsed into the nearest empty seat, next to a man trying in vain to listen to a Brooklyn Dodgers game on his transistor radio. Everybody else was reading—most of them the *Daily News,* although there was a smattering of *New York Posts* and *New York Times.* A few were reading books, mostly *Anatomy of A Murde*r, which was number one on the bestseller list that week.

She got off at the fifth stop and exited at the northwest corner of Broadway and 96th Street. Ahead of her *Vertigo* was playing at the Riverside Theatre, and *Indiscreet* at the Riviera beside it. She remembered going with her mother to see *A Tree Grows in Brooklyn* at one of them and a funny Disney film at the other all in one weekend. Both were double features and one of them had a travelogue about a floating market Sophie said she was going to see one day. Just up the street was another theatre, the Symphony, where they'd once seen *Bambi.* She'd cried for an hour afterwards.

How different it all was from the Millersville drive-in, which played mostly horror movies and an occasional western. People had to go to Poughkeepsie to see a decent movie.

Sophie continued up Broadway and found that Braun's Market had taken over the greengrocer next door and become Braun's SuperMarket. Babka Bakery hadn't changed though, and the *La*

Primadora sign still marked the corner store that had sold everything she wanted when she was twelve — pencils, notebooks, chocolate bars, movie magazines and trading cards. The owner, Frau Handler, short, square little woman who spoke German and almost no English, had always squinted at her through her glasses —little round ones like the ones Nazis wore in the movies. *My how you've grown*, she'd said every time Sophie went in, finishing with a scowl and a *I hate tall girls*. There was no doubt which side of the war *she*'d supported. Sophie was relieved to see a man behind the counter now, chatting and laughing with a customer.

She turned onto 100th Street and as she walked toward the Hudson River, her heart began to race. Without realizing it, she'd missed Uncle Harry's street and turned onto hers. She clutched the handle of her suitcase. There on the left, between West End Avenue and Riverside Drive, was the small turn-of-the-century apartment building where she'd lived with her mother. She turned around and ran, her suitcase banging against her leg, until she reached Broadway again. She thought she'd buried that grief long ago. Taking a deep breath, she made her way back to 98th Street, turned right toward West End Avenue again until she arrived at Uncle Harry's three-story brownstone. Three steps up to the black-and-white tiled foyer floor. Six brass mailboxes on the wall. The one marked Whittaker looked full. Hopefully, Uncle Harry had remembered to leave the key. Up the stairs to the second floor, Number 3 on the left.

She pulled out the house key Uncle Harry had sent and unlocked the door. The front room was just as she remembered it except for a new Emerson television squeezed between two of the overfilled bookcases that lined two of the walls. His green sofa, even more faded than before, sat opposite between a chair she remembered from his office, and a Formica-topped table on which his old, black Underwood perched like a crow next to a note written in Uncle Harry's large, loopy handwriting.

Sophie — Make yourself at home. You can use my bedroom. The dresser is empty. Feel free to write a novel on my typewriter (I bought myself a Hermes Portable for traveling) or move it off the table and have a dinner party. You can read my books but don't lend them out willy-nilly — people forget to return them. I've put a folding bed in the closet for when I'm in town or you have a friend over. Get out and see the world!

Well, maybe not the floating market yet. But at least she'd made it here. It was a beginning.

Sophie hung up her dresses and skirts, put the smaller items in the dresser, and pushed her suitcase under the bed. Aunt Bessie said she'd send her winter things once she'd settled. It would be a while before she needed them.

She changed into her nightgown and opened all the windows, but the July evening was so still and hot that there was no cross-ventilation at all. If it got any worse she'd have to sleep out on the fire escape.

Aunt Bessie's sandwich was still in her bag, and there was a bottle of ginger ale in the refrigerator. They would do until morning. She made herself comfortable on the sofa and started reading a copy of an old *New Yorker* she'd found in the bedroom. She decided to explore the city before she made any decisions.

The next morning she started her exploration by walking down Broadway to Columbus Circle and back through Central Park. The day after she walked from Columbus Circle to Greenwich Village. On the third, she took the subway down to Wall Street, and worked her way up through Chinatown and Little Italy to the Village.

She loved the architectural details on the city's old buildings. Every street had its own character and life. Young mothers wearing pastel sundresses pushed their strollers down Broadway, or laid out a picnic lunch for their children in the park; men battled the heat in their seersucker suits as they walked from the subway to their offices; dirty-faced boys played stickball in the side streets, while their mothers gossiped on the stoops. Blue-haired ladies with white gloves drank coffee in Rumplmayer's Café on Central Park West, while others crushed into Ohrbachs for a sale.

Sophie bought giant dill pickles straight from the barrel at a deli on Broadway, and hot knishes slathered with mustard from street vendors on 6th Avenue. She had chocolate egg creams at a neighborhood soda fountain, and nibbled on marzipan potatoes and rum balls from the bakery. She ate egg rolls in Chinatown and cannolis in Little Italy. With every bite she recreated moments from her childhood.

She was tempted to keep walking until she'd seen Manhattan from top to bottom, and then move on to the other boroughs— but that wasn't why she'd come. She'd come to find direction for her life. So she gave herself one more week before looking into enrolling in City College. It was time she finished her degree.

Sophie spent all of the next day at the Metropolitan Museum of Art. Exhausted and inspired, she returned home to find a man in a hat and trench coat—much too hot for July—struggling to unlock one of the mailboxes. He was standing with his feet on either side of a battered suitcase, and with an even more battered leather bag over one shoulder, and a bulging paper bag on the other arm.

"Excuse me, sir, can I help you?"

He turned and said, "Oh, good. I was hoping you were here already. Here, hold this bag. Hope you don't mind putting up with me for a few days."

Without waiting for an answer he picked up his suitcase and started up the stairs. She ran ahead to unlock the door.

"Of course not, it's your apartment, Uncle Harry—but how come you're here? I thought you were—"

"In Egypt? I was and have to go back so I won't be here long," he said, putting his suitcase down and giving her a hug before closing the door behind him. "It's great to see you, Soph'."

"I wish you could stay. I haven't seen you in ages and there's so much I'd like to talk to you about."

"Me too. But first, how long have you been here and what do you think of the old neighborhood?" he asked.

"Just a few days and it's just as I remembered it, except for the new supermarket."

"Frau Handler's gone."

She laughed. "I noticed, and I'm thrilled."

Uncle Harry pulled a bottle of wine out of the paper bag he'd brought.

"Let's have a drink and you can tell me all your plans."

She took two glasses out of the cupboard.

"I've decided to finally get my degree and was thinking I might like being a librarian."

"A noble profession, but you can't bury yourself in books forever, Sophie."

She blushed.

"I sure have missed you, Uncle Harry, even if you do see through me."

"I've missed you too. And you're old enough now that you can drop the uncle and call me Harry. I'm starving. How about we eat while I tell you how adventurous you should be."

She jumped up.

"We can't, I forgot to buy food! I'll run down and—"

"No need, I stopped for Chinese," he said, as he removed two plastic tubs and four white cardboard containers from the paper bag.

Sophie set the table and arranged the containers neatly in the middle.

They worked their way through won-ton soup, egg foo young, sweet and sour pork, and both fried and white rice while she plied him with questions about all the places he'd been since she'd seen him. They cracked open the fortune cookies and laughed at how vague and interpretable the messages were, although Harry's said *you will soon take a voyage* which was certainly true.

Hers read *you will soon meet someone from the past.*"

"Little chance of that," she said.

"Unless you count me, of course." He suppressed a yawn.

"You'd better get to bed, Uncle … I mean, Harry. You look exhausted. I'll sleep on the cot tonight and we'll talk more tomorrow. And no arguing."

When she woke the next morning, Harry was already up and on his knees rummaging through the coat closet.

"What are you looking for?" she asked, peering over his shoulder.

"Stuff I've been saving for you—if I can find it. I know I put it in a safe place."

She'd dressed and made coffee before Harry finally found the large tin box he'd hidden behind two other boxes in the back of the closet.

"This was your mother's. I'm not sure what's in it. I've wanted to give you this for years but Bessie wouldn't let me in case it brought up painful memories. But you're out from under her protective wings now and I think it's time. Are you up to looking at it on your own? I have to run down to the paper and talk to my editor but I'll be back in a couple of hours if you'd rather wait and look through it together."

"I think I can manage."

He smiled and handed her a box of tissues.

"Just in case," he said and left.

Sophie took a deep breath, opened the box and pulled out two large manila envelopes. She spread the contents of the first envelope on the floor—a passport, a small white envelope, an address book, and two packages wrapped in tissue paper and tied with gold ribbon.

The passport was her mother's, issued in Vienna, 24 March 1931. The photo showed her younger than Sophie remembered her, with her thick curly hair down to her shoulders, her expression serious but unworried. Sophie's name had been added in 1938, and all the visas and entrance and exit stamps were dated between then and 1941.

The address book was small, well-worn, and covered in green canvas. Inside the front cover, she had written a list of telephone numbers, the first four in black ink, *Emma, Léonie, Otto/office, home*; the last four in blue. *Harry, Bessie, work, home* — the numbers most important in her two lives. Funny, Sophie always wrote her home number in the front of her address book too in case she couldn't remember it, or if she lost it someone would see the number and could call her. Or if she died in an accident so they'd know whom to call.

The small white envelope contained two black-and-white photographs.

The first was a scallop-edged snapshot, broken off in one corner, of a young woman with her hair held back with combs, sitting on the grass with a fair-haired man. A little girl with short, dark hair sat between them, her head against the woman, her toes wiggling into a space under the man's arm. A happy family that could have been anywhere and now no longer was. *Am Kahlenberg Juni '37 - Sophies 4ter Geburtstag* it said. The last birthday she'd spent with both her parents.

In the second snapshot she was about ten and her hair had grown long. She was leaning against her mother, who had one arm around her. Looking down on them, his hand on her mother's shoulder, was Harry, in all his tall, lanky friendliness. On the back he'd written: *With my two favorite girls - Central Park 1943.*

Sophie reached for the tissue-covered packages and unwrapped them. The smaller item was a delicately engraved silver case. She remembered her mother tracing the design with her fingers before opening it to pull out a cigarette. She held it up to her nose and her eyes welled with tears as she smelled the remnants of tobacco. Blinking her tears away, she slipped the case into her pocket.

The second tissue wrapped package was a leather journal with a miniature lock and key. The binding cracked softly as Sophie opened it. Its white pages were still crisp and blank—except where her mother had written:

For my dearest daughter on her 13th birthday
a little book to write your memories and dreams in.
May all your days be filled with hope and promise,
all my love always, Mama

The pain of her mother's death seared through her as if it had just occurred. But it hadn't just occurred. Thirteen years had passed since that day—half of Sophie's life. Half her life without the one person who understood her and loved her completely.

Tears cascaded down Sophie's cheeks as she smoothed the ribbon that had been around the package and placed it between the first two pages. She blew her nose and wiped her tears so often that she was sitting in a sea of crumpled tissues when Harry returned.

She handed him the two photographs.

"Look at this one of Mama in Central Park, Harry. You'd never know all she'd been through. She was so strong and brave."

"She was, and you're more like her than you think, honey. Did you read all the articles she saved? Is that why you were crying?"

"What articles?"

"Didn't you get to the second envelope yet? Your mother saved every article that could provide her a clue as to what happened to your father and their friends. They're pretty grim. How much have you read about the war?"

"A lot, though whenever I brought any books or magazines home, Aunt Bessie would sneak them back to the library and say she thought they were overdue. She thought it would be too upsetting—which, of course, it was and still is but I have to know, don't I? For a long time, she wouldn't even let me watch the evening news. When I was old enough to drive to Poughkeepsie by myself I'd go to the library and read there. I wish you'd been around more. We could have talked. I had a lot of questions— though sometimes I wonder why I torture myself with it. I can't change it and it just makes me angry."

"So put the articles away for a while. We'll take a ride up to the Cloisters. It's the most peaceful place in New York."

The next day she and Harry took the ferry to Staten Island and back, and ate lunch at his favorite deli, In the evening they went down to the village and listened to jazz. It was a good day and Harry said they'd do it again next time he was in town.

It wasn't until days later that she noticed she'd overlooked a small notebook still in the bottom of the manila envelope. It was a little thing, its once-soft leather cover long dried out and cracked. Her mother must have brought it with her from Vienna because the stationer's stamp was still legible in the inside cover. There weren't many pages left in it as most had been torn out at some point, but those that remained were filled with her distinctive handwriting.

Cradling the little book in her hand, Sophie started reading.

Lyon, 2 August 1939
I dream of Otto night after night—running after me, reaching out to me, never catching up. I call to him, wanting him to know that Sophie is safe, but he can't hear. Other times he shouts at me from behind a barred window that I should escape, that he will find me, all the while Sophie is pulling at my skirt, pleading with me not to leave him.
I've lost track of how long we've been in Lyon endlessly waiting for papers, paying bribes, waiting for more papers: new papers, revised papers, extended papers, applications for entrance visas, exit visas, transit visas —papers with nationalities that make no sense. I was born Czech because my parents were, became an Austrian because I married one, was unwillingly

Anschlussed to Germany—none of which helped me at all — until an overworked young American consul took pity on me and found that he could put me on the Russian quota because I happened to have been born there. Even then, the struggle wasn't over. Sophie could not leave without her father's written permission. After days of arguing that it wasn't possible, the young consul gave in—whether out of compassion or exhaustion— and put her on my papers. Now the next journey begins. There is talk of war everywhere.

Havana, September 1941, a Wednesday, I think
It is hot and I close my eyes and am in Casablanca again listening to the languages of people displaced by history mingling with those of people who have lived there for two thousand years: Arabs, Jews, Berbers, Spaniards, Portuguese, Austrians, French, Germans, even Americans. And now some of those sounds have found their way to this little island. They say that we will leave here soon—in New York there will be a cacophony of a different kind—one that is underlined with hope that, although displaced, we can find a future, not merely shelter.

New York, 20 November 1941
New York is filled with people and sounds and smells so familiar that sometimes I forget where I am and think I see one or the other of my friends crossing a street or entering a doorway; or hear them speaking or laughing as I wait on line at the market. Most often, though, it is Otto I see turning a corner. Without explanation, I grab Sophie's hand and pull her behind me as I run after him. At times, my longing for him is unbearable, and so unfair to Sophie that I must train myself to look away.

She often asks about her father and wants to hear about our life in Vienna. I tell her how kind and good and courageous Otto is—was?—I struggle with what tense to use. I tell about our friends and how much fun we had, but instead of making her happy, it makes her sad. I must stop telling her. I will not let her dream only of what should have been.

Sophie sat and cried for both of them and pushed away the realization that even though they'd stopped hoping, her father could still be alive. With a shiver she remembered her fortune cookie — *you will soon meet someone from the past.*

50.

VIENNA

Emma was glad to have at least two of her rooms booked all winter and into early spring to distract her from Hannah's absence, which she felt more acutely than she'd expected. They'd written each other almost daily the first few weeks, but settled into writing once a week after a while. Hannah and Stefan returned for Christmas and plans were made for Emma to visit them as soon as their house renovations were completed. With every letter, Emma felt Hannah grow stronger and more confident—although that made Emma miss her even more.

Emma's boarders, as friendly and interesting as they might be, were strangers, so Emma was grateful that Hanns and she had continued to see each other after the wedding. Although they rarely spoke of the past, it bound them together and was the lens through which they viewed the world. That was why, she supposed, it was her that he called late one night in April.

"Forgive me, Emma, for calling at this hour but I need your help. I was walking home from visiting a patient when I found a young girl curled up in the doorway of a shuttered store. I might have mistaken her for a bundle of discarded clothes had she not moaned as I passed. Seeing the terrible state she was in, I told her I was a doctor and insisted she come back to my office with me. She only agreed because a police car drove by and she was more frightened of them than of me."

"I don't understand. What can I do?"

"Well, I was hoping you could take her in for a while."

"I already have two guests coming—"

"She's only sixteen—still a child—and pregnant. She has no one. I'll pay her way—"

"Oh Hanns, it's not the money," Emma said, ashamed she'd even hesitated. What would have happened to Hannah had she let the police decide, or to Sophie if Mrs. Stone hadn't taken her? "I'll come and get her now, Hanns. We'll manage. When is her baby due?"

"She wouldn't let me examine her but she thinks September or October so not for another few months."

It was almost midnight when Emma reached Hanns' office. The poor girl cowered like a wounded animal when Emma handed her the coat she'd brought along.

Her face was streaked with grime, her body gray with dust. Strands of her long black hair stuck to her cheek and neck. She looked as if she hadn't washed in days—or even weeks.

"Do you want to bathe before we leave?" Emma asked.

The girl shook her head no and wrapped her torn cardigan more tightly around her.

"Never mind then. We can do that at home."

Emma hung the coat she'd brought over the girl's shoulders, took her hand and felt it tremble.

"You needn't be afraid, dear child. You're safe now."

The girl's eyes flitted nervously between Hanns and Emma. He nodded and that seemed to reassure her.

When they arrived home Emma gave her the room off the kitchen because it was small and warm, and less intimidating than the high ceilinged rooms in the rest of the apartment. She seemed to appreciate that, and pointed to the adjacent bathroom which had a *Sitzbad* rather than a tub.

"I'll wash now," she said, speaking with an accent Emma couldn't quite identify.

Emma gave her a bathrobe and two towels and said she would wait for her in the kitchen. When she came out the gray dust that had covered her was gone. Her long hair was still tangled but clean.

"Come sit here," Emma said, "and I'll comb your hair. My hair was once black like yours and my mother always had to comb the tangles out."

She placed a towel over the girl's shoulders and gently pulled the comb through the long wet strands.

"We even have the same color eyes. Artists call it burnt umber."

One could mistake them for mother and daughter, Emma thought, although the girl's skin was more olive, and she wondered where she was from.

She tucked her into bed and wished her sweet dreams. The girl did not answer. In fact, they hardly spoke at all the first few days. Not wanting to pressure the child, Emma waited for her to begin. When she didn't, Emma began with questions so gentle they could be answered with a nod or a shake of the head. Did she like milk? Fruit? Was she warm enough? Then, at last, she asked her name.

"Magda."

"That's very pretty. And your last name?"

Magda shrugged and looked away. Emma did not press her lest she was afraid to tell her, or worse, that she did not know.

One day Emma noticed the heavy callouses on her feet and said her feet might feel better if she used a pumice stone.

"I can do it for you," Emma offered, and they talked while she rubbed them, and then smoothed them with lotion.

"That feels good," Magda said.

"You must have walked a lot."

She nodded. "Every day."

"Where did you live?" Emma asked softly, smoothing lotion on her legs and arms.

"Many places."

"And your home, where was that?"

"I don't know—far away."

"Are your parents there, Magda? Did you run away?"

She shook her head.

"I'm tired. May I sleep?"

"Of course."

Magda went to her room and lay down. Emma stroked her head, and pulled a cover over her.

"Tomorrow we will buy you new shoes and something to wear."

Magda's eyes welled with tears.

"Do I have to leave?"

"Oh no, I only thought…but there's no rush. I just remembered that I have things here you can wear. We'll worry about the shoes later. I think the first thing we should do is make something pretty for your room."

Emma sat with her until she fell asleep and then went to call Hannah.

"Poor girl," Hannah said. "Who knows what she has been through. I hope you can find her parents. I wish I could come see you and meet her but … I was waiting to tell you until I knew everything was going to be all right. Stefan and I are going to have a baby … Emma, did you hear me?"

"Yes…I…"

"Are you crying, Emma?"

"A little. I was thinking of the first time I saw you in the hospital, gently cradling a little boy in your arms. It was our first Christmas after the war. In a world that seemed broken almost beyond repair, you were so brave. You gave me the strength to go on. I will be grateful to you forever for that. You will be a wonderful mother, my dearest girl. How are you feeling?"

"Fine. The doctor says my blood pressure is a little high and I need to rest, but there is so much to do."

"Hannah, be sensible. Nothing is more important than your health. I only wish I could be there."

She laughed. "You have your hands full, but don't worry, Stefan's sister was finally granted asylum, so she is here to stay. She and Stefan hardly let me lift a finger. So I'm back to sewing."

"Me, too."

Sewing was what Emma could do for Magda, so the next day she and Magda searched through her stack of fabrics and she chose one with daisies.

"Mama loved daisies," she said.

"Then we'll use this to make you a bedspread."

It took them two full days, but Magda's smile as they laid it on her bed was worth every minute.

"Mama and I stayed on a farm once that had a big field filled with daisies, and she wove them together and made a crown for me. The field was so beautiful I wanted to stay there forever."

"Was your father with you, too?" Emma asked.

Magda shook her head and lowered her eyes.

"No. It was after they took him to the *Zigeunerlager*."

"Oh." Emma caught her breath for she knew what that meant. *Zigeunerlager* was where the Nazis put Roma, before they exterminated them.

"But not your mother?"

"No, because my father hid us. Mama said he was very brave."

"Yes, he was," Emma said, realizing he must have had no time to save himself. "Is that when you went to the farm?"

"No...Can we stop talking now?"

"Of course."

Emma put her arm around her shoulders but felt her stiffen so she let go.

It was a while before she told Emma anything else.

Emma started bringing her little gifts from the market to lift her spirits—a fancy ribbon for her hair, colored pencils, a pretty notebook to draw in, although after a while she noticed Magda didn't use them, just kept them in a box under her bed. Emma wasn't sure if it was because she didn't like them or whether she was afraid someone would take them. Trinkets couldn't make up for what Magda had been through anyway.

Little by little Magda began to trust Emma, although it wasn't until July that Emma was finally able to piece together all the circumstances that had brought her to sleep in the doorway of a shuttered store.

Emma gleaned from something Magda said, that they must have lived in Silesia, the part of Poland that expelled all its Germans after the war.

"We walked for a long time. So many of the buildings everywhere were broken. Sometimes we saw people sleeping on the street. Mama said they were Nazis and it was their own fault. They were the ones who took Papa. So I started thinking that maybe the people who fought Nazis had saved Papa and we should go home so he could find us, but Mama said we couldn't."

As she spoke, Magda twisted her hair around her finger, or fidgeted with her sweater. Anything so her eyes wouldn't meet Emma's.

"We stayed in a camp where lots of other people were who had no home. It was very crowded and we didn't know anyone but they gave us food, and some of the children would let me play with them, but then they left and new people came and some of them didn't like us. Mama said she was afraid things would never get better for us. That's why we ran away."

Although Magda didn't say, Emma thought she must have been about seven or eight then. She said sometimes people didn't know they were Roma and her mother would find work for a while, but then they'd have to leave again. Between jobs they'd sleep in farmers' barns and eat what they could steal or glean from the fields at night. Emma could only imagine the cold and hunger they'd survived. She felt ashamed once again at having been more fortunate than she deserved.

"Then we found a village where Mama could work and I could go to school. We stayed a long time, but one day Mama said we had to leave right away. She had bruises on her face and when I asked her what happened she wouldn't tell me. She said everything would be fine as soon as we left."

"How old were you then?" Emma asked.

"Twelve, I think. That's when Mama decided we should go to Vienna because she had a cousin here. So we walked again and came to a farm. They had no animals so Mama asked if we could sleep in the barn. It was nice there, but the next morning, I couldn't wake her. I tried to shake her but she didn't move and felt so cold, so I covered her with straw to warm her and ran to ask the farmer for something warm for her to drink. When he saw her he was so angry and screamed at me that Mama was dead and he should never have let us sleep in his barn. He'd be in big trouble if anyone found out. I didn't understand why. It wasn't his fault but he frightened me so much I ran away. I wanted to go back when it was dark but I got lost."

Magda stroked her growing belly as if to reassure her child that it was safe, just as Emma had done when she couldn't find Theo. She never imagined then that things would get even worse.

"What did you do then?" I asked.

"I walked and walked until a policeman found me and asked who I belonged to. No one, I said ... he took me to an orphanage. I didn't want to go but he said I had to, children couldn't live by themselves ... but I didn't like it there. You won't send my baby there, will you?"

"Never," Emma said. "You mustn't worry about that."

Several days passed before Magda would tell Emma that, without the protection of her mother, the years in the orphanage had been her most difficult. She escaped when a boy there decided to run away and she ran with him.

They stayed together for a while, wandering from one village to another, until one day he told her he couldn't take care of her anymore.

She began walking again, and after some time she fell in with a group of young people. She stayed with them for weeks or perhaps months. She'd lost her sense of time by then. One of the boys took an interest in her—even teaching her how to work with numbers —which she interpreted as kindness, so when he demanded that she do something for him in return, she acquiesced.

"I didn't like it," she said, "but he said that's what girls like me had to do. But when my belly began to grow he was very angry. I promised not to eat so much, but he grabbed me and shook me and screamed, *You're going to have a baby, you idiot Roma girl*! I didn't know...the next morning everyone was gone and I was alone again."

"You're not alone anymore, my dearest, sweetest child," Emma said, putting her arms around her and holding her tight. And for the first time Magda let her.

51.
NEW YORK

Sophie had one more day before she was to start classes at City College. She was nervous but excited. At $14 a semester, and with a rent-free apartment and what she'd saved, she wouldn't have to work for a while and could sign up for a full fifteen credits of history courses, so that in a year she would get her degree.

She put two slices of bread in the toaster, poured herself a cup of coffee from Harry's dented percolator, and was thinking about where to go on her last free day when the phone rang.

"Harry? Where are you? You sound like you're next door."

"Stockholm. Have you started classes yet?"

"No, tomorrow."

"Good. Caught you in time then. Tell them you can't start this semester, and go down and apply for a passport. Tell them you need it immediately. It'll cost a little more but you can afford it. I've booked you on the *SS America* leaving a week from Thursday. That's the 21st."

"What are you talking about?"

"Sorry, can't talk long—these calls cost a fortune—but this is your chance and you have to go. Your uncle will be on the ship."

"What uncle?"

"Don't be dense, Sophie. The one married to your aunt, your father's sister. Friedrich von Harzburg is his name. Ask for him when you're on board. Then when you get to Le Havre you can take the train to Vienna together."

Sophie felt the cold sweat of fear trickling down her sides. She couldn't possibly do that.

"This is crazy, Harry. I don't want to go."

"Why not?"

"Because I'm finally getting on with my life. There's nothing for me there."

"Maybe not, but how do you know until you know what happened to your father? Honey, I know it's hard but do it for your mother. She never had the chance. And look for her friends. They meant a lot to her."

Sophie felt a wave of panic rising to her throat.

"I can't!...I can't afford it," she said, in a last ditch effort.

"You can't afford not to. Besides, I'm paying. In fact, I've already paid. And Bessie's put money in your account for expenses. She'll explain everything. Oh, and if you get seasick don't stay in your cabin—I could only afford an interior one in tourist class—go upstairs and out on deck. The fresh air really helps. Have to go. I'm out of coins."

"But —"

Sophie stared at the receiver in her hand and was so lulled by the sound of the dial tone, that she almost forgot to hang up before dialing Bessie's number.

"I was about to call you," Bessie said. "It wasn't my idea, sweetie. All I did was tell Harry that I read in the society pages that your uncle was in Chicago for some exhibit. It's Harry who decided you should go and he said he'd give me hell if I tried to stop you. Then the more I thought about it, the more I thought he might be right. You're old enough now. It'll be good for you to reconnect with your family. I'm sure they'll be really happy to see you."

"Maybe. How long have you two been planning this anyway?"

"This isn't a conspiracy," Bessie said, sounding hurt. "And you should be grateful. Not everyone gets an opportunity like this."

"I'm sorry, Aunt Bessie. I didn't mean it to sound like I wasn't. It's just that —"

"It's all arranged, sweetie, so enjoy it, and don't forget to send us postcards with pretty stamps. My friends collect them. I wish I could see you off but I'm president of the women's club now and have responsibilities. I've sent you a special delivery package with some of your warmer clothes just in case, and a list of what you need to buy and take with you. They say you have to dress for dinner on the ship, so buy yourself a cocktail dress. You'll probably need it in Vienna, too. Who knows what fancy parties you'll be invited to there. Your uncle is some kind of aristocrat, it seems."

The idea of partying in the city that had caused her mother so much pain struck Sophie as awful and inappropriate, but she didn't want to sound ungrateful again so she thanked Bessie as enthusiastically as she could and told her she'd call again before she left.

Bessie's special delivery package arrived promptly at ten the next morning, giving Sophie time to have photographs taken before she went to the passport office. Following Bessie's advice, she bought a second Samsonite Streamlite suitcase to match the one she came to New York with. She also bought a large shoulder bag with multiple pockets, a passport case, and a guidebook and map of Vienna. With so much to carry home, she put off the search for the cocktail dress she didn't really want.

By Sunday Sophie's shopping was complete and her nerves calmer. She was ready to pack: clothes in the big suitcase; shoes, stockings, gloves, a small handbag, toiletries, stationery and the manila envelope with all the articles she still hadn't read in the small one. Into the shoulder bag, she put her passport, wallet, her mother's address book, a small German-English dictionary—just in case—and three paperbacks: *Doctor Zhivago* because it wasn't about Vienna, *Compulsion* because maybe it would help her understand why people did terrible things, and *Auntie Mame,* just to have something that wasn't depressing.

At the last minute she bought herself a new 35mm Kodak Pony II with flash attachment, three rolls of film, and a camera case.

On Tuesday she purchased ten American Express traveler's cheques and bought enough French Francs to get her from Le Havre to Vienna. By Wednesday, she had finished everything she had to do. She was still nervous, but it was far too late to back out.

When she arrived at Pier 11 the day of departure, she was awestruck at the sheer size and beauty of the great ocean liner, with its long, elegant lines and red-white-and-blue funnels—far grander than the ship she and her mother had sailed on from Cuba to New York.

She removed her new camera from its case and took a picture, then left her suitcases with the porter and walked up the ramp. At the top she was greeted by friendly ship's officers who assigned her her tourist-class stateroom and dining room table number, encouraging her to explore the ship until her luggage was delivered.

The ship had multiple decks—open and closed—a ballroom, dining room, pool room, gymnasium, library, children's playroom, smoking room, beauty parlor and barber shop—all decorated with American artwork.

As sailing time approached, visitors started leaving the ship to gather on the dock below, while the passengers lined up on the open decks. The prolonged blast of the fog horn announced their imminent departure, and the ship's band began to play as visitors and passengers waved frantically to each other and the ship began its move out to sea.

Sophie watched with tears in her eyes as they passed the Statue of Liberty, remembering the day they had first sailed into New

York. Her mother had lifted her up to see it better, whispering again and again *we are safe now, darling, we are safe*—words almost drowned out by the cheers of the other passengers.

When it came time to go to their staterooms, Sophie followed the plan she'd been given down to Deck B, stateroom number 51 and found that her suitcases had been delivered and placed neatly next to her berth—one of four, though two seemed to be unoccupied.

"Oh, hello!" a voice said, startling her. A freckle-faced redhead stepped from behind the door.

"I'm Mary Marjorie Quinn but you can call me Margie. I'm so glad you're not old," she said.

"Hi. My name's Sophie Bruckner."

"I'm going to Germany to join my parents. My Dad's in the Army and was just posted to Bamberg. I thought it was a good opportunity to see something new and learn a language at the same time, so I took a term off and won't go back until classes start in January. Why are you going?"

She practically said this all in one breath, and her friendly directness made Sophie laugh.

"Good question. I'm not sure yet, but I might borrow your answer next time someone asks me,"—which made Margie laugh.

After they'd unpacked and organized, Margie said it was time for dinner and they'd better not miss it. Margie chatted happily all the way there and Sophie wondered if Harry had had a hand in stateroom assignments.

Also at their table were a young American artist returning to Florence after a month at home, an older couple who, fortuitously, owned a gallery on Long Island and offered to look at his work, and a history teacher from Pittsburgh going to France on a teacher-exchange. With Margie's enthusiastic prodding, conversation flowed easily.

The second day, there was a lifeboat drill after breakfast, after which Margie became their activities director, making sure she and

Sophie played ping-pong and shuffleboard, swam in the pool, walked the decks after meals, and listened to the Meyer Davis Orchestra in the ballroom.

Margie let no chance for conversation escape her, and Sophie was sure that by trip's end Margie would know all one thousand passengers and most of the crew by name. It wasn't until they'd settled into bed the second night that Sophie told her — or even remembered — that her uncle was somewhere in first class.

"Golly, I've always wanted to see first class!" Margie burst out. "We'll ask George. He'll know how to sneak us in," she said, referring to the young steward she'd already managed to befriend.

Margie was so excited Sophie didn't have the heart to say she wasn't ready to meet him, no matter what Harry had intended.

Margie had little trouble persuading George to help them. He confided that many famous people were in first class—Marlene Dietrich for one.

"And John Kennedy," he said, pointing to a handsome young man leaning against a railing. "He's an American senator."

"This is your chance, Sophie," Margie whispered, nudging her forward.

"Are you crazy? I can't just go up to him because he's good-looking."

"No, I mean to look for your uncle."

"Oh." Sophie's face must have turned red it felt so hot, but Margie was too busy looking for other famous people to notice.

"What does your uncle look like?"

"I don't remember."

"What's his name? George can find out and send him a message, couldn't you, George?"

She pulled a piece of paper and a pen out of her bag. "Write down his name and that you're his niece and want to talk to him. And tell him our cabin number."

"I don't want him coming to our cabin," Sophie said, suddenly panicked. "But I guess I can write that I'm on board and see what he answers. If he answers."

Margie took the note out of Sophie's hand and handed it to George.

"Thanks, George. Tell him it's important."

George seemed very pleased at the smile she flashed him.

52.
ON BOARD

When Marion was chosen to represent Austria at the *Europe: Art Nouveau to Art Deco* exhibit in Chicago she cited "health issues" as her reason for not being able to accept. Of course, Marion was not ill at all. She merely preferred to spend the month at the spa in Bad Gastein as she now did every year.

After some discussion as whether it was appropriate for German-born Friedrich to represent Austria, he was approved to go in her stead. He was delighted.

After a relaxing week onboard ship, Friedrich was whisked into modernity in New York, a city crackling sleeplessly with life and light. Had he had the courage, he would have given up everything to stay there. Of course he didn't and went on to Chicago. There he found its slower-paced friendliness and magnificent lake such a welcome contrast to cranky old Vienna that he was tempted to ask for asylum on grounds of peril to his mental health if he returned to chez Bruckner. But he was no fool, and knew that if he stayed he would have to make a living—a hurdle that would be an even greater peril to his mental health. He had no choice but to return to New York, board the *SS America* bound for LeHavre, and head for home.

His Europe-bound stateroom was even better situated than the one on the U.S. bound voyage. He was seated at the captain's table opposite an enchanting young Parisian lady with whom he hoped to spend more than just the dinner hours.

On the third day at sea, a steward from tourist class delivered a note with the surprising words: *Your niece Sophie is in tourist class*.

The steward left before Friedrich could ascertain whether he was being warned or invited. Sophie had been a sweet child. If she were going on to Vienna he could introduce her to Klaus who'd never had relatives even vaguely his age. But then, who knew how the war had affected the girl—or had she and Greta escaped the worst and been in New York all this time? But why come now, after so many years? She was traveling tourist class, the least expensive, so there could only be one answer—she was coming to claim her share of the Bruckner estate. He dreaded to think what mayhem would ensue once Marion found out.

Friedrich thought of not answering. But then Sophie might arrive at their door unannounced—a frightening thought. No, it was best to meet her and see what her intentions were. But he had time. If he answered too quickly it might interfere with his plans for the lovely Parisian lady. Sophie had waited all this time. She could wait a little longer.

To Friedrich's delight, the lovely Parisian moved to the chair beside him at dinner, after which they strolled the deck in the moonlight—his arm around her slender waist. She turned her face up toward his and smiled. He felt encouraged and held her closer. Then, quite in passing, she mentioned that her husband was the Minister of Defense and would be meeting her in LeHavre— along with their children and their nanny. And probably their dog. A large German Shepherd, no doubt.

The next morning Friedrich sent his steward to tourist class with his card, inviting Sophie to tea the following afternoon. So it is that plans change.

53.

VIENNA AGAIN

Relieved not to have gotten an immediate answer to her message, Sophie was almost disappointed when she found her uncle's calling card slipped under her stateroom door.

Dear Sophie -
What an unexpected and pleasant surprise.
Please join me in the cocktail lounge tomorrow at four o'clock. I have arranged for the steward to bring you.

Margie was thrilled when Sophie insisted she come along for moral support, and suggested that they rehearse potential conversations.

"I hope the steward takes us to him since I have no idea what he looks like," Sophie said.

Margie predicted he'd be tall with a shock of white hair and a monocle—like aristocrats in the movies.

The first class cocktail lounge was decorated in a stylish blue-green, from the walls to the curved chairs' upholstery, with vases of fresh flowers on every table.

"That might be him," Margie whispered, pointing surreptitiously to a man sitting alone and reading a book. "He looks suave, like a combination of David Niven and William Powell."

Friedrich stood up as the steward led them to his table.

"Good afternoon. I'm delighted you could join me," he said, kissing Sophie's hand.

"This is my friend, Margie," Sophie said, "I hope you don't mind."

"Not at all. It is my pleasure," he said, leaning over to kiss her hand too.

Margie giggled and pinched Sophie's arm.

"Oh, it's so nice you speak English, isn't it Sophie?" she said. "How did you like our country?"

"I was especially impressed by New York," he said. "So dynamic and full of energy."

"Where else did you go?" Margie asked.

"Only Chicago, which I also liked. Where are you from, Fräulein Margie?"

"Lots of places," she said, and listed all the bases she had lived with her Army father. "He's in Germany now, which is where I'm going."

Friedrich smiled and asked if they'd like tea or cocktails.

"Tea, please," Sophie said, thinking it was better to keep a clear head.

Friedrich ordered tea and a selection of pastries.

Sophie should have been the one asking questions, but Margie made it too easy to just sit back and listen, so when their tea was over she realized neither she nor her uncle knew any more about each other than before.

"Why didn't you tell him you were going to Vienna?" Margie asked when they'd returned to tourist class. They found two empty deck chairs and sat down. "I thought you were going to take the train together."

"It was just an idea — until I saw he wasn't interested in me. He never asked me anything, not even where we were during the war."

"Maybe he already knew."

"I don't see how."

A gust of wind made Sophie shiver and she pulled a blanket over her legs. "He couldn't know. We've had no contact with them for twenty years."

"Your aunt might be friendlier. After all, she's your real relative."

Margie was the eternal optimist.

"I don't know. Maybe I should just forget about relatives and go to Paris or London."

"Or maybe you should send a message to that good-looking senator instead," Margie giggled.

That night, after Margie had fallen asleep, Sophie pulled out the address book she'd found in the Lebkuchen tin and opened it to B for Bruckner to see what their address in Vienna had been and noticed that her mother had written something on the last pages.

> *8 December 1941*
> *America is at war. Terrible of me, but it brings me hope. I found a newsletter for refugees. Afraid I'd have to wait for hours to speak to someone, I arrived early and found the office was just one room in the back of a hardware store staffed by only one man. His name is Harry Whittaker and he's offered me a job.*
>
> *New York, January 1942*
> *Thanks to Harry we have found a school for Sophie and a small apartment on West 100th Street in an area called the Upper West Side. It is full of newly arrived European refugees (mostly Jews), whose worlds have been turned upside down like ours. Lawyers work as waiters; professors push carts in the garment district. Fine ladies mend stockings for money on little machines in their dining rooms.*

My mind is so cluttered with people and places that they tumble out of my head like papers out of overstuffed files. I think of the woman on our ship to Cuba who'd been going back and forth for months because no one would take her in and no one would take her back, the captain angry because no one was paying her fare; and of the couple with the black-eyed child, who looked poor and frightened, but evoked a terrible envy in me because they had each other. How I yearned for Otto then—and how I long for him still. In the life I now share only with Sophie, I find I must talk less about him. How do I tell her that my hope of finding him is fading? Am I realistic or disloyal? The question torments me.

Our doctor is a refugee—also from Vienna, only blocks from Léonie's apartment. I asked if he knew Josef, but he didn't. He understood what was happening early and left Vienna in '36. We reminisce sometimes about our favorite cafés or going to the opera—but not too often. They have opera here, he says.

"Oh, Mama! I'm so sorry!" Sophie cried into her pillow so as not to wake Margie. If only she'd known. Her mother had always been so strong. Sophie had envied her that and relied on it. Why hadn't she realized that it had been a mask put on just for her, that underneath she might have been as lonely and afraid as she?

Harry was right. She had to go to Vienna for her mother's sake. Sophie dreaded it, knowing that being there would be harder than just reading books about it. In her heart she felt her father was dead, but the how and why of his death could be more terrible than she wanted to know.

The next morning, Sophie and Margie were too busy saying farewells and watching the tug boats pull them to shore to give Friedrich any further thought. Once disembarked, Sophie booked train tickets to Vienna and was happy to learn that she would have a few hours in Paris before the evening train left for Vienna.

In Paris, Sophie hailed a cab and asked the driver to take her past the Louvre, Notre Dame and the Left Bank. It cost her more than she expected but he explained everything they passed with such enthusiasm that she didn't mind and was in a better mood when she boarded the Vienna train. It didn't last. The other people in her compartment were so grumpy and sullen that she found her mood sinking with every clickety-clack of the train.

Sophie pulled out the manila envelope filled with the newspaper articles she'd put in her little suitcase to read later. As she opened it, she saw yellow papers stuck randomly between the articles. She pulled one out and found that it was another of her mother's notes to herself.

> *Millersville, July 1942.*
> *Bessie is so content with her life, so sure of its permanence, I wonder if she's ever questioned anything. When I was a child living with Tante Resi, I was consumed with anxiety about how heaven was organized. How do dead people know where they belong? If they're sorted by family, how can they also be with friends? What if people are organized by the date of their death? Then I would be with strangers and never meet my parents. Tante Resi held me tight and told me not to worry, God is much smarter than we are and has it all figured out. I believed her. After all, hadn't He made sure I met Léonie and Emma? Why else would our teacher have lined us up in alphabetical order instead of by size, as the other teachers did? Where is God now?*

Sophie gently folded the note, put it in her handbag, and pulled out another.

New York, 16 May 1945.

As soon as Sophie left for school, I heard a thud. The mailman must have been in a rush because I found the newest issue of LIFE crushed against the wall. Anxious, I brought it in, poured myself a cup of coffee. lit a cigarette, sat down, then got up again and opened the kitchen window to take a deep breath of fresh air. Too late. The light shaft was already filled with the scent of Mrs. Kaminski's cabbage. I returned to the table and found a long gray ash where my cigarette had been. Anxious, I sat down and smoothed out the wrinkled corners of the magazine. May 14,1945, it said: an American soldier, his right hand raised in a mock Nazi salute, stands victoriously before a monumental stone swastika. It isn't right. It should be an American salute, the swastika smashed beyond recognition so that I would never have to see it again.

Line by line, page after page, I read through articles entitled The War Ends in Europe *and* Displaced Persons: Millions of People the Nazis Uprooted Start Their Great Trek. *Inch by inch I examine each photograph with a magnifying glass, afraid both to find and not find my Otto among the survivors.*

The coffee's cold and my search is unresolved—again. I reach into my pocket and pull out my silver cigarette case. It holds only a few cigarettes, and now that I smoke too much, I keep having to refill it. I remember the day Otto gave it to me. It was my twenty-fifth birthday and we'd spent the day with our friends, walking through vineyards in the Wachau. Just yesterday, it all seems, though I know it's a lifetime ago.

Sophie looked at the sullen faces of the people sitting opposite and felt like turning around as soon as the train got to Vienna and going back to New York, where people talked to you and made jokes.

She folded her mother's notes, put them in her handbag and looked out the window until they pulled into the Westbahnhof station.

Following her guidebook's advice, she went to the *Zimmernachweis* and booked a room in the *Pension Johann Strauss,* which turned out to be a narrow three-story building squeezed in between two larger apartment buildings in the third district. It was a tiny room but clean and would do for her stay.

She asked the desk clerk where the nearest market was and bought herself a hot sandwich from the vendor with the longest line, figuring the food there must be good. It was called *Leberkäse* but had nothing to do with liver or cheese, and was nothing more than a fat slice of something like bologna. Not quite the delicious Viennese food her mother used to talk about. She only finished half of it and might have thrown it out if she hadn't noticed a dog following her. He was a scrawny little thing, so she ripped the remainder of the sandwich into little pieces for him. They had a nice conversation about the perils of a dog's life before she left him happily licking the grease off the paper the sandwich had been wrapped in.

The market was crowded—mostly with old women. Many had swollen ankles, just visible under their raincoats as they pulled their rickety shopping carts from one vendor to another. There were men too—some one-armed, or one-legged, leaning heavily on crutches as they made their way through the market. War-wounds, probably. She saw a couple of men wearing those little round Nazi glasses Mrs. Handler had worn, which made her wonder if they had been Nazis, and how would she know? She was glad she didn't see anyone with a Hitler mustache.

She brought some fruit and cheese up to her room and spent the evening on her bed, leafing through the manila envelope in search of more yellow papers. Down in the bottom she found three, written by her mother at different times.

April 1943.

I so want Sophie to be happy but she has no friends her own age to laugh and be silly with, to plan the future with. Instead she spends her afternoons working at the office with me. "I like helping you, Mama," she says, "I don't want to go to the zoo or the movies." Or the park, or the ice cream shop, or anywhere she might have fun. I'm afraid she will look back one day and wonder if she'd ever been a child.

7 June 1945

Almost a month since my letter was taken to Vienna, and still no response. Please God I need to know what happened to Otto. Does anyone know? I cannot help but picture them together as I left them—suspended in time, awaiting my return. Poor, gentle Josef, sitting numbly at Frau Huber's table with Léonie standing behind him, her delicate hands firmly on his shoulders; Frau Huber, holding a bundle wrapped in newspaper, containing sustenance for our journey; and our beautiful Emma, her black hair sweeping over her shoulders, standing stiffly at the door, knowing she can no longer delay the moment of our departure. I'm so afraid of what I'll hear from them, yet just as afraid I won't hear at all.

The last was a short note, but one that made Sophie's hands tremble and her heart ache.

New York, June 10, 1945.
Sophie's cough worries me and New York's hot humid
summers only make it worse. Dr. Löwy says I should get
her out of the city for a while. I'm taking her to Bessie's
in Millersville though it frightens me, the thought of
being without her.

The next morning the clouds hung heavy making the sky look as if the sun had taken the day off. Even Margie couldn't have lessened the dreariness.

Not yet ready to face family ghosts, Sophie checked her guidebook and decided to start her stay with a tour of the city and, more specifically, the opera. The guidebook predicted that standing room tickets were inexpensive but the line for them might be long. She was relieved when it wasn't and asked for a ticket for that night. The cashier waved her hand dismissively in the direction of a poster advertising *Ballo in Maschera* on September 30th.

"Nothing today. Can't you read? Come back on the 30th. You can't buy standing room in advance."

"People are much nicer at the Met," Sophie grumbled under her breath.

She pulled the street map out of her purse to find the route to St. Stephen's but felt too annoyed now to sightsee. Knowing Margie would have laughed it off made her feel even worse and she wished her scrawny little canine friend from the day before was there to tell her woes to. She would have bought him a *Wurst* and felt better,

Sophie wandered aimlessly through the oldest part of the city, finding interest only in the names of the streets. *Essiggasse.* Vinegar Street. Had they once fermented grapes and apples there, filling the gloomy air with even more sourness? She imagined butchers flinging their cleavers on the street called *Fleischmarkt,* and bakers pounding their fists into dough on *Bäckerstrasse.*

Goldschmiedgasse had clearly beckoned the wealthy to sell their gold, but had there really been a cacophony of preacher voices on *Predigergasse?*

Eventually, she wandered into *Blutgasse.* Blood Street. How gruesome, with its connotation of murder and vampires — yet a name that was oddly familiar. She was already a few blocks away from it when she realized it had been a street in her mother's address book. She reached into her bag and fished the book out. There it was under H—Emma Huber, Blutgasse 4—one of her mother's best friends. She should have remembered.

Sophie ran to number 4 and skimmed the short list of tenants' names posted on the right of the building's door. No Huber. She turned to walk away then turned back and rang the bell for the *Hausbesorgerin.* Silence at first, then, with a soft scraping sound, the door opened a crack, revealing only half a face.

"Yes?"

"Can you help me, please? I am looking for Emma Huber."

"We have no Emma Huber here," the half-faced woman answered and slammed the door.

"Do you know where she went?" Sophie said, too late for the woman to hear. The only response was a rumble of thunder as it began to rain.

"I hate this place," she shouted as she ran for cover. "I bet New York is having a sunny Indian Summer."

By the time she reached her *Pension*, the rain had washed away some of her frustration. She was being childish. She hadn't come all this way to give up at the first setback.

She returned to her room, changed into dry clothes and thought about the people she had seen on her walk. No children, which was strange. New York had been full of them. Didn't people have babies here?

She read for a while, then, feeling hungry, she decided that if she took her book with her she could eat alone at the little

Gasthaus down the street without people thinking she'd been stood up.

When she went to bed that night she realized she'd been speaking German all day. It was the first time since her mother died. It troubled her that it had come back so easily, as if nothing had changed when actually everything had.

The next morning Sophie woke to a streak of blue forcing its way out of the clouds. A good sign, she thought, as she washed her face in the small sink beside her bed. She pulled her mother's address book out of her bag again and tried to recall what her mother had told her about her friends. There'd been three of them —inseparable when they were kids—her mother, Emma and another one whose name she couldn't remember. She had to find them.

Sophie went through the address book page by page. After a while every name sounded familiar as she'd heard many of them in New York. *Altman, Birnbaum, Finkel, Goldberg, Katz, Mandlblatt, Rubenstein*...but then *Salzmann, Léonie, Josef, Valerie — Ungargasse 39/7*. That was it—Léonie. She'd go there next.

54.
VIENNA

Emma flung open the French doors to the balcony and was pleased to see that neither the rain nor the wind had harmed the delicate lobelia she'd planted alongside her sturdy geraniums.

Soon the dining room would be filled with lively conversations again as two young English students were due to arrive on the afternoon train.

Emma hoped it would cheer Magda to have girls not much older than she in the house, for the last days of her pregnancy seemed to rob her of her strength. She was pale, her face drawn. Hanns would have sent her to the hospital had she not resisted so fiercely.

Day after day, they'd had the same conversation.

"Emma, you will make sure my baby's all right, won't you?"

"Of course. But —"

"No matter what, you won't let them take my baby away from me."

"Of course not, Magda. But why would they?"

"That's what they did to the girls at the orphanage."

"But not here."

"Do you promise?" she said.

Every day, Emma would place her hand on her heart and promise, for nothing less would comfort her.

Magda was sleeping and Emma was about to make herself a cup of coffee when the doorbell rang. Thinking her new guests had arrived early, Emma rushed to the door.

"Hello, welcome," she said, before she realized there was only one person at the door and she had no suitcase. "I thought there'd be two of you."

"I'm sorry if I'm disturbing you. I'm looking for Léonie Salzmann."

Emma felt her knees start to buckle, and a hand grasping her arm as she began to fall.

"Are you all right? I didn't mean to startle you. I should have rung your bell downstairs, but the door was open ..."

Emma heard her talking but could make no sense of her words. Time seemed to collapse as she absorbed the features of her face: the auburn hair, the freckles across the bridge of her nose, the high cheek bones, the eyes ...

"Greta ...?" she murmured, though it couldn't be.

Not understanding, the young woman repeated that she was looking for Léonie. "She was a friend of my mother's."

"Your mother?... Are you Sophie?"

It was all Emma managed to say before she burst into tears.

At that moment the elevator clattered to a stop and spilled out two noisy girls and their suitcases.

Emma squeezed Sophie's hand and whispered, "Here they are. Please, come in and wait. Don't go away."

She took a handkerchief out of her pocket, blew her nose, pushed the button for the elevator to go down, and greeted her guests. While she showed them to their rooms Sophie stood nervously in the foyer, her heart racing. The woman must be Léonie. How else would she know her name?

"Forgive me," Emma said when she returned. "I—"

Sophie nodded. "It's all right. You're Léonie, aren't you? That's why you know my name."

"No, I'm Emma, Emma Huber," she said, her eyes welling up with tears again.

Neither of them knew what to say next though they both realized that a great distance had been crossed. As their minds struggled to untangle the images their memories recalled, Sophie realized that if it weren't for the photographs Harry had given her she would no longer have been able to describe her mother's face.

"You look so much like her when she was your age," Emma said, as if she'd entered Sophie's thoughts.

Sophie felt a sob rise from her chest, as she grasped the full import of who Emma was—her mother's friend, who had known her as a child, an adolescent, a young woman, married and filled with dreams and plans. This Emma could tell her about her mother's world—a world that should have been hers.

Sophie felt Emma's arms folding around her. For a long time they didn't speak. Then Emma said, "Where are you staying?"

"Not far. In a little *Pension* called *Johann Strauss.*"

"Yes, I know it. Are you traveling with someone?"

Sophie shook her head.

"Then please, will you stay here? I have a free room —"

"Are you sure? But maybe not til tomorrow? I should give notice…"

She was shaken by the intensity of emotion she felt and needed time to think.

Miss Huber? Can we ask you something? a voice called from the hallway.

"I'm sorry. I have to…" Emma said, turning toward the voice. "You won't change your mind?"

"No. Please go. I can let myself out."

"Tomorrow then."

55.

VIENNA

Friedrich returned to Vienna later than scheduled, having stopped in Paris for a few days—not to continue his acquaintanceship with the charming Parisian lady, for that had clearly come to naught, but merely to postpone his return.

As his schedule would not interest Marion, he did not tell her.

Paris was still not welcoming to Germans, which should not have surprised Friedrich—his father had said the same after the first World War. Nevertheless, Friedrich admired the city's beauty and loved that it still attracted young people—unlike Vienna, whose glow had faded long ago. Had Paris been a part of Sophie's travel schedule? He hadn't asked. In fact, he hadn't asked her anything, lest it open the door to questions he was not willing to answer.

Had he asked about her mother, he would have had to ask about her father. If she knew he was dead and said so, he would have had to feign shock. If she didn't know, he would have had to lie that he did not either. Then she definitely might have felt the need to come to Vienna and might have asked his assistance in finding out. By saying nothing, he could tell himself that she and her friend were merely tourists going to Paris. It's where he would go if he were young.

Sophie had grown up to be an attractive young woman, taller than her mother but with the same striking auburn hair. Friedrich had recognized her immediately, though she didn't recognize him.

Although it was she who had contacted him, she said very little, leaving most of the conversing to her more outgoing friend. Even as a child, Sophie had been shy, clinging to her mother. Klaus never clung to Marion, and it pleased Friedrich no end that Klaus preferred him. At seventeen his son had begun to live his own life, yet on occasions when they spent time together they still found each other's company as enjoyable as ever.

Friedrich decided not to mention Sophie to Marion unless necessary. He no longer found pleasure in testing his wife's reactions.

Shortly after Friedrich's return, Marion announced that she was giving a dinner party for some minister or other and needed him to be on his best behavior. Although he was not in the mood for another evening of cultural and intellectual pretension, he said he'd make the effort.

Marion seated him next to the minister's wife, a most unpleasant and unattractive woman, so Friedrich found himself drinking more than perhaps he should have. As a result, he fell asleep. In his seat. At the table. He might even have heard himself snore for a few seconds until he felt Fritz' discreet nudge at his shoulder. He turned, hiccuped rather loudly, and knocked over the woman's still full glass of Château Lafite Rothschild Red Bordeaux, 1952. It spread like blood over Marion's Belgian lace tablecloth, and dribbled relentlessly into the woman's unpleasantly ample lap. She shrieked, apparently not pleased, and lifted her skirt so that the liquid could glide down onto Marion's two-hundred-year-old Persian carpet.

The sight of the woman's hairy thighs made Friedrich gasp and then laugh, which made the other guests react in a variety of ways —none of which were sympathetic to him. Quite understandable, of course. He had, in Marion's terms, misbehaved atrociously.

A cacophony of voices followed, most of them, if Friedrich understood correctly, indicating that the guests were ready—if not desperate—to depart, despite dessert not having been served yet, let alone after-dinner drinks, which he rather desired at that point.

Within minutes, wraps and hats were found and distributed and the guests' cars lined up in the driveway.

"I am terribly sorry, my husband is still recovering from his travels," Marion explained, to guest after guest.

When Friedrich saw the front door finally close, she turned and walked back to the dining room, where he was still seated in his chair of shame.

Her eyes and voice were filled with fury.

"You pathetic, impotent excuse for a man!"

"Pathetic, perhaps, but hardly impotent. You forget the magnificent son we created."

She approached the chair and leaned over him, her eyes on fire.

"You fool! Do you really think you fathered that child?"

Oh, the dagger she thrust into Friedrich's heart with those words. It was true. His blond-haired, blue-eyed son could not possibly be his, a man descended from generations of brown-eyed, brown-haired people. Turks, probably. Descended—how cruelly appropriate a word for someone fallen from fatherhood to nothingness. Whose progeny was his splendid boy? The answer should have been obvious all along. It was that perfect specimen of Aryanhood that had lived in their midst, roaming the halls of their house, eating in their dining room. Friedrich had admired him. Young and beautiful of body, he'd worn his well-pressed Nazi uniform with manly style. He'd been Friedrich's contact, his colleague. Friedrich had been his spy. One reported, the other conveyed. It had been a professional relationship—until the brute attacked his wife and she was forced to defend herself. Oh double fool! What delusion! There'd been no attack, no need to defend.

"Say something!" Marion said, spitting out the words so that her saliva hit Friedrich's chin. "Or don't you want to know that we made love in our bedroom while you drank cognac downstairs? His brow was still damp when he went down to drink with you. And you were too much a fool to suspect."

Oh, woman, thy name is cruelty.

"He sired well, Marion," Friedrich said, in his softest, smoothest voice. "He might have fathered well too, had you not murdered him."

"Stop that!" She slapped his face. "Why do you care, anyway? You only married me for my money."

"And you me for my title."

"I didn't choose you," she said. "Mama did. You didn't care how I felt. You never loved me."

"I tried," he said. Perhaps he had. He couldn't remember.

"Not hard enough, Freddy. I needed someone who wanted *me* and I found him in Siegfried. He adored me and I would have left you if Mama hadn't interfered when she found out I was pregnant."

"So you killed him because your mother—"

Marion pushed him—lightly—but drunk as Friedrich was, it almost knocked him out of his chair.

"No! You don't understand anything. What if Siegfried had been sent to the front and was killed? What would I have done then? When I told him I couldn't be with him, he was furious—"

"Yet another reason to kill him."

"He threatened me! He said if I didn't leave with him he'd say that I was in the resistance and I'd be arrested and the baby would be born in prison. I was frightened. I had no choice."

Friedrich stood up and looked straight into her eyes.

"So you devised a clever plan. Congratulations. But knowledge is power and I have the upper hand now. Klaus is my son and will remain my son."

He turned and walked unsteadily out the door and to his study.

56.

VIENNA

Emma's apartment was grand—the kind of apartment Sophie imagined one would find in the Dakota in New York. Twelve-foot ceilings, eight-foot lace-curtained windows, French doors between the dining room and living room. Yet the furniture was incongruously plain and unpretentious, as if Emma had bought it at a wholesale place just for *Pensions.*

Emma introduced her to Magda and the English students.

"It's very kind of you to have me," Sophie said, as Emma showed her to her room, which was next to hers and across from the bathroom. It too was grand, with tall Palladian windows, and so spacious that, although it accommodated two single beds, a comfortable looking chair, a dresser, wardrobe, table and even a sink, it appeared almost empty. Quite a difference from the narrow single at the *Johann Strauss.*

"Tell me, Sophie, how does it feel being back in the city where you were born?"

"Not so great yet…I may not stay long."

"Oh, I see," Emma said, as she turned away and lifted Sophie's suitcase onto the luggage rack. "Even so, you're welcome to hang up your things."

"I'm sorry, that sounded ungrateful. The thing is, I'm not sure how I feel. It wasn't my idea to come. It was Harry who insisted … but, of course, you don't know who Harry is."

"I do. Your mother told me about him in her letter."

Sophie sat down. She hadn't expected that.

"When? When did she write you?"

"As soon as the war ended, although it was weeks before I received her letter. You can imagine —"

"I didn't find any letters from you."

Emma sat down next to her.

"Before I found a way to answer, I received Mrs. Stone's telegram about…about the accident."

"So you knew that too?"

"Yes, I —"

Sophie pulled her hand away.

"You never wrote me."

"She asked me not to…She wanted to protect you."

Sophie swallowed hard, and pounded her fist on the bed, unable to suppress her anger.

"I'm sorry, but it really upsets me that Bessie has never understood that every day of silence made my mother seem farther and farther away."

Emma put her arms around her.

"I'll try to do better."

57.

VIENNA

Emma promised herself that there'd be no more hiding, no pretending that the past had not occurred. Whatever Sophie asked she would answer to the best of her ability.

Not knowing what to ask, or perhaps afraid, Sophie's questions were simple at first and questions like *How did you meet? Where did you live?* were a good way to begin for both of them.

"We met on the first day of school. We lived near each other, although quite differently. Your mother lived with her aunt, as you probably know, in a wonderful big apartment, but we rarely played there because of the boarders. Most of them were old and cranky, it seemed to us then. My parents would have enjoyed having us but our apartment was small, and my father's woodworking projects ate up most of our space. So we were usually here at Léonie's because she had an abundance of dolls and games, and her mother made sure we were well-looked after and properly fed."

The answers to many of Sophie's questions could be woven easily into short sight-seeing trips through the city. *Here's the school where we met, the university your parents attended, here was our favorite café, and Léonie's parents' store, here they ... here we ...* but after a while it became clear to both of them that they were avoiding the most difficult question — what had happened to Sophie's father.

"Do you know, Emma?"

"We tried to find out," Emma said, and told Sophie about Frau Mandl's visit to the old typesetter. "Otto must have been arrested the day you left, otherwise he would have found a way to join you —if not at the train, then in Lyon. If he had escaped, or survived the war or even the Russians, he would have looked for you by contacting me. I was here—alone at the end—but I was here."

Sophie nodded silently. Emma could see that she accepted her conclusion because it was what she already believed.

"I don't want to know if he suffered or how. Is that terrible of me?"

"No. He wouldn't have wanted it either," Emma said. "He would want you to go on with your life, to —"

"Have you done that? Have you come to terms with everything that happened?" Sophie asked. "It's been a long time."

"Has it? I wasn't tortured or beaten. I did not starve or find myself homeless, but I lost the people that meant the most to me, and I lost faith in my country and in me. So to answer your question, no, I have not come to terms," Emma said, surprising her. "All of Europe has to come to terms with what it did and what it allowed. I fear it will take a long time. Perhaps generations. After that, maybe we can talk about coming to terms."

The return of Hanns and now Sophie to her life made Emma realize what a strange relationship she'd had with time, for in her mind she'd chopped it into amorphous chunks whose sequence had become random and irrelevant. She recalled or abandoned each moment at will—or rather, as needed.

She'd protected her memories of *Before*—the golden days when life seemed both complete and full of promise—as she'd once wrapped up and hidden her photographs. Unshared, they would remain whole and unscarred by grief, she'd thought.

Then were the years of tragedy and loss. Yet, even *Then* had moments of unexpected joy. Later, when she was filled with guilt and self-recrimination at what she had done and not done, she looked upon those moments of joy as stolen and undeserved. She had survived but took no pride in it. Others had suffered so much more.

In the twelve years that followed the war—*The Hannah Years* —Hannah had grown from child to young woman. In their quiet way she and Hannah had helped each other, but they'd lived suspended between past and future, unable to face either fully — not until Stefan appeared. Loving him and being loved in return had set Hannah free—and had allowed Emma to remember when she too had felt like that.

How strange the mind was, with its memories collapsing haphazardly into one another like children's building blocks. How was she to make sense of it all?

58.

VIENNA

Friedrich had time on his mind as well. Two weeks had passed as if nothing had changed. The loss of his son had not stopped the sun from rising or the postman from doing his rounds.

Klaus, who was a boarding student at Vienna's prestigious Theresianum, did not know he was lost, of course.

When people saw Friedrich and Klaus together, they'd comment on how straight they both stood, how elegantly they both walked. A sign of their aristocratic genes, he thought. Now he knew that is was merely imitation. Not unlike the baby duck that follows the first creature it sees, be it its mother or a chimpanzee. But no matter how much the chimpanzee loves the duck it will never be its parent. Such were the foolish thoughts that swirled through Friedrich's mind. He was neither duck nor chimpanzee. Nor a mother who knew for certain that the infant she had borne was hers. Alas, there was no such certainty for fathers.

He and Marion had not spoken the last two weeks. He would have relished a dramatic departure from their conjugal bedroom, but that pleasure had been usurped some years previously, when Marion moved to her mother's room upon Elsa's death. Their connubial relations, as they were, remained undisturbed. That is, nothing changed—then or now—except his soul, which, until now, had gone unexplored.

Friedrich retreated to his study, eating at his desk, sleeping on the leather couch. Even Tibor's prattle became too much of a burden. He told him he'd decided to grow a beard and he needn't come anymore. Tibor begged him to reconsider—something about Vera's condition—but Friedrich couldn't be bothered.

To such selfish disregard did Friedrich descend when faced with the only loss that ever mattered to him.

59.

VIENNA

"Sophie and Magda seem to have grown quite close," Hanns said as Emma accompanied him downstairs. He'd come to check on Magda, as he'd been doing every few days.

"Yes, they understand the other's loss so well. Both of them were only twelve when their mothers died. I'm a little envious of their closeness, I have to admit."

Hanns smiled. "You needn't be. They feel close to you in a different way. You are the wiser, older woman they can turn to for answers."

Emma laughed. "Oh no. We'd better disabuse them of that belief. I have no answers."

"But you do, Emma. Young people need to know that they can get through difficult times. Their mothers couldn't do that for them. But you can, just as you did for Hannah. But right now I am more concerned about Magda's physical health. She has been through so much already and pregnancy can be hard on such a young body. She really should be in the hospital when the time comes—it would be safer—but she refuses every time I mention it."

"She's afraid, Hanns. I've tried to convince her to let us at least call a midwife, but she begs me not to. She doesn't want any strangers, and says all she needs is us."

They stood in the small courtyard by the front door. Although sheltered from the wind outside, the chilly October air seeped inside and made Emma shiver.

Hanns put his arm around her shoulders.

"Then we'll be there for her. Go on up now, Emma, it's too cold down here. I have to go to the office, but Magda's labor could start at any time, so call me if and when it does, no matter the time. And tell her to lie on her left side."

"I will," she said and kissed him on the cheek. "You're a good man, Dr. Menzler."

On October 10th, only days later, Magda was too tired to get up for breakfast. The English girls had left for Salzburg and wouldn't be back for several days, so Emma thought it best to stay out of the kitchen and let Magda rest.

Sophie was helping Emma change the guests' bed linens when Emma said, "You don't have to be stuck here all day, Sophie. Why don't you go out and see something new."

Sophie tucked in the corners on the last of the beds and said, "I was thinking it was time I went to see where my parents lived. Do you think I need to call ahead?"

"Don't go there! They are awful, greedy people. I'm not so sure Marion didn't...never mind, ignore that. It's just better you don't go."

Emma regretted being so vehement but was relieved when Sophie said, "It's okay. I'll do something cultural instead—maybe I'll go see all the Dürers at the Albertina."

"Yes, that would be better. And there's a lovely print shop across from there. Do go in and take a look."

After Sophie left, Emma sat down at her desk and was catching up on bills when she heard Magda cry out. She rushed to her room and found her standing with her legs apart, staring at the floor.

"I'm sorry," Magda said, beginning to cry. "I don't know what happened but everything is wet."

"Your water broke. Remember, Hanns said that would happen. It means your baby is coming—don't be frightened. Are you sure you don't want to go to the hospital?"

"No! Please don't make me."

"I won't, sweetheart. I promise."

Magda moaned.

"I have cramps, Emma. They hurt."

"Those are the contractions. Walking might make you feel better."

Emma took Magda's arm and they walked up and down the hall several times.

"Let's move you to my room," Emma said. "It's bigger and I've already set aside all the things Hanns said we will need."

Emma sat Magda down in a comfortable chair while she stripped her bed, covered the mattress with a rubber sheet, two layers of towels, and fresh sheets. Then she placed gauze, string, scissors and a large bowl for water on the night table next to the bed.

"Now, Magda. Go lie down. I'll call Hanns."

"Have the contractions started?" he asked.

"Yes, but they're not very regular yet."

"It could be another few hours, but since her water has broken she is more susceptible to infection. Keep her bed clean and wash your hands often. And call me as soon as her contractions become regular. Make sure she has enough to drink but don't let her eat, in case she needs a cesarean."

Sophie returned just as the contractions were becoming stronger although they were still progressing at a snail's pace.

"Have you ever helped anyone in labor before?" Sophie whispered to Emma.

Emma shook her head.

She and Sophie did everything they could to make Magda more comfortable—walking with her, massaging her back, changing her position.

"Are you sure you don't want the midwife, Magda?" Sophie asked.

"No, Mama didn't have a midwife with me. I can do it."

A few more hours passed. When the contractions were finally regular and closer together, Emma called for Hanns to come.

Olga, his nurse and receptionist, answered.

"He is not here, Frau Huber. He was called out on an emergency and I don't know when he will be back. I had to cancel his evening appointments and I'm about to close the office."

Emma asked her to leave Hanns a message that he should come as soon as he returned.

They were on their own. It was a frightening thought. Emma took a deep breath and told herself that they'd just have to do their best.

"Sophie, look at your watch and keep track of how often Magda's contractions are coming. And Magda, turn onto your left side. I want you to breathe slowly and steadily. Hanns says if you concentrate on your breathing you won't feel as much pain. The baby is coming and we are here to welcome it, so you mustn't worry."

Magda closed her eyes and concentrated. Soon Emma and Sophie were keeping the same rhythm as she. Inhale…exhale… inhale…exhale.

Instead of defeating her, the pain of the contractions seemed to become something Magda could conquer. Inhale…exhale… inhale …exhale.

Emma stroked her legs.

"Not much longer, Magda."

The phone rang.

"Sophie, can you answer? It might be Hanns."

"I feel the baby," Magda called out. "It wants to come."

She turned onto her back and Emma put a pillow under her bottom. She could see the top of the baby's head.

Sophie came and stood by the door, holding the phone, its long cord stretching out to the foyer.

"Dr. Menzler says don't pull or push the baby, Emma. Can you see the umbilical cord?"

"No."

"Good. He says that's good. But if you see it around the baby's neck you have to move it—gently. Now push. Magda, I mean."

Magda squeezed Emma's hand and pushed.

"Again, Magda. As hard as you can. As soon as the baby's shoulders are out it'll be quick."

It took all the strength her young, frail body could muster. Emma thought those few minutes would never pass. Then, at last, with a whoosh, the baby landed in Emma's hands.

'You did it, Magda. You were wonderful!"

Emma was shocked at how small and almost weightless the baby was. She dried it gently with a towel and held her breath until she heard it cry. A strong, powerful complaint.

"It's a girl, Magda. A beautiful, healthy baby girl."

Emma laid the baby on her mother's chest and covered them both with a sheet and blanket.

Sophie dropped the phone and ran over to see the miracle. She gave Magda a kiss and both their cheeks were wet with tears.

Sophie whispered to Emma, "Dr. Menzler says she'll deliver the placenta in ten to twenty minutes. You have to make sure all of it comes out and keep it. I'll get a bowl and more towels. He said it'll be messy. Make sure to keep the baby warm. He's coming now and we can wait until he gets here to cut the umbilical cord."

By the time Hanns arrived, all the towels and sheets had been exchanged for fresh ones, and the old ones put in a bucket of water to be washed. Magda was on Emma's bed, propped against a pillow, her baby against her chest. A soft light from the night table lamp illuminated them like an Old Master Madonna and Child. It was the most beautiful sight Emma had ever seen.

Hanns put his arm around Emma's shoulders and said, "Well done, dear, well done."

She couldn't speak.

60.

VIENNA

Emma's apartment became an oasis filled with happiness, all because of an enchanting 53.3-centimeter, 4309-gram creature with jet-black hair. Every time they measured her Sophie would convert the units to ones she understood. The latest showed that at one month Magda's baby was 21 inches long and weighed 8.5 pounds —a little on the small side, but then so was Magda.

Emma had suggested Magda name her daughter Theodora because it meant gift from God—which is what Theo had once been to Emma—but Magda thought that was much too heavy a name for such a little thing. Emma said she could shorten it to Dora, but Magda said it didn't matter what the baby's official name was, because she was going to call her Xenia. That's what her father had called her mother.

Xenia must have been as happy to be with them as they were to have her because she rarely cried. When she squeezed Sophie's finger with her tiny hand, Sophie's heart swelled, making her realize how protective her mother must have felt about her. And maybe even how Aunt Bessie felt.

Magda never took her eyes off her daughter, and Emma was the fairy godmother, showering them with gifts. She even managed to find one of those grand English prams—left behind by some British general's wife when the occupation ended.

"I'll use it as her bed and take it everywhere I go," Magda said —which wasn't very far. The weather was too miserable for long walks, and the pram too awkward to carry up and down the stairs very often, but when the sun was shining they rolled it out to the balcony and pretended they were in the mountains overlooking a valley of daisies.

Magda moved back to her room near the kitchen and hung birds she'd made of colored paper so that Xenia would have something to look at. Xenia's every smile was proof that she knew how much her mother loved her. Together they lived in a happy bubble of baby smells and gurgles, of whispers and soft caresses. Even their guests would rush back from class and tell Magda that Xenia was the prettiest baby they'd ever seen.

To capture Magda's happiness, Sophie fished out the camera she'd brought and took dozens of photographs, wondering why she hadn't thought of it before.

Only Hanns was concerned.

"Why? Is something wrong with my baby?" Magda asked.

"She's perfect," he said. "It's you I'm worried about. You haven't regained your color or your strength."

When he examined her, everything looked normal—no swelling or jaundiced eyes. Magda said she felt fine, though Emma wondered if it was because she was happy or because she didn't want to be a bother. Sophie remembered Bessie insisting she take vitamins, so she asked Hanns if they should get some for Magda. It couldn't hurt, he said.

61.

VIENNA

It was cold and rainy, as it had been most of November, but as much as Emma hated leaving their happy nest, she put on her old Loden coat, slipped on her galoshes, and walked out into the dreariness to do her morning's errands.

Buildings that had once looked gray in the sun, now looked like they'd been smeared with soot. Vendors at the market grumbled that they didn't have enough business, while customers complained that the lines were too long. But nothing could ruin Emma's good mood. Xenia was six weeks old and they were going to celebrate.

Emma bought fruit, vegetables and veal *Schnitzel;* then stopped at the bakery for bread and an *Apfelstrudl*—Magda's favorite, and something Emma didn't have the patience to make.

She was taking off her coat in the foyer when she heard Magda's scream, followed by a thud and Xenia's wail.

Terrified that Magda had dropped the baby, Emma rushed through the kitchen—still in her galoshes—and found Magda on the floor in her room, in a pool of blood, her face drained of color. Thankfully, Xenia lay safely in her pram.

Sophie heard the scream and came in seconds later.

Together she and Emma lifted Magda onto her bed.

"I'm sorry, Emma," the poor child said. "I couldn't help it. I felt a rush and it poured out of me like when my water broke."

"I'll call the ambulance—"

"No, please, Emma! Not the hospital. They'll take Xenia away."

"I would never let them do that," Emma said. She turned to Sophie and mouthed, "Call Hanns. Tell him to hurry."

She raised Magda's legs on pillows in the futile hope that it would stop her bleeding, but the the stain under her was still spreading, turning the bedspread's yellow daisies into a giant ghastly splotch.

Magda grabbed her arm and pulled her down toward her, her face streaked with tears, her voice already grown weak.

"Promise me, Emma. Promise you'll take care of her. Don't let them take her."

Emma wiped her tears and took Magda's hand in hers.

"Never, my sweet child. I promise."

Magda's hold on Emma's arm was now merely the touch of her fingers on her sleeve.

Emma stroked her face. "Look at me, Magda. Stay strong. Hanns is coming."

Again and again Emma reassured her that everything would be all right if she would just hang on a little longer.

But Magda grew weaker, barely able to keep her eyes open, until her hand slipped off Emma's sleeve and her arm dropped, lifeless, off the side of the bed.

"No! Magda, don't give up. Hanns is almost here."

Emma put her arms around her, drawing her toward her chest, but Magda's head fell silently to one side. Emma laid her cheek on hers, feeling for a breath, a flutter of a pulse. But there was nothing.

"Oh God, oh God, not again!" Emma cried. She kissed Magda again and again as if she could bring her back to life.

Hearing her cry, Sophie rushed into the room.

"Hanns is on his way," she said.

Emma shook her head, her hands and face now streaked with Magda's blood.

Sophie unclasped Emma's hands and laid Magda back on the bed. Gently, she closed Magda's eyes and folded her arms over her chest.

"Come, let me wash your face," Sophie said, leading Emma out of the room.

"Xenia," Emma said.

"I will get her in a moment," Sophie said.

Emma sat on the edge of the bathtub as Sophie cleansed the blood off her. She handed Emma her robe and returned to Magda's room. She lifted Xenia out of the pram and returned to Emma.

"Come, we can wait for Hanns in the foyer. He's on his way."

Emma nodded and reached for the baby.

Shifting her weight from one leg to the other as she held Xenia to her chest, Emma hummed a wordless lullaby as they waited for Hanns to arrive.

When they heard the elevator rattle into place, Sophie threw open the front door.

"Thank God, you're here!" she said, bursting into sobs.

Seeing Emma's ashen face, Hanns placed his hand firmly under her elbow, and said, "Give Xenia to Sophie."

"I'll take her to my room," Sophie said. She wiped her eyes with the back of her hand and took Xenia out of Emma's arms.

Emma's legs threatened to buckle under her.

"I thought I'd finished with such grief, Hanns."

He shook his head. He knew better.

With his arm still supporting her, they entered Magda's room. Emma gasped at seeing how much blood there was—on Magda, on the bedspread, the sheets, in a puddle on the floor.

She took the towels that hung on the back of the door and dropped down on her knees to mop up what she could.

Hanns rolled up his sleeves. "Don't," he said. "I'll do it."

She raised herself off the floor.

"Was it my fault? You said if the placenta —"

"It was whole. This was not your fault. Will you bring me some towels, and a basin of water. And a sheet."

By the time Emma returned, Hanns had removed the blood-soaked bedspread, and together they laid Magda on two fresh towels. Gently, they washed and dried her body, and wrapped her in the sheet.

"Don't cover her face," Emma said. "Not yet. I couldn't bear it." Gently, she caressed Magda's cheek. "What happens now?"

Hanns gave her a long look before he answered.

"I have to make out her death-certificate. If I say she died of a postpartum hemorrhage—which I think is what happened, though I won't know why until I examine her—and even then I may not—we will have to report the birth of the child, and Xenia will be taken into custody—"

"No! You can't. I promised I would —"

"I know, but are you sure, Emma? It's a big decision."

"I am. I have to…I want to."

Hanns looked at Magda, then said, "I will say that she suffered from severe cardiomyopathy and went into cardiac arrest from which I could not resuscitate her."

"What if they find out that it's not true?"

"I'll take the risk. I didn't take risks I should have when they were rounding up our friends. Now I will. You and Sophie take the baby and go for a walk somewhere. The rain has stopped. I will take care of things here."

Sophie and Emma carried the pram downstairs, settled Xenia in it, made sure she was well bundled up, and started walking. They walked aimlessly for a while, both of them so deep in thought that they could not talk. Only when they found themselves on Blutgasse, did Emma realize that she had traced the path she had walked so often years before—with Theo, with Greta and Léonie. With her mother.

She turned to Sophie. "My mother lit candles when she thought God's intervention was needed. It's too late for that, and I no longer believe in his benevolence anyway, but I'd like to light a small candle for Magda to honor her."

"I'd like that too," Sophie said.

They wended their way through the oldest streets of the *Innenstadt* to Maria am Gestade, the Gothic church Emma had always liked best because of how the nave was slightly bent so it could follow the course of the Danube. She had found that accommodation touching.

There, sitting in the back of the church, with the pram at her side, Emma's tears flowed sloppily, rolling down her cheeks and nose, dripping their saltiness into her mouth, sliding down her neck to the collar of her coat. A woman in a pew opposite her, scowled, as if Emma's public sorrow were unseemly. Sophie, wordlessly, placed her hand in Emma's—while Xenia, in her innocence, slept through it all.

Eventually, they made their way back home and found both Magda and Hanns gone. There was only a note, left on the kitchen table:

Emma, I will come to see you in the morning. Much to do.
Hanns

Emma couldn't sleep and alternated between tossing and turning in her bed and pacing back and forth as she looked out her window at the deserted street below.

Would Xenia sense her mother's absence? How could she, when Emma could barely comprehend the enormity of her loss. Their loss.

They would not allow Magda to be forgotten. Emma could promise Xenia that, but to the world outside Magda had not existed. She had not known her last name; had had no way of proving who she was. No birth certificate, no baptism, no identification card or passport. If her mother had had documents, they were gone, lost or destroyed. Emma feared that without them, even a proper burial or cremation was impossible.

Yet to Hanns, who tended to the needs of displaced people, this was not unfamiliar. To help them he'd often confronted challenges that seemed insurmountable. He'd learned to build relationships and found his way past bureaucratic roadblocks and blind alleys — so when he returned to Emma's the next day, he had done what she could not have. He'd arranged for Magda to be officially cremated, and for her ashes to be brought home to Emma, to where she'd been loved—not thrown into a pauper's grave with strangers. Emma was so grateful and deeply moved that she kissed his hand. But when it came to words, all she managed to say was, "I made coffee."

"Coffee would be good. Where is Sophie?" Hanns asked.

"Out for a walk with Xenia."

"We have to decide what to do about her," Hanns said, sitting down at the kitchen table.

Emma poured them both coffee.

"I've already decided, Hanns. Xenia is staying with me."

Hanns shook his head. "It's not that simple. We have to register her birth. Without that she cannot get the documents she needs to go to school, to work, or get married."

"Don't we have time for that?"

"No, Emma. If you are to raise her you need to be her official guardian. Without Magda's authorization, Xenia will go into state custody. There is only one solution. I have to make you her mother. Officially."

"And how can you do that? You don't have a magic wand."

"No, but I have a pen. I will—after an explained delay—register that I delivered your child at home."

"Who will believe that? I'm forty-nine —"

"And I'm a doctor."

Her heart began to race. Was it really possible? Could Xenia be hers, as legal as the baby she had once carried would have been.

"And the father?" she asked.

"Me," Hanns said, color rising to his cheeks. "Do you mind?"

Emma felt the sting of tears, and shook her head. "No."

"Then it would be best if we got married," he said, calmly, as if he'd said it would be best to take the tram rather than a bus. But when his eyes met hers she was overcome by a rush of happiness, so ill-timed and undeserved she felt like a thief.

When he took her hands in his, she broke into sobs—uncontrolled gasping, gulping, kind of sobs—as her memories tumbled out in an incomprehensible jumble of names and words, and the walls she'd built around her collapsed, revealing every grief and guilt, every hope and failure she'd hidden from herself for more than twenty years. Hanns took her into his arms and she felt the warmth of his tears on her shoulder.

"It's always the unlived future, isn't it?" he said. "The children not born, holidays not celebrated, joys not shared. Those are the things that break one's heart. But Xenia is new and fresh. We can and we will make sure she has a long and bright future."

62.

VIENNA

Sophie lay in bed rocking Xenia's pram, hoping the gentle, steady rhythm would lull them both to sleep.

"I know, little one," she whispered into the dark. "Someone who suffered so much shouldn't have so little time to be happy. But your mother wouldn't have seen it that way. She knew life wasn't fair. She was brave and never complained or felt sorry for herself. Loving and protecting you was the only thing that mattered to her."

Eventually, Sophie slept, and when she woke the next morning, the pram and Xenia were gone. Emma must have come and gotten them. Sophie threw on her robe and went to look for them.

"We're in the kitchen," Emma called out. "Are you ready for breakfast?".

"Just coffee. I have something I want to do. Xenia needs memories."

In the days that followed, Sophie bought a leather photo album, had Magda's name embossed on it, and had enlargements made of all the photographs she'd taken of her and Xenia. Then she wrote down everything she could remember about Magda's life and the day Xenia was born, and had Emma do the same.

When she finished, Sophie realized that to move on with her own life she would have to face some of her own memories. She'd have to go see where she and her parents had lived. Even if Emma was against it.

Not knowing how she'd be received if she arrived there unannounced, she decided to check things out from a distance first, then send a note asking if she could visit at a time that was convenient for them.

Emma had already left for the market with Xenia when Sophie made this decision, so she left her a note saying she'd be back by early afternoon. After taking a tram and then a bus to Döbling, she found the house was only a few minutes walk away.

Her mother had told her that they'd lived in a big house, but Sophie did not expect it to be as palatial as it was. As she stood at one end of the curved driveway and took a picture, she imagined parties there with guests arriving in Rolls Royces, chauffeurs opening the doors so their passengers could step out in their long gowns and tuxedos and walk up the marble steps to the majestic double doors where a butler waited to announce them. Yes, definitely palatial.

Margie would have been at the front door in a flash. Sophie thought of her every time she was hesitant to do something Margie would jump at, but then she'd always been afraid to step into the unknown. She would have left Millersville long ago otherwise. But she was here now—though only thanks to Harry. She took several pictures and might have ventured toward the door if she hadn't seen a curtain move in a front window. Someone was watching her. She ducked behind a hedge and was about to slink back to the bus stop when an old man walked up to the entrance of the driveway and stopped her. He was wearing a black three-piece suit and a bow tie—surprisingly formal for the time of day—and was carrying a newspaper and two loaves of bread

"May I help you?" he asked.

"Oh, no. Thank you. I was just looking. I used to live here as a child."

He stared at her, took a deep breath as he pulled the bread to his chest, getting flour all over his vest.

"Fräulein Sophie? Is it really you?"

"Yes, who —"

"Fritz, I work here," he said, inclining his head in a little bow. "You won't remember me but I remember you and your parents very well. Have you come to see your aunt?"

"Oh no, I was just —"

"Good." He looked down the driveway and back at her, then whispered, "I can't give it to you now. Not with her here."

"What can't you give me?" she asked, though she was starting to think he wasn't quite clear in the head.

But then, quite firmly, he added, "Come back in a week. She'll be away then. Your uncle may be here but he was always fond of you …"

"Sometimes things change," Sophie said.

Fritz put his hand on her arm, getting flour on her sleeve, and said. "I have to go, but do come back. I will make sure it's the right time. You have every right." And with that, he turned and walked toward the house.

On her way home—funny, she thought, how one always says home, even when it isn't. Maybe Emma was right and she shouldn't go to the house. In fact, maybe it was time to let this all go and get on with her life. Emma was responsible for Xenia now and didn't need her hanging around occupying a room she could rent otherwise. Besides, the weather was dreary and City College would be starting a new semester in January.

She stopped at a *Tabak-Traffik* and was pleased to find a *Paris Herald Tribune*. It had been a while since she'd read a newspaper and thought she might as well catch up on what was going on at home if she was going back.

They were standing in the foyer when Sophie returned— Hanns in his good suit and coat, holding his hat in his hands, Emma in a blue silk dress, busy bundling Xenia into a puffy sleeping bag-looking thing covered with daisies. Emma must have made it because it looked just like the daisy bedspread she'd made for Magda.

"Thank goodness you're back, Sophie! We've been waiting for you. Hanns and I are getting married and we need a witness."

Sophie thought she must have looked peculiar with her mouth hanging open because Emma laughed as she handed Xenia to her. Before Sophie could say anything Emma had put on her coat, arranged her hat carefully on her head, put on her gloves, and taken Xenia back. They were out the door in less than a minute. That's when Sophie finally closed her mouth.

"It's the only way," Hanns said cryptically.

"To make sure Xenia can be ours," Emma explained.

On the way to the Third District Registry Office, Sophie suggested they stop to buy Emma flowers.

"Just one flower for each of us," Emma said, choosing a rose for herself and for Sophie, a carnation for Hanns' lapel, and a daisy for the pram.

It was after one o'clock when they climbed the stairs to the marriage office only to find a sign firmly stating that marriages were only performed until noon and never without an appointment.

"Don't worry," Hanns said, pushing the door open. "I have a friend here, don't I, Viktor?"

"Certainly, Herr Doktor. I'd do anything for you," the man behind the desk said. "But you know we only do marriages here."

"Exactly what we're looking for. Will you do us the honor, Viktor?" He gestured toward Emma. "I'd like to introduce my bride, Emma Huber, our friend Sophie Bruckner, and our little Theodora."

Viktor raised himself from his chair, supported himself on two crutches and hobbled over to them. Sophie noticed that he only had one leg.

"An honor," he said, bowing his head. "Herr Doktor saved my life, you know. And more than once."

He reviewed Hanns and Emma's application, and stamped it *approved*. Then they raised their hands and signed another document that Viktor then reviewed and stamped. It was all rather short and bureaucratic but everyone grinned happily through the whole thing. Even Viktor. Xenia, on the other hand, just slept.

"One more thing, Viktor," Hanns said. "In the excitement of all these wonderful events in my life, I forgot to register our little Theodora's birth. Is there any chance you could help us with that while we're here."

Viktor raised his eyebrows and then winked.

"Of course, Herr Doktor. You're a very busy man. I wouldn't want you to have to come back."

And so it was that Hanns and Emma became husband and wife and father and mother on the same day. Xenia was now officially Theodora Magda Xenia Menzler.

They celebrated over a lovely lunch at Hotel Sünnhof near the market, and Sophie held Xenia while husband and wife toasted each other with a glass of champagne. A quite romantic day, after all.

When they returned home Sophie asked when Hanns was moving in.

Emma blushed. "I don't know. We haven't talked about that yet."

"Soon," Hanns said, looking a little uncomfortable himself.

Figuring they needed some time to make plans, Sophie excused herself and went to her room to read the newspaper she'd bought that morning.

A small personal ad on the second page caught her eye.

Historian seeks research assistant fluent in German and
English.
Contact M.Millington c/o American Express Vienna

The ad intrigued her. She could put off leaving a while longer and answer it. Besides, it was silly not to go Döbling if she was already here and see what it was that Fritz wanted to show her.

Margie and Magda would go. And Harry would give her hell if she didn't.

63.

VIENNA

Marion went about her life, indifferent to the damage she'd wrought in Friedrich, her perfidy a mere detail to her, no more important than a run in her stocking.

As the days and weeks after her revelation passed, Friedrich vacillated between a burning desire for revenge and disdainful resignation. One week, *I will kill her!* morphed into *what difference would it make?* The next week, *I will have the adulterer arrested for murder!* dissolved lazily into *what's one more murder after millions.*

As entertaining as he might find Marion's downfall, it would be a public disgrace for Klaus. Friedrich could tell Klaus privately, forever ruining his mother in his eyes. Or would the boy defend her, a young woman desperate for a love? He would sympathize with Friedrich, wouldn't he? A faithful man betrayed? Or would he view him as a cuckold, pathetic and diminished? Klaus was seventeen. What did he know about such things?

Alone in his study Friedrich resolved to write a memoir to be published when Klaus was old enough to withstand a scandal. He juggled possible titles in his mind: *An Aristocrat Diminished, A Betrayal Exposed*, or merely, *A Life Revealed.*

He took pen to paper and wrote *It was in the bleak days of late autumn when I first learned...*

He rang for Fritz.

"I need a typewriter. A new one. And reams of fresh paper."

"Yes, Herr Graf."

By the time they were delivered, Friedrich had lost interest.

While Marion shopped and dined, and attended theatre and opera without him, he grew a beard, and let his hair hang down to his collar and over his ears, disgusting even himself. He called Tibor. The old rascal told him that he'd taken a position elsewhere and would find it difficult to find the time, but he came, looking more moth-eaten than Friedrich remembered.

Even Fritz seemed to have suddenly aged, or had Friedrich just not noticed until then that he shuffled when he walked, his feet barely lifting off the floor. Emil had retired, or was fired by Marion —without a word to him—for one day there was another, younger man polishing the car. Friedrich decided then that a fitting title for his memoir, should he ever write it, would be *And So We All Decayed.*

Of course he wouldn't write it. Why would anyone want to read about the many things he hadn't done. He hadn't created a life nor saved one. He couldn't help it, he was weak. Perhaps he should have tried to save Otto—his own brother-in-law and Sophie's father—but what could he have done, one little man against the Nazi party?

Poor Léonie's undoing was to have seen Marion and her growing belly in the company of the man who had impregnated her. But Marion wouldn't have known if he hadn't coerced Léonie to come back with him just to irk Marion. He would have insisted on taking her home if he'd known what Marion would do. Wouldn't he?

He might have given more thought to his moral failings had he not looked out the window of his study just then and seen a young woman at the foot of the driveway. She stopped, took a picture, and disappeared behind the hedge. For a moment Friedrich thought it was Sophie, though he had heard nothing from her. He could have gone out to make sure, but it would have meant running down the driveway in pajamas. As it was already early afternoon, she might have mistaken him for a mental patient, and had she been interested in knowing deranged people she would have gone to Steinhof. Although not all insane people were there. Some hid in their studies making excuses for their failings and thinking up titles for memoirs they'd never write.

64.

VIENNA

Days earlier, Emma and Hanns had been friends. Old friends. Nothing more. Today they were married and parents of a child without a notion as to how those new arrangements—this new family—would work.

Emma had never lived with a man other than her father. She and Theo had stolen time alone but they'd never woken up together in the morning, never had breakfast still in their nightclothes. The life she had dreamed of with Theo had not been realized. Her life had gone on but she'd stopped dreaming.

Had it been different for Hanns? Had he ever been in love? Engaged? Perhaps even married? She didn't know. They'd never talked about that aspect of his past or hers.

She tried to recall the Hanns she'd known when they were young, but could only see the man before her now—a man still fifty who looked sixty, with thinning gray hair and circles under his eyes. His suit hung loosely on his body, as if it had once belonged to someone bigger. His sleeves were worn at the wrists, his shoes perpetually dusty from walking from one patient's home to another. Yet his tired eyes were warm with compassion as he treated even strangers as friends. "Suffering isn't limited to the righteous," he once said. "So I try to remember that everyone is someone's father or son, wife or sister."

In the Austria they'd once loved, that had so betrayed them, Hanns was paying the debt every day that they all owed as survivors. Emma did not need to alter or mend or polish him. He was a man she could love.

On the day of their marriage, Hanns returned to his apartment to sleep. Emma told herself that the first step toward being a family had been taken and the details would follow in good time — but when he did not call the next morning, she convinced herself that he regretted his decision and did not know how to extricate himself.

"Emma, I have been thinking about our situation," he said, when he called late in the afternoon.

"It's all right, Hanns. I understand. You have enough responsibilities. It was too much to ask. Xenia and I can manage."

She might have straightened her back then and replaced the receiver with a firm hand—in a show of courage and resolve — had she not been holding a wet, dripping baby in her arms, having just lifted Xenia out of her bath.

"Emma, you haven't changed your mind, have you?" he said, the words tumbling out more quickly than usual.

"No. I just thought —"

"Well, then it's all right. I have a few more patients to see, but can I come see you after that, if it's not too late for you, and tell you what I think we should do?"

Emma found herself smiling and nodding eagerly, though she didn't realize until after she'd hung up that she hadn't answered him.

"Everything will be fine now, my precious child. You'll see," she cooed as she gently patted Xenia dry.

As if they were part of an unspoken plan, her two English guests announced that they had decided to leave early so they could spend a few days in Paris before returning home in time for the holidays.

When Hanns came, he said that he'd been thinking all afternoon and under the circumstances—their new life, not just the girls leaving—Emma should not have to rent out rooms anymore.

"If I give up my apartment we can manage on what I earn," he said. "I know I could earn more if I worked here, but—"

Emma took his hand and kissed it.

"You can't leave your patients. They need you. You're right about not renting out rooms now but I want to contribute. I'll sew again. There's always a need for that."

That night, after Sophie and Xenia were both asleep, Emma fretted whether she should prepare space for him in her room or whether he would prefer having a room of his own, next to hers.

By morning, it all seemed clear. She could do both. She prepared a room for Hanns to the right of the one they would share, and moved Xenia to the room on the left. Then she moved Sophie into the room facing the back garden where she and Hannah had worked for so many years.

When Hanns moved in that evening he brought little with him —only his doctor's bag, a briefcase, and some clothes in a battered leather suitcase he'd had since he was a student. His books would follow, along with a small chair that his father had made for him when he was a boy—the only thing he still had from home. It would be perfect for Xenia, he said.

The next day Emma removed the plaque that said *Pension für Junge Damen* and replaced it with one that said *Menzler.*

65.

VIENNA

Sophie wrote to M.Millington, historian, and said she was interested in working with him. She asked him to call or write to her at Emma's. Four days passed. No answer. Tired of holding her breath she decided she might as well return to Döbling in the meantime.

She called the house to see when a good time would be and was relieved that Fritz answered.

"Come tomorrow morning, if you can, Fräulein Sophie. We'll have the house to ourselves."

So as not to worry Emma—Sophie could tell her the truth later —she said she was going to the Natural History Museum.

Fritz must have been standing by the door when she arrived at the house, for he opened it the moment she rang the bell.

"I'm afraid we won't have as much time as I'd hoped." he said, craning his neck to look both ways as he let her in. "I won't take your coat. He could be back any minute."

"You mean my uncle? I don't think he'd mind my being here. We met on the ship."

"Really? He didn't mention it, but then he has not been himself." He gestured for her to follow him. "Come, we can talk in the kitchen."

"Could I look upstairs for a minute? I'd so like to see where my parents and I lived."

"Oh," Fritz said, looking chagrined. "I suppose … but we must hurry."

They crossed the foyer, past a large marble table, to the grand staircase which curved up to the second floor and turned at a landing bigger than Harry's whole apartment. A crystal chandelier at least five feet wide shimmered brightly over their heads. Sophie wondered how they cleaned it.

A long row of portraits lined one wall of the hallway, landscapes the other.

"Are these relatives?" she asked.

"Someone's."

"Not ours?"

He shook his head and she detected a smile as he said, "Frau Bruckner bought them at the Dorotheum during the war. She thought they gave her…lineage."

Toward the middle of the hall, he stopped and opened a door.

"This was your parents' room but it's completely changed. Frau Bruckner took it over after they left. But now it is your aunt's."

The drapes were closed and in the darkness all Sophie could make out was a large canopy bed and an intricately carved and gilded vanity.

"Frau Gräfin admires opulence," he said, pulling the door closed before she could turn on the light. "Quite different from your parents' taste," he added as he led her to the next room.

"This was yours. A lovely room then. Now young Klaus has it," he said, opening the door only half way before closing it again. She would have liked to look inside, to imagine what it had been like before, but Fritz had already continued down the hall to the last door, which opened to a small landing and a steep, narrow stairway   .

"This is the way to the attic," he said, pointing up. "Your parents' things are up there—in boxes, under the eaves. There's no time to look at them today, but perhaps you can come back." He pulled a flashlight out of his pocket. "You must hurry down now and wait for me in the pantry by the kitchen. It's better he doesn't see you up here."

Sophie ran down the narrow stairs and opened a few doors before she found the one into the pantry. There she waited, surrounded by mops and brooms and jars of pickled vegetables. By the time he came her heart had stopped racing and she felt rather foolish.

"Why am I hiding, Fritz?"

He was holding a leather portfolio in his arms.

"Because of this. I kept it for your mother. She was always good to me. I thought she would be back long ago. Now you will have to give it to her."

Sophie put her hand gently on his arm. "My mother died shortly after the war."

She felt him slump as he blinked away tears.

"Then it is up to you, Fräulein Sophie."

"What is, Fritz?"

"You'll see, but please, you must leave now before he sees you."

"I'll be back."

"Yes, yes, another day," he said, pushing her out the kitchen door.

The phone rang shortly after Sophie returned to the apartment. Emma and Xenia were out. A man with a warm, resonant voice but little knowledge of German said, "*Bitte*, may I *mit* Miss Sophie Bruckner *sprechen?*"

She laughed. "You must be Mr. Millington."

"How did you know?"

"A lucky guess."

"I am looking for someone who can translate for me."

"I'm fluent in both languages, Mr. Millington, but I am not a trained translator."

"Oh, that's all right," he laughed. "It doesn't have to be perfect. Could we meet and I'll explain my plan and you can tell me if you're interested in helping me? It's still a bit fluid at this point."

"Fluid may be just what I'm looking for, Mr. Millington. When and where would you like to meet?"

"How about now? You can decide where."

She suggested the Aida Café across the square from St. Stephen's and said she could be there in fifteen minutes.

She put the portfolio Fritz had given her on her bed, left a note for Emma and went out.

Sophie imagined Mr. M.Millington to be gray-haired with a small gray goatee, a bow-tie and blackboard chalk on his suit—an absent-minded professor writing about the Congress of Vienna.

On the other hand, people rarely looked like their voices.

As she approached their meeting place, an old derelict staggered toward her and she had a moment of panic that he was Mr. Millington. Relieved when he walked past, she entered the café. As she stood at the door, looking for likely prospects, a man at the table nearest the door stood up.

"You must be Sophie Bruckner," he said, holding out his hand as he approached her. "I'm Matt Millington. It's good to meet you."

They shook hands. He was better than his voice. Far better. Tall and slender, with a full head of sandy hair, a Roman nose, and remarkable eyes the color of a cloudless sky. And young. Whatever the job was, Sophie was ready to take it.

"Are you a history professor, Mr. Millington?"

"Oh, no just a graduate student." He laughed, and his laugh was even more appealing than his voice. "I thought of going into law, but decided it was too precise for me. One word in the wrong place and there goes the case—so I studied history instead—European history, to be exact—and am getting my master's at

Columbia. I'm not sure what I'll do with it, actually. Journalism, maybe."

"So, why did you place an ad for a research assistant?"

"Oh, because I have to write my thesis and then maybe later I can turn it into a book. See, I got interested in Austria because my uncle attended the 1943 Moscow Conference where the Allies issued the declaration that the Anschluss was null and void, which made Austria Hitler's first victim rather than co-perpetrator—did you know that? I've always wondered how they came to that decision and why and what effect it had on Austrians during the war. Now they seem to think it absolves them of culpability but I'd like to know how people here felt about it at the time. To do that I have to talk to them, and to do that I need a translator. So far I've found that people are unwilling to admit to knowing anything about the war. Makes you wonder what secrets they're hiding. don"t you think? So, what brought you here?"

"I was born here, but we left when Hitler came. That is, my mother and I did. My father was supposed to go with us but he didn't make it. I don't know all the circumstances."

"That must be why you've come, then, to find out?"

"Sort of. I was kind of coerced into it at first, but I'm glad now. I've been staying with one of my mother's best friends who was here throughout the war."

"Do you trust her?" he asked.

"Of course! Why would you ask that?"

"Sorry. Guess I've seen *The Third Man* too many times. Having been here through the whole thing she must be a font of knowledge. Do you think she'd talk to me? There's so much I'd like to know—or would she think I was being too nosy? It gets me into trouble sometimes."

He smiled sheepishly and it made her smile. It felt good, like the sun coming out after a wet, dreary day.

"I've always liked research myself," she said.

"Perfect. Then you'll make a great assistant. But how about some coffee? And what kind would you like? There seem to be an awful lot of choices."

"It's what Vienna's famous for," Sophie said,. "I'll have an *Einspänner*, which is espresso with *Schlagobers*. That's whipped cream."

He ordered a *Melange* which had steamed milk instead.

"I could write about something medical instead," he said. "Did you know that it was Dr. Semmelweiss, who practiced here in Vienna, who discovered that the mortality rate of new mothers went down dramatically when doctors washed their hands? He was treated very shabbily for it, because doctors felt he was insulting them. He died after being beaten trying to get out of an asylum he'd been tricked into."

"How awful. Where did you hear that?"

"I read it. My grandmother thought every child should have an encyclopedia. It got me interested in everything—which has been my problem. Too many choices, sort of like Viennese coffee. There's so much good material here—besides Dr. Semmelweiss— a rich imperial history, with all its music and art, and Freud, of course, but still it's hard to get away from thinking about the war, isn't it?"

They talked through another cup of coffee, and then pastries, and yet another coffee—about how different Vienna and New York were; about movies and books, and Sputnik and Senator McCarthy; about where to find the best knishes in New York; about how children practicing how to hide under a desk if they were attacked with atomic weapons was ridiculous; and how the U.S. would never live up to its ideals as a country if it continued to allow segregation. For the first time since she'd come to Vienna, Sophie felt pulled back into the present.

When they realized how late it had gotten, they said their farewells and made plans to meet again in a couple of days. Sophie couldn't wait.

66.

VIENNA

As Sophie had not returned yet, Emma decided to take advantage of the unseasonably mild afternoon by bundling Xenia in her pram and taking her for a long walk through the *Innenstadt* to see her first Christmas decorations.

The first really good Christmas Austria had after the war was five years earlier, in 1953, when inflation and devaluation were stabilized and—despite still being occupied—the war finally seemed to be over. Economically, things continued to improve after that and people had more money to spend, but then they complained that Christmas was becoming too commercial. Emma wasn't surprised. Complaining had long been a well-developed art in Vienna.

As she and Xenia made their way along the shops on Kärntnerstrasse, they saw their first American Santa Claus. He was surrounded by a group of very excited children who called him the *Weihnachtsmann*, the Christmas man, quite different from the St. Nicholas who visited Austrian children every December 6th with his devilish companion *Krampus*.

Emma kept Xenia out until almost dark. When the old grandfather clock in the foyer struck six and Sophie still hadn't returned, she didn't know whether to be concerned or pleased that perhaps she'd met another young person to keep her company instead of just her and Hanns. She knew Sophie missed Magda— yet she rarely talked about her. Perhaps she'd taken Bessie's lessons to heart not to talk about things that couldn't be changed. Emma's mother would have agreed with Bessie, having often scolded Emma for wallowing in her grief after the war. Even young Martin, with his kindness and British provisions, had not been enough to pull her out of her self-pity. Taking care of Hannah had been her salvation. And now it was Xenia who brought her joy — despite the tragedy that lay behind her being with them. Her ability to absorb sorrow enough to find joy had often been the truce Emma negotiated with life.

When Sophie finally returned, her cheeks were flushed and she was more animated than Emma had ever seen her.

"I found a job!" she said. "Remember the notice I saw in the paper? His name is Matt, he's working on his thesis and I'm going to translate for him, maybe even help him interview people. That is, if it's okay for me to stay here a while longer."

"Of course, my dear, as long as you want."

"Where's Xenia?" Sophie asked, hanging up her coat.

"Fast asleep. We went for a long walk and I think the fresh air wore her out. Come into the kitchen. You can help me bread some schnitzel and tell me all about this Matt of yours. Where is he from?"

"He's from New York, about my age, and he wants my help doing research."

Emma handed Sophie three soup plates and told her to put flour in the first, a beaten egg in the second, and breadcrumbs in the third.

"Research on what?" she asked, as she showed Sophie how she had to coat the schnitzel in the same order as the bowls.

"He's not sure yet. He's interested in everything!" Sophie's enthusiasm made Emma smile. "One thing is the Moscow Declaration and how people felt about it. I thought maybe he could talk to you. You would tell him the truth."

"I don't remember it having any effect on me at the time. My memories of the war are personal and filled with regrets. I'm not sure that's what he wants to write about."

Emma understood that for Sophie the war had meant leaving home and her father. But Sophie hadn't experienced bodies on the street nor felt the earth shaking as bombs fell. She hadn't done all the wrong things…she could never understand the fear that Emma had felt, and the guilt—toward Theo, toward Léonie, toward everyone who had not survived when she had.

"I'm sorry that I do not know what happened to your father," Emma said. "He was a very courageous man and spoke out against the Nazis long before the war. *Lügenpresse*—the lying press—is what they called him and all who disagreed with them. He was their enemy because truth was their enemy, and it cost him."

"Do you think he was sent to a camp?" Sophie asked.

Emma took her hand in hers.

"It's the first time you've asked that. It could be, but I don't know. If he was, there might be proof somewhere—they kept good records. But not every death was documented or explained. I'm sorry. I wish I—"

Sophie reached over and embraced her.

"Please don't ever feel you've let me down in any way. By sharing your memories you've returned my parents to me. I will love you forever for that. In my heart I've always known my father must have died. He would have found us otherwise—even in Millersville."

Emma nodded.

"I will talk to your Mr. Millington. But now, tell me how was the museum this morning? Did you enjoy it?"

Sophie looked away and didn't answer at first.

"I didn't go there. I'm sorry, Emma. I know you told me not to, but I went out to Döbling. I wanted to see the house."

"I understand, and I was wrong to tell you not to…How were they? Did they welcome you?"

"They weren't there, but a man named Fritz was —"

"Fritz is still there? He's someone you should talk to. He's been there since your father was a boy. Did he show you around?"

"Only a bit. He was nervous about having let me in and rushed me out as quickly as he could—but he gave me a portfolio he said he'd been saving for us."

"What kind of portfolio?"

"You know, one of those leather envelopes. I haven't even had a chance to look in it yet. I was about to when Matt called and I went out again."

"Well, go on, go get it. Aren't you curious?"

"What are we going to look at?" Hanns said, coming into the kitchen.

He looked tired. Emma worried that he was working too hard, though he would never admit it.

"Sophie got a mysterious gift today."

Sophie returned and placed the portfolio on the table.

"Open it, Sophie," Hanns said. "Don't keep us in suspense."

Sophie pulled out two envelopes. The first and thicker one was marked in carefully written block letters:

HERR BRUCKNER'S COMPLETE EDITORIALS.

Inside, in what appeared to be chronological order with the most recent on top, were all of Sophie's father's editorials neatly cut from the newspapers in which they'd been published.

"Fritz must have saved all these," Emma said. "He always admired your father. He took a risk keeping them."

"What does it say on the second envelope?" Hanns asked.

Sophie held it up. In large shaky letters were the words *Please deliver immediately to Dr. Lothar Wolff, Notar.*

She opened it and pulled out three pages with a brief letter stapled to the top of them—all written in the same shaky handwriting.

19 January 1937

My dear Lothar -

As my friend, you will understand that it is with some reluctance that I have come to the decision to change my will, but I have no choice. I have listed my reasons and concerns, should there be any legal opposition or dispute.

I regret that I am unable to leave my bed, but my man Fritz will bring this to you in person today. I know that I can trust you to register the new will as soon as possible and that you can vouch for my mental stability and health.

> *Gratefully,*
> *Your friend,*
> *Heinrich Bruckner*

CONCERNS and RESOLUTIONS

1. As you have always known, Elsa was already with child when we were married, and that the child was not mine. Elsa worked as a secretary in my office and was a great comfort after my dear wife's unexpected death. I had hoped that once we were married she would be a loving mother to Otto, but she showed no interest in that. (Nor has she shown any interest in his daughter Sophie). Her focus has been solely on her own child, Marion. I understood —at first—for Marion was easy to love as a small child, but she has grown into a young woman who finds pleasure only in the most shallow things. This might have been reparable had she fallen in love with a man of character, but Elsa has manipulated her into an engagement with someone whose most positive quality seems to be his title. I fear he is only interested in Marion for her money. I have expressed my concern to Elsa but to no avail.

2. Legally, Elsa is entitled to one third of my financial estate but has no claim to property that I owned before our marriage (our home, and the buildings in which the newspaper and factories are located) unless I grant it, which I no longer wish to do. Legally, she has the right to continue residing in my house after my death.

3. Although I allowed Marion to use my name, she is not my natural or adopted child, and so I hereby disinherit her, with the recognition that she will inherit what is left of Elsa's share of the estate. This will not be as much as she desires.

4. For that reason, and as I do not believe Marion's fiancé has the resources to provide for her properly, I would ask Otto to ensure that Marion not be left homeless.

5. Otto and Greta are to have all furniture and art work that was in the house before my marriage to Elsa.

6. Otto is to receive all property as mentioned above.

In the event of Elsa's death, he will be free to sell the home should he so desire. He can then use a portion of the proceeds to provide Marion another place to live.

7. In the event of Otto's death, his share of my estate is to go to his daughter, Sophie and any other children he and Greta might still have.

8. In the event of Marion's death, her remaining share of my estate is to go to her offspring. If she does not have any, her share is to go to Otto's children as well.

I trust Lothar Wolff to revise my will with all these considerations reflected.

It too was signed, *Heinrich Bruckner.*

"I don't understand," Sophie said. "What does this mean?"

"It means you will have to go to a lawyer," Emma said, as shocked as she.

67.

VIENNA

Every day Friedrich did less. Thought less. Felt less. He refused Fritz entry into his study, so that his daybed remained unmade, his clothes unwashed, the books on the floor unread. He blamed his increasing inertia on depression. He had every reason to feel depressed—but can one refer to *increasing* inertia? Isn't one either inert or not? Just as one is either dead or not.

He might have continued paddling in that murky sea of self-pity had Marion not kidnapped Klaus. They were going skiing for Christmas and he need not come, she told Fritz to tell him.

Friedrich felt only a small frisson of anger at first, but even that flutter energized him enough to allow the image of a young woman sneaking out the kitchen door with something flat under her arm to enter his consciousness. She had been young—though not young enough to be a friend of Klaus, who wasn't there anyway. She must have snuck in just as she'd snuck out, else she would have come to the front door—but for what purpose? Whatever item she'd stolen, it couldn't have been anything of value for no one reported it.

As Friedrich's mind began to clear, he remembered the young woman's auburn hair. The same color hair he'd seen in the driveway some weeks earlier. The same color hair as his niece. Sophie. It had to be.

How delightfully ironic if the young woman he'd been too distracted to pay attention to aboard ship should now become the person he most desired to bring into his home. Marion's home. Tibor would appreciate that Friedrich's awakened interest in his wife's long-lost relative could in fact be a way to exact a most delicious revenge. After all, what reason could Sophie have for coming to Vienna if not to claim her half of the Bruckner inheritance? Not one to share, Marion would see Sophie's sudden appearance as catastrophe. How marvelous! Or would Marion merely shrug it off? That would be disappointing.

He raised himself from the day bed, moved to the chair by his desk and rang for Fritz. He only tinkled the bell once, lightly. Fritz would come no faster if he rang it with urgency.

After a few minutes there was a soft knock followed by the slow opening of the door. This process evoked the image of a sauce slowly overflowing.

"Fritz? Do you know who that young woman was who left by the kitchen door?"

"When, Herr Graf?"

"A few days ago."

Poor Fritz. His hand clutched the door knob so hard it turned his knuckles white. His mouth opened without a sound.

"I believe it was Sophie Bruckner," Friedrich said.

Fritz's eyes dropped as he tried to avoid Friedrich's gaze, his mouth emitting only the smallest indication of a response. More an *oof* than an actual word. Friedrich smiled, knowing then that he was right.

"She and I met on the ship when I was returning from America. I don't know if I mentioned that to you. You don't by any chance know where she is staying? I would like to invite her to visit."

Fritz shook his head.

"Is she planning on returning?"

"I wouldn't know," he said, though a slight flush to his cheeks made Friedrich think he did. He didn't push. There was no rush. Marion wouldn't be back until after Christmas.

"When she does, you must let me know."

"Yes, of course, Herr Graf," Fritz said, bowing a little. He was not a rebel.

"It's almost Christmas, Fritz. Do you have plans?"

"No, Herr Graf."

"Neither do I, my good man, so I've been thinking that I would like to spend the holiday in a more festive setting. Perhaps at the Hotel Sacher. Many a king has stayed there so why not us? I will reserve us each a room."

Friedrich was amused to see Fritz' tired eyes widen in surprise.

"Have you ever stayed there, Fritz?"

"No, of course not," he said with just a hint of annoyance.

"You will have to bring your best Sunday suit. I fear we are too late for the finest rooms, but I have found that even the attic can be pleasant. It's the food we are going for and the reception rooms. One can sleep anywhere. I understand they will be very decorated this year. Thanks to a little American influence."

"What should I tell Frau Bertha, Herr Graf? She was planning the menu."

"Just tell her there'll be no cooking this year. She'll be free to visit her family. We're closing the house. Go on, tell her while I call and make the arrangements. No time to waste."

Fritz bowed and left, a look of shock still on his face.

Friedrich laughed with more abandon than he had since he was a boy. This would be a Christmas to remember. He must make sure his dear wife hears all about it.

68.

VIENNA

"I wanted to invite you for coffee at Café Central," Matt said, when he called. "It's where Freud and a lot of other intellectuals used to hang out, but it's closed. So I asked around and was told we should go to Café Sperl for the same sort of atmosphere. Do you have time?"

"I'm doing something with Emma this morning but I could meet you this afternoon. I have lots to tell you," Sophie said.

In business since 1880, the Sperl was elegant, with its tall ceilings, arched windows, and crystal chandeliers. Ladies in hats sat in red-upholstered booths eating strudl with their coffee while old men in Loden coats or gray *Trachten* suits sat at marble-topped tables reading newspapers and smoking cigarettes.

"Listen carefully, Sophie," Matt whispered conspiratorially after they'd sat down. "We wouldn't want to miss any great intellectual breakthroughs."

She laughed. "I think they're just gossiping."

"Oh well, guess it's up to us then to come up with revolutionary new ideas."

"I'm afraid I'm fresh out, but I do have some interesting news," Sophie said and told Matt about receiving all her father's editorials.

"I would love to read them," Matt said, "though you'll have to help translate when I get stuck. Maybe we could even write an article about your father."

Sophie stirred what was left of her coffee as she thought of how to answer.

"I'm not sure I want to share him with anyone yet. I feel I only just got him back."

Matt leaned back in his chair, as if to give her space.

"When you're ready. I just thought your father would be an inspiration to people who believe in the importance of a free press."

"Can I think about it?"

"Of course, but would you let me read them in the meantime?"

Sophie nodded.

"And that's not all I got," she said, and told him about her grandfather's letter.

"Wow, that's like something out of a Dickens novel where the orphan girl gets an unexpected inheritance that will change her life."

"Not *Bleak House,* I hope. The last thing I want is to spend my life in court."

They both laughed, but it made her worry. Unexpected changes didn't always turn out so well.

When Sophie returned home Emma and Hanns were on the living room floor playing with Xenia.

"How was your afternoon?" Emma asked.

"Good," she said, "though after talking to Matt I started worrying about what I might be getting myself into with the will."

"Marion is a greedy woman. She won't hand everything over to you without a fight," Emma said.

"Don't let Emma scare you," Hanns said. "The changes to the will may already have been registered. If so, it might not be that complicated."

Xenia gurgled happily as Emma picked her up and said, "I wonder how Fritz came to have that letter."

"I was wondering that too, but does it matter?" Sophie said.

"It might. It might mean that the lawyer never received it. Then you'll have to prove that it's authentic. It also makes me wonder if Marion knows about it. She'll definitely fight you if she has to."

"I'm not sure I care. She can have the house. I just wanted to see it, not live in it."

"You don't understand. There's more to the estate than the house," Emma said. "There are all the Bruckner businesses and the properties they are on. Your grandfather was a very wealthy man, and Marion and Friedrich have lived quite well off it all, even through the war. Perhaps even because of the war."

"What are you saying? I don't want blood money!"

"Oh God, no. They made paper, not weapons. And the value of the estate would change your life—just as Matt said. It's what your grandfather wanted and the estate is certainly more yours than Marion's — and should be."

"I don't know…"

Sophie almost wished Fritz hadn't given her the letter. The last thing she wanted was to be drawn into an ugly battle in which she was completely over her head.

"Talk to Fritz," Hanns said, as if reading her mind. "See what he knows."

"I was planning to go back," she said. "Fritz said there were still things in the attic that belonged to my parents."

"Good, that gives you a reason to go," Hanns said.

"Be careful," Emma interjected. "Marion and Friedrich may not know about the letter, but they know that as Otto's daughter you already have a claim. Perhaps you should take your friend Matt with you. You can tell them he is an international lawyer with a prestigious American company. That'll put the fear of God into them."

The next day Sophie called the law office of Lothar Wolff, only to be told that he had died eight years earlier. His son Helmut might be of assistance but he was away and would not return until the new year. Sophie was relieved not to have to fight anyone yet about what claims she might or might not have.

"We'll think about Christmas instead," Emma said. "With everything that's happened none of us have given it a thought yet and it's almost here. We have to make it special. It's Xenia's first. It's a shame Hannah and Stefan can't come this year, but do ask your friend Matt if he wants to join us. It's sad to be alone on Christmas Eve."

When the 24th arrived, Emma and Hanns set up and decorated a small tree while Matt helped Sophie wrap the presents she'd bought. The teddy bear for Xenia was a bit of a challenge, but in the end they put it in the box Matt's champagne had been in.

Matt entertained Xenia and even managed to have long conversations with Hanns—whose English was not much better than Matt's German—while Emma and Sophie cooked.

After dinner, in the light of the candles on the Christmas tree, they ate pastries baked by Hanns' grateful patients, and listened to an old recording of Richard Tauber singing *Silent Night,* each of them lost in memories of Christmases past.

As midnight drew near, Matt and Sophie walked through the rain to mass at the little Rochuskirche on Landstrasse just so they could hear the bells. Emma told them all the church bells in Austria toll at midnight, carrying their sounds from village to village, over hills and down valleys. The greatest bell of all was St. Stephen's own *Pummerin* whose deep and unmistakable sound thundered over the Danube to the far corners of what was once the Austro-Hungarian Empire.

69.

VIENNA

They were an odd pair, so Friedrich should not have been surprised at the questioning looks and whispers he received. Here he was, a known face in Viennese society, in black tie, having Christmas dinner at the opulent Sacher not with his wife but with an old man in a shabby blue suit. It might have struck them as even odder if he'd explained that this was a man he had lived in the same house with for twenty-one years; a man who knew everything about him, but about whom he knew almost nothing. Poor Fritz. He behaved quite well, considering he had never stepped outside his position in society before. If he felt uncomfortable he did his best not to show it. So Friedrich did the same.

It seemed to Friedrich that they were like two children on a see-saw. He, high up in the air, oblivious to the world beneath him; Fritz, his feet firmly on the ground, looking up, and seeing only his underside. Perhaps the most realistic view.

For the two days and nights they resided in adjoining attic rooms at the Sacher. Once they'd dismounted their imbalanced perches, Fritz became visible to Friedrich, and became a man who had a brother, three sisters, and any number of nieces and nephews. He read books and collected stamps. He'd never been outside of Austria, and thought it remarkable that the countries that had once been part of the Empire now had borders he needed papers to cross. Papers he didn't have.

He marveled at the grandeur of the Sacher and confided that he'd only once been inside a hotel at all. One evening, after sharing an aperitif, a bottle of fine French wine, and two after-dinner cognacs, Fritz confided that he'd been very fond of the first Frau Bruckner and that Elsa could never hold a candle to her. He was not inebriated enough to express his opinion of Marion, and Friedrich forgot that his purpose in bringing him had been to embarrass her. In that moment it seemed unimportant.

This newly revealed Fritz was much more interesting than Tibor—who'd probably never read a book in his life. Friedrich regretted having wasted friendship on the wrong man all those years. Yet, when they returned home Fritz removed his blue suit and with it—as if it had been a reverse magic cloak—his visibility. His steps slowed, his shoulders slumped—even his eyes seemed to lose their brilliance. He was hiding again. Friedrich understood and wished he could do it as well.

1959
The Will

70.

VIENNA

Sophie finally reached Lothar Wolff's son by phone the day after he returned from his Christmas holiday ski trip to St. Moritz.

According to his files, no amendment to her grandfather's will had been received or registered, which meant that at this time she only had claim to one fourth of the estate. Marion, as Elsa's only heir, had claim to Elsa's half plus her own fourth.

"For anything to change, I will require incontestable proof that Herr Bruckner wanted it to be otherwise," Dr. Helmut Wolff said, brusquely yet emphatically, as if he knew for certain that an American would have no such thing. "And anything in English will have to be officially translated—at your expense, of course. We do not handle foreign documents here."

It was clear to Sophie that she would have to find a more sympathetic lawyer. Before she did that—and before the lawyer contacted Marion—she had to go back to Döbling and talk to Fritz. And, if there was time, look through what was stored in the attic .

"Make sure to take Matt with you," Emma said, "and don't alert the von Harzburgs that you are coming. Don't even tell Fritz. Just go."

Sophie and Matt arrived in Döbling shortly after two, though the overcast sky made it seem like late afternoon. She suggested that they go to the servants' entrance where she had managed to escape last time she was there. Maybe there, they could talk to Fritz before anyone else.

As they crept along the hedge, trying their best to keep out of sight, Matt pointed to the row of dormer windows on the mansard roof and whispered, "Take a look at the size of that attic! It'll take you a month to look through that."

When they reached the kitchen door, they could see Fritz sitting alone at the kitchen table, reading a newspaper and drinking coffee. Sophie knocked on the window and waved.

He cracked open the door.

"Fräulein Sophie, I did not expect you."

"I just want to ask you a few questions about the portfolio you gave me."

"Oh no, today is not a good day. They are on their way back. They must not know—"

"It's all right. We can talk another time— but I'd like to get my parents' things from the attic. My aunt and uncle shouldn't mind that, should they?"

Fritz looked at his watch.

"We don't have long. You must hurry, it's best your aunt doesn't know."

"Thank you, Fritz."

She introduced Matt, and as before, Fritz led the way upstairs and down the hall to the last door.

"It's a little longer this way. I'm sorry, Fräulein Sophie, but the narrow stairs are a little difficult for me."

"Is one of these your grandfather?" Matt whispered as they passed the row of portraits in the hall.

Sophie shook her head. "They're all strangers. Stuff they bought during the war."

"How sad. They're probably someone's relatives. Someone who needed the money."

They reached the end of the hall, and Fritz opened the door to the stairwell. He took a flashlight off a small shelf and led the way upstairs to the attic, where he pulled a long cord hanging from the ceiling, and turned on the overhead light.

"Here," Fritz said, handing Sophie the flashlight. "You'll still need this. Your parents' things are under the eaves, on the left." He pointed to a dark corner at the far end. "I'll wait here, Fräulein Sophie, so I can hear if they come back. Please hurry."

Sophie and Matt threaded their way through neat rows of stacked chairs, rolled up Persian rugs, and miscellaneous suitcases and boxes, pushing aside cobwebs hanging from the rafters, until they reached a large uneven lump covered by an even larger dust-covered sheet. Sophie carefully lifted it off, revealing two wooden steamer trunks on which a smaller, sticker-covered trunk and three neatly marked boxes balanced precariously.

They scanned the labels for the containers' contents. *Linens*, said the small trunk, *Clothes* one of the large trunks, and *Objects* the other—which inspired some curiosity but would have to wait for another time. It was the three boxes marked *Photographs*, *Letters*, and *Archives* that were important now.

"Hurry, please hurry!" Fritz called from the top of the attic stairs.

"We're coming."

They unfolded the sheet again, trying to avoid getting covered with dust, carefully laid it over the containers they were leaving behind, and pushed the boxes toward the stairs. They had almost reached Fritz when he cried out. "They're back! Turn off the light, and hurry downstairs to the kitchen. I'll go meet them."

As Fritz turned he tripped over a loose wire and, failing to grab the bannister in time, he plunged down the narrow steps, hitting his head against the wall as he landed.

Sophie left Matt with the boxes and ran down the steps to help him.

"Fritz, are you all right?"

He did not answer, and she saw that his ankle was twisted at an unnatural angle.

"Stay with him, Matt. I'm going for help."

Hearing voices rising from the foyer, she rushed down the hall to the main staircase, shouting as loudly as she could, "Help! Someone call an ambulance."

Sophie looked over the landing railing and saw a woman in a long fur coat looking up at her, and a man in a gray coat and hat standing by the door with his back turned.

"Who are you? You don't belong here," the woman said.

Sophie continued down the stairs until she stood in front of her.

"Actually, I do. Now, where's your phone? We have to call an ambulance."

"How dare you! Who do you think—" She was practically sputtering when the man at the door turned and said, "That's enough, Marion. It's your niece, Sophie. I'll call from my study."

"Thank you, Uncle Friedrich. It's Fritz. He fell down the attic stairs. I'm going back up."

As Sophie reached the upstairs hall, she saw Marion come up the stairs, still glaring at her, then turn, and stalk off to her room, slamming the door without another word.

"Was that your aunt?" Matt asked when Sophie reached him "Not exactly an auspicious beginning to your relationship."

"No. And I'd better explain to my uncle what we're doing here. I don't want him thinking we broke in."

But Friedrich had gone outside to wait for the ambulance so it wasn't until after it had left for the hospital, that she had a chance to tell her uncle why she had been in the attic.

"So you found something?" he asked, his mind still more on Fritz, than on her presence.

"Just some photographs and things like that," she said. "There are also some clothes, but I'll come for them another time."

"Yes, another time. Perhaps when Marion—"

"I'll call first," she said. "And could I use your phone to call a taxi? The boxes are a little heavy."

"Certainly. What address should I say?" he asked, and then added, "I am sorry it ended like this."

It didn't seem the right moment to say things were far from ended.

Matt and Sophie barely spoke on the way home. If they hadn't insisted on going up to the attic Fritz wouldn't have fallen. What if he died or suffered brain damage?

The boxes marked *Letters* and *Archives* sat on the seat between them, one atop the other so that Sophie could only see the top of Matt's head as he looked out the window. She held the box marked *Photos* on her lap, her arms tightly around it for support, while Matt looked out the window, lost in thoughts of his own.

As the taxi made its way back to the third district, all she could see was gray—empty gray streets with sooty gray buildings under heavy gray skies. Even the trees were gray. Bereft of leaves, the bony fingers of their branches stretched toward the sky, searching for who knows what.

Why had she come to this depressing place? To fight for real estate? How would that make up for anything?

When the taxi arrived at Emma's building, Sophie reached into her bag for money to pay. The driver said it had already been paid. Friedrich. She should have been pleased but she felt like she'd been bought off.

Matt helped her load the boxes into the elevator and she invited him to come up to Emma's to look through them.

"You should do that with Emma first. It'll mean more with her. I can wait."

He smiled and kissed her on the cheek, and she felt her gloom lift a bit.

She closed the elevator doors and pushed the button for the fourth floor.

Matt waved, then turned and walked toward the front gate.

Sophie hadn't ridden in the elevator since Emma told her that you weren't allowed to ride it down because it might crash to the ground. She didn't understand why it was more dangerous going down than up but figured it wasn't worth taking chances and avoided it completely. She didn't want to die in Vienna, but just this once taking a risk seemed better than carrying heavy boxes up four flights of stairs one at a time.

71.

VIENNA

At two in the morning Emma and Sophie were still awake, sifting through piles of papers and photographs spread from one end of the dining table to the other. Hanns had suggested a glass of wine for fortification. By midnight they'd finished the bottle.

They'd started with the photographs, each bringing back an afternoon, a conversation, a meal, a dance, an argument, a laugh Emma could now share.

How wrong she had been to think that hiding her memories would keep grief at bay. Memories would have kept her friends close, would have comforted her with their warmth. Without them, she had let herself forget what happiness was and what it had felt like. Had she hidden her memories out of fear, or had she done it to punish herself? If she hadn't been so foolish, she might have given Hannah more hope for the future instead of Hannah having to wait for Stefan to do it.

By the time Emma and Sophie reached the final photograph, they'd soaked through three handkerchiefs with their tears and were wiping their eyes on their sleeves.

"We never imagined we'd run out of time," Emma said. "But, one by one, we did and I could do nothing to stop it."

She reached out and put her arm around Sophie's shoulders. "I'm so grateful you took those photographs of Magda. They will mean the world to Xenia one day."

At the bottom of the photo box, Sophie found a folder filled with the autographs Greta had collected after every opera. On the back of each one she'd pencilled the date.

"Jan Kiepura was our favorite singer then. He and his wife made it to America too," Emma said. "I wonder if your mother ever saw them again. It would have made her happy."

In the box marked *Letters* were mostly letters written to Otto by his readers, but a few were to Greta's aunt from her parents.

"From Russia. What were her parents doing there?" Sophie asked.

"Her father worked there—but something happened to them there which is why your mother was raised by her aunt. I don't know what. I'm not sure your mother even knew."

In the *Archives* box they found all of Otto's articles and editorials in neat folders organized chronologically and by subject.

"Your mother did that," Emma said. "She knew how important your father's work was. If only people had listened to him."

If only. How many times had they uttered those heartbreaking words?

72.

VIENNA

Sophie woke before anyone else the next morning, and tiptoed back into the dining room to look at the photographs again. She had seen so few until then. To see so many now at different stages of her parents' lives, was like walking into another dimension. People used to tell her she looked like her mother because of their auburn hair, but it was in her father's face that she saw her eyes and nose.

She put the photos back in their box and went to the kitchen to make coffee and found that Hanns had already prepared it.

"I'm glad you're up. I have a patient to visit at the hospital this morning. Would you like me to check on Fritz?"

"Can I go with you? I'd like to see how he's doing. If he's up to it and there are no von Harzburgs about, it might be a good time to ask him questions."

Fritz was finishing breakfast when Sophie entered the room he shared with another man. The green walls made Fritz look sallow.

"Forgive me, I'm not dressed," he said, fumbling with his hospital gown.

"How are you feeling? You gave us quite a scare yesterday."

Sophie sat down next to his bed.

"I'm all right. Are they angry with me?" he said in a low voice.

"No, why…oh, do you mean for letting me in? I wouldn't worry about that. I'm sure they've forgotten all about it and are just concerned that you are all right."

Fritz shook his head and lay back on his pillow.

"Herr Fritz, do you mind if I ask you about the letter — the one in the portfolio? Where did you get it? Why did the lawyer not have it?"

He closed his eyes and didn't answer for so long that Sophie wondered if he'd fallen asleep.

"Your grandfather was very fond of you … and your mother. He explained everything in the letter…"

"Yes, but why did *you* have it?"

Fritz struggled to pull himself up, and took a deep breath.

"You have to understand…your grandfather called me into his room. He gave me an envelope, and said I should take it to his lawyer immediately. He was very agitated. I would have gone but when I opened the door Frau Elsa was standing there, blocking my way. She must have heard us talking because she grabbed the envelope from me. 'I'll take it' she said. Your grandfather was so upset I had to call the doctor."

Fritz leaned forward and grasped Sophie's hand, causing his pillow to fall off the bed.

"You won't tell them I gave it to you, will you? They will fire me and I have nowhere to go. They might even have me arrested. They've done that before…never mind, I didn't mean to say that. You won't tell her, will you?"

She bent down to pick up the pillow and put it back behind his head.

"No, Herr Fritz, I promise. But please, you must tell me how you came to have the letter. Herr Wolff's son said he needs incontestable proof. Will you speak for me?"

He shook his head. "In court? I couldn't do that."

"Don't worry, it may not be necessary. But can you at least tell *me*?"

Fritz pulled his blanket higher, as if to protect himself.

"Frau Elsa must have read it immediately for I heard her yelling while I was running downstairs to call the doctor. By the time he came, your grandfather was dead. A heart attack … I'm not sure why she kept the letter—no one would have known if she'd destroyed it. I wouldn't have found it if she hadn't asked me to move her things to a sunnier room. She'd taped it to the back of her vanity mirror. I only took it because of what she had done to your father—"

Sophie leaned forward. "What did she do to him?"

"Oh, no, I didn't mean…I shouldn't have said anything."

"What is it? What did she do? You have to tell me."

"She…she turned him over to the Gestapo," he whispered.

Sophie jumped up.

"What do you mean!?"

Fritz grabbed her hand to pull her back down and pointed to the curtain separating him from the man in the next bed.

"Sshhh."

She lowered her voice. "When? When did she do that?"

"Minutes after you and your mother left. The Gestapo came looking for him. I told them he was at work, but Frau Elsa told them he was upstairs…You can't tell them I told you. That's why I hid the letter. I had to keep it safe for you…I never thought it would take you so long to return."

Sophie felt his hand tremble as two tears trickled down his cheeks.

The door opened and Hanns poked his head in.

"Forgive me for interrupting…is everything all right?"

"Yes, thank you, Hanns."

Sophie gestured for him to come in and introduced him.

"Dr. Menzler is married to my mother's friend Emma. You may remember her, Herr Fritz."

Fritz wiped his cheeks with the corner of his sheet and offered his hand.

"Oh yes, I remember Fräulein Emma very well—a very beautiful young woman she was. Please be so kind as to give her my regards."

"I certainly will," Hanns said, shaking Fritz' hand.

After he left, Sophie told Fritz she'd been at Emma's since she first arrived, in the apartment that had once belonged to Léonie Salzmann.

"Of course. You must have known her also," she said, seeing his eyes widen at the mention of her name.

His breathing faltered for a moment as he looked down at his hands clenching and unclenching the edge of his blanket.

"Are you all right, Herr Fritz? Should I call a nurse?"

"No, no, it's just…I'm a little tired."

"I've stayed too long. Forgive me. I will let you rest now."

She tapped him gently on the shoulder and left.

On the way to the tram she stopped at a post office and tried to call Matt, but he was out. She took the tram only as far as the Ring and decided to walk home from there. As she passed the grand old buildings along it she tried to remember that her family had once been happy in Vienna. She found it difficult.

When she returned home, she played with Xenia and tried to put her anger aside for a while.

Hanns returned from work to find Emma stirring a large pot of goulasch while Sophie set the table for dinner. Xenia was propped up against a pillow in her pram so she could watch, and gurgled happily when Hanns kissed her head.

"How was your visit with Fritz?" he asked. "I had the feeling I'd interrupted something."

"He explained why he had the letter." Sophie turned to Emma. "He also told me something else. He said that it was Elsa who turned my father over to the Gestapo."

"I called her that very day…" Emma said. "She said she didn't know where he was. Did Marion know?"

"I don't know. Fritz didn't say anything about her…oh God, Emma. I thought coming to Vienna would give me answers, not more questions."

"It's always the same questions—*how could they?*" Emma said. "I'll never forgive them. I was only collateral damage, but I can't forgive what they did to others. My mother said to forgive is divine. I told her that means only God can forgive—but why expect that since He allowed it to happen in the first place."

"So how do we make the future better than this?" Sophie said.

"Learn from your mistakes and fix what's fixable," Hanns said.

"One act at a time, one person at a time, as Hanns does," Emma said. "Good acts accumulate, not just bad ones." She smiled affectionately at him.

"And you think that's enough?"

Emma shrugged.

"It's a beginning."

73.

VIENNA

Once he'd started sleeping on the daybed in his study, Friedrich asked the cook to serve him his meals there. But the morning after Sophie's unexpected visit, he rose early and asked Bertha to set the breakfast table for two.

When he entered the dining room, he saw with amusement that she had placed Marion's plate at one end of the long table and his at the other—for fear of a physical altercation, he wondered. A silver bread basket and butter dish, and a collection of English jams on a revolving silver platter sat in the middle, too far for either of them to reach. He pushed it all toward Marion's end, moved his plate next to hers, and waited for his wife to come down from her room.

He waited at least an hour, sitting at first, then walking back and forth in front of the ornately framed paintings that lined the walls—all bucolic themes that meant nothing to Marion. She'd only bought them because she could.

"Where is Klaus?" he asked, when she finally made her entrance. "Why didn't he return with you yesterday?"

"He went off with friends," she said, without a glance in his direction as she poured herself coffee from the pot warming on the sideboard.

"His classes start again in a few days. Does that mean I won't see him at all?"

"I suppose not," she said, shrugging as she sat down and slathered butter on her roll.

"Here, have some marmalade, too," Friedrich said, wishing he could stuff it down her throat, like the farmers do to geese to fatten them up.

The phone rang in the living room. She didn't move, so Friedrich stood up and started for the door.

"Fritz will get it," she said, her mouth full.

"He's in the hospital, remember?"

After a few minutes Friedrich returned, energized.

"My deár, it's Dr. Wolff again. I forgot to tell you. He's been trying to reach you. Says it's urgent."

"About what?"

The moment was quite delicious and he wanted to savor it.

"It appears," he said, spacing his words, "that there may be a claim on your father's estate."

She licked a smudge of marmalade off her fingers.

"That's ridiculous," she said, wiping her hands on her dressing gown as she walked to the living room. "But I suppose I have to talk to him."

As Friedrich poured himself a cup of coffee, he could hear Marion yelling. Sometimes the woman lacked all sense of propriety.

"That damn girl!" she shouted when she returned. "I don't care if she's my niece. She hasn't lived here in years. Who knows if she really is who she says she is. After all, just because she says she has proof doesn't mean...oh, really, the whole thing is absurd!"

She sat down. Friedrich waited for her to calm herself, then said, "It's easy enough for her to prove who she is."

"So what? Even if she is my niece, why should she have any right to anything? She doesn't even live here."

In a soft, comforting voice, as if the words didn't matter, he said, "The court will be swayed in her direction, I'm afraid... After all, your mother had her father—*your* brother— arrested."

"Don't be ridiculous!" Marion threw her spoon at him. "Mama told me Greta and Otto left together without saying anything. They should have let us know where they were. Mama was worried about them."

"Not so worried, my little cabbage." He shook his head sympathetically.

"Otto was always good to me—why would Mama do what you say she did?"

There was a flash of hurt in Marion's eyes—a rare sign of vulnerability—yet Friedrich could not help himself and had to turn the knife a little more.

"She did it for you, so all this would be yours," he said, opening his arms in an all-encompassing gesture. "The Gestapo came looking for him, and she gave him up—right there in our foyer. I heard her...Don't look so shocked, Marion. You had Léonie arrested for no reason at all."

Marion sprang up and slapped him. Not lightly, like a woman whose beau had been too fresh, but hard and touched with venom. It stung but it made him laugh.

"Stop that, Freddy! What does it matter after all this time?"

"Oh, my little turnip, that is cold even for you. Your action sentenced the poor woman to death—quickly, if she was lucky. They were quite insane at the end, those Nazi friends of yours."

"*Of mine*? They were not *my* friends."

"Lovers, then."

"That was a mistake. It's all so long ago. It's this girl we have to worry about now, not some old grievance of yours. The girl can try to have Otto's share, but no more than that. The rest is mine. I'm sure that's what the law says."

"Ah, my sweet Marion—it won't help you once they know about Siegfried. That was murder. They would have to arrest you for that."

Friedrich saw a flash of fear in her eyes, but it only lasted a second. He was no match for her.

"You'll never do it, Freddy, for I can implicate you. I can tell them how you covered it up. Then she would get everything and you'd have nothing."

"We could give people a laugh, couldn't we, Marion? Empty title, empty treasury. What a pair."

"Stop babbling and concentrate. We can't let her succeed."

"Can't we? I've managed on little before. I can do it again. Poor old thing, it will be so much harder for you."

If she could have picked up something heavy, she would have hit Friedrich over the head with it, but all she managed was to throw her plate. He ducked and it smashed to the floor. She cried out and left the room, slamming the door behind her, breaking one of its small panes of glass as well.

Friedrich rang for Bertha to sweep up the shards and have the glazer come and repair the door.

Break it and someone will fix it. Such were the prerogatives of wealth. Perhaps he should not, need not, give them up quite yet.

74.

VIENNA

After her visit to the Bruckner house in Döbling and to Fritz in the hospital, Sophie was much more motivated to speak to a lawyer.

Emma was pleased at the thought of the von Harzburgs losing what mattered to them most, though she warned Sophie what going into battle with Marion might entail.

"Until now she has always gotten her way. She will not want that to change."

As usual, they were talking in the kitchen while preparing dinner. Xenia sat in her pram giggling and banging on the side of it with a wooden spoon.

"If I succeed," Sophie said, "I want to sell everything and do something with the money that can make a difference to more people that just me."

"Do it in America, not here. Americans still believe change is possible."

That night, with only a glimmer of moonlight shining through the space between the curtains, Emma lay in bed, with Hanns' body touching hers, and asked him—for the first time—-how it was to have fought for *them*.

"How could you reconcile it with what the …with everything that was happening?" Even now it was difficult for her to put those times into words.

"I didn't even try. My job was to help the wounded—ours or theirs—not to fight. That made it morally easier—at the time."

"Did any of the soldiers resist? Matt said that was the Allies' goal with the Moscow Declaration. At least, one of the goals. Greta asked me whether it had made a difference when she wrote me at the end of the war."

"Perhaps, but resistors and defeatists, as some were called, were severely punished. I remember one young soldier who'd been sent back from the Russian front after being wounded. He made a joke—a light-hearted remark about a higher officer that would not have drawn attention before the war. He was beaten and demoted. Had he made the joke about the Führer he might have been executed."

Emma turned toward him and saw a sliver of moonlight cross his face.

"Will our Austria ever atone for its sins, Hanns, or even admit to them? It is a question that has made me ask myself again and again why I've stayed here. Germans have no choice but to face their culpability. We hide behind the Allied lie that we were Hitler's first victim—though there are enough of us who know better. I'm afraid that if we don't publicly, officially admit our guilt, children will remain ignorant of their country's complicity, or worse, find a way to accept it or even defend it. It will be left to *their* children or their children's children to face the truth with honesty. But then I worry that if too much time goes by people will lose interest and make the same mistakes again—if not here, then somewhere else."

Emma turned and lay her face on his chest.

Long ago, Theo had been the love of Emma's young self—a love that had filled her with excitement and promise. But she was not that person anymore. Without her having to explain, Hanns understood all the sorrows and terrors she had absorbed since then and how they'd changed her. His acceptance comforted her, and she curled her arms around him. She hoped she was as much a comfort to him sometimes, for she knew that he had survived even worse.

"We won't despair yet," Emma said.

"No, dearest, because we must be strong for Xenia and do what's right for her, for Hannah and her baby, for Stefan and Sophie and Matt, so that they will know how to do what's right for all who come after them. Otherwise there'd be no point in our having survived."

75.

VIENNA

The next day, Sophie and Matt went to the U.S. Embassy and Sophie returned with the name of a lawyer who'd agreed to accept her case.

"And Matt wants to write about it," Sophie said, "because it might spur others to claim restitution or compensation for all that was taken from them."

"I wish you well," Emma said, shaking her head, "though I fear nothing will happen until Austria admits its guilt. I'm afraid by the time that happens most of the people may be dead. And even if everything that was taken by force is returned, the world, the culture we knew is gone. There is no restoring that. All we can do now is remember it."

Emma bent over to pick up a blanket that had fallen out of Xenia's pram, then straightened her back and said, "Forgive me, Sophie. I've been in a mood recently. You don't have all those memories. I don't know if that makes it easier or harder. In any case, you are right, justice is worth fighting for."

The doorbell rang. Emma looked at her watch.

"Are you expecting Matt?"

"No."

"I'll get it then, you stay with Xenia," Emma said.

She recognized him immediately, though he looked older, grayer, and no longer had that distinctive pencil-thin mustache she remembered.

"Friedrich. How did you get in?"

She placed her foot firmly against the door.

"The downstairs door was open. I'm flattered you recognized me. You're looking very well, Emma—as beautiful as ever."

Her hand tightened around the doorknob. She did not move her foot.

"Why are you here?"

"Pardon me for coming unannounced, but I need to speak to my niece if she is here. It's important."

He spoke in that cultivated *Hochdeutsch* accent that Viennese society had admired at one time. It was less acceptable now. The Viennese lilt that had charmed the Germans was also gone, replaced by a more vulgar dialect adopted after the war as a way of separating themselves from Germany. A little late, Emma thought. They should have kept their distance in '38.

She stared at Friedrich for several moments, lost in a swirl of disconnected thoughts. Did his German title still carry weight in their post-war world? Was his suit Italian? Or from London? No Austrian green-and-gray Loden for him, even after all this time. And why was he smiling?

"Is Sophie here?" he asked again. "I need to speak with her."

Emma loosened her hand and stepped back.

"Very well, if you must."

She let him in but made him wait in the foyer while she fetched Sophie.

"You can talk in the living room," she said.

"Please stay, Emma, Xenia's sleeping," Sophie said. "Should I bring us some coffee...or wine?"

"Water will be fine," Emma said.

She and Friedrich remained standing, awkwardly avoiding each other's eyes, until finally she sat down on the sofa, and gestured for him to sit in the chair furthest from her.

Friedrich's eyes scanned the room, no velvet sofas here, no gold, no pretense, just ordinary, comfortable furniture, a few pictures on the wall—how different from what he was accustomed to. He smiled as if he found it amusing.

"What a lovely room, Emma," he said. When she didn't answer, he went on. "I haven't seen you since that evening after the war when we met at the opera."

"I remember."

Sophie returned, carrying a tray with a pitcher of water and three glasses and sat down beside Emma.

"Fritz told me you went to see him, Sophie," Friedrich began. "That was very kind of you. He'll be home soon. No broken bones or concussion, thank goodness."

"Is that why you've come?" Emma said. "To give us a medical report?"

"No...I...I've come about the change my father-in-law wanted to make to his will. I understand you are engaging a lawyer, Sophie."

"Yes,...I—"

"I think that's wise, because Marion will fight you," he continued. "She'll take you to court."

"I think it will be the other way around. Sophie will take Marion to court," Emma said.

"That may be," Friedrich said. "And although it would be best to let the lawyers battle it out, I have come to offer some information that your lawyer may find useful."

Emma squeezed Sophie's hand.

"Be careful," she whispered.

"And what might that be?" Sophie asked.

"I understand you are already aware that Marion—unlike you —is not a Bruckner by blood. Marion did not know that until now, and feels that a lifetime of living as a Bruckner should be viewed as being as important as blood in this case."

"Is that all?" Emma said, rising from her seat.

"No, no. That is not the information that will strengthen your case."

He leaned back in his chair as if he were planning to stay.

"Please get to the point, Friedrich," Emma said.

He leaned forward and looked only at Sophie.

"The first thing you should know is that it was Elsa that gave your father up to the Gestapo."

"Which led to his death," Sophie said.

"Oh. So you know that?"

Sophie nodded.

"You're sure it wasn't Marion?" Emma said.

"Marion was actually shocked when I told her. In her way, she loved her brother," Friedrich said. "It was Elsa. I was in my study and heard her do it."

Emma's cheeks grew hot.

"And you did nothing?"

He shook his head.

Emma turned to Sophie and said, "At least he has the decency to not make excuses."

"There's something else," Friedrich went on. "It has to do with Léonie."

"What? What do you know about her?"

Emma glared at him and as their eyes met, he lowered his.

"One day," he said, "near the end of the war, I was on my way home from the *Innenstadt*. Emil was driving and I was in the back when I noticed her. She was carrying a package. It had been a few years since I'd seen her, but she still had that gentle elegance about her."

"Just tell me what you did," Emma said, her fists clenched and pressed against her.

"Of course, I made Emil stop and offered her a ride. Unfortunately, I fear it startled her for she tripped and hit her head against the curb. Her head was bleeding so I had her get into the car to make sure she was all right—."

Emma's chest tightened. She could barely breathe.

"The white car... that was yours?"

"Yes, why?"

"Go on."

"We delivered her package and I suggested she come back with me and stay for dinner...She didn't want to come, but I insisted... to be honest, I did it to annoy Marion."

"You thought that *fun*? Didn't you realize the danger you put Léonie in?" Emma asked, almost choking on the words.

"I didn't think...I had planned to take her home after dinner but Léonie said something that enraged Marion. Something about having seen her when she was pregnant. I didn't understand why Marion was so angry until much later. I was ready to drive Léonie back but Marion said she...It was too hard to argue with her. I never expected she would call that man—"

"What man?"

"The officer assigned to us...an SS—you know how it was then..."

Emma gasped, and Sophie reached out and grasped Emma's hand.

"It was awful," Friedrich went on. "It turned my stomach to see the lout put his coarse hand around Léonie's arm but it was the flash of terror in her eyes that has haunted me... "

"Haunted *you?*" Emma shrieked.

Freeing herself from Sophie's grasp, she knocked over the tray of untouched glasses as she lunged at him, pulling at his shirt, battering his chest with his fists. Sophie put her arms around her and pulled her away from him. Emma was still screaming.

"Did your SS friend tell you that they shot her? That the Russians found her body thrown into a cell at Gestapo headquarters. *You* did that."

She began to sob, not with her head in her hands as if to hide her grief, but wailing, her head thrown back, no longer caring if the whole world knew the depth of her pain.

Friedrich stood motionless at first, his hands hanging limply down his sides, his face blotchy.

'You must understand," he said, barely audible, as he tried to tuck his shirt back into place. "It was because Léonie said she'd seen Marion with Siegfried. He was my son's father—Klaus doesn't know that. He still thinks I'm his father, and I want that." His voice grew stronger. "I want that very much. He's just a boy. I don't want him to be known as the son of a Na—"

"But he is, isn't he?" Emma said, her face inches from his now. "He was born to the lot of you, raised by the lot of you. Don't you think that counts?"

Friedrich stepped back.

"Coward!" she said, grabbing for his shirt again.

He pulled away.

"I never joined the party, Emma. I never believed their propaganda. Klaus will understand that."

Emma pulled a handkerchief out of her pocket and blew her nose. She would not cry in front of him again.

"Oh, I don't think so, Friedrich. Not if he has a conscience—which he might not, given his parents. What he will understand is that his mother and grandmother were collaborators, and you—at best—were and always will be a coward."

Emma felt a sudden odd pang of sympathy for a boy she'd never met, who, through no fault of his own, had to live with the consequences of his parents' indecencies.

"Your son will be changed if this comes out in court. You can't really want that," Sophie said, breaking into Emma's thoughts.

"Why not? Let it come out," Emma said, putting aside her moment of sympathy. "It's time the ugly truth was finally out in the open."

"But my son…" Friedrich said.

"You should have thought of that before you came," she said. "How is it that even now you have no concept of right and wrong? No idea of what hurts people."

Shoving him as she passed, Emma left the room. She could not bear to be in his presence a moment longer.

Soon after, she heard the front door close and Sophie's footsteps in the hall. Sophie knocked softly at Emma's bedroom door and asked if she was all right.

"Yes, dear. We'll talk later."

"I'll take care of Xenia," Sophie said.

Emma changed out of her clothes and folded them neatly as if doing so could put order back into the chaos Friedrich had unleashed. She had wanted to kill him with her bare hands.

When Hanns came home, late that night, he found her standing, shivering, at the window, looking out into the darkness. He gathered her into his arms and held her as she told him what had happened, how every loss, every grief, every fear she'd ever had, had come flooding back. Gently, he made her get into bed and lay down beside her. She nestled into the curve of his body, the warmth of his chest against her back, his arms enveloping her, and drifted slowly, gratefully, to sleep.

76.

VIENNA

Emma was right. He was a coward. "But aren't we all?" Friedrich mumbled to himself. "I doubt Emma risked her life smuggling messages to the Allies. And Sophie, who was just a child, was safe in America. What test of courage did she have to pass?"

It was not easy telling right from wrong. The world was complicated. It required compromise. Sometimes a little moral ambiguity could save one. How else could one protect oneself?

He'd given Sophie ammunition. It was up to her now to use it or not.

77.

VIENNA

Sophie rose early and found Emma and Hanns in the kitchen already finishing breakfast, the table still set for her.

"I'm glad you're up, Sophie," Hanns said. "Emma needs company and I'm afraid I have to leave. One of my patients is having emergency surgery and I want to be there when he wakes."

He kissed Emma and Xenia, who was in her arms, and promised to return as early as he could.

"How are you feeling, Emma?" Sophie asked. "I feel quite shaken."

"Frau Mandl said it must have been someone Léonie knew, but I never imagined it was Friedrich. You would think nothing could shock us anymore, until the long arm of grief grabs us by the throat, revealing betrayals we didn't know about. Every betrayal, every cruelty we didn't know about shocks us all over again. The war is over, but its shadow will always linger over us."

Emma sat down and held Xenia on her lap. Sophie reached over and caressed the baby's cheek.

"Will you tell Valerie?" Sophie asked.

"I don't know that she would want to know. She's never asked. She was so young when she left and escaped the worst of the war. I could ask Martin, but maybe it's best to let Valerie be. She's known since she was thirteen that Léonie died. She doesn't need to know it was for nothing."

"May I ask you something, Emma? Why didn't you leave Austria after the war?"

Emma shrugged.

"Where would I have gone? I couldn't go to England, not without Léonie, and I doubt Bessie would have welcomed me in America. Which is all beside the point because there were so many refugees clamoring for countries to accept them. And by then, I had Hannah and she needed me. But why are we talking about me? Eat some farina. It's nice and warm, and if you add chocolate the sweetness will make you feel better. What have you decided?"

Sophie put a spoonful in her mouth.

"Mmm, this is good...I haven't decided. Not yet. I don't want Marion to get away with what she did, and I know that Friedrich told us what she did just to get even with her—but I do feel for their son who has done nothing to deserve his name being dragged through the mud. How would you feel if I put in my claim without revealing what Marion did to Léonie? There'd be no justice for Léonie, but Marion might come to some sort of civilized agreement. I don't want this whole business to destroy everything in its path just to get revenge. I should see what the lawyer says before I decide."

Emma held Xenia and swayed back and forth while she thought for a moment.

"The lawyer will want a quiet settlement no one has to hear about. In court you'd be seen as the American going after money they would say belongs here—and he'd look bad if he won and bad if he lost. So it's up to you. Give yourself time to think about it and then do what feels right for you. Meanwhile, call Matt and do something fun. All this can wait a few more days. It's waited this long."

Sophie helped Emma make the beds and vacuum, and then called Matt and suggested that they wander through the *Innenstadt*.

"Again?" he said.

"Yes, please. It's my favorite part of the city, and it's sunny so it'll seem new, like you've never seen it before."

They met at noon, and after meandering through the old streets and taking pictures for two hours without once talking of Friedrich or the war, Matt asked if she was hungry. He pointed to the *Griechenbeisl* sign hanging high on a wall of a vine-covered medieval building connected by a narrow arch to another, larger building whose double gate implied a large courtyard behind it.

"I read about this place and was going to bring you here for dinner," he said, "but as we're here already, how about now?"

"Is it Greek food? I've never had that."

"No, just Viennese, I think it was named for the Greeks that once lived in this area. It's the oldest restaurant in the city, and was already an inn in the 15th century. All your favorite composers ate here—Beethoven. Brahms, Strauss."

Matt grinned. "Aren't you proud that I remember everything I read?"

She took his arm and they walked in.

Every room in the restaurant was different, though most had stained glass windows and Persian rugs on the floor. The *Music Room* had a vaulted ceiling covered with signatures—Mozart's among them—whereas in the *Mark Twain Room*, where they found a table, the walls were lined with autographed photographs of international artists and politicians.

Matt ordered *Gulaschsuppe* and a *Wiener Schnitzel*. Sophie ordered *Leberknödlsuppe* and assured him that the oversized liver dumpling was much more delicious than it sounded. Sophie couldn't resist ordering the *Kaiserschmarrn* after that, a fluffy torn apart pancake with powdered sugar and stewed plums.

"The name means Emperor's folly. I haven't had it since my mother made it for me. She said Emperor Franz Josef loved it."

She didn't think about lawyers once all afternoon.

78.

VIENNA

In the evening, as Emma was giving Xenia her bath, Friedrich rang, acting, Sophie said, like nothing happened.

"You should have hung up or told him you'll only talk to him through your lawyer."

"Probably, but he asked if I could meet him for lunch."

Emma lifted Xenia out of her bath and wrapped her in a towel.

"Why? What does he want?"

"He didn't say. I was going to say no but I said I'd let him know later. Maybe they're ready to come to some sort of agreement."

Emma scowled.

"Don't agree to anything without a lawyer."

"I won't."

"And let him wait before you call back."

"I'll tell him that I have an appointment in the morning but can meet him for coffee tomorrow afternoon. And I've decided that I'm not calling him uncle anymore. After all, Marion's not really my aunt."

Emma laughed.

"It might make you feel good, but I doubt he'll notice. Tell him you'll meet him at Café Demel."

"Why there?"

"Two reasons. One, because it's only steps from where the Grünbaums' store was, which you should point out in case he doesn't remember. It'll make him uncomfortable. And two, because they make the best Sachertorte and he'll appreciate the symbolism. Demel and Hotel Sacher have been fighting forever about who has the right to call their cake the *original* Sachertorte. Hotel Sacher went bankrupt before the war, and Herr Sacher's son went to Demel and took the recipe with him. The new owners of the Sacher think they should have the right to call their cake the original." Emma smiled. "So it's a bit like you and Marion—she, not a real Bruckner, in the Bruckner house whereas you, a real Bruckner come from America to stake your claim."

The two-hundred-year old Café Demel, steps from the Hofburg, was grand, with high ceilings, tall windows and endless mirrors. Friedrich was waiting when Sophie arrived and walked over to greet her.

"Thank you for coming. I think you will find the pastries exquisite here."

"I'm looking forward to the Sachertorte. And a melange, please," Sophie added, when the waitress appeared. She turned to Friedrich. "So which do *you* think is the original?"

"Both, neither. Does it matter?"

Sophie gave him a sharp look. It wasn't the answer she'd expected.

"You're right. It's only cake," she said.

With nothing left to say on the subject they sat in silence until the waitress returned.

'What is it you wanted to talk to me about, Friedrich?"

Emma was right. He did not notice that she no longer called him uncle.

"Philosophy. Or perhaps psychology. I very much regret not having taken advantage of our time together on the ship to get to know you."

"By psychology, you mean you want to know how I think so you can help Marion figure out her best defense? You needn't look hurt. You and I both know it's in your interest to have me fail."

Friedrich laughed.

"You are clever, Fräulein Sophie, but you misjudge me. I am willing to live a much simpler life, and have little sympathy for my wife's need for wealth and position. I am only concerned for my son. Whether he is biologically mine matters only to Marion. In my heart he will always be mine and I want to protect him."

"Then you shouldn't have given me the means to hurt him. Not being rich wouldn't kill him, you know."

"There you are gravely mistaken. Poverty is precisely what killed my mother."

Taken aback by both the harshness of his reply and the sorrow in his eyes, Sophie stammered, "Sorry…I didn't know."

"You couldn't. It's not something the von Harzburgs publicized."

"Please understand, Friedrich. I have no desire to hurt your son, but if I ignore my grandfather's letter I would be rewarding Elsa and Marion for actions that are unforgivable—and you for allowing them."

Friedrich reached for the cigarette case in his pocket, then changed his mind.

"I had no choice, Sophie, but I was no Nazi. I did not share their views nor did I join their party."

Sophie stared at him.

"You went along. You could have resisted."

"Oh no, my dear, the SS was living in my house, remember? They would have arrested me immediately."

"You are muddying the waters, Friedrich. What Marion did would not have happened if *you* hadn't taken Léonie to your house.

And now you are willing to betray your wife for betraying *you*—even if your son gets hurt in the process. What kind of morality is that?"

"Exactly what I wanted to talk to you about. The psychology of morality. What would you do in my shoes? What if you learned that Emma had collaborated, or had done something else you knew to be wrong and against your standards or ideals, or whatever it is you call your moral code?"

"She wouldn't have! You can't compare her to Marion," Sophie answered hotly, startling the two women at the next table. Leaning forward, she continued more calmly. "If anyone accused Emma of collaborating, I would not believe it. She hid Léonie and her husband for years, at great risk to herself. I don't think you realize that."

"No, I did not know that, but my question still holds, even if it's only hypothetical. What if she had, and you were given proof?"

"If Emma did anything bad, she would have been justified."

"So you are more loyal than I, Sophie. That's to be admired—but even good people do bad things sometimes, and then one is forced to choose between loyalty and truth. Which do you hold to be the higher good?"

"Truth," Sophie answered without hesitation. She would not let him manipulate her into justifying his acceptance of Marion's treachery.

"Very wise. One can't always trust loyalty. It's too subjective. One has to weigh which would bring the greater reward—loyalty or truth. Or rather, which would cause greater harm—disloyalty or truth? Deciding what is right and what is wrong is a challenge … more coffee, Sophie? Another *melange?*"

She shook her head but he gestured to the waitress anyway.

"You are enjoying this, Friedrich, but I suspect you only care whether it will harm or reward *you,* not others. To answer your question: assuming that being loyal can make you complicit then justice would require—"

"... that you turn the evil-doer in, even if you love her? I'm afraid, my dear Sophie, that even that may not be as simple as it appears. What you view as justice may be a way to self-glorify. *Look at me, look at me, I am noble. Far more noble than she or he.* Denouncer-pride, one could call it. Though, often, it is merely a pretense for revenge."

"You think *I'm* taking revenge? All I ask is to have my grandfather's letter accepted as his wish. It is *you* who came with ammunition against your wife as a way to exact revenge."

"Ah, you are too quick for me. You are right. I would love revenge, but I love my son more So it is *you* who must decide what is just. I am not qualified."

The waitress arrived with their coffees and Friedrich asked if she'd like another pastry—their Dobostorte was divine. She declined.

"Next time then," he said.

Not if she could help it, she thought.

He offered her a ride home but she declined that too, preferring to walk and clear her head. Vienna was a complicated place.

79.

VIENNA

"WHERE WERE YOU?"

Marion's voice was even shriller than usual. She was standing in the foyer in her dressing gown, her hair uncombed, her face bare of make-up, as if she'd been lurking there since she got out of bed, ready to pounce the moment Friedrich returned home. *Home?* - a strange word to use for a house that after twenty-two years was still known as the Bruckner house, although the brass plaque on the door had long said von Harzburg.

"I had business in town," he answered quietly, as he turned to hang up his coat. "Nothing to concern yourself with."

"You met that girl, didn't you?"

"What girl, dear?"

"Don't play the idiot, Freddy," she said, tugging at his sleeve. "How did she get hold of my father's letter? Did she tell you that, or was it you that gave it to her?"

"Interesting that you still call him your father but you won't let me call Klaus my son."

"Don't start, Freddy. Tell me what the girl said."

Marion's face was so close to his that he could feel her breath. It was hot.

"Two of your teeth are crooked, darling, did you know? You probably should have that corrected. They can do that now."

Her hand tightened on his sleeve but he shook her off and walked away. As he opened the door to his study, he saw that the drawers of his desk were open, their contents scattered on the floor.

"My God, Marion, why did you bother? The lawyers already have the letter. And I'm sure they've made copies."

"What else do you have?" she said, pushing past him to look under the bed.

"Nothing. I had nothing and I have nothing."

"Then why did my lawyer say that I might lose everything if that girl takes it to court? What did you tell her? I know you met with her."

"I did, but I didn't tell her about Siegfried. About how you killed him. All we talked about was philosophy, nothing else... What is your philosophy, by the way? I've always wondered."

She glared at him and dug her nails into his arm like a cat.

"Survival, that's my philosophy."

Friedrich removed her fingers from his arm. Nothing ambiguous about Marion.

"Then you'd better talk to her."

Before she ruins us in Klaus' eyes, he wanted to say, but instead said, "She seems reasonable."

Marion flicked her hand at him, as if he were a fly to be swatted away.

"Don't be stupid," she said. "Her mother hated me. In fact, she probably had that letter all along—but I won't let that girl defeat us. And if you don't stop her, I will."

79.

VIENNA

Sophie returned from her meeting with Friedrich looking like she was carrying the weight of the world on her shoulders.

"What is it, Sophie? Did something happen?"

"I'm just tired. I need some baby cuddling time," she said, lying down on the living room floor where Xenia was practicing her rolling-over skills on the rug.

"What terrible things did Friedrich have to say this time?"

"Nothing. No new revelations. He just wanted to talk. About psychology, he said, but all he really wanted was to make excuses for himself. Not that he cares how *we* feel about him, but he does seem to care what his son thinks—so maybe it was just a practice run and he figured that if I swallowed his rationalizations so would his son."

The phone rang. Emma hoped it wasn't Hanns saying he wouldn't make it home for dinner again. He'd been working far too much. Winter was always harder on poor people. One widow, who had severe bronchitis, had been using her husband's army coat as a blanket and burning his old boots for heat. Soon she would have nothing left.

"Hanns?"

"No, Emma. It's Friedrich. I beg your pardon if I am disturbing you, but is Sophie there? I need to speak to her."

"Haven't you upset her enough for one day?"

"If I did, I apologize. I had no intention of doing that. Please tell her I have information that will guarantee that she win her case."

"Tell me and I will tell her.'""

"No, I have to explain it in person. It's important. May I come to see her? I won't keep her long."

Emma took a deep breath before she answered.

"But no tricks. I'll be right here watching you."

"No tricks. I'm leaving now. I've already called for a taxi."

She immediately regretted having agreed.

She returned to the living room and told Sophie he was on his way with information. "If he doesn't behave we'll put arsenic in his tea."

Sophie smiled, but then sighed. "I'll be glad when this is all over with."

The *Hausbesorgerin* rang from downstairs a half-hour later saying a well-dressed gentleman was there to see them.

"You can send him up. We're expecting him."

Emma opened the door and waited, teeth clenched, as the elevator made its way slowly up the wrought-iron shaft to the fourth floor.

Friedrich opened the elevator doors and stepped out, his hand outstretched.

Emma did not take it.

"You said this wouldn't take long," she said.

"No longer than it requires."

She might have slammed the door in his arrogant face, but Sophie came up behind her in time.

"We can talk in the kitchen," Sophie said, and turned to lead the way.

Emma pushed the button for the elevator to descend, then quickly followed them, offering Friedrich the one kitchen chair that had a rip in the seat.

He smiled—a smirk, Emma would have called it—and laid his coat over the chair before sitting down.

"What is it you so urgently need to tell Sophie?" Emma asked, placing herself directly opposite him.

"It's about Léonie."

"You may not speak about her anymore." She reached for his arm to make him leave.

"Sophie, listen," he said, looking only at her. "I told you about Siegfried. He wanted Marion to leave me. He wanted his child. *My* child. And Marion would have gone with him, but Elsa wouldn't let her. Siegfried didn't like that. Marion said he threatened her when she told him. They had a fight—in a hotel room. Even Marion didn't dare to have this meeting in our house, in the house where we all lived."

"Why are you telling us this? We don't care about you or Marion," Emma said.

Disconcerted at her interruption he stammered, "You must! She took my son from me. You have to understand…I need you to know how Marion came to shoot him. They struggled—she said it was an accident. She was distraught when she called me. He was dead—we had to…There was nothing else we could do but make it look like suicide. He was SS. They would have arrested her. Perhaps even executed her."

Emma looked down at her hands and saw that she had unconsciously balled them into fists.

"Why should we care? What does it have to do with Léonie?"

"Léonie said she saw Marion when she was pregnant, talking to an officer. I don't think she meant anything by it, but Marion panicked because she thought Léonie was telling her she knew everything. That's how it is, isn't it, one little thing can lead to—"

"Oh God…"

"Why tell us now?" Sophie broke in.

"Because you can use it as leverage. Tell Marion that you know. You must come to an agreement for Klaus' sake. It is a terrible burden to be the son of a perpetrator. So much better to be the child of a victim, like you, Sophie. People have sympathy for them."

Emma felt the bile rise to her throat and jumped up, almost knocking over her chair.

"Get out! If it's revenge you want, do it yourself. We are not your pawns."

She pulled him by the sleeve and walked him to the door, Sophie following behind them.

As Emma opened the door, the elevator rattled to a stop in front of her.

Friedrich turned toward Sophie and handed her an envelope.

"Take this and tell Marion that you know."

Emma heard a gasp as Marion opened the elevator shaft-door, dressed in a full length mink coat, and holding an umbrella threateningly in her upraised hand, ready to strike.

"Know what, you snake? What did you tell her?"

"Everything!" Emma screamed, and slammed the elevator door so hard the whole shaft shuddered. Frightened, Marion stepped back into the wrought-iron cage, slamming the interior door as well. With a swift movement, she turned the handle and pressed the button to descend.

"No! Stop, you can't go down!" Sophie shouted.

Too late. The ancient elevator had already begun its descent, picking up speed as it approached the ground floor. With a grinding screech, it crashed to the bottom, and the lights inside went out.

Emma started running, with Sophie and Friedrich close behind her.

"No, Sophie, stay with Xenia—and call an ambulance."

By the time they reached the ground floor, the concierge was standing by the elevator, wailing and wringing her hands.

"That won't help, Frau Novotny. Open the door for the ambulance and turn on all the lights."

The ambulance arrived within minutes, but during that time Marion did not move and Emma could see a long gash on the side of her head. It took the paramedics several minutes to pry open the elevator door because the cage had slipped below the ground floor level. Gingerly, they removed Marion and lifted her onto a stretcher and into the ambulance. In all that time, Friedrich watched in stunned silence. When they told him he could follow them in his car, he simply nodded.

"You came by taxi, Friedrich. Should I call you one?" Emma asked.

He looked bewildered, then nodded again. Emma asked Frau Novotny if she could use her phone and then waited with him until the taxi arrived. His face was ashen. Emma almost felt sorry for him.

It was not the end she'd expected.

80.

VIENNA

With the shock of the accident and the news that Marion had killed someone, Sophie forgot all about the envelope Friedrich had handed her until late that night when she was getting ready to go to bed. She'd stuck it in her skirt pocket and found it just as she got to her bedroom door.

"Wait, Emma, I still have the envelope Friedrich gave me... How strange, it's addressed to Elsa."

"Go on, open it."

Inside the envelope was a yellow manila card with an embossed Nazi letterhead—the state eagle above a wreath-encircled swastika.

"I'm not sure I can read it, Emma, it's quite faded, and the print is so dense."

"It might be *Fraktur,*" Hanns said, coming out of their room. "Let me see. The Nazis loved *Fraktur* because it was so gothic and Germanic. Later, when the Nazis wanted the countries they conquered to be able to read their propaganda they abolished it, saying they were *Jew-letters* because Jews had owned all the printing presses. One of their many insanities...Here's what the card says:

The Führer is grateful for your sacrifice in recognizing that loyalty to the Reich must supersede even that to family.

The traitor has been dealt with. There will be no public
announcement. Do not be concerned if you see
his name in print.

FJH

12.38

"I don't understand …"

"Look at the date. They are thanking Elsa for turning in your father—but I'm afraid it also implies your father was secretly executed."

"So they could use his name in the paper," Emma said. "Remember, I showed you the paper the typesetter gave Frau Mandl."

"It's real now, isn't it?" Sophie said. "Even though deep down I knew …"

"It's still a shock. I know," Emma said.

"The long arm of grief…" Sophie murmured.

"It would have been quick, Sophie," Hanns said. "No concentration camp. He was spared that—as well as the knowledge of the horrors that were yet to come."

She nodded. "At least that …Who was FJH?"

"It must be Franz Josef Huber—no relation to Emma—he was the Gestapo chief in Vienna. A terrible man, guilty of thousands of tortures and deportations. He was arrested and tried after the war but served no time. I understand he lives in Munich now and works as a bookkeeper."

"I wish I could go and shoot the bastard myself. I'd claim I was only meting out justice. That would be sweet!"

"Be glad you won't," Hanns said gently, "because evil just begets evil. There will always be new victims to avenge, but then evil would just beget evil again. Revenge never cures anything."

But that night, thoughts of evil avenging evil again and again for centuries upon centuries, kept Sophie awake half the night.

In the morning, exhausted, she woke to the realization that she had to do something about her future. Mourning the past was not enough.

82.

VIENNA

AS THE DECADE ENDS

Friedrich lifted Marion from her bed and helped her into her wheel chair.

"You're hurting me, Freddy! If that girl hadn't been so selfish I could have someone who could really help me."

"We had someone, remember? You fired him. You do realize that Sophie was quite reasonable about the will."

"Reasonable? She took everything!"

"Just the businesses and the house. It was a small price to pay for your sins, don't you think, darling?"

Marion's eyes flashed.

"And what price have you paid for yours, Freddy?"

He smiled.

"You're my price, my sweet."

She glared at him. For one foolish moment he thought she saw through the glibness of his answer to the truth that they'd paid no price at all. But there was no chance of that.

"My father said I wasn't to be left homeless."

"And you're not, are you? Sophie could have made sure you went to prison. Instead, here we are free and safe in this apartment."

"You call this an apartment? It's a hole."

"It's the best we could afford. And you have to admit, dearest, that with the modern elevator that management just put in we are much more mobile than we would have been in Döbling."

Marion scowled, taking all mention of elevators as a personal affront after the accident at Emma's. She had been severely injured, remaining in a coma for more than a month, and suffering from speech as well as physical problems after she regained consciousness. She could have viewed this as the price she'd paid but she'd only felt fury at the unfairness of such a fate befalling her and refused all therapy at first, as if that would somehow punish Sophie — or him. She changed her mind, of course, and her speech —if not her mood—returned to normal, although it became clear that she would never regain the use of her legs.

"I've told you a hundred times, Freddy, I have no room for my things."

Friedrich wheeled Marion down their narrow hallway toward the kitchen.

"You're right, my little fox. I am a selfish beast. You must take the second bedroom. I'll move my study to the dining room."

He'd been waiting for this opportunity, as the dining room was larger and captured the morning sun, but when he first suggested that perhaps they did not need a dining room—it had been a long time since they'd entertained dinner guests—she'd been incensed.

"People will assume we eat in the kitchen with the servants," she said.

Of course, they did eat in the kitchen, but their days with servants were over, Friedrich had had to let Fritz go but Sophie had assured him that Fritz would be well-provided for. He didn't tell Marion that. She blamed Fritz for everything—everything, that is, that she couldn't blame on Friedrich or Sophie. Their cook Bertha went to live with her family in Meidling, but returned occasionally to tend to housekeeping duties Marion and Friedrich had no experience with.

"The girl even stole my father's paintings. She had no right to do that," Marion said, still grumbling. She had only two ways of speaking anymore—grumbling and shouting.

"She did, actually," Friedrich said. "It was in your father's letter. He specified that all the furniture and paintings from before your mother's time would be Sophie's."

"He didn't mean it!" Marion yelled, waving her fist in protest as he wheeled her into the kitchen.

"He did, Marion. He wanted your brother to have them, but as he's dead, thanks to your mother, they're hers now. And lest you forget, the old man wasn't your father anyway. Besides, we have more than enough paintings. You've managed to cover every inch of every wall with them as it is."

"That's only because the ceilings are so low. We live in a box!"

"Stop fretting, darling, and let me prepare you breakfast. You slept so late it's almost lunchtime."

He poured muesli into a bowl, added milk, put in a spoon, and handed it to her.

"She's a very greedy young woman, Freddy," she said, licking a drop of milk from her lower lip.

"I think she was remarkably fair, considering. She made sure that Klaus was well-taken care of. That's the most important thing, isn't it? And you know that she's hardly keeping any money for herself. She's created some sort of foundation in America."

"What a fool. America doesn't need her money. *We* need it. Look how we have to live."

They'd had this same conversation every morning since Marion was released from the hospital. She spent her nights counting grievances the way others count sheep.

Thanks to a small investment Otto had suggested when Marion and Friedrich were first married and he was given access to her money, they had a small but steady income that covered their expenses. It had occurred to him recently that if he'd had any business acumen at all, his life might have been quite different. But no matter, their needs were few now that their social life was dramatically reduced—extinguished, more accurately—which he didn't mind at all. And thanks to the socialists Marion had always looked down on, her medical expenses were also covered.

Constrained by their limited finances, Friedrich had found perverse pleasure in being forced to look for apartments in districts Marion considered far below her station. He chose an apartment in working-class Ottakring for its proximity to a lively market and a variety of places to eat, none of which Marion enjoyed in the least but which freed him from cooking—a skill he certainly did not possess. Their immediate neighbors spoke languages Marion and he did not understand, so there was little communication. Their apartment could be described as a well-appointed cell in a prison of their own making. Friedrich saw it as penance of a sort. His, at least. Marion felt no need for penance as she felt no remorse for her sins. Regret, perhaps, but no remorse.

Marion hated her wheelchair, although she managed it quite well, and resisted angrily every time Friedrich wanted to take her out for a stroll through the neighborhood. Like it or not, she had to face the world, he'd tell her. She'd glare at him, take a deep breath, put on sunglasses and a hat lest she be recognized—although there was little chance of that in Ottakring—and command him to hurry, she hated to be kept waiting. She was not one to admit defeat, which was something to be admired, he supposed.

After the Döbling house was sold, they saw little of Klaus. Their small apartment and Marion's condition were not conducive to having him bring his social life home.

Klaus said he planned to go to university but had not yet decided where, or what he wanted to study. He was thinking of traveling for a year first. He seemed happier after he was on his own. It made Friedrich sad—but he suffered no illusions. He had done nothing to deserve better—or much of anything, actually. Through luck and an inherited title, he lived in an Austria no longer tied to Germany's sins. At least for now. Eventually the truth would come out, for the proof lay in bones and ashes, and the detailed records dutiful bureaucrats left behind.

If anyone had asked, Friedrich would have said he was doing penance for his sins by taking care of Marion—though, if truth be told, he did not find her disability a burden. Perhaps it was the power her dependence gave him. Power brought pleasure, even in such feeble incarnations. It was insidious that way. He liked to remind Marion that she would hate it even more if he were dependent on her.

With little else to do, Friedrich resolved to use his time to finally write his memoir. But in the end all he wrote was this:

I would not be surprised if Marion didn't try to kill me one day—as she had Siegfried years ago— although it will be so much harder from a wheelchair.

1960
A New Decade

83.

EN ROUTE

The new decade brought an unexpected change to Hanns' practice. He hired an assistant, a young doctor who had fled East Germany and shared Hanns' compassion for refugees, having encountered many in his short life.

This change made it possible for Hanns to take his first vacation since before the war, knowing his patients would be well cared for.

He and Emma discussed various possibilities, having until then seen little of the world—except for Hanns' time in wartime Russia where he saw little but blood and snow. In the end they decided nothing could be nicer than to spend two weeks in late spring with Hannah, Stefan and their baby.

So one sunny May morning, Emma, Hanns and Xenia boarded the regional train to Eisenstadt. They were joined in their compartment by two young Americans.

"What brings you to Burgenland?" Emma asked, happy to practice her English again.

"We think our ancestors were from here, but we started our trip in Germany…Our father fought in the Battle of the Bulge," the older one said, questioningly, unsure where Emma or Hanns stood on the matter of the war.

"What scars his heart must bear," Hanns said.

This surprised the young American for his eyes welled up for a moment, and he asked if they were German.

"Austrian," Hanns said.

"Ah," the young man said, with a smile, as if that exonerated them.

"But equally guilty, I'm afraid," Hanns said. "It's the burden *our* hearts bear."

There was an awkward silence, and then the younger man asked, "And where are you folks going?"

"To family," Hanns answered.

"It's sure nice to have family. My brother and I have twenty first cousins and we're all pretty close. It'll be fun for your granddaughter."

"Yes," Emma and Hanns said. An explanation would have been too complicated, but the young men were right. It was nice to have family.

Lulled by the rocking and the steady clicking of the train wheels against the tracks, Xenia leaned against Emma and fell asleep. Emma held Hanns' hand and closed her eyes. She could almost see their faces, all the people she had loved and lost. Yet she felt grateful. She had a husband she loved and two daughters whose futures looked brighter than she ever thought possible again.

As the train pulled into the Eisenstadt station, Emma looked out the window and saw Stefan on the platform waving, and Hannah leaning on her cane, smiling, her baby daughter clinging to her hip—reminding Emma of how Sophie had clung to Greta all those years ago.

Emma lifted Xenia to the window and waved back.

1961
Into the Future

84.

NEW YORK

Sophie lowered her head against the October wind blowing up the hill from the Hudson River and opened the door to Hirsch's bakery.

"Is the Fourth Reich still standing?" Mr. Hirsch asked with a smile. It was the name Jewish immigrants had given their Washington Heights neighborhood—and the question he asked daily to emphasize their survival and the Third Reich's demise.

"Still standing," she said, returning his smile as she hung up her coat and reached for an apron.

She'd been working weekends at the bakery on 181st Street in Manhattan since Matt and she got married and moved into an apartment on Cabrini Boulevard. Matt finished his thesis on the Moscow Declaration and his article on it was accepted by the prestigious *Foreign Affairs,* and Sophie finally completed her degree at City College—but soon everything would change and she would have to tell Mr. Hirsch that she was leaving.

She'd already told Harry when he called from Berlin where he had been sent to cover the construction of the Berlin Wall and the East Germans' order to shoot anyone trying to escape to the West. He said Hanns' assistant had been lucky to leave when he did but if he left any family members behind, they'd be looked at with suspicion.

Sophie was glad the changes she and Matt were about to embark on did not involve dealing with worsening U.S-Soviet relations. They would be going to a completely different part of the world. She had been chosen to be in the first group of volunteers to enter President Kennedy's Peace Corps, and they were going to Colombia.

She was to help with community development, and although Matt had not been selected to the Corps himself, he was determined to make the most of their time there. With the new Zeiss-Ikon 35mm camera his parents had bought them as a wedding gift, he planned to keep a thorough record of everything they did and saw, and the people they met, so that he could write articles—maybe even a book about this new American initiative to promote world peace and friendship.

"I'm proud of you, Sophie," Harry said. "And your mother would be too. It's just the type of thing she would have loved to do herself."

Matt's family hadn't been too sure about the young President's scheme, as they called it, but they loved Matt and Sophie and said they were behind them all the way.

Aunt Bessie worried that they would get sick.

"I'll send you a first-aid kit. Don't drink the water and wash all your fruits and vegetables—and be wary of strangers," she said the last time Sophie called.

"Don't let her scare you. You'll be just fine," Uncle Bill said, when he got on the line. "I'm sure people down there are just as nice as people up here and will appreciate any help you give them."

"You're out from the shadows now, my dear Sophie. Stay safe and keep making the world a better place," Emma wrote, as she did in every letter.

It had taken Sophie a year to figure out what to do with the money that was left after selling the Bruckner house and businesses and fulfilling the obligations she felt toward Marion, Klaus and Fritz. As it was quite an enormous amount, she wanted to do something important and had dreams of setting up a Magda

Human Rights Foundation in her friend's honor. She realized quickly that she had no experience, knowledge or skills to improve on what the International Rescue Committee was already doing— helping refugees of persecution and government oppression—so she set up a fund for Xenia and made a large donation to the IRC. The rest Sophie left in the capable hands of her in-laws' financial advisors until she and Matt returned from the Peace Corps, hopefully filled with new ideas on how to fix the world.

"I met President Kennedy once," she boasted to everyone at the farewell party Matt's parents gave them. "Well, not exactly met and he wasn't president then—but my friend Margie and I did see him from a distance when we were sailing to Europe on the *USS America*. It must have been a good omen because everything for me has gotten better since then. Thank you, Mr. President!"

Sophie raised her glass. "Here's to the future!"

All That Lingers

NOTE FROM THE AUTHOR

For over fifty years Austria chose silence over truth.

At the Moscow Conference of 1943 the Allies declared the Anschluss null and void. Austria was to be seen as Hitler's first victim. Glossing over the declaration's urging that it take responsibility for its participation in Hitler's regime, Austria excused and even denied its complicity with a public face that blurred the differences between active perpetrators, reluctant participants, and silent witnesses. Most of its victims were no longer there.

The first real cracks in Austria's whitewashed facade appeared in 1986, when Kurt Waldheim, once Secretary General of the United Nations, and now candidate for president of Austria, was exposed as having lied about his service in the SA during the war. He won the election, but the effects of his exposure continued into the 50th anniversary of the Anschluss in 1988 and were compounded by the controversial play "Heldenplatz" by Thomas Bernhard which despaired at Austria's continuing anti-Semitism.

Until then nothing that happened after 1934 had been taught in schools.

Compensation to Nazi victims was not even begun until more than fifty years after the war was over.

A movement to the far right with its populism, nationalism, and anti-immigrant stances became more and more popular in the early 21st century in much of the world.

And so it is that lies linger and spread.

Readers' reviews and comments are very much appreciated and can be posted on Amazon, Goodreads, or social media.

This Vienna street scene was created by the Austrian artist, Béla Husserl who was born 26 January 1898, and died in 1940 in Austria's Hartheim Concentration Camp, a victim of Nazi euthanization, after having spent almost fourteen years as a patient in Vienna's Steinhof Psychiatric Hospital. The image was provided to me by his niece, Susan Husserl Kapit.

To see this image in color, and to explore the Vienna of this novel, please check out my website https://all-that-lingers.com. You will find many interesting videos, audios, articles, photographs and even recipes.

ACKNOWLEDGMENTS

Above all, I thank my husband Wayne without whose unending support this book would never have been realized.

Special thanks to Martin Ouvry and Richard Hermann for their invaluable early assessments; to my fellow writers, Sally Holland, Jane Anderson, Megan Murphy and Diana West, who kept me working; and to Susan Kapit for her copyediting and shared memories.

And thanks to my children, Caitlin and Timothy, and my grandchildren, Rachel, Ben, Cyrus and Lorna, who hold in their hands the promise of a fairer and more just future.

All That Lingers

Made in the USA
Monee, IL
13 February 2021